When in trouble, when in doubt,
Run in circles, scream and shout.
And when the shit all hits the fan,
Duck and cover, quick as you can.
—from "I'd rather get stoned than die"
by Rapper I.C.

Chapter 0

Cut to the Chase

"There's that moment of suspension, when the coyote looks down, realizes that he's run off the cliff, and the only thing holding him up is inertia and his imagination."
– Excerpt from "What Makes Us Laugh?" A.P. English thesis by Isaac Cohen (June, 2018)

"Go faster!" Charlie yelled.

"Don't go faster!" Helen yelled back. "The speed limit is 25!"

"Rover?" Jesús hissed through gritted teeth.

"Turn right. Right!" Dave Rover screamed. His head ducked down as he squinted at his phone's screen. "No, nono! Left! Left!"

"Hey," I shouted. "Anyone have any gummies?"

Usually, it was a tight squeeze when the seven of us were crammed into Jesús's Dartmobile, but because of our royal blue nylon graduation gowns we were sliding around like frozen fish on ice.

My stomach lurched as we topped a hill and went airborne for a moment before bottoming out with an excruciating thud of antique

Detroit iron scraping on asphalt. We heard Helen's wheelchair crash around inside the trunk.

"Stop bouncing the car!" Helen shrieked.

My cousin, Adam, didn't say anything, but he had a big wide smile on his face as he held Helen securely in his lap. His arms were wrapped around her like a shoulder strap safety belt, which actually hadn't been invented back when the car was manufactured.

"Graduation's supposed to start in fifteen minutes," Charlie said.

"Rover, I need to know the next turn now," Jesús said. Even from the back seat, I could see that his knuckles were white on the steering wheel.

"I'm working on it," Rover said, squinting as he tried to tap something on his phone. "My battery's about to die."

"We're all gonna die!" Sean and I said simultaneously. We high fived over Helen and Adam, laughing hysterically. "Jinx!"

Looking back, it was probably way too much to expect that our last moments of bondage in the Groston public school system would be uneventful. Considering the monumental prank we had set up, and our recent history of back-to-back shitstorms, it seemed entirely possible that we really would die before crossing the gym floor and collecting our diplomas.

My heart was pounding. I could have sworn I heard a police siren.

"Rover," Jesús said. "This road dead-ends in about five hundred feet."

"Go right!" Rover shouted.

"NO," everyone else screamed. "LEFT!"

Chapter 1

New Year's Eve 2018

"Comedy is when really bad shit happens to other people. Tragedy is when it happens to me."
– My cousin, Adam Siegal, paraphrasing something he'd heard

There was a shriek in the darkness, then a low black moan, then the grinding of gears and the sickening thud-thud-squirtch of a body being run over.

We ignored it.

It was the last half-hour of 2017, our final New Year's Eve in high school, and we were stoned. The seven of us were down in the basement of Dave Rover's house, watching some South Korean horror movie on a pirate stream.

Yes, we were "good kids" but yes, we were breaking the law. On the advice of my attorney, I don't advise this. Not only were we teenagers, but this was just before recreational marijuana was "legal" in our state. Six months before graduation, and only a few days left of winter break, so we were making the most of it.

Rover's parents were out at a grown-up party. His sister was at a sleepover. In a few hours, Rover's Mom and Dad would come home in a ride share, half wasted and slur, "Everything ok down there?" from the top of the stairs.

The edibles were sort of legal, provided by my cousin, Adam, who'd scored a medical marijuana card after a massive hip injury during his first-degree Aikido black belt test.[1]

To ring in the new year, Adam had brought us a big red heart-shaped box of "cherry bombs" – thirty-six dark chocolate covered cherries, each injected with two milligrams of THC.

I don't know how many cherry bombs I'd eaten. They were tasty. More than three and fewer than seven? I was wasted. We all were.

Yes, it was wrong. And we knew it.

But it was fun, and we weren't idiots. Sure, we were a bunch of high school seniors left alone and unsupervised with popcorn, pizza, mini-egg rolls, soda, and lots and lots of inexpensive medical marijuana. But we weren't drinking beer, wine or liquor, or planning on driving anywhere.

If you're expecting a moralistic "young adult" story with lots of lessons and high school melodrama about relationships and drug abuse (or vampires, racism, psychosis, homophobia, gang violence,

---

[1] During his Aikido test, Adam dodged three attackers by bouncing off a wall, which dislocated his hip. He finished and received his black belt, but as soon as his Sensei pushed the hipbone back in, Adam had collapsed in screaming agony and went to the emergency room. The pain didn't go away. So, he did some research and told his mom and stepdad that he wanted to try medical marijuana. He'd expected stiff resistance; my Aunt Dot is an elementary school teacher, and Uncle Paul is a retired navy officer who runs a security firm. But Paul had seen guys come back from Iraq and Afghanistan with pain and opioid addiction, and knew that medical marijuana worked for some people. They set three conditions: Adam's grades couldn't drop, he couldn't drive while impaired, and he could never ever sell the drugs. The only mistake my aunt and uncle made was not telling Adam that he couldn't share...

incest, magic, superheroes, or politics), this isn't it.

We were basically a bunch of pretty good middle class kids from decent families, who had known each other since way back in the day at Jerome Marco K-8. We'd been best friends that long.

We called ourselves "Team Bombshelter" and our plan was simple: hang out, have fun, slog through school, get to the finish line, and graduate from Ashby Bryson High School without incident. As it turns out, that went horribly awry, but that wasn't our fault. Mostly.

My English teacher, Mrs. Maxim, told us that authors usually describe their characters early in a book. I would prefer not to.[2] I've hung out with these guys since the beginning of time, and I don't want to piss anyone off. It's one thing to write down what someone said and did. That's verifiable in a "You said… No I didn't… Yes you did!" sort of way. But to set down your impression of a good friend's body in words is like jumping rope near a field full of land mines – foolish and probably suicidal.

Take me. My full name is Isaac Shlomo Cohen, which is probably the most Jewish old man sounding name on the planet. My parents and teachers call me Isaac. My sister, Ellen, calls me, "Echh". My friends, and most kids at school, call me Izzy, or Ike or "The I-Man" or variations on Izz, Ick, Ickster or Icky.[3]

When I was in middle school I dreamed of becoming a hip hop poet rapper called I.C. But my best rap was: *You know that my funk is smooth as silk/'Cause I always dunk my oreos in my milk.* Yeah, I know. It sucks. As far as talents go, I'm the least exceptional of our bunch.

I'm five-ten, very White, a bit pudgy, with brown hair and blue eyes that I wish were romantic-looking. Without glasses I'm almost blind, so I wear soft contacts, which Adam and I got around the time of our Bar Mitzvahs. I almost always wear our crew's unofficial uniform – blue jeans and tee shirts, with a hoodie when its cold, and

---

[2] She also said that most books only introduce one or two characters at a time, because it's "confusing for the readers," but that's just not going to be possible because there were seven of us. Besides, I think that underestimates the intelligence of most readers.

[3] Only Adam knows about my middle name. Of course, I also know that his is Hyman…

whatever pair of semi-trendy sneakers I can convince my parents aren't too expensive.

As the last cherry bomb hit, I grinned and looked around the basement at my best friends.

Fat Charlie was swigging from a liter bottle of high fructose corn cola. We used to joke that Charlie Johnson was globular – shaped like a globe – but he'd stretched out since our years at Jerome Marco K-8. Charlie and Adam (who also used to be really short) were both about six feet tall. Side by side, they looked like Laurel and Hardy, though Adam was more buff than skinny. Charlie wore his weight well, never let his jeans expose butt-crack, and he liked to dance. Laughing, he sometimes showed off by resonating a wave of fat across his back from shoulder to shoulder.

Oh, and Charlie was black.

Honestly, I never really thought about what "color" my friends were. Maybe it's a privilege thing. It always pissed me off when my Dad complimented me on being part of such a diverse group. "I'm proud of you," he'd say, like I had picked my buddies based on some ethnic scatter chart.

Charlie was Black, with a skin tone halfway between dark roast and skim milk latte. Jesús Ramirez was Hispanic, which meant he always looked tanned. Sean Chang was Chinese-American, with skin color like New England beach sand on a bright summer day. Helen Beagle's ancestors were from England, so she was milky White, almost ghostly but not Goth. She just didn't get out in the sun much. Adam and I were White Jews of Eastern European descent. Technically we were a minority at Ashby Bryson High School, but it really doesn't count.

Rover was White too, but somehow you never thought of Dave Rover as being any particular ethnicity. I don't know where his family was from. He was just Rover. Considering how much time he spent indoors, why he wasn't as pale as Helen I never knew. Maybe radiation from all the screens. Rover was behind his keyboard, as always. His sandy brown hair stood up like he'd gelled it, but probably he'd just forgotten to rinse out the shampoo.

Jesús and Sean had started a standing thumb wrestling match, which they treated like a full-contact contortionist competition.

An inch shorter than Sean's five-ten, Jesús was sneaky and would pop up onto his tiptoes when we did group selfies. He mostly kept his straight dark brown hair in a ponytail, although sometimes he let it down in what must have been the only cool mullet in the history of the world.

When we thumb wrestled, Sean was quick and limber. Unlike the rest of us, he cared about his clothes. He liked to keep himself neat and tidy. His dark black hair was cut short and always styled with product. He studiously rejected our uniform, wearing pressed slacks and starched button-down shirts with an assortment of sweaters and cardigans, that we teased him about mercilessly.

Sean liked to stay clean, so, Jesús fought dirty. Literally. Jesús's jeans and tee shirts were always covered with charcoal and paint splotches, so he knew that if he went down to the floor with the thumb-wrestling, Sean would bail to avoid staining.

Maybe I was just really really stoned, but for the first time I realized had absolutely no idea how tall Helen really was.

Unless she was in the back of Jesús's car, I always saw Helen in her wheelchair. She was sort of small, and (if I can be a bit fanciful) pixie-like, but her baggy sweat pants and sweatshirts hid her shape. Adam, of course thought she was beautiful. I often caught him staring at her with his hazel eyes. For me, it was like checking out my sister, but if I squinted I could see it. Helen had light blonde hair pulled back in a ponytail, a great smile and her eyes were Caribbean Sea blue. When she laughed at Adam's jokes, which she was doing just then, her teeth were orthodontically even and pearly white. I knew that Adam had planned on giving Helen the big red velvet box of chocolates (certain that she'd share them with the rest of us), but Rover had spotted it first and made him open it before she got there.

I'm not going to get into the nitty gritty details of our scars, acne and pocks. I'm not going to tell you what other tics and quirks we all had. Nobody was bulemic, and the only ones who were obese were me and Charlie. His was obvious. Mine was based on the pediatrician's weight and height chart. Fortunately, standing or sitting next to Charlie always made me feel thin, so unless my Dad was riding my ass, I never let my weight get to me.

We were a normal pretty-good-looking bunch of well-fed middle-class American teenagers partying and having a kick ass time. It was the kind of moment that you want to last forever.

Helen laughed hysterically while Adam pushed her wheelchair around the room, trying to figure out how to make it do new dance moves. Rover was on his computer.

Sean had tickled Jesús into declaring the thumb wrestling a draw. Now they were playing poker with Charlie and me.

I was trying to remember the odds of filling an inside straight flush, but my brain wasn't working right.

On the big screen TV the Korean horror movie streamed along, but no one was watching because we were checking our phones, bantering, joking, giggling, yelling, arguing and laughing like crazy.

• • •

That's when I glanced up from my four-five-seven-and-eight of hearts, and saw there was a soybean harvesting truck with rotating knives breaking through the wall, and heading straight toward us!

I panicked and screamed. Loudly. It wasn't a high pitched shriek like a little girl, but the full-out bellow of a guy who thinks he's about to die. (In my defense, I was totally baked, the movie was filmed for 3D, and Rover has a ginormous high-def display.)

My yell scared the shit out of Fat Charlie, who threw his cards up into the air.

Helen and Sean began shrieking along with me and the families of Korean Christmas shoppers in downtown Jeonju.

Adam jumped in front of Helen into his martial arts ready position.

We all stared up at the screen as buckets of blood spurted, and an arm flopped on the sidewalk, fingers still wriggling. Rover's subwoofers shook the room with the sounds of concrete and metal, grinding of gears, whirling knives, and the shrieks of innocent families becoming shredded bulgogi.

Composed as always, Jesús grabbed the remote and hit mute.

Rover looked up from his keyboard, "Huh? What'd I miss?"

We all laughed, our hearts pounding.

Jesús shook his head at me. "Izzy, man, you sounded like my cat Paco, when one of my little brothers stomps on his tail."

"Sorry," I muttered.

"Shit, I almost squeezed off a niblet," Charlie said.

"Did you have to go there?" Sean asked.

"Right?" Helen seconded.

Charlie shrugged.

"Hey, guys, hey!" I said. "It's nearly midnight. Quick, change the channel!"

"Why?" Fat Charlie said. "I'm into this movie now. I think that guy with the glasses is about to get sliced."

"Just pause it," I insisted. "We've got to watch the ball drop. Rover?"

"On it." Rover tapped some keys. "I found a local TV station out of West Virginia that's broadcasting an animated avatar of Dick Clark superimposed over Times Square."

"Who's Dick Clark?" Jesús asked.

"I dunno," Sean shrugged.

"He was one of the world's first DJs. He was famous forever," Rover explained. "Some people claim that he was the guy who started the whole dropping the ball on Times Square thing. He died a while ago, and everybody was bummed out. But this backwoods station is putting together a video mashup, and has a live actor in a computerized body suit, like Andy Serkin, playing Dick Clark."

"The guy who played Gollum in *The Hobbit*?" Adam said. "He's awesome! He did *The Planet of the Apes* too…"

"So, it's a combination of live action and color commentary?" I asked.

"Let's find out." Rover switched the channel.

Rover's giant video screen showed Times Square in New York City, full of people freezing in the cold. You could see all the police officers, hundreds of them everywhere, scanning the crowd.

"That does not look like fun," I said.

"Back in the nineties," Sean said, "my father went to Times Square for New Year's and had a great time. Now, everybody probably gets cavity searched."

"SHH!" Helen hissed.

"Seven, Six!" everyone on TV was chanting along with the on-screen digital countdown.

A guy who looked like a cross between a Botox frozen plastic surgery victim and a giant version of somebody's favorite uncle was climbing up the side of a building like King Kong, reaching for the huge neon ball at the top of the spire.

"Five! Four!"

We all joined in. "Three! Two!"

Fake Dick Clark grabbed the ball from the top of the building and spiked it into the crowd.

I wondered what would happen when the ball hit the bystanders on the ground...

"ONE!"

We cheered and waited for the explosions.

Fake Dick Clark thumped his chest, and then his face drooped like he was having a stroke. Maybe his animated plastic surgery had failed.

Everyone in Times Square cheered and confetti fell. Fireworks shot up into the sky. Nobody screamed or dropped dead.

The spiked ball had been a CGI special effect. Of course.

"That was lame," Fat Charlie grumbled.

"I kinda liked it," Sean said.

"Happy New Year," I said.

"Happy New Year!" Helen sang out.

"Happy New Year," Adam answered. He smiled at Helen. Everyone, except Helen, knew that Adam had been interested in her for years.

Jesús and I watched out of the corners of our eyes to see if they'd kiss. We had a bet with Sean that this would be the moment.

They didn't.

Because Sean cheated. He slapped Helen a quick high five. "Happy New Year!" And Adam's romantic moment passed.

Jesús and I pulled out our wallets to pay Sean his five bucks.

"Can I watch the rest of that horror movie now that we've

interrupted all the suspense?" Charlie held up the remote.

Everyone threw popcorn at Fat Charlie. He caught half of it in his mouth and laughed, nearly choking.

It was a new year, and a new beginning.

It was also an ending, although we didn't know that at the time.

We could have gone on peacefully and blissfully ignorant of the level at which our lives could be fucked up by an incredibly fucked up world. Everything was still normal. Nothing would change. It was the home stretch of high school. We were looking forward to coasting toward that finish line. We'd graduate, go to college and become professional this-es and thats. We'd work together to successfully solve the challenges of climate change, racial prejudice and income inequality. We'd procreate and raise kids who would finally grow up in a world without violence and trauma.

Could we have avoided the bad shit that was coming?

I don't know. Maybe.

If we'd made different choices, we might have sidestepped some of the pain and drama to come. Of course we would have also missed the dreams and the memories. And we wouldn't have pulled off the wild accomplishments nor experienced the moments of touching beauty.

On that last New Year's Eve, if we'd thought about it, we should have known that everything was going to change.

We just didn't know how much.

Sidetrack

New Year's Day with Helen

The world was spinning when Helen Beagle woke on New Year's morning. Even with her eyes closed, she felt the vertigo. Took a few deep breaths. No nausea. That was good. A few more breaths. Stability reestablished itself.

One eye, then the other. She was in her room at home. In her bed. That was good. She patted her chest and her legs. Fully clothed. She glanced down. Same clothes as last night. Also good. Ish.

Helen realized that she had no idea how she'd gotten home. Or rather no clear memory of it. Probably Jesús had driven her. Adam had almost certainly escorted them. But how had they gotten her inside the house and to her room? Had they talked with her parents?[4]

---

[4] Isaac's note: I journaled this book as it happened. After many drafts, my editor suggested that I didn't know my friends very well. I angrily explained that I could only reveal what they'd told me at the time. We argued, and eventually I added several "Sidetrack" chapters, which I based on later conversations. When my editor suggested that I should also preface these with amusing quotes from my English thesis, I told her to stuff it.

Trying to dredge up that memory, she shook her head, and then immediately regretted it, as the room spun like a lazy roulette wheel.

The problem with Adam's medical marijuana edibles was that Helen never knew how much to take, how long before lift-off, nor how long it would last.

It also seemed to give her a hangover. How many of those cherry bombs had she eaten? They were delicious, and clearly more powerful than she'd thought.

She looked left and saw the glass of lemon-infused water that her Mom left on the night table every single morning, along with the little cup of medications. She smiled. Stability and routine were good. If she'd said or done anything stupid on her way in, at least she knew that Mom and Dad still loved her. Or cared enough to keep her healthy.

Honestly, Helen wasn't sure if she wasn't still stoned. Waking up this confused was something new. And the blackout? You weren't supposed to get that with THC. The thought of being high for the rest of her life horrified her. She imagined following some jam band around the country, selling tye-dye tee shirts....

She pulled herself up to sitting, picked up the glass and the med cup. Mom and Dad had drilled her to always check the meds to make sure that they were correct and the right dosage. Yellow, yellow, blue, green: four this morning, which meant it was Tuesday or Thursday. She tossed them back and swallowed with a swig of lemon water.

Had Adam finally kissed her last night? No, she didn't think so. Helen shook her head.

Whoah! Stop doing that. This time the spin was like a merry-go-round. Helen watched the half-full glass of water float up and down. When it stopped moving, she set it back on the night table.

Her everyday wheelchair was next to the bed, a little further south than she or her parents would have left it. So someone else had helped her into bed. Was it Adam? Jesús? Izzy? Charlie? Sean? It could have been any of them. Or the whole team. Probably not Rover, because they'd been partying in his basement.

Helen blew air out her lips. Fuck.

She tried so hard to make her disability invisible. Never show weakness. Frustrated, she leaned forward and grabbed the ankle straps from their clips on the wall. She attached one to her right ankle, and the other to her left.

She yanked the hand-pulls from their clips, and then wound the resistance tension up to six.

When her father had built her strength trainer twelve years ago, Helen had hated the daily exercises. It had been so hard just to pull and lift one leg.

"Hellie, if you don't work the legs and the muscles, they'll atrophy," Mom had told her. "You're doing so good." Cheering after just three pulls.

"I'm not doing so good," Helen had said. "My legs are broken and they'll never be fixed."

Helen had been born with *fibular hemimelia*, which meant she was missing two inches in each of her fibula leg bones. For some kids this meant a life with deformed feet. For some, if you only had one bone with missing parts, it meant that they could break bones, or perform leg grafts, or lengthen the missing part to the point where you could walk. For other kids it meant amputation.

"Everyone's broken, honey," Mom had said. "Some people just don't know it. Do two more reps on each side. Make yourself strong."

As always, Helen had been both lucky and unlucky. She was lucky that, aside from the missing parts, her legs grew in normally. Her circulation was good. Amputation wasn't necessary. She was unlucky, because it meant that walking was something she'd probably never do.

That first time she'd worked with the pulley-system, Helen had only managed seven reps on each side, and nearly passed out from the effort.

Over the years, however, the routine had become… well, routine. Twenty minutes every morning. Get the heart going. Pull with the hands and arms and shoulders. Resist with the thighs and calves. Push with the toes. Extend through the imaginary missing bone. Then pull down with the glutes. Resist with the arms.

These days she could do it for an hour, if she wanted. More than

17

four hundred reps.

This morning, though, the first pull up brought another bed spin, but Helen worked through it. The bed spins weren't real. Weakness was.

• • •

It was nearly noon by the time Helen wheeled into the kitchen and poured herself a mug of coffee.

"Morning," her mother said brightly. "Happy New Year!"

Dad just looked at his watch and raised an eyebrow.

"Didn't hear you come in last night," Mom said.

"Happy New Year," Helen grunted, but breathed an internal sigh of relief mixed with a bit of anger.

Her parents slept like logs. Dad had bought an alarm system from Adam's stepdad that sounded like an air raid siren. If they hadn't helped her into bed that meant one of the guys had.

Helen sat next to the coffee maker, drank her mug halfway down and refilled it. "I wasn't that late."

"It's okay honey, we trust you," Mom said.

Dad shrugged and sighed.

Really? They still trust me? I guess they don't know about the medical marijuana. Or the Ecstasy that we tried last year. That was fun. And the cocaine Isaac had stolen from his sister. Which they all agreed totally wasn't worth it.

Helen didn't say anything, but rolled up to the table, set the cup down and headed toward the fridge.

"Can I make you breakfast?" Mom asked.

"Brunch," Dad said. Monosyllabic. Dad usually talked more. Was he upset?

"I can get my own food," Helen snapped.

"It's just that I haven't made you breakfast in a long time, Hellie," Mom said. She had a long sweater on over her workout gear.

Helen looked at her mother and suddenly wanted to cry. There wasn't a hidden agenda, nor a secret scolding. Mom really wanted to do something nice.

Mom was only forty-three, but she looked like she was sixty. Her hair was white and her cheeks were thin. If she'd been a smoker that would have been understandable. But it was the stress of raising a girl with a disability that had aged her. Everyone knew it. Nobody said it. First staying at home every day. Then, when Helen went to school, going to work every day at the craft store, and then rushing home to make dinner and take care of things.

Dad was sixty and looked sixty. But he was Dad. He'd always looked the same to her. Short greying hair and a close shave. This morning he was reading the news on his tablet and dressed business casual. Even though it was New Year's Day, Dad was ready to go into the office if there was an emergency. What kind of an emergency did insurance company managers ever have to deal with?

Helen looked at the fridge, thinking through all the steps... Get the eggs and butter out, get the frying pan from its drawer, ferry them to the stove. Get bread from the breadbox and put it in the toaster. Sidle her chair up to the burner, light the stove, break the eggs, and flip the eggs. Get a plate, fork and knife. Get the toast from the toaster. Butter the toast. Turn off the burner and slide the eggs onto the plate. Then edge her chair away from the stove, over to the table. Then eat. Then clean up.

"Okay," she said, slowly.

"How about pancakes?" Mom said.

"You didn't offer to make me pancakes," Dad said, looking up from his tablet.

Mom smiled and sighed at him. "Do you want pancakes?"

"Yes, please," Dad said, smiling back.

"What about you, Hellie?" Mom said. "Pancakes?"

Helen imagined herself bursting into tears. She wanted to cry. She wanted to tell her parents how much she loved them. She wanted to tell them how confused she was about everything. About the drugs. About Adam. About going away to college in the fall. Would they understand? Would they be angry? Helpful? Indignant? She depended on them for so much. She needed to stand on her own two feet, which was a laughable phrase because Helen had never and probably would never be able to stand on her own.

"Yeah. Sure. Whatever," she said, cursing herself. "I'll do the

19

dishes."

"You don't have to…" Mom began, but Dad interrupted with, "That's great. I love it! I get pancakes and I don't need to do the clean up. Total win."

Mom shot Dad a look. He nodded his head at Helen, and Mom nodded back.

Like she didn't notice their body language.

– You're not making it easy, Mom was saying.

– She has to learn to take care of herself, Dad was saying

– She can. She will. She does. But she's still our little girl.

– You're not helping her by coddling.

– I'm not coddling. I'm making her breakfast. And for you too.

Helen stared into her coffee and wondered if she'd ever be with someone long enough to have that kind of shorthand conversation with just a few glances and shrugs.

The pancakes were delicious. Hot and filling with warm real maple syrup. She'd have to do another twenty minutes of exercise to burn them off, but it was worth it.

Mom gave her a kiss on the cheek, and then left for a New Year's Day yoga gong bath.

By the time Helen was done with breakfast and the dishes it was after one.

"You left your phone over there last night," Dad said, pointing at the table near the back door where everyone kept their keys, wallets and phones. "It's been buzzing all morning."

Helen nodded.

"Helen," Dad said with that tone of voice that meant, here-comes-a-lecture.

"Yah?"

"Don't leave your phone at home," he said.

"I was with the guys in Rover's basement," she said. "Phones don't work down there."

"It doesn't matter," Dad said. "I need you to keep it with you. There are enough things in this world for me to worry about. Losing track of you is something that I don't want on my list."

"Fine," Helen said. She snatched the phone, dropped it into her chair's left side pocket, and spun down the hall into her bedroom.

"I love you," Dad said to her back.

• • •

With her bedroom door tightly closed, Helen glanced at the phone. About a dozen messages from the guys in their group chat. She did not want to deal with that right now. Probably a bunch of dick and poop jokes because, let's face it, the guys were all guys.

Helen opened her laptop and stared at it for a moment before logging in.

Maybe writing some poetry would help.

Flashing on the screen was a friend request from Robyn Franklin.

Really? Helen rubbed her forehead. Why was Robyn Franklin making a friend request? They were both seniors at Ashby Bryson High, and had been in school together for three years without ever becoming friends. There were certain rules to social media friend-ships. Whenever you started a new class or signed up for a new ac-tivity, you could add people to your list. Or when you were moving away to go to a new town. But it was the middle of the year going into their last semester. What had changed?

It was probably a mistake. Helen was just about to delete it when she saw that Robyn had also sent her a really long direct message: "Hi Helen. I know that we haven't been friends before this, but I made a New Year's resolution to reach out to people I don't know. You're really the only person that I don't know at Ashby B who isn't a jerk or a bitch. That's not what I meant to say. I'm just trying to connect with someone who doesn't have a Big Opinion of me. This is awkward, and I'm tempted to delete it, but I already sent the friend request. You can ignore me if you want. I won't take it personally."

What the fuck? Helen stared at the screen. Did that girl not have any filters?

Robyn was what, asking Helen to be her friend because of a New Year's resolution? So she was like a project? Befriend the crip-pled girl. Have a laugh and feel good about yourself. Sanctimonious altruism always made Helen instantly angry.

This really was a morning for outrage, wasn't it? She was

completely triggered.

Helen clicked on Robyn's profile picture. It showed a normal-looking black girl with perfect coffee-skin and an orthodontic smile busting out of her tight cheerleader squad sweater. Everything about Robyn exuded clean wholesome bubble-headed fun.

Was that accurate or just a Big Opinion? Robyn was in Helen's AP European History class, and had once made a few interesting points about how the world would have been different if the Ottoman Turks and Suleiman hadn't been stopped by the Holy Roman Empire. So maybe she wasn't a complete airhead.

Helen shook her head and was momentarily pleased to notice that this time the room didn't spin.

She went to Robyn's page, looked at her friends list and realized that Robyn was right. Everyone at school who wasn't already a friend was either a jerk or a bitch.

Helen's own friend list hadn't changed in months. Every interaction there was always part of the whole social currency economy. If you like this, I'll like that. If you share this, you'll be in the know. Very surface and shallow.

But that's the kind of relationship Helen had always had with girls. Girls either treated her like she was learning disabled and fragile, or like she was dangerous, and contagious – as if being born without bones was something you could catch by association.

That's why she hung out with the guys. They didn't treat her like she was breakable. They respected her brain. They included her completely. They even made cripple jokes, which was great because it meant she could make jokes about their problems, disabilities, quirks and maladjustments right back at them.

Yeah, she had a lot of fun with the guys. They were the best.

But they were guys.

Sometimes, often if she was honest, Helen wished she had a girlfriend to talk with.

How much did it really cost to accept a friend request? A little bit of humility. A little bit of danger, because the whole thing might be a prank. An elaborate cyber-bullying plot. But the little Helen knew about Robyn told her that it probably wasn't a gag. Just in case, she took a screen shot of the IM. Evidence for the prosecution if necessary.

Crap. What a world. Back when her parents were kids they'd pick up the phone and say, "Hey, you wanna hang out?" and then the other person would say, "Yeah." Or "Fuck no." and that would be it. Now it was this whole transactional evaluation process and always with the risk of being called out on social media.

What was it Robyn wrote? "I'm just trying to connect with someone who doesn't have a Big Opinion of me." Capitalized the words Big Opinion. On purpose? Maybe.

Helen nodded and whispered "Okay Robyn. I don't have a Big Opinion about you. Let's see what happens."

She clicked "Accept."

Worst that could happen, it wouldn't work out.

A moment later, another DM came through from Robyn, "Excellent! Want to get a cup of coffee?"

Helen laughed. Desperate much, Robyn? But yeah. Sure. Why not. Tomorrow was a school day, and Helen would be back rolling her chair in the educational hamster wheel. She'd bring her laptop and do some work in case it was a bust or Robyn didn't show.

"Hey Dad, can you give me a lift somewhere?" she yelled.

"No problem," Dad yelled back. Thank god she had good parents who didn't ask too damn many questions.

Then Helen typed, "Meet you at Chucklehead Café at 3?"

Robyn came back with a thumbs-up.

• • •

Dad pulled the van into the spot next to the two-seater sports car parked in the handicapped space. He started cursing, his typical rant about people not respecting the law.

Helen let his words roll off her as she pushed the button to open the door and lower the ramp. If she got pissed off every time someone blocked her way then she'd spend her whole life angry.

"Thanks Dad," she called over her shoulder. "I'll text you when I'm ready to go."

"Twenty minutes notice, if you can," Dad called back.

"Yep." And she would, as always. Back in ninth grade, when she'd just started at Ashby Bryson, there had been a period of rebellion, when Helen had broken every house rule on a consistent basis. Those had been rocky days, until Helen learned that it was easier to conform with the stupid rules than fight all the time.

She pulled the S-hook from its sling behind her chair, looped it on the coffee shop's door handle and the front armrest of her chair, pushed the open lever, and backed the chair away enough to pull the door open. Then she used the hook and pulled herself forward enough to block the door from closing. She unhooked the hook, put it back in its sling, and wheeled inside.

That's when Robyn jumped up from her table, ran over, and said, "Oh, I'm sorry! I should have helped."

Like Helen, Robyn was wearing sweat pants and a sweatshirt, but on her the workout wear looked stylish rather than schlumpy.

Helen waved her away. "Don't be sorry. I do this all the time."

"Really?" Robyn looked aghast. "Don't people help you?"

Helen shrugged. "Sometimes. And sometimes it's not worth it. They hold the door open, but then stand in the way. Or they let go and it bangs the chair. You do what you have to do."

Robyn nodded her head as if Helen was the Buddha dispensing wisdom.

"Can I buy you a coffee at least?"

"Sure," Helen said. "Tell Chuck I'll have my usual."

"Chuck?"

"Yeah. He's the owner. Chucklehead… Chuck?"

"Really?" Robyn glanced at the old man behind the counter. "I never put that together."

"People either talk to me or they avoid me," Helen said. "It's one or the other."

"Well, I'm done avoiding you." Robyn smiled. Then she bopped to the counter and placed the order.

Helen, meanwhile, rolled her chair toward Robyn's table, reached over and moved a chair out of the way, and then pushed herself up.

"I should have done that too," Robyn said when she returned with the lattes.

Helen shrugged. "Just because I'm disabled doesn't mean I'm a helpless cripple."

Robyn's eyes widened in dismay. Then they narrowed. "Are you making a joke?"

"Yep," Helen said. "One of the benefits of the chair is that I can make as many jokes as I want."

Then Robyn smiled and started to giggle. "You're pretty bad-ass aren't you?"

"Bad ass?" Helen made a face. "Are you talking about my bed sores from sitting all the time?"

It took another moment for that one to land, and then Robyn threw her head back and laughed. She had a nice laugh, Helen decided, as she joined in.

After that, the afternoon flew by. They talked about everything and nothing.

By nature, Helen was wired to avoid gossip. It was too easy to take pot shots at her, so she avoided conversations that demeaned others. That didn't mean she wasn't curious about Robyn and Robyn's life.

Robyn told her about growing up down south in Maryland, and moving to Groston the summer before high school.

"Back home, ninth grade was still middle school," Robyn said, with a hint of a southern lilt. "So I felt younger than everybody else. And clueless. Plus our school was huge and mostly so-called minority. Here in Groston, black folks are scarce, in case you didn't know. Sort of as a survival tactic I joined all the popular activities. Cheerleading and gymnastics. Not basketball. I wasn't going to be that black girl superstar on the all white team. And besides, I can't play that well."

Helen nodded, not saying anything.

Rather than continuing, Robyn paused. "You couldn't do that, huh?"

"What?"

"Any of those things. Gymnastics, cheerleading or basketball."

"No. Not really." Helen shrugged. "I thought about becoming a team manager, but it felt kind of pathetic."

Robyn nodded. "I can get that. My tits got too big for gymnastics, so I quit that."

Helen laughed. "That's a thing?"

Robyn nodded. "Yeah, it screws up your balance. Look at all the Olympians. They're all tiny, or else they have to bind themselves so they don't bobble. And the big-boobed girls never win the golds."

"So you were stuck with just cheerleading?"

"It's not bad," Robyn said. "Sometimes it gets catty, but the girls are pretty good. Susie's a good captain."

Susie Wardle was the most popular girl at Ashby Bryson High. Everybody liked her. She was pretty, maybe even beautiful. Every girl wanted to be her. Every boy wanted her. The only thing she and Helen had in common was blonde hair.

Helen sighed.

"You'd like her," Robyn said. "She's tough. And smart too. You actually remind me a lot of her."

"Really?" Helen snorted. "My naturally curly hair?"

"You've got nice hair," Robyn said. She eyed Helen. "And wow, you have a pretty nice body under all the baggy clothes you always wear."

Helen blushed and looked at her coffee.

"No, I understand," Robyn said. "Camouflage. It's a good tactic. Being invisible. That's one possibility."

"I'm never invisible," Helen said, feeling a bit sorry for herself. "Everybody always sees me. After that, though, I'm just someone to be ignored or pitied."

"Bullshit," Robyn said, shaking her head. "You dress like that to be one of the guys that you hang out with."

Helen got very still. Robyn was right, but Helen wasn't sure she wanted to have this conversation.

"It's okay," Robyn said. "I'd be invisible if I could. But I'm too tall, too dark, and I'm too curvy, and I've got a big mouth. So invisibility's not an option."

Then Robyn stopped talking and waited. She stared at Helen until Helen finally looked up.

"What?" Helen said.

"I think you're awesome," Robyn said. "You kick ass in school.

You have really good friends. You don't take shit. There are so many more kids that I know whose lives are infinitely more fucked up and they don't have the challenges you have to deal with every day."

"What the fuck do you know about me?" Helen said. She pulled her phone from her saddlebag and punched the quick, "Twenty minutes, please" text to her Dad.

"Hey, I'm not trying to piss you off. I'm trying to compliment you. Half the girls on the squad are on diet pills or cocaine. Half are dumbasses. Another half pretend they're dumbasses. Another half can't wait to get married and have kids. And another half think high school is going to last forever."

"That's two-hundred and fifty percent," Helen snapped.

"There's overlap," Robyn shot back. "Think of a Venn diagram."

Helen had to laugh. Robyn joined her.

"What I was trying to get at," Robyn said, "is that there are a lot of people I know who screw up their own lives. You got born screwed up. And you're just making the best of it."

"Can I put that on my tombstone?"

"Sure." Robyn smiled. "Just don't die soon."

"Not planning on it," Helen said. "Unless…"

Then they both chorused, "Live fast, die young, and leave a good-looking corpse!"

Their laughter made everybody else in the small coffee shop turn and stare, which kept them laughing even longer.

• • •

When Helen's dad arrived, Robyn pushed the wheelchair down to the curb and watched as the door opened and the ramp extended.

"Pretty cool van," Robyn said.

"Yeah," Helen said. "In theory I can pull out the drivers seat and operate it by myself, but my parents don't want to let me, and to be honest I kind of like being chauffeured."

Robyn nodded. "My parents hate each other. I don't know why they stay together. They yell all the time."

Helen reached back and put a hand on Robyn's. "Sorry."

"Is what it is," Robyn said. "Going away to college and never coming back."

Helen's dad tapped the horn and shouted, "Come on, we've got to go. Another asshole is parked in the handicapped spot, again, and we're blocking the road."

Helen wheeled herself up, turned and waved.

Robyn waved back. "See you tomorrow."

"Not if I see you first," Helen said.

The door closed and Helen positioned herself up in the passenger area, locking the chair to the floor.

"Who's that?" Dad asked. "New friend?"

"No," Helen said. "Her name's Robyn. She's an old friend that I just didn't know."

Dad made a puzzled face, then shrugged, put the van in gear and asked, "Do you have any homework?"

Helen sighed. Back to life, as usual.

Well, it could be worse.

She leaned over and kissed her dad on the cheek.

"What's that for?" he said.

"Everything." Helen smiled. Got to keep them guessing.

Chapter 2

In Rover's Basement

"Comedy is when you laugh, even if you don't want to."
– Charles "Fat Charlie" Johnson

January in New England sucks.

It was freezing outside, and Dave Rover's basement felt like a dungeon. The walls were cement. The floor was cement. The cross-beams were steel. It was stark and ugly, and we usually loved it. In the summertime the concrete kept us cool. In the winter, though, it was often dank and chilly.

Originally built as a bomb shelter in the 1950s, Rover's basement had been our primary hangout since elementary school.[5] Our games had evolved from Clue to Risk to D&D to Magic: the Gathering to

---

[5] Rover's grandfather, who had designed the shelter to withstand an H Bomb, had hung a framed picture of his hero, Winston Churchill, flipping the reverse peace sign with the caption, "Never, never, never give up." The photo was still nailed to the wall. Beneath it, I'd scrawled another one of Churchill's quotes, "If you're going through hell, keep going."

Call of Duty to Texas hold 'em, and Rocket League, but the mood of the place was the same. Rover's basement was our home away from home.[6] Cell phones didn't work down there, so our parents knew that if they needed to get in touch with us they'd have to call Rover's mom or dad and have one of them yell down the stairs. This was always awkward and only happened in emergencies, so over the years they'd lowered their expectations. In other words, when our parents called or sent a text that we didn't want to answer right away, we always had the shrugged excuse, "I was downstairs at Rover's." Boom. Kismet.

Like I said, Rover's basement was our home away from home. We were sheltered from the world, and problems did not exist.

That morning there were just four of us hanging out – the original crew – Rover, me, Fat Charlie, and my cousin Adam. Jesús, Helen, and Sean weren't in just yet.

We were lounging about doing nothing, except an informal gum spitting contest. Rover's mom had bought a huge box of Bazooka bubble gum for Halloween at a wholesale membership club, but none of the trick-or-treaters had taken any of it. I didn't blame them. The gum was pink, brick-shaped and rock hard. After you chewed it for two minutes, it lost all flavor. But, we'd also learned

---

[6] There was only one one real rule in Rover's basement: stay out of Rover's dad's basement lab, which was a cross between Dr. Frankenstein's workspace and an EPA HAZMAT site.* Rover's dad was a weird activist blend of chemical engineer and environmental scientist. Come to think of it, even though we were there all the time, never once did Rover's dad come down the stairs and interrupt, or emerge from behind the locked door with a stench of chemistry. Maybe there was another way in and out, which now that I think of it seems likely, since the basement was designed to survive a near miss of a nuke.

*We did stay out. Mostly. The lab was locked, and every year or so, Rover's dad changed the whole security procedure, which usually only took Rover a week or two to crack. Rover was, as we liked to say with a Boston accent, "Wicked smaaht." We'd open the door, peek in on an experiment bubbling in some delicate stage of incompletion, and then shut it before the stank could escape.

that the gum wouldn't stick to anything, so we'd started rebounding the chaws off the walls, aiming for an old spittoon Fat Charlie had found in his Uncle James the cop's basement.

I had just shot a big gob off the ceiling and into the spittoon, where it landed with a perfect three-point thuck, when Rover asked me, "So, Izz, did you hear yet?"

My stomach dropped. I shrugged.

We were in the thick of Early College Acceptance Time, and all anybody in our age and demographic group could think of was who got in to what schools.[7] Someone should do a sociology study about what happens to a group of friends when they're all waiting for the news that's going to determine their entire future. The level of anxiety and stomach churning is huge. When one person gets good news there's a blend of cheering on the outside and bitter cursing on the inside.

For instance, we all knew that Rover had applied to MIT "Early Action" and got in – of course. He'd found out way back in early December, which was just crazy. Even before Christmas, he'd known that by next fall, he was going to be living in Cambridge and hanging out with a whole bunch of geeks like himself. For Rover, high school was all done, except for the showing up part. He didn't need to ace anything, he just needed to pass. The relief we saw in Rover's body and mind was visible. He could breathe.

"What about you guys? Hear yet?"

Fat Charlie shrugged. "Soon." Charlie was always cool like that, never concerned about anything.

But a grin flashed across Adam's face, and then vanished when he noticed I hadn't reacted.

"Um…" Adam said.

Rover squinted at Adam. "Dude, what did you hear?"

"Nothing." Adam was a nice guy, always a peacemaker. He avoided trouble like the plague. Adam knew that if he shared his good news, I'd probably feel like shit. "Never mind."

But I could tell that he had good news, so I already felt like shit.

---

[7] I am not even going to go into the special kinds of high school hell that we'd been through during the previous three and a half years.

"I'll be fine," I lied. "Spill it."

"I got into Columbia." Adam grinned. "In New York City! NYC! They even came through with a great financial aid package."

"That's awesome," I said, forcing a smile.

"I don't know about that," Adam demured. "My real dad went to Columbia, so I'm sort of a legacy. I don't know if I deserve it."

"Bullshit, man," Rover yelped. "You have a four-point-oh, you're captain of the fencing team, and you have a first degree black belt."

"Actually," Adam said, "I passed my second degree black belt test just after Christmas."

"Really?" I glanced at my cousin. "You never said."

Adam shrugged. "It was sort of a surprise."

"Oh, you deserve it," Charlie said. Then he banked a clump of gum off two walls and landed it on the spittoon's rim. "That's a point for style and one for sticking, right?"

"Only if nobody knocks it off," I said, reaching for another piece of gum.

"You're a second degree black belt in Aikido!" Rover continued. "Plus your real dad, the Columbia grad, was killed in action. And your stepdad's a vet too. You got all the ducks lined up. Somebody's got to get into Columbia. Might as well be you."

Adam paused, like he did every time he thought about his real Dad. "Yeah, but…" His voice trailed off. He looked at me. "So, Isaac, did you hear anything?"

"Not recently," I said. "Crickets."

I had applied to Harvard early decision. I'd visited and been charmed by the campus and Cambridge. It looked like what a college was supposed to be. I really wanted to go there. I knew it was a long shot, though. Even though their reply deadline was past, I hadn't heard. I hadn't heard from anywhere else either, which was to be expected.

I wasn't feeling optimistic. My grades weren't as good as Adam's. My extracurriculars weren't either. Our SATs were about the same. Adam had a varsity letter from the fencing team and now his second degree black belt for Chrissakes. My biggest sports challenge was running through the hall to be on time for Mrs. Hendry's AP

World History class. My application essay was better than his, but that wasn't much.

If I didn't get into Harvard, I'd be okay going to Columbia. Or maybe Princeton. All I really wanted was to get into any good school that was nowhere near home.

"Did you check your email this afternoon?" Adam asked me. "I just found out like an hour ago."

"And you didn't say anything until now?" Rover made a face.

Adam shrugged. "Check your email. Log onto Harvard's site."

"Check your email, man," Fat Charlie said.

"No." I shrugged. "Phone won't work down here."

Rover nodded his head toward his hyper-gaming-computer-stack. "We've got the Internet. Use the wifi. Open a private browser. I'll turn off the keyboard logging. Sign in. Check."

I did not want to. There were only four possibilities: acceptance, rejection, nothing, or worse, the wait list. And the odds of acceptance seemed to get smaller with every day that I didn't hear.

"Let it go," Adam told Rover. "Anybody else coming in today?"

"So, we're just going to pretend nothing's going on?" Charlie said. "Ignore the gorilla in the room?"

"What gorilla?" I felt the weight of my phone in my pocket.

Adam ignored Charlie.

Then Charlie pointed and yelled, "LOOK OVER THERE!"

Rover's eyes widened as he too pointed over my shoulder. "There's a big fucking gorilla!"

"AAAAAH!" I yelled, playing along.

"What? Where?" Adam shouted, and in one fluid movement jumped up out of his chair and assumed a defensive Aikido posture. "What?"

"Second degree black belt, my ass." Charlie sniggered.

Rover and I cracked up.

Every time Adam got startled he leaped into his martial arts ready mode. We had a running challenge about how often we could get him to react. The record was three times in one afternoon. Just before Halloween, Jesús and Fat Charlie had planned the whole set-up with a series of escalating pranks involving a prerecorded news

33

bulletin about a serial killer, a fake stabbing, and a starter's pistol.

I high fived Rover, got up and chalked another mark on the wall.

"Am I winning yet?" Rover asked.

"We've got to split that one," Charlie insisted.

"You're still behind by six," I told him. I was way ahead of everybody, but of course Adam was my cousin, so I knew which buttons to push.

"A gorilla? Really?" Adam was pissed, checking around the room to make sure that nobody was hiding. With our friends, it could have been Sean or Jesús in a gorilla suit. But there was nobody in the basement, just us four. "What the fuck was all that shit about a gorilla?"

Rover and I were still chuckling.

"Come on. Don't you get it?" Charlie grinned. "There really is a gorilla in the room."

Even though he'd just checked, and completely embarrassed himself, Adam's shoulders jerked and his head and eyes twitched.

Rover and I laughed again.

"Does that count?" Charlie asked.

"Almost, but no," I ruled.

"There is no gorilla," Adam insisted.

"Yeah, there is," Rover said, pointing behind Adam.

Despite his best efforts, Adam's eyes darted and he turned his head. "Cut it out!"

We couldn't help laughing.

"You are so easy," I teased.

"A gorilla in the room is when you don't talk about something, but everybody knows it's there." Charlie explained, pedantically.

"It's that like an elephant joke" Rover said. "An elephant walks into a bar and says, 'Make me a grasshopper.' The bartender says, 'I can't, you're an elephant.'"

"What the fuck?" Adam said, exasperated.

"Adam, you really need to cut back on the coffee," I told my cousin. "Speaking of which, make me some."

"You're the caffeine addict. I'm just sensitive to potential threats."

"You're a jittery jumpy mess, Adam" Charlie said. "Maybe you should bump up the dosage of your medical marijuana."

"No. I'm trying to taper off the weed," Adam said. "I think that the hip pain's finally going away, but it's hard to tell when I'm stoned all the time."

"Do they do drug testing for college?" Charlie wondered.

"Do they?" Rover suddenly looked worried.

"I don't think so," I said. "But of course I haven't gotten in yet."

"Hello!" Charlie said. "There's that gorilla! Right there."

Adam closed his eyes and took a deep breath.

Yeah. It was a gorilla all right.

"Listen, I've got an idea," Adam said when he opened his eyes. "If you don't get in to a good school, then we'll all defer college a year."

"A gap year is an awesome idea," Rover said. "We'll keep you company. We can form an entrepreneurial Internet startup, get some venture capital, vest our stock, sell it off, and make millions. Billions! Then, when we finally go to college, we can study whatever we like. We'd be like Gates, Jobs, and Zuckerbutt, except we'd all cash out before we become douches."

"What the fuck?" I shook my head. "That's just stupid. You guys would never do that."

"Why not?" Charlie said. "I'm not in anywhere yet either. I'm not making any big plans. My Dad's always bugging me to get some real life experience."

"Sticking together is not stupid," Adam insisted. "We've been friends forever. College is going to break us apart. This much we know. But there's no reason for you to get left behind."

"Nobody gets left behind!" Charlie boomed.

"I'm not going to be left behind," I said. "I can always go to good old Fectville State University. They'll take anyone."

"Fect U?" Rover and Adam stared at me like I was stupid, which I'm not, but I always felt stupid compared to them. Rover turned the knife, "Do you really want to go to Fect U?"

"There's nothing wrong with Fect U, except the nicknames," I said. "It's a good school, and my folks can afford it."

"Fecting Useless." Charlie said.

"Come on," Adam said. "Money's not an issue. Your dad's a

doctor. Your mom's a shrink. They can afford to send you pretty much anywhere."

"Well, I have to get in somewhere first."

"Maybe you're in now," Rover gestured toward the keyboard. "Izzzzzzz… You've got to check it. Go on. You know you want to." His sing-song voice was insinuating. "Izz-zy…"

Again, with the sinking feeling.

At almost eighteen, you have no idea who the hell you are.

Growing up, your identity is first set by your parents and then by your friends. During school you become your activities, grades, and extracurriculars. Then you're supposed to mature and become something new, usually based on work or higher education.

Well-meaning teachers talk a lot about self-validation. You see Zen monks on TV lecturing about being in the moment. The entire history of the United States of America is supposed to be about rugged individualism and self-reliance.[8] Add on the completely weird ideas about being a man these days, which is a blend of respectfully taking care of your family while offending no one, but also being self-sufficient but dependent on no one. It's all so confusing.

I don't even know where I get all this shit. It sort of floats around between social media, pseudo-fake news, real fake news, peer pressure and real real news, but all of it had been rattling around in my brain ever since I'd applied to college. Maybe before.

I wished I could be like Fat Charlie. Big and calm and centered.

Fact was, I had no idea what I was going to do or be, nor where I was going to do or be it.

Our world seemed very arbitrary and artificial. One day you're a normal high school student trying to survive parents, hormones, dating, standardized testing, grades, drugs and sex. The next day your entire life is about waiting for the email that tells you to log into the college's portal for your "admission status update". Some kids stalk their status, keeping themselves logged-in 24/7, obsessively refreshing their browser hoping for a change of status. Or you can watch the snail mail for the thick envelope that has the golden ticket, or the

---

[8] With a dollop of Westward expansionism, occasional religious tolerance, and a strong undercurrent of racism.

skinny one with the bad news. Or you could be wait-listed, which means more agony for months to come.

"Dear Student, We won't say that you are laughably unqualified. Instead, we want to thank you politely for spending money to apply, and wish you the best for your future. Here at Top One Percent University, we accept only the best. You're not it. You're fucked. Oops. Did we say that out loud? Sorry, but it's true. Maybe there's a job opening in our sanitation removal department…."

Needless to say, I hadn't been checking my email vigilantly.

"Listen," I began.

Suddenly, Fat Charlie jumped up from checking his phone and yelled, "Rover, you rock! I got into NYU! I got into NYU!"

I gaped at Charlie.

Rover gave him two thumbs up. "Congratulations. You and Adam are both going to be in New York City!"

Adam grinned and slapped Charlie five.

Charlie started dancing. "Whooo hoo!"

"Great," I said, glumly.

"Fuck you, Ike!" Fat Charlie grinned. "Be happy for me."

"I am," I mumbled.

"Then fucking check your fucking email. I personally know that waiting sucks balls. My folks are laid back and I was going nuts! You, with your overeducated high-pressure professional parents, man you must be completely insane."

Yeah. Thanks. I wanted to hang myself.

"Fine." I gave up. "Rover, turn off your keystroke logging."

Charlie didn't care, but one reason I almost never logged into Rover's network was that he was an incorrigible hacker. He loved collecting passwords, and had been known to send emails or post on other people's social media accounts.

Rover tapped a few keys. "Viola!"

"You mean voila, right?" Charlie said.

"Nah, I like Classical music more than French," Rover answered.

I pulled my phone out of my pocket and logged into the wifi.

"Well?" They all crowded around. "Well?"

Spam, spam, spam and more spam.

My friends looked at me expectantly.

With a sigh, I logged onto Hah-vaad's admissions portal.

Suddenly my eyes widened. "HOLY SHIT! I GOT IN!"

"Woohoo!!" Adam yelped.

"All right," Charlie bellowed, pounding me on the back.

"Really?" Rover asked. "Lemme see!"

"Psyche!" I shouted, grinning through gritted teeth.

"What?" Adam said. "Which? Did you get in or not?"

"Not." I shrugged. "Not yet."

Rover and Charlie deflated. "What?"

"I didn't get in," I admitted, somewhat abashed. "Not really."

"What the fuck, man?" Charlie shook his head.

Even Adam looked pissed.

"Look," I snapped, "I was just bullshitting. Nothing yet. No change in status. Still awaiting decision."

"Shit," Adam said.

"FUBAR!" Rover said.

I wanted to throw up.

"Hey." Fat Charlie grinned. "No news is better than bad news."

"Yeah," I said. "Maybe."

I felt like a racehorse ten feet from the finish line with a broken leg. I wanted to get up and hobble away. Everybody else was either cheering me on or wanted to put me out of my misery.

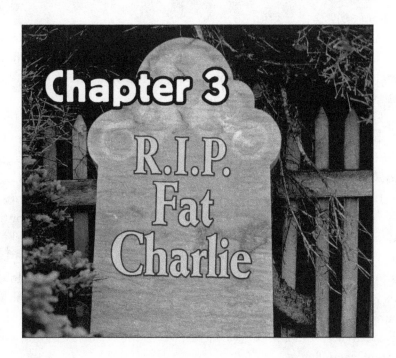

Chapter 3

R.I.P. Fat Charlie

"You wanna know what makes me laugh? It's simple. A guy in a white suit falls into a pile of shit. I'm a visual person."
— Jesús Ramirez

The weather in Rover's basement was always the same. No matter which season, whether the hottest days of the summer or the coldest of the winter, the temperature was always sixty-five degrees. Rover's dad was big into energy efficiency and had installed a geothermal system. Some kind of viscous liquid was pumped up through the floor of the basement and circulated through the house, cooling or heating, depending on the time of year.

In the wintertime, though, it got a little dank, so we kept an assortment of old sweaters hanging from a rack under the staircase. Everybody but Sean would wear them. Sean, of course, wore his own designer sweaters. Once a year, Rover's mom came down, collected the ones we'd outgrown, and donated them to a women's shelter.

Add into the ambiance the complete lack of windows and no clocks on the wall, and, in my memory, Rover's basement was utterly timeless. Like a Las Vegas casino without the lights, bells, slots, roulette wheels, bartenders and waitresses.[9]

Or maybe I'm just romanticizing it. Probably. When I look back on those last days before everything changed, it blurs like a movie montage or a time-lapse, with people racing around from seat to seat showing days or months or years passing in a matter of moments.

It was the Friday of the MLK long weekend and we were unusually quiet. Rover was playing a game of solitaire on his computer. Adam and Helen were doing their homework for next week, which they always did first thing, rather than putting it off until the last minute – which probably was why they got straight As and I didn't. I was writing in my journal. Jesús hadn't arrived yet; he was still home taking care of his younger siblings until his mom got back from her job. Sean was out for the weekend, visitating with his father, who lived in Fectville.

Fat Charlie still hadn't arrived, which was worrying. He'd been called out of class in the afternoon, and had never returned.

Every few minutes one or another of us would glance up the stairs that led to Rover's kitchen.

"How come there's no music on?" Helen asked.

Adam shrugged.

"I mean, unless you guys are blowing each other up with video games, it's always so quiet in here. We could listen to something," she continued. "Rover, your sound bar's got Bluetooth, right?"

Rover nodded.

"Can I pair with it without you downloading my phone?"

"Sure." Rover shrugged. "Are you on the wifi? There's no cell down here."

Helen shook her head. "I've got lots of stuff downloaded on my phone. My parents won't let me run up the cell data anyway. What do you guys want to listen to?"

---

[9] We did play a lot of cards.

None of us said anything. We were all waiting for Fat Charlie.
We looked up the stairs and then looked at each other.

"All right then, my pick," Helen said.

She put on the original cast recording of *Hamilton*, which everybody likes. Historical revisionism combined with rap on Broadway.

"Does anybody know what the fuck happened to Fat Charlie?" Rover finally said, while Alexander Hamilton was starting out from nothing.

Adam and Helen shook their heads.

"He got called out of Mrs. Hendry's class over the loudspeaker just after lunch," I said. "He didn't come back. He hasn't texted me. Or at least he didn't before I came down here."

Getting called out of class in high school was never good news. Back when we were all going to Jerome Marco K-8, it seemed like every fifteen minutes some kid or another was called out of class for a doctor or dentist appointment, or something like that. At Ashby Bryson High, though, interruptions were rare. Every time somebody's name flashed over the loudspeaker, everybody else in that kid's class sing-songed, "Oooh, you're in trouble!"

Most of the time kids were called out was because they'd gotten caught – cutting classes, smoking cigarettes in the bathroom, or swiping somebody's homework.

But Fat Charlie was a good kid. He had good grades. He didn't get into trouble.

When he got the call over the loudspeaker, Fat Charlie had shrugged at me, grinned at the jeers, taken a bow, grabbed his backpack, and vanished.

At the end of the day, we'd looked for him. Usually after the last bell, especially on a Friday afternoon that kicked off a long weekend, we'd gather near the school's library to figure out our plan for the next few days. Fat Charlie's locker was just down the hall from the library. He didn't show.

Alexander Hamilton. His name was Alexander Hamilton...

We didn't hear the door, but we all felt the slight air pressure change as the back door to Rover's house opened upstairs.

All eyes went to the staircase.

The door to the basement creaked open.

We listened.

Everybody in our gang[10] has a different stepsound tromping down the stairs. Adam is kind of bouncy but quiet. Rover thumps regularly, like clockwork. Jesús has a quickstep. Helen, of course rings the back bell, then uses the ropes system to roll her wheelchair down the ramp we'd installed in the bulkhead for her. Sean does a kind of "rap-a-ta-tap" down the steps. I have no idea what I sound like. Fat Charlie thuds like a bass drum. Sometimes it's quicker than others.

Today Fat Charlie's thudding was slow. Real slow. Funereal. Shit.

We all pretended to ignore it and went back to what we doing. Rover was flipping digital cards. Helen and Adam focused on their calculus.

I wrote this in my journal, "The basement smelled like cinder block and grease and sweat, but faintly and not in a bad way." Not much in the way of memorable prose, but that was the only way I could keep from watching as Fat Charlie reached the bottom of the steps.

"Hey, Fat Charlie," Rover said, also not looking up.

"Fat Charlie!" Adam and I said as a chorus, like a bunch of regular characters in a TV sitcom.

If Helen hadn't been there, we might have tried to put together a serious poker game, so we wouldn't have to talk about it. Whatever it was.

Guys and girls must be wired differently. Guys respect other guy's right to privacy. Girls, however, have no clue about male silences or emotional boundaries.

By then, Charlie had moved into the basement proper. He hung his coat on a hanger and pulled on a sweater. His face looked pale, or as pale as a black kid's face can be.

"Fat Charlie, what's wrong?" Helen asked. "You okay?"

The guys all froze. You just didn't do that. When a guy wanted

---

[10] Yes, we were a gang. No we weren't gangbangers or criminals or troublemakers (mostly). We were, as the dictionary said, "a group of people, especially young people, who regularly associate together."

to talk, he'd talk in his own time.

Fat Charlie licked his lips and said, "Stop fucking calling me Fat fucking Charlie."

"What?" Helen yelped. "I'm sorry."

"Hey!" Adam leapt to Helen's defense. "Don't talk to her like that."

"Yeah, man," Rover said. "What the hell?"

"I don't need you to protect me, Adam," Helen said, testily.

"What's going on?" I asked.

"My dad is in the hospital," Charlie said. "He had a heart attack."

"Shit!" We all said it at once.

"Is he okay?" Adam asked

Helen spun her wheel chair around and stared at Charlie. "What happened?"

"Are you okay?" I asked.

Fat Charlie's dad was a manager at a Japanese car dealership. Like everybody in the Johnson family, Mr. Johnson was big and tall and wide. George Johnson was nice and kind and funny and very popular. His wife was an amazing cook, but Mr. Johnson loved to barbecue too. Every summer their family had a neighborhood cook-out and Mr. Johnson fired up two huge rigs, roasted a whole pig and grilled most of a cow. Everybody loved Mr. Johnson.

"He's not dead," Charlie said.

"That's good," I said.

"Whew!" Rover added.

"Dad was just getting ready to take some customers out for a test ride," Fat Charlie said. "One of the sales reps didn't show up to work because of the long weekend, so Dad was filling in, doing his job. He opened the passenger door to a brand new SUV hybrid and just collapsed in the parking lot."

"So, will he be okay?" Helen asked.

"Yeah. Maybe. I don't know. Yeah, he's okay. He's still in the hospital. But you know what we had for dinner last night? Fried chicken."

"I love your mom's fried chicken!" Rover said.

We all nodded. My mouth started watering.

Charlie's dad was a good cook, but his mom was even better.

Mrs. Johnson made everything from scratch. Her food was delicious, hot, crunchy and savory – except for her desserts, which were fatty, crunchy and sweet. She came from Louisiana. Her family was a mix of Creole and East Texas, so she knew how to make fabulous Southern food that was unmatched in our small New England town.

"And I had leftover fried chicken for lunch too," Fat Charlie said. "And potato chips. And a big soda. And chocolate pudding. Like I do every day. Like my dad did every Friday. You know how many chickens Mom fries when she fries chicken on Thursday? Four. Two for dinner and two for leftovers. And these are big chickens, about seven or eight pounds each. They're huge, probably shot up with growth hormones. There are only four people in our family, me, Mom, Dad, and Desiree, who's off at college. That's half a chicken or more each for dinner and another half for lunch. Tuesday is pizza night. Mom makes four to six pizzas, depending on company. Wednesday is chili. She makes three gallons. Some of that she takes to the homeless shelter, but most of it gets eaten at home. Friday night is either brisket or ribs. Saturday is either ribs or brisket. Sunday is fried catfish with hushpuppies and grits. You know what we have for vegetables? Fried okra, mashed potatoes or French fries. Monday is leftovers or meatloaf or chicken pot pie."

"Oh my god, Fat Charlie, you're killing me!" Rover said. "That all sounds so good!"

Rover was never the quickest on the social cues uptake.

"Don't fucking call me FAT FUCKING CHARLIE EVER AGAIN!" Charlie yelled. "All that fried fatty food put my daddy in the hospital. All four of my grandparents are dead of heart attacks. My Uncle Bob has had two heart attacks this year. Uncle Jeff's had gastric bypass. Uncle James, the cop, is a fitness nut, but he says his cholesterol's still off the charts. Every time I go for a checkup, the doctor tells me that I am morbidly obese. Morbidly fucking obese. My pediatrician says I need to lose weight, or I'm going to die. He laughs when he says this. Like he knows I'm a dead man walking. Like he's pronouncing my death sentence."

Alexander Hamilton was babbling about not throwing away his shot.

Helen turned off the music.

The room was dead quiet. Sometimes we could hear Rover's mom walking around upstairs. If she was up there, she had stopped moving too.

Charlie looked at us. "I'm just another black kid in a moderately integrated school…"

"Hey, you know that doesn't matter to us," Adam interrupted.

"Shut the fuck up, I know," Charlie snapped. "But for everybody else, I'm the big fat black kid, who's supposed to be jolly and happy and chubby and everybody's friend."

"But that's who you are, man," Rover said. "Everybody likes you. You're awesome. It doesn't matter what you look like…"

"I am a fucking stereotype!" Charlie yelled. "I am a goddamn stereotype waiting to become a death statistic. I love my family. I love my dad. I don't want him to die. And I don't want to die either. So I'm killing Fat Charlie now. Today. As of this moment, Fat Charlie is dead."

"Wait, I'm lost," Rover said. "I thought you said you didn't want to die."

"Rover," Helen hissed, "Charlie is changing his life. Get a clue."

Charlie nodded. His voice got thick and slow. "I don't know how I'm going to do this shit. I'm supposed to lose like a hundred pounds. But one thing I do know is that being called Fat Charlie has got to stop. Are you guys okay with this? Shit, even if you're not okay with this, I need you to be."

He waited.

"Yeah." I nodded.

Helen and Adam nodded. "Of course."

"Sure, sure. No more Fat Charlie." Rover nodded. "How about we call you Skinny Charlie Wannabe?"

"Rover!" Helen barked.

Adam snorted and tried to cover his smirk.

I held back my chuckles.

Rover looked like a deer in the headlights. "What?"

Charlie's eyes grew wide and angry. For a moment he looked like he was going to lose it. Then he relaxed, nodded and forced a smile. "Yeah. No. Let's wait on the new nickname."

"All right," I said. "Charlie it is."

"Charlie!" Rover and Helen echoed.

Adam went to the fridge. "Anybody want a diet soda?"

We laughed. Adam passed out cans. We raised them high in a toast. "To the death of Fat Charlie!"

"May he rest in peace!" Helen said, nervously.

"A big fat piece!" Rover said.

I winced, but Charlie managed a small grin.

"Yeah," Charlie said, lifting his can. "Farewell, to Fat Charlie. You're big and round and you're in the ground."

Chapter 4

Oranges

"I am in awe of the comedians who get laughs with language and wordplay. I like puns and witticism. I like concept dissection. But when they make a sentence dance and then turn it on the last word, it makes me laughgasm."
– Helen Beagle

I'd never seen a real fight. Not until that Tuesday morning when everything went off the rails.

As a young American, I've watched a gazillion life or death battles, with billions of punches thrown, high kicks snapped, brutalizing explosions and trillions of bullets fired in endless sprays resulting in heaps of bodies and oceans of blood – all on video, in the movies and on TV.

And of course in video games, I've killed and maimed more than my share. I've participated in duels to the death, firefights, extractions, hijackings, carjackings, ripoffs, beatdowns, smackdowns, and home invasions. I've run suicide missions and died horribly again and again until I figured out the flaw in the Kobayashi Maru and finally won.

None of it was "real."

We all lived in Groston, which rhymes with Boston, and is a somewhat scenic partly-suburban partly-derelict New England mill town, with relatively little in the way of gang violence. Close to zero. Ok, none. Somehow, despite a hunkering bunch of old-time Yankees, a well-established African American community, a close-knit Hispanic neighborhood, and all the various world music types who'd ended up there, Groston was too lame to muster much in the way of tribalism. Even though my group of friends jokingly called ourselves a gang, we didn't have colors, treaties or deal fentanyl.[11] Of course over the years, the town had seen its share of scuffles and shoves and the occasional thrown punch, but nobody ever pulled a knife or a gun or even got taken to the hospital.

Until that Tuesday morning, I never realized how quick and brutal a real fight could be.

It was a Day C schedule, so I was coming out of chemistry, heading toward calculus. Chem and calc back to back was mind numbing. With no time to stop at my locker, I was seriously considering eating the four-month old protein bar I kept buried in my backpack for emergencies.

My cousin Adam had just finished his AP Bio in Room 315, which was two doors down from my chem class.

Adam and I were in Calc together, so when I saw his head bobbing about fifteen feet ahead I started hurrying to catch up.

Coming toward us from the other direction were Doug Hawthorne and Butch Batten, the fearsome twosome of the Groston Pioneers football team. These two guys had been big since forever. For four years, they'd been the star high school football players. Now as seniors in their last semester, they were right at the top of the social and sports food chain.

---

[11] Although we did print up "Team Bomb Shelter" tee shirts. Jesús drew an illustration of a nuclear explosion on the surface, and all seven of us below ground playing video games while the world topside burned.

Doug was the tall handsome quarterback, lithe and quick and precise with a pass. He had an amazing way of connecting with a receiver and dropping the ball exactly where and when they'd be open. Doug had been scouted by colleges, had an agent, and was in a bidding war negotiation between UCLA and Notre Dame. Rumor was that he was holding out for a full ride for both himself and Butch, plus housing, food, travel and expenses.

Butch was Doug's front line. His entire front line, because the rest of the players on the Pioneers front line were fairly useless. Butch had been a mean-ass bully from third grade on. Toward the end of our K-8 school years, Butch had grown from merely large to fucking huge. He was six-four and wide as a door. During games, when anybody came close to Doug, Butch flattened them like a steamroller. They had literally carried seven rushers off the field that year, scaring the hell out of every defensive line in our division, and leaving Doug wide open to do his thing. Butch was a brutal cross between an enforcer, a wall, and a football terrorist.

During their senior year, the fearsome twosome had won every regular season game, slaughtering the opposition like sheep. Groston went all the way to the state finals, and we would have won, except for a lucky kick in the closing twenty seconds of overtime by Springfield West High.

I was in the stands for that game, and it was heartbreakingly close to a movie ending. At first, people in our school were pissed that we'd lost, but since Groston had never gotten that far in the history of Ashby Bryson High School football, ultimately nobody cared, so Butch and Doug were still feted as heroes.

Doug had his pick of any girl he wanted, which was Susie Wardle, the head of the cheerleading squad. Butch took any girls Doug didn't want, which turned out to be a revolving string of Susie wannabes.

It was Tuesday morning at 9:57. The fearsome twosome were on their way to their remedial Geology class in room 320.

I was catching up, about five feet behind Adam, when it happened.

Doug and Butch were walking toward Adam. Butch almost had

a smile on his face and seemed to be raising his hand in a wave.

Back in the day at Jerome Marco K-8, Adam and Butch had gotten into an almost-fight, which Adam had somehow defused. He'd made it out alive and become somewhat friendly with Butch. Their friendship had dwindled as Butch hulked out and his ego had grown bigger than his shoulders.

From where I was standing, it looked like Butch walked right into Adam, who rebounded like a tennis ball off a brick wall.

Adam bounced straight back but didn't fall. Then, he said something to Butch.

Butch looked confused, and then angry, like he'd been poked with a cattle prod.

The hallway cleared in an instant as every high school student's monkey instincts kicked into gear and they got the hell out of the way.

Butch went from zero to sixty straight at Adam with his head down and both fists clenched ready to mow my cousin over.

When Adam was elementary age, he'd been a short and small kid with glasses. Now Adam was grown, wore contacts, and for the previous few weeks, he and Charlie had been working out regularly at the gym. Adam wasn't anywhere near Butch's size, but he wasn't tiny anymore either.

Still, Butch was moving like a sledgehammer and Adam was the tent spike Butch was going to pound into the dirt.

Except when Butch was six inches away, Adam moved, did something with Butch's shoulder and sent Butch flying into the wall, missing the lockers, and cracking Butch's skull against the cinder blocks, where it hit with a sound like a watermelon splattering on cement.

Butch dropped.

By then, Adam had already turned to face Doug, who paused for a moment in disbelief, and then came to his downed teammate's rescue.

Adam walked toward Doug, dodged Doug's fake left, moved inside Doug's roundhouse right, grabbed Doug's wrist, spun around, and broke Doug's right elbow with a quick and loud snap.

Doug's face turned white. He inhaled for a long long time, and then screamed, a horrible high-pitched wail, as he looked at his right forearm and hand dangling limply below his elbow at a visibly wrong angle.

In twelve seconds the fearsome twosome were down and out of action.

Adam didn't even break stride. He kept walking toward Calc as if nothing had happened. Meanwhile, because of the screams from Doug and some of the bystanders, classroom doors flung open, teachers came racing out.

I edged to the wall and pulled the fire alarm. The bells and emergency lights started ringing and flashing. Before anyone noticed, I wiped the handle clean of prints with my tee shirt.

The last I saw of Adam that day was him lifting Helen off her wheelchair and carrying her toward the emergency stairs.

Helen looked stunned.

Adam had a grim smile on his face.

• • •

The rest of that day at school passed in a blur. Classes let out at two-fifty, and by three-fifteen, everybody except Adam and Helen were downstairs in Rover's basement.

We were quietly concerned. Rover and Jesús were searching social media for updates. Sean, Charlie and I were playing a three-person game of cribbage. Nobody was saying anything about the fight.

Finally, Rover pushed himself back from the keyboard in disgust.

"There is nothing anywhere on social media except gossip and chatter," he said. "There are no pictures and no video. How is that even possible?"

"Butch and Doug are in the hospital," Jesús said. "There's a brigade of cheerleaders and footballers in the waiting room. Everybody's talking, but nobody's saying what really happened."

"This is bullshit," Rover said. "An entire hallway full of teenagers, and nobody had a cell phone out?"

"It was wicked fast," I said. "Nobody had time to pull out a phone before everything was over. Unbelievable."

Charlie and Sean looked over their cards at me.

"You saw it?" Charlie said, his voice quiet.

I shrugged.

"And you didn't say?" Sean said. "You didn't tell us first thing?"

I sighed. These guys were my friends, but Adam was my cousin. Maybe back before instant communication, I'd have led with the news, but in these days of internet infamy, the last thing I wanted was to say anything or start a rumor that would get Adam in deeper trouble or make matters worse.

And what did I really know?

Yeah, Butch and Doug were in the hospital. We'd all watched from the field, shivering in the cold during the fire drill as the ambulances had taken them away. Like Jesús said, word on the web from cheerleader gossip was bleak. The football team was furious. Butch was still unconscious. Doug's right elbow was severely fractured, and it seemed unlikely that he'd ever throw a pass again. Already the rumor was that Doug would never be able to sign his name with his right hand.

College for Doug and Butch had been a done deal. Now they were just done.

Besides, I kept replaying the twelve seconds of what I saw in my mind, and I couldn't believe it. From what I read later on social media, nobody else could either.

"It was really really fast," I repeated. "I saw it and I don't even know what I saw."

"Ike, that's bullshit," Charlie said. He always could cut through the crap. "You know exactly what happened."

"Naw man," Sean said. "Not necessarily. You ever see those Rashomon-effect movies where they show the same scene from different points of view? No matter what anyone thinks, we all only get a small slice of reality."

Charlie glared at Sean and then turned back to me. "Maybe we won't get the whole picture, but what did you see?"

Did I break down and tell them? Of course I did. They were my friends. They were Adam's friends, too. Everyone else in the school was in the midst of carpet-bombing Adam's social feeds with blistering and violently threatening accusations and attacks. The football team had already created a "Lynch Adam" page. Except for us, nobody in school realized that Adam had a second-degree black belt. Not yet. When that fact emerged, it was going to get even darker.

Somebody needed to have my cousin's back. Besides, if our gang didn't stick together, we'd all get torn apart by the wolves.

Quickly, I spilled the details. "Adam bounced off Butch. Butch ran full speed at Adam, missed and hit the wall. Doug tried to punch Adam, but Adam ducked and broke Doug's arm. Then the fire alarm went off, and Adam picked up Helen and carried her outside."

"That's it?" Sean said.

"Yep." I don't know why I didn't tell them I pulled the alarm. I didn't want any credit, and I certainly didn't want to get caught.

"So, it looked like Butch started it?" Rover asked.

"I don't know," I said. "Adam doesn't usually bump into anybody. He doesn't let people bump into him. I think it's one of his martial arts things."

"Yeah, that's right." Jesús nodded. "When we used to play tag, Adam was almost always impossible to get."

"Moving through the empty spaces," Charlie said. "That's what he calls it."

"But you saw Butch bump into Adam," Rover persisted. "And then Butch charged right at him?"

"Yeah, but before that Adam said something to Butch."

"What'd he say?" Sean and Jesús asked simultaneously.

"Jinx," Sean said. "You owe me a coke."

Jesús flipped him off.

I shook my head and raised my hands in a shrug. "I don't know what Adam said. I didn't hear it. But whatever it was got Butch totally pissed. I know Adam and Butch haven't been hanging lately – for years – but I didn't think they were enemies or anything like that. They used to be friends."

"So, you think Adam provoked Butch on purpose?" Jesús said it quietly, like we were discussing evidence that might convict a killer. Which is kind of what it felt like.

"I don't know," I said. "Adam has always been a peacemaker. But shit, he put those guys down hard and fast and…"

The sounds of Butch's skull and Doug's elbow replayed in my

mind, and I suddenly threw up my half-digested peanut butter and jelly sandwich.

"Oh fuck!" Sean said, looking at the puke on his sneakers. "Those were brand new!"

"Sorry," I muttered, looking around for a tissue.

My friends are pretty great. Rover got paper towels and a black plastic garbage bag. Jesús helped me clean it up. Sean wiped off his new shoes and told me it was okay. Charlie patted my back.

It was quiet for a while.

Then Rover asked, "Anybody hungry? Mom's making chili."

• • •

All the details came out over time. Adam told me his side of what happened about a week later.

During the fire drill, he'd taken Helen out to the student parking lot. Helen's friend Robyn Franklin kept a spare key hidden under the fender of her car, so Adam had unlocked the car, put Helen in the passenger seat, started the engine so she could stay warm, told her he needed to go, and then jogged off.[12]

He skipped the rest of school, heading across town to his stepdad's office.

It was a long hike, and Adam, who had left his coat in his locker at school, had been shivering when he opened the door to A1 Security and Alarms.

There was a beep, and Uncle Paul shouted from the back, "I'll be right out."

After retiring from the Navy, Uncle Paul had parlayed his military service into a struggling private security firm. Groston wasn't exactly a hotbed of crime. There was no secretary and no support staff. Uncle Paul did everything from answering the phone and sales, to installation, repair, break-in call response, and the occasional on-premises surveillance.

"Adam?" Paul said as he came into the waiting room. "What happened? Are you all right?"

---

[12] Helen texted Robyn, who went back into the building after the drill and got her wheelchair. I wish she'd called one of us, but she was pretty shaken.

"I'm fine. I was in a fight," Adam said. "I need a lawyer. A good one."

"Did you kill anyone?" Paul said.

"No." Adam shook his head. "No. I don't think so."

"No, or you don't think so?" Paul's voice was even.

Adam shook his head, and shrugged. "I don't think so."

"Shit."

Adam nodded. Then he started shivering.

Paul wrapped Adam in his arms. Uncle Paul probably wanted to say it would be okay, but he wasn't sure.

He got a blanket, put it around Adam's shoulders, and gave him some hot burned coffee.

Then he called the lawyer, who told Paul to tell Adam to keep his mouth shut and say nothing to anyone, not even his parents.

Then Paul called Adam's mom, my Aunt Dot.

Then Paul put Adam in the back of his SUV and they drove out of town.

Fortunately, the lawyer Paul called was really fucking good.

Bob Billings was an ex Marine, who had billboards all over Fectville and Groston with his picture in uniform and the tagline, "Ready to fight back? Call Bob." Until he worked on Adam's case, everybody thought Bob Billings was just another ambulance-chasing joke.

Billings met Adam and Paul at our family's vacation house in New Hampshire. He sent Uncle Paul out to gather firewood, and took Adam's statement. Later on, Billings joked that even listening to Adam's story ten times, and going over every detail twenty more times, took less time than driving to New Hampshire and back.

Shortly after Aunt Dot arrived, Billings told Adam and his family what he had in mind.

"That's risky as hell," Uncle Paul said.

"If we don't take care of this right away," Billings said, "then your lives in this town are going to be over. This is the kind of thing that can ruin people. Even if I manage to acquit Adam, or get him off on self-defense, everybody in Groston will hate him. Messing up two high school football heroes? Everybody will hate your whole family. You'll have to move out of town. That's how bad this thing is. I think we can do this, but the decision is yours."

Billings looked at Aunt Dot, whose face was red from crying, and then at Paul. Then they all looked at Adam.

"Whatever you want, Adam," his mom said. "I trust you."

"It's up to you kid," Paul told Adam. "We'll back you no matter what."

Think about that for a moment. I know that there are a lot of fucked up families on the planet. Imagine going to your parents with something that messed up, and getting nothing but unconditional support. Just then, despite everything, Adam was the luckiest kid alive.

"Yeah," Adam said. "Let's do it."

Then Billings got way out in front of everything.

He put together a conference call with the school department and the police department and told them that he wanted a public hearing.

Dr. Pedro Gonzales, the superintendent of the Groston school department told Billings that he already had enough evidence to "exclude" Adam from school for the rest of the year.

Kevin Brennan, Groston's police chief, told Billings that Adam was a "person of interest" in the "incident." Butch and Doug's parents wanted to press charges, but hadn't yet.

Billings said he was relieved, and told them both that Adam would be glad to come in and explain everything, but only in a public statement and at the high school. If they wanted, they could arrest him after that.

To cover their asses, Chief Brennan conferenced in the county's district attorney, Jeffrey Johnson.

Right off the bat, D.A. Johnson accused Billings of grandstanding, and said that he couldn't and wouldn't entertain a plea bargain without knowing what Adam was confessing to.

Billings said Adam wasn't confessing, he was making a statement, and wondered aloud why the District Attorney was even involved at this stage. Then they all waited to see if anyone else was going to chime in to the call.

Dr. Gonzales kept ringing the mayor's office, but they weren't answering the phone. Sandra Kopel had served as Groston's mayor for nearly two decades. She knew how to keep herself far away from a political nightmare.

Finally Billings told everyone else on the conference call that there were two ways the process could go. Either they'd hold a hearing immediately, on Wednesday morning and in public, or else Adam would remain silent, and the case would go to trial and drag on for years.

"These are kids we're talking about," Adam heard Billings say. "No matter what happened, they deserve to have this resolved quickly and fairly. My client will waive a trial, but only if he can directly face the court of public opinion."

All the politicians agreed that a quick resolution was a good idea, so it only took fifteen minutes for most of Groston's city government to come to an agreement, probably setting a speed record for inter-agency cooperation.

The hearing was set for nine a.m. Wednesday morning at Ashby Bryson High School, in the gym. It would be an open public meeting. Everyone was invited.

We were still in Rover's house at midnight when we heard that bit of news.

None of us slept well that night.

• • •

Classes were canceled on Wednesday. Everybody was at the hearing.

The gym at Ashby Bryson High was packed to the rafters. There were TV news crews from all the major broadcast and cable networks. It was a media circus.

In the middle of the floor, at center court, were two facing tables. Each table had four chairs. Each chair had a microphone. Wires ran all over the place to a brand new portable speaker system with a sound engineer that Bob Billings had hired from New York City.

It was loud as hell. Imagine every single kid in your high school attending a public hearing about the guy who wrecked the football team's star players. The whole football team was there wearing their jerseys and letter jackets. They were angry. The cheerleaders were crying. Susie Wardle had seated her whole squad on the floor in front of the bleachers, like they were ready to jump up and start a cheer. I could just imagine them leading off with one of their favorites: "We're dynamite. We're Dynamite. We're tick tick tick tick. Boom, Dynamite. BOOM DYNAMITE!"

Nobody was interested in hearing anything.

Our principal, Martin Douglas, stood up and in his deep and resonant voice tried to get everybody quiet, but Ashby Bryson's gym is old, made of cinder blocks and metal beams with a rippled basketball floor and aluminum bleachers.[13] On normal days we rarely paid attention to Principal Douglas when he spoke over the school loudspeakers. His nickname was "The Snore." This morning, even with the temporary new sound system, we couldn't hear a word.

It was only when Mrs. Capamundo, the tiny principal of Jerome Marco K-8 took the microphone that the room got quiet.

She didn't even have to use it. Mrs. Capamundo was a rock star elementary and middle school principal. Everyone in high school had been terrified of her when we were little, and we all listened to her now.

"I know that each of us here has an opinion," she said, her soft voice carrying. "But you will all be civil. If anyone is disruptive, she or he will be asked to leave. Am I clear?"

A kid named Frank Jackson, who had transferred into Groston from Alabama in eleventh grade, stood up near the back of the gym and shouted, "Who the hell are you?"

Before anyone could answer, the boy was surrounded by three police officers and whisked away to a round of quiet applause.

One by one the superintendent of schools, police chief, and district attorney walked into the middle of the gym and took their seats.

I had my notebook out because I was planning on documenting it in an article for our official school blog, *The Ashby Brysonian*.

---

[13] Our basketball team sucked because of that warped court. They won some home games but couldn't play for shit on a flat floor.

Jesús was seated next to me with his sketchpad. He's an amazing artist. Some of the graffiti he's done on the walls of the bomb shelter are truly sick.[14] Our idea was that we'd cover the meeting like it was a real trial. I'd write the text and Jesús would do some of those cheesy courtroom drawings where everybody looks guilty, including the judge, except of course he'd make Adam look innocent. I didn't really think they'd post our stuff. To be honest, I didn't take a lot of notes[15], but I did jot stuff like this down:

"Parade of town officials. −Supr. Gonzalez: brown suit, brown shoes, brown hair, brown mustache, red tie. −Chief Brennan in full uniform. Pressed blue. Shiny black shoes. Big 'fruit salad' of medals on left chest. No gun visible. −D.A. Johnson: dark suit, black shoes, kind of pointy. Black briefcase. Mayor: ?? Where?"

Even though the mayor's office said she'd be there, at the last minute, the mayor had a "family emergency" and decided not to show up. Smart on her part.

I probably should mention that the county District Attorney, Jeffrey Johnson, was Charlie's uncle. We knew him as Uncle Jeff. Uncle Jeff knew Adam. He looked very uncomfortable.

Jesús was bored. Instead of drawing the kangaroo courtroom scene, Jesús had done a detailed cartoon of the gym's back wall as a "History of Student Slavery" with kids chained to desks and teachers lashing them with whips. Blood dripped from the students' backs, and the teachers looked gleeful. Even in pencil, it was a vivid and disturbing picture.

Then, Adam and his family and lawyer came out and sat at the other table.

Someone on the football team started to boo, but a glare from Mrs. Capamundo shut them up.

If it was possible, the gym got even quieter.

---

[14] If you're an old fart reading this, "sick" doesn't mean perverted. Jesús's work was highly detailed and vivid. For instance, he did a picture of Helen jumping over the Breakneck River in a wheelchair equipped with rocket afterburners. It looked real, right down to the expressions of total terror on the faces of her parents.

[15] And I never did write the article.

Even though he was a senior, Adam looked very small. His hair was combed. He wore his fencing letter jacket. His mom was on his right. His lawyer was on his left. Uncle Paul was further right, on the other side of Aunt Dot.

Charlie's cousin, District Attorney Johnson started with the obvious: getting everybody's names and saying that the hearing was being recorded – which was kind of obvious considering all the TV cameras. He swore Adam in. Then he shook his head and said, "Mr. Billings, are you sure that your client wants to waive his right to a trial by jury?"

"No," Billings said. "We are not waiving any rights. This is not a trial. We are agreeing to making a statement at this hearing as a way of ensuring that my client, Adam Siegal, as a student in this high school is given fair judgment in front of the people who really matter – his peers."

There was one of those loud whispering scenes that you see in all the TV and movie court shows – until Mrs. Capamundo stood up and said, without a microphone, "If everyone is not quiet, this is going to take a very long time." She really was very good.

When the room was again silent, Billings said, "Can we get on with it?"

D.A. Johnson was open-mouthed. Finally, he closed it.

"My client," Billings said, "would like to read a prepared statement, and then he will take questions from the table."

Another rumble started.

Billings turned and looked out at the crowd of students and teachers. "At this time, my client will not answer questions from the bleachers. I believe that through this process, we will be able to satisfy everyone."

"You should know," D.A. Johnson said, "that we have testimony from both of your client's victims."

That was a surprise, and a bit of a relief. Not that Doug had given a statement, everybody had expected that. But until just then, nobody knew if Butch had regained consciousness.

Another whisper rose through the crowd, and just as quickly got quiet as Mrs. Capamundo began to stand.

Billings glanced at Adam, who looked visibly relieved at the news that Butch wasn't dead. Some tension left his shoulders, and Adam nodded.

"Remember," the D.A. said. "You're under oath."

I scribbled, "Timeline? Adam…"

Adam nodded again. He looked down at a piece of paper that was in front of him. Then he looked up and spoke into the microphone.

"I was coming out of class, and I saw Butch and Doug…"

D.A. Johnson interrupted. "That would be you were leaving your biology class on the third floor of Ashby Bryson High School when you observed Bailey Batten and Douglas Hawthorn…"

There was a brief hubbub as everyone realized that Butch's first name was really "Bailey". Somehow, even with all the hullabaloo around the football championship, Butch had managed to keep that a secret. Mrs. Capamundo frowned and shook her head, and silence resumed.

"Yeah." Adam nodded. "Biology. Butch and Doug."

He glanced down at his notes, and then looked up again.

"I saw that Butch and Doug were harassing another student…"

D.A. Johnson interrupted. "You allege that they were harassing another student?"

Billings banged the table, and everyone in the gym jumped.

"Mr. District Attorney," Billings said. "This isn't a trial. This is a statement. My client is reporting what he saw and what he did. He is not here to play games with a lawyer."

Jeffrey Johnson looked really anxious. On the one hand, as district attorney, he was an elected official, dealing with an incredibly important local issue. On the other hand, he knew Adam personally from some of Charlie's family's backyard barbecues. He nodded. "Please go on."

Adam started from the top.

"I was coming out of Bio when I saw Butch and Doug harassing another student. Butch and I bumped into each other. I called Butch a name. Butch attacked me, and I defended myself. Then Doug attacked me and I defended myself. Then the fire alarm went off, and

I left school."

Adam looked down at the piece of paper. He read it over silently. Then he nodded. "That's it."

The gym was very very quiet.

I scribbled, "Name? What Adam say? Who Butch/Doug harass?" Seems that when I take quick notes, I write like a caveman.

"That's it?" D.A. Johnson began. "That's all?" He shook his head. "You don't have anything else to add?"

Adam shook his head.

"My client will now take your questions," Billings said.

Johnson looked flummoxed. He hadn't even had time to write anything down on his legal pad.

"You said that Doug and Butch... Bailey... were allegedly harassing another student?"

Adam nodded. "Yes."

"How do you know?"

"I could see it on their faces and on that student's face. The other student was mortified. And Butch and Doug were laughing. At the other student."

"So, you believed that you saw Doug and Butch... Bailey... and this other student having a problem. Did you hear what was said?"

"No," Adam said. "But I could tell from their faces..."

"This is such bullshit!" somebody on the football team screamed. I couldn't see who it was from where I sat in the bleachers, but the whole team jumped up. The cheerleaders on the floor crab walked out of the way. Mrs. Capamundo appeared directly in front of the football team and told them quietly to sit down. They did. Everyone settled down.

I wrote, "Football team pissed. Susie Wardle wears blue panties."[16]

"You inferred that there was a problem," Johnson continued. "Who was that other student?"

"I would prefer not to say," Adam answered.

"Really?" Johnson said. "You won't say who..."

"My client declines to give that information."

---

[16] I know that I'm not supposed to objectify women. I'm trying to be honest. It's where my mind goes. Deal with it.

"I'm saying that Doug and Butch were bullying this person, and no I will not say who it was. What happened to Butch and Doug was not that student's fault. I don't want them blamed. I won't have them be part of this."

Paul reached over and put his hand on Adam's shoulder.

"Did you bump into Butch on purpose?" Johnson said, giving up on the whole Bailey thing.

"I don't know," Adam said. "I was walking one way. Butch was walking toward me. Neither of us got out of the other's way. We bumped into each other."

"So, you could have avoided the bump?"

"Maybe," Adam said. "But of course maybe Butch could have avoided it too."

My notes read: "Noise from crowd. Muttering. Glare from Mrs. Cap."

"Were you injured during the bump?"

"No. Neither was he."

Johnson made a few notes. I looked at my notebook and wondered what he'd written down. I had nothing, so I wrote, "No injury?"

Then Johnson asked the question everybody had been dying to know.

"According to witnesses, both victims, and your testimony here, you said something to Butch. Doug says he didn't hear it. Butch says that he doesn't remember. Memory loss is a symptom of a concussion. What did you say to Butch?"

Adam cleared his throat.

"I called him a name."

"What did you call him?"

"I would rather not say."

"Really?" Johnson said. "It seems to me that whatever you said was incendiary. No one else heard or remembers it. I'm very interested in hearing what you said."

"It was ugly and… kind of graphic," Adam said. "And there's a rule against using that sort of language in school."

"My client would like to ask that anything he says now be exempt from the school's policy on swearing."

"He's going to repeat what he said?" Johnson glanced at Superintendent Gonzales, who nodded. "We can do that for this instance, but not for the instance of swearing yesterday."

Adam glanced at his attorney. Billings shrugged.

Adam leaned into the microphone.

"I called Butch a weak and cowardly tree fucker."

Shit. I wrote, "Butch –>TREE FUCKER?!!!" And underlined it three times.

I glanced at Jesús. Grinning, he lifted his pad and showed me. He'd done a quick sketch of a pine tree with a small hole in it. Maybe it was sap dripping… probably not.

Meanwhile, the gym went crazy.

• • •

Teenage boys are all insane. As they grow from children into men, their hormones make them crazy. I've heard about research that boys going through puberty think about sex once every three minutes. Personally, having been through the process myself, I think it's significantly more frequent.

Essentially, as soon as their voices deepen, they get hair on their crotch, and their balls drop, boys want to have sex all the time.

This is normal.

What's not normal is the way the world deals with guys growing up. Or rather I guess it's normal by definition, but it's certainly weird. We start as innocent children, who begin to experience feelings and emotions and desires that are brand new. We're looking for guidance. Some parents talk with their kids, but a lot of us get misinformation from other kids or the line of bullshit they feed us in health class. And on another hand,[17] there's an Internet filled with tits, asses, pussies, and every single kind of kink ever imagined.

It all messes with you.

Mostly, guys going through puberty don't talk about sex. If we do, we confine sex talk to close friends. And if we do talk about sex, we brag to each other. And we lie. A lot.

If you ask a group of thirteen year old boys if they've ever had

---

[17] Usually the right hand.

sex, there's a pretty good chance that all of them will say, "Damn straight!"

Probably not true.

That said, back when we were younger and not enemies, a bunch of us were having a campout in Breakneck River Park. There was me, Charlie, Adam, Jesús, Butch, Doug, and a few other guys. Sean and his mom hadn't moved into town yet and Rover never camped out if he could help it.

It was late. The fire was still going. We were wired on cocoa and too many toasted marshmallows and 'smores.

Talk was about football and video games, and eventually about sex. Lies mostly. But then someone asked the question, "What was the weirdest thing you jacked off on?"

It got a laugh and guys began shouting out stuff like, My hand! My cat! My pillow! My leg. Your momma!

(That got another laugh, mostly because it wasn't directed at anybody's momma in particular.)

Then Butch Batten said, "I fucked a tree!"

And we all stared at him.

"A tree?" Charlie said. (He was still called Fat Charlie at the time.)

"A pine tree!" Butch said, gleefully. He was a bit slow on the up-take that this was a strange thing to have admitted.

"How did you possibly jack off on a tree?" Adam asked. I clearly remember that it was Adam asking. Probably he was interested in doing it himself. Hell if I'm honest, at that moment we were all considering it. Albeit briefly.

"I didn't jack off on a tree," Butch said.

"Oh, okay," Charlie said, relaxing a bit.

"There's this tree in our backyard with a squirrel hole right at dick level," Butch said. "Just the right size. Extra wide. I fucked it."

"You came in a tree?!" Jesús sputtered.

"With a squirrel in it?" I asked.

"No way. There was no squirrel at the time," Butch said. "I'm not stupid."

I rolled my eyes, hoping Butch couldn't see across the fire.

"How was it?" Adam asked.

"Rough." Butch laughed. "Very rough. And sticky. But good."

We all laughed with him. Sort of.

And because Butch was a beast even then, we never mentioned it again.

But we also never forgot.

• • •

After consulting with Superintendent Gonzales and Principal Douglas, District Attorney Johnson called for a twenty-minute bathroom break.

Nobody, except Adam's family and lawyer left their seats.

The town's administration that had been brave enough to attend the hearing were busily conferring.

Adam, Aunt Dot, Uncle Paul and Billings came back into the gym and sat down.

Mrs. Capamundo stood and raised two fingers in a peace sign. She probably could have done this from her seat on the bleachers, but she was very short and half the crowd wouldn't have seen her.

The room fell silent.

"Mr. Siegal, remember that you are still under oath," District Attorney Johnson began.

Adam nodded. "Yes."

"You said that after you insulted Butch, you defended yourself?"

"Yes, Butch and Doug both attacked me."

"How did they attack you?"

"Butch charged at me. Doug tried to punch me."

"Two members of a championship football team tried to hurt you, and yet they went to the hospital, while you walked away untouched?"

Adam shrugged. "Yeah."

"Is it true that you study the martial arts?" Johnson asked.

Shit, I thought. Now everybody knows.

Mrs. Capamundo preemptively raised her finger before any whispers could even begin.

"Yes," Adam said. "I practice Aikido. It's a martial art, but for peace."

"And are you a black belt?"

"Second degree."

"Did you use this Aikido on Butch and Doug?"

"Yes," Adam said. "But I was defending myself."

"What did you do to them?" Johnson said.

"I moved out of Butch's way and gave him a bit of a push," Adam said.

"So, you were able to get out of his way when he charged at you, but not while you were just walking?"

Adam snorted. "The second one seemed a lot more threatening than the first."

"You say you pushed Butch. How? Where?"

"I gave his shoulder a little bit of a shove so he couldn't immediately turn around and flatten me," Adam said.

"You pushed Butch so hard that he cracked his head on a cinder block wall and has a concussion."

"Objection," Billings said. "This is not a trial."

There was no judge to rule, so Adam continued.

"No, I didn't," Adam said, shaking his head. "I pushed him a little. He was running at me so hard that he slammed his head into the wall and gave himself a concussion."

Adam closed his eyes as if replaying the incident. Then he nodded, opened them, and looked up.

"And what did you do to Doug?" Johnson prodded.

Adam licked his lips, and glanced at his attorney, who nodded. "Go ahead."

"Doug was trying to hit me. I dodged one punch. He swung again, so I caught his hand and performed an Aikido technique called shihonage. It means four-direction throw."

"So, you tried to throw Doug and you broke his elbow?"

"No," Adam answered quickly. "I wasn't trying to throw him. I wanted to put Doug into a position where he would have to stop fighting and we could talk. Instead, he resisted and pulled away from me. He jerked back so fast that I couldn't let go. I didn't have time."

"Mr. Siegal." District Attorney Johnson looked at Adam skeptically. "You're saying that it's not your fault that two members of our championship football team are in the hospital. You admit that you decided to rescue somebody, provoked an attack, and used martial arts violently, but deny responsibility for the subsequent injuries?"

Adam opened and closed his mouth several times. "I'm telling you what happened. It's clear that you and many other people blame me for this. Whether or not Doug and Butch were tormenting another student is irrelevant. This is what happened. I bumped into Butch. I called him some names. Both he and Doug violently attacked me. I responded. They are hurt. Those are the facts. Personally, I wish that none of this happened. But there is nothing that I could or would have done differently, except let go of Doug's hand quicker and maybe not call Butch a... I'm not going to say it again. We were friends once a long time ago."

Johnson was scratching his head, trying to figure out what to do next. The school superintendent and police chief were conferring.

The room was getting restless.

Helen was halfway into the middle of the room before anybody noticed her wheelchair.

Adam saw Helen and started shaking his head. He whispered "No," to her.

Helen kept rolling across the bumpy basketball court, until she settled into the spot at the table where the Mayor was supposed to be.

"May I please speak?" Helen said.

We could all hear her even though she wasn't talking directly into a microphone.

"Are you sure?" Police Chief Brennan asked Helen in a whisper. She nodded.

Superintendent Gonzales got up and moved the mayor's empty chair out of her way.

Helen wheeled up to the microphone.

"My name is Helen Beagle. It's me that Adam is protecting," Helen said.

Even through the microphone, her voice was quiet, so everyone had to settle down to listen.

"Not that I needed it. People look at me and think, 'Oh, poor thing. She's so small and… disabled." Helen paused, nodded. Then she shrugged and continued. "I've been like this my whole life. I was born this way. Like some of you are white. Some of you are black. I can't walk. I've got a good brain, though. I keep my body in shape with a lot of exercise. I actually like my body." She smiled.

"Yesterday, as I was rolling through the hall, Doug and Butch were saying things to each other. About me. They often did this to girls. You all know they did things like that."

A ripple went through the gym as lots of girls looked at each other and nodded. Even the cheerleaders. Actually, all of the cheerleaders were nodding.

If it was possible, D.A. Johnson looked even more uncomfortable than ever. The two football stars had been teasing a girl in a wheelchair?

"Guys say things to girls all the time," Helen said. "These days it's kind of more known about, but they still get away with it because they're big shots. Usually I laugh and ignore them. I would have walked away, but I can't walk and besides, at the time we were all going the same direction."

Everyone laughed a little.

Helen frowned, and then continued. "So they just kept talking. Kept talking about me like I wasn't even there. I was upset. Adam must have noticed."

Adam's eyes kept darting from Helen back to his hands, which had gone white on the table.

"Ms. Beagle," the district attorney said, "may I ask what they were talking about?"

Adam jumped up. "No! You don't have to tell them anything."

Helen shrugged. "It's okay. I've been thinking about it a lot. I can't keep quiet. I won't."

Helen looked out at the gym and spoke to our classmates. "Nobody wants Butch or Doug to be hurt. But I don't want Adam to get the blame either. It's not his fault that they were talking about my boobs."

There were a few laughs, but the room quickly silenced.

"Yes. They were talking about my boobs," Helen continued.

"They talked about every girl in the school like that. They had a whole rating system. They were always saying what kind of fruit they thought girls' boobs were like, and how they would like to eat them."

"Fruit?" District Attorney Johnson made the mistake of asking the questions before he thought it through. "What do you mean fruit?"

Helen nodded. She looked at Adam and smiled softly.

"Oranges. Two ripe navel oranges"

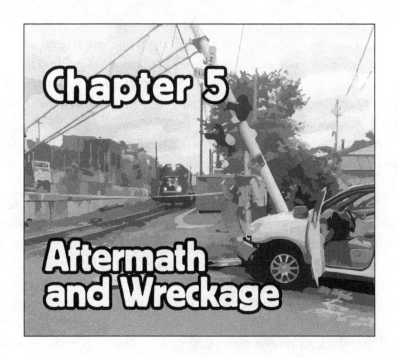

Chapter 5

Aftermath and Wreckage

"The most perverse things make me laugh. Exploding penises and guys getting run over by steamrollers crack me up. If a guy with an exploding penis got a steamroller dropped on his head, I would die!"
— *Sean Chang*

We all expected the shit to hit the fan after Adam's un-trial. We expected a real nightmarish scenario with all the students at Ashby Bryson High turning on Adam and Helen like in a YA novel or teen angst movie. We also expected Adam to be suspended, expelled, tried, convicted and imprisoned.

That's not what happened.

The gym stayed quiet. Then a whole bunch of girls in all the different grades stood up and started clapping for Helen.

D.A. Johnson gave up. He shook his head and said, "I have no more questions."

Principal Douglas tried to dismiss everyone, but it took a loud wolf whistle from Mrs. Capamundo followed by her trademark yell,

"Class people, class!" to get them moving.

After the hearing, Adam peeled off from his parents and told me that, unless they suspended him, he was planning on going back into school tomorrow morning. I told him to forget about it. The football team still looked pissed. They stared at us and mouthed things like, "You're dead!" and "You're fucked."

We looked across the gym at Adam's attorney, Bob Billings, who was in furious conference with the district attorney, school superintendent, and police chief.

"Billings thinks that if they suspend me for fighting, they'll have to suspend Butch and Doug too." Adam shook his head. "It was self defense, so legally I didn't do anything wrong. If I act like I'm guilty, then everybody at school will treat me like I'm guilty. So, if I don't have to, I'm not staying away."

"You did smash Butch's head into a wall and break Doug's elbow," I reminded him.

Three flickers passed over Adam's face: first a grin that quickly morphed into a shadow of regret, which was replaced by a neutral empty expression.

"Butch forgot he wasn't wearing a football helmet," Adam said. "And Doug…" His voice trailed off and he shrugged. "I really didn't mean to hurt him that badly. But he was being a real dick to Helen. They both were."

Adam glanced across the gym at Helen, whose wheelchair was surrounded by a crowd of girls.

"Anyway, I want you guys to know and to be ready," Adam said. "In case there are problems for you. Blowback."

"For us?" I shrugged. "You're the guy that everybody hates."

"Yeah, but you're my cousin, and the rest of the gang are my friends. Guilt by association? People can be real assholes."

"Yeah, but no." I shook my head. "We're all going to go in together. Like we used to do back at Jerome Marco K-8. We'll form up over by the flagpole and escort you to homeroom."

"You don't need to do that," Adam said. "And you can't do that every day."

"No," I agreed. "We can't do it every day. But we can do it

tomorrow morning. Like you said, if you look guilty, you'll feel guilty. If we act like we're together, then we're together. I'll make it happen."

My cousin smiled. We shook hands.

As promised, the next morning, there was a posse of us at the flagpole when Adam's mom dropped him off.

Me and Charlie and Rover opened the car doors. All of them except Adam's.

"Very funny," Adam said, as he got out.

I gave my Aunt Dot a kiss on her cheek. Sean and Jesús were arguing loudly about who would carry Adam's backpack. Adam flipped them both off.

Helen was there too, smiling on the sidewalk. As far as I knew then, she and Adam hadn't spoken since the hearing. Later on, he told me that they'd been texting each other until two in the morning.

You know what the scene would be like in a movie. The slow motion walk – or in Helen's case roll – toward the school building with some catchy but dark anthem slowly building in volume and anticipation.

Sean and Charlie peeled off and held the front doors open.

Adam let Helen go first, and then followed, walking beside her.

We were ready for rocks and jeers.

We weren't prepared for applause.

Literally, as soon as we cleared the main office and got to the west hallway, they started clapping. Kids at their lockers turned toward us, smashing their hands together. There were lots of whistles and "Woo!"s and "Yeah!"s.

We couldn't help but grin. It was like an unexpected ticker tape parade.

Yes, the football team was there, but they kept in the background and seemed to have cooled down too. Maybe it was the cheering crowd. Maybe they all knew Butch was a dick.

Guys were doing drumrolls on their lockers. Girls had their fists up in solidarity with Helen. Teachers stepped outside to see what was going on, and while all of them were smart enough to keep from joining in, most of them smiled at us as we passed.

We took Helen to her homeroom first. Her teacher was nowhere in sight. The kids in there were cheering and banging on their desks. Helen rolled her eyes, waved us off, and then rolled to her desk.

Adam's homeroom was dead quiet. Mr. Jenson was the Latin teacher, and he was incredibly strict; if you weren't in your seat when the bell rang, Jenson marked you late.

"Glad you could make it, Mr. Siegal," Mr. Jenson said. He looked at the rest of us. "We're not going to have any trouble, are we?"

Mr. Jenson had the quiet ability to make us feel like we were six and had just done something embarrassing and inappropriate.

We all shook our heads.

"You going to be okay?" Charlie asked Adam.

Adam shrugged. "Fine." He slid into his seat.

The bell rang and Mr. Jenson told us, "The rest of you are all late."

And just like that, school began.

• • •

Classes dragged on forever. At the end of the day, Charlie and I escorted Adam to Sean's car, but again there was no trouble. We dropped Adam at his house for his home confinement, and then drove over to Rover's and gathered in the basement, as usual.

"I had no idea that everybody hated Butch that much," Helen was saying.

"Doug too," Sean said.

Helen, Charlie, and I were playing spades. Jesús was drawing something on his sketch pad. Sean was texting someone. Rover was on the computer, as usual.

"Butch was a real asshole," Jesús said, not looking up from his drawing. "He was big and he was mean. He thought he owned the whole world and he treated everyone who wasn't on the football team like they were expendable. He liked to call me a spic, a wetback, and a greaser. Once, when I told him I was an American and he was a racist, Butch explained that he couldn't be a racist, since he slurred on everybody equally – niggers, kikes, gays, rednecks, slant-eyes, and even swamp Yankees."

"At least his bile was consistent," Charlie said. "Though to his credit, he never gave me any racist shit."

"Your uncle's the district attorney," I reminded Charlie. "And your other uncle's a cop."

"It was kind of sad, though," Helen said. "I mean how vicious everybody was about Butch now that he's been beaten down."

"High schoolers are like sharks," I said. "They swarm when they scent blood in the water."

"I still feel kind of sorry for Doug." Helen said. "I mean he could be a jerk too, but he wasn't as bad as Butch."

"Doug was a dick to you," Sean said.

I agreed. "The people who collaborated with the Nazis were probably nice too, except for the whole death camp thing."

"Really?" Charlie said. "You're gonna go play the Holocaust card?"

"Yeah," I said. "Why not? Where do we draw lines? Doug and Butch were harassing Helen. They deserved what they got."

Helen blushed as we all avoided looking at her and focused on our cards. I tried not to think about oranges.

Jesús spun his pad around and showed us a Ralph Steadman-style black ink drawing of Butch in a Klansman robe with his head flattened and the inscription, "Wall Meat Head."

I laughed.

"Shit!" Rover said. "Shitshitshitshit SHIT!"

"Wha?" Charlie asked.

"Fox News picked up Adam's story," Rover said. "It went national."

He clicked a button and the story came up on the basement's widescreen TV.

"And in the tiny New England town of Groston, a young man rescued his disabled girlfriend from the taunts of a football team. Adam Spivak, a martial arts expert stoned on medical marijuana, destroyed the careers of the Groston Pioneers championship quarterback and front lineman in the hallway of Ashby Bryson High School. Spivak, who is still facing charges of assault and battery, seems to have emerged from the incident unharmed."

"Fuck!" Charlie said. "You were never charged with anything. They don't get anything right!"

"So, are you and Adam actually a couple now?" Sean asked Helen, who was frowning, but she didn't say anything.

"Adam wasn't stoned," Jesús asked. "Was he?"

"Hey, at least they got Adam's name wrong," I said. "They called him Spivak not Siegal!"

"Dude, they mentioned the medical marijuana," Rover said. "That didn't come out at the hearing. Somebody told them. Somebody leaked it."

"Oh, shit," I said. "Fuck!"

• • •

I texted Adam about Fox News. He already knew. He caught me up later.

He was now grounded indefinitely from everything but school and work. No phone calls. No video. His parents said that he wasn't allowed to come over to Rover's ever again. His stepdad, my Uncle Paul, told him that although playing the hero could be a good thing, Adam had been incredibly stupid and reckless and needed time to reflect on his mistakes. His mom, my Aunt Dot, just didn't want Adam out of the house. Ever again.

That afternoon, after school, he'd been allowed to go to his Aikido dojo, where he was paid to do janitorial work. Adam had been training almost daily for years. There was a kids' class in progress, so Adam had quietly bowed into the dojo at the back door. The rugrats all stopped practicing their rolls and started cheering, until the sensei shouted them to silence.

Adam's Aikido instructor, Sensei Joseph Leguzamo, had nodded Adam into his office, and told my cousin that he was banned from the martial arts school for a month.

Adam was surprised. As a kid, Joey Legs had been famous for getting into fights. "But Sensei, I did the techniques perfectly. I don't think I did anything wrong."

"Really?" Sensei said. "Two months."

"What!? Are you serious?"

"Four," Sensei said.

Adam opened his mouth and then closed it.

"I warned you when you started taking the medical marijuana that there could be a problem with control," Sensei said. "That's one. The fact that you don't see that you are ultimately responsible for your actions? That's two. I don't want the students of this school to try and emulate you. That's three. Mostly, though, I think you need to take some time to get your head together. Who are you? What do you stand for? Who are you going to be?"

Adam kept his mouth shut, nodded, and bowed. He collected his white gi uniform, blue hakima, and black belt from his locker.

"Adam, meditate on it," Sensei Legs had said. "We'll still be here when you get done thinking."

Later Adam told me that the click as the dojo's back door closed was one of the loudest sounds he'd ever heard.

That evening, Adam's lawyer, Bob Billings went to Adam's house for dinner. Aunt Dot made her famous turkey meatloaf. Uncle Paul had a six-pack of local microbrewed beer. Adam drank iced tea.

The celebration was muted. Although Billings had managed to delay Adam's suspension from school, he wasn't sure that he could make it stick.

"You publicly admitted to using indecent language," Billings told Adam. "And you got into a fight in the hall. Both of those are listed as 'severe disciplinary offenses.' You still could be expelled. The only reason you haven't been kicked out already is because Butch and Doug provoked the whole thing with your girlfriend in the wheel-chair, so they would have to be expelled too."

"She's not my girlfriend," Adam said quietly.

"Don't tell anyone else that," Billings said. "Whether it's true or not. Sympathy is good. Chief Brennan seems indifferent. He hinted to me that he already had a file on Butch's activities. Evidently, Butch and Doug's parents want to let it go. I told your friend D.A. Johnson that if they change their minds and decide to press charges, we'll press counter-charges. Most of the eyewitnesses in the hall agree with your account. At this point, the D.A.'s on your side, too, but he has to follow the law himself."

Adam shook his head. "I don't want to press charges."

"Yeah," Billings said. "You never want to go to court if you can help it. How come you all didn't tell me about the medical pot?"

The table at Adam's house was quiet.

"It was private," Adam's mom said. "Confidential. Medical records."

"Were you high at the time?" Billings said. But before Adam could answer he interrupted. "No. Don't answer that. That's a question that will come up if we go to trial. That's the question that they're going to be asking on the news. Don't talk to reporters. Any reporters. Don't talk to anyone about it. Not even your friends."

Adam nodded.

Then the wall phone in the kitchen rang. Adam's family was probably one of the last in the world to have an old-fashioned land-line.[18] They all looked at the black receiver.

The answering machine picked up "You've reached the Davis-Siegal house. Leave a message."

"Hello, this is Dean Chalmers from Columbia University calling for Adam Siegal..."

Adam ran and picked up the phone. "Hello? This is Adam."

His parents and attorney watched from the dining room.

"Yes, sir," Adam said. "No. But... I... No. I understand. Yes, sir. Thank you."

Adam hung up.

"What was that?" Adam's mom asked.

"That was Columbia," Adam said. "They... They're suggesting that I defer enrollment for a year."

"What?" Paul shook his head. "No. They can't make you do that. You're not guilty of anything."

"Actually, they probably can," Billings said. "Most colleges have a clause that allows them to rescind an offer based on anything that

---

[18] Uncle Paul was a bit of a disaster preparation freak. He insisted that the copper wires still carried electricity, which meant that communication was possible even during a power outage. Actually, my family still had a land line too. So did Rover's. And Charlie's. I don't think Sean, Jesús or Helen did, though.

reflects poorly on your character, or on the school, or just for discipline. Columbia is a private institution. You don't even have to be legally guilty of anything."

"That is such bullshit," my Aunt Dot said, swearing for the first time in Adam's memory.

"Mom, I'm sorry," Adam said. He sat back at the table. "The dean said it was my decision. He didn't say they were rescinding. He said that the publicity might follow me. And that I might need time to sort things out. Why does everybody seem to think I need time?"

"Adam," Billings said. "It's all up to you. We can sue them. You aren't under arrest. Your medical history can't be used to bar you from attending…"

"I know!" Adam shouted. He banged his hand on the table and the silverware jumped.

"Settle down," Paul said. "You've already seen what losing your temper does."

"I can't," Adam said. "I can't do anything." He stood up. "May I be excused? I'm not hungry."

Adam's mom nodded.

Adam cleared his plate, dumped his meatloaf into the trash, and put the dish in the dishwasher.

He went to his room.

There were ten texts from Helen. He ignored them and texted me.

"Guess we'll both have to go along with Rover's plans now."

At the time, I didn't have a clue what Adam was talking about.

Sidetrack

Rover's Plan

Four in the morning, and David Rover stared at the giant screen on the wall and wondered what he should make.

His fingers itched with the need.

But his mind was a complete blank.

The house was quiet. One of the best things about the basement bomb shelter was how silent it could be when everybody else was asleep. You couldn't hear the hum of the refrigerator upstairs, and he'd modified the basement's mini-fridge to run silently. The only time it got noisy was when his computers' fans started whirring, and that mean that he was too busy working to care about the buzz.

What to make was more than a momentary problem. It was the immediate question based on a larger issue: what to make of himself?

Dave Rover hated thinking about shit like that. He was an action man, albeit a technological action man rather than a physical one. Get shit done. Make it happen. Do the work. Solve the problem. Create the app. Fabricate the prototype. Just do things, right?

Next year… This year really. In the fall, he was supposed to go to MIT where he'd be surrounded by hundreds if not thousands of guys like himself. Girls too, if the rumors were true.

In Groston at Ashby B, he was unique and special. A quirky weirdo maybe, but the only one. He ruled the tech world.

At MIT he'd be a minnow in a pond full of piranhas, which was a shitty metaphor that needed work, but a pretty apt description of how he felt.

He didn't want to go.

He didn't want to leave his friends. He didn't want to leave his family and his home. He liked his room upstairs and he loved his room in the basement. Sharing a tiny dorm room with one or two other people like him? Jeez, that sounded like hell. If either of his roommates were as whacko as he was they'd be planning to poison each other within days.

He needed to make something. Stop thinking about this stuff.

He wished he could talk with someone about it. His friends would just laugh and make a joke, which was fine, but wouldn't help.

His parents still weren't talking to each other and he didn't dare go to one for fear of the other getting offended.

These days, Mom and Dad didn't talk to each other at all. Not a word. They slept in separate bedrooms and drove in separate cars. Even things like passing the salt were done with gestures or by asking Elspeth or himself. There weren't any arguments or yelling. Which was good. Maybe they dealt with their issues by sending each other emails or texts. He didn't know. Maybe they weren't dealing with their issues.

They'd been like that for almost a year now. It was almost normal. Almost.

The cursor was blinking. He moved his trackball so that the computers wouldn't go to sleep.

He'd tried a dozen times to figure out what had happened to his parents, or when it had started, but nothing came.

Rover knew that he was a self-obsessed tech geek, and that he missed out on a lot of social cues. That meant that whatever had broken his parents marriage was going to be one of those mysteries he'd probably never understand.

Elspeth might know, but somehow he knew that talking to his little sister about it would provoke her to tears, and he hated that because he didn't know how to comfort her. It wasn't his job. That was supposed to be the job of the parents. And they were busy doing their own separate things, leading parallel lives which only intersected around their children, and even then barely.

He really did want to go away to school – to learn the massive amounts of stuff that he had no clue about and to be challenged and pushed to go beyond and further than he could on his own. That was the whole point. Get the training. Get the teaching. Learn from the best of the best. And then make something happen. Make something amazing happen.

Make something that would get his parents to look at each other and say, "Yeah, we did something right together."

Fuck that. It wasn't about his parents. This was about him and his life.

He tapped the keyboard, hitting the space-bar and then control-h to back space over and over again.

He knew that he'd make new friends in college. That there would be a different crowd. He'd make contacts and connections.

But his friends here in Groston would be left behind. And they knew him. And they didn't care how crazy or quirky he was. For them he wasn't David Rover or Dave Rover. He was just Rover.

He didn't want to leave them. He didn't want to go. He wasn't ready.

He put his hands on his head, plugged his ears with his thumbs and pressed on his eyes with his middle and ring fingers until all that he could hear was the whoosh of his blood circulating and all he could see was the dark flashing of his optic nerves and the outlines of floaters.

What was wrong with taking another year? Defer everything. Keep the band together. Don't lose your shit. Don't lose your friends. Don't lose yourself.

All of a sudden all Dave Rover wanted was to overwhelm himself with sound and light. Like a total sensory overload. Not deafening or blinding, but loud and bright and all-encompassing.

Surrounded by total input that overloaded the mind and got the brain to stop thinking and just experience that moment. And that moment. And that moment. And the next.

It would have to be constantly changing, but not so much to be jarring or provoke epileptic seizures. Not soothing, nor frightening. Challenging, beautiful. Dark. Resonant. Melodic but not fixed to any one song or visual. Abstract sometimes but real as well. Human.

What the hell? Crazy talk.

Dave Rover pulled his hands away from his head and shook his skull to let the garbage fall out.

How do you project and vibrate that kind of shit? The engineering part of creating the sound and visuals wasn't rocket science. It was doable, but would depend on the environment. Each space, each vicinity would have different challenges. You could map it and design it, but in the field, the actual installation would have to be tuned.

And how the hell do you program that? Do you go random? There's enough random shit in the world that you could pull images and sounds from almost anywhere. But the mind tends to draw meaning, so do you try to break that by increasing randomness or do you try to create something that defies meaning? Or creates meaning?

This was the kind of thing that the other guys were good at. Dave Rover knew that he could do the mechanics and electronics. For everything else, he needed his friends.

He missed them already – and he wasn't even gone yet.

He laughed at himself out loud. Fuck that bullshit. Don't get caught up in what you can't do. Focus on what you can do.

Can't fix Mom and Dad. They're probably going to get a divorce as soon as Elsepth goes to college. Can't fix Elspeth's sadness. Or his own.

But maybe designing a flexible component-based audio and visual projection system that could be scaled to almost any environment?

Think outside of the loudspeakers and point-projection metaphors.

Did any of that make sense? Not yet. But it would.

Rover flipped from keyboard control to drawing, and began to sketch ideas.

He grinned.

Yeah. It would.

Chapter 6
The Rains

"*I've always enjoyed black, dark, and sarcastic comedy. I know that's not what you'd expect, but fuck you!*"
— *Doug Hawthorne, quarterback*

It was raining. It was pouring. And that was wrong.

It was February, and we lived in New England. February in New England is supposed to be wintertime. It's supposed to be cold. Cold enough for snow and snowmen, snowball fights, ice-skating, and hot chocolate. And it was raining. Pouring buckets. It was a fucking deluge, and it had been going on for four days.

The hysterical weather reports called it a "bomb cyclone". Others claimed it was just an old fashioned gigantic nor'easter, the kind of storm that hits every century or so. They all said that if it had been cold we'd have been buried in snow to the rooftops.

But it wasn't cold. It was fifty-five degrees outside. In February. In New England.

Groston is one of those stereotypical New England towns that

Norman Rockwell painted, except not quite as pretty. There are nice parts and shitty parts. Our downtown's quaint, with the Museum of Natural History and City Hall and the library all done up in red brick and civic architecture. On top of Steeple Hill is the old Central Church that dated back to Groston's founding. We've got the railroad tracks running through the middle of town, and the Breakneck River acting as the western and southwestern boundary. There are a few derelict mills upstream toward Fectville. Of course there's the old box factory that used to employ lots of people. Then there are a bunch of shuttered shops. There are still a few old houses downtown, dating back to Groston's founding, and a couple of apartment blocks, but almost nobody lives downtown anymore. Quaint is one thing, but people in Groston do like their lawns and backyards.

Groston is a normal place. I've lived there my whole life, and I've never seen anything like The Rains.

That's what they were calling it in the *Groston Gazette* – The Rains. With capitals. Like The Flood that wiped out Biblical civilization back in the time of Noah.

We were out of school on our February break – a welcome and much needed week off from the pressures of our insane senior year at Ashby Bryson High – and it had been raining every single day.

We'd all run out of school on Friday with our jackets over our heads, just as the rain had started, and got drenched on our way to Rover's basement for a quick vaycay planning session. Not that there was much to plan. Get up late. Eat. Hang out at Rover's. Eat. Go to bed late. Repeat.

So, I'd gone to bed with the full intention to avoid my parents' well-meaning proposals of visits to the library or cross-country skiing day trips in favor of investing some quality time in a week-long video game binge with my friends.

Instead, I woke to ducks floating down the middle of the street. And my street wasn't even close to the river.

The river hadn't actually overflowed. Not yet. But the sewers and storm drains were full, and water was coming out of them instead of going in.

And the ducks evidently hadn't flown south for the winter.

Rover's dad, who's a chemical engineer for an environmental activism non-profit, said that there was a good chance the whole public water supply – and even the private wells – could be contaminated by fecal coliform bacteria from the sewage overflow. That made the news.

My dad was busy doing extra shifts in the emergency room, treating people who'd been stuck in their cars when they'd driven into four-foot deep puddles and gotten trapped. Some had airbag injuries. Some had hypothermia, because the water from the river was colder than the rain.

My mom, the shrink, was manning a crisis hotline, talking to people who were filled with anxiety.

And personally, I was terrified of climate change. We all were.

I know there's a belief that kids today are ignorant and don't care about anything except getting the latest cell phone. That's so not true – at least not about my friends. We understand science, and have vivid imaginations. We just don't know what to do and have no political power.

Our AP World History teacher, Mrs. Hendry, explained that all civilizations rise and fall. Sometimes it's due to warfare. Sometimes it's due to overpopulation or bad sewage. And sometimes it's due to natural disaster.

Just before the February break, Mrs. Hendry had cited the fall of Rome, the decline of Egypt, and the annihilation of the Native American tribes as just some of the biggest and most obvious decimations.

"History only pays attention when a million people die," she said. "It doesn't really care when a few hundred are wiped out – unless somebody escapes and writes the story. The Roanoke Colony was a mystery. But you've never heard of Feverton or Glassville. You can't even find them online. These were small American communities that simply vanished."

It was like she was seeing our future. And had assigned us all to write papers on it over the break. Fun.

My folks were busy being heroes, were using both cars, and refused to drive me anywhere, so to get to Rover's house, I had to put on rain gear and overshoes.

When I say overshoes, I don't mean dinky rubbers, but good old-fashioned galoshes – the Brits would call them Wellingtons – giant rubber boots that went up past my ankles. Which was actually a fortunate thing because they kept my feet dry as I sloshed across town through waterlogged streets.

The door at Rover's house was unlocked. It always was. The lights in the kitchen were dark. I sloshed in to the mudroom, dripping on the tiles, pulled off my galoshes, and called out. "Anybody home?"

"You are late!" Charlie yelled. "Get your fucking ass down here and give us a fucking hand!"

I ran down the stairs in my socks, careful not to trip, fall and plunge to my death by cracking my head on the concrete basement floor.

Rover, Charlie, Adam, and Jesús were struggling to get Helen and her wheelchair down the bulkhead ramp we'd built for her a few years earlier.

I've mentioned before that Rover's basement is a reclaimed bomb shelter. The bulkhead is deep and steep. We'd laid boards over the steps and made a ramp that we'd rigged with a rope, tow hook, and block and tackle pulley system so that any one of us could easily help Helen up or down. She's not heavy. In fact, the setup was so sweet that Helen could hoist herself in and out of the basement by herself, which is what she usually did. "It's good for my upper body strength," she always said.

Today, though, with the rain dumping down and the wind blowing gales, Charlie and Jesús were holding open the bulkhead doors. Rover was on the belay. Adam was up the ramp from Helen, sliding down behind, guiding the chair in one hand and the rope in the other, trying to keep everything straight.[19]

Usually we just lower Helen backwards to keep her in her chair. But because of the rain, she was facing forward so she wouldn't

[19] Adams parents had given him a temporary furlough from home confinement over the break. "It's like parole," he told us, "except one strike and I'm out. Mostly, I think they want me out of the house."

drown, and clutching her armrests to keep from falling out of the chair. She had a look on her face that flitted between bewilderment, amusement and abject terror. Sort of constipated, really.

"Izzz, Give me a hand!" Rover shouted.

I joined him, grabbed the rope and looped it across my back for the friction, like I'd been taught way back when I was in Cub Scouts.

"This is slippery," I said. "The rope is soaked."

"No shit, Sherlock," Rover snapped.

"Will you two shut the fuck up until we're done with this?" Charlie yelled.

I did, and we did our best.

We slipped and slid and grunted and groaned. At one point the rope slipped, and Helen started to roll full speed straight at us.

She screamed. Adam howled.

Rover and I yelled as the wet rope ripped the skin from our palms but we grabbed harder, kept Helen from smashing into Rover's knees, and wheeled her, finally, into the basement.

That last bit jerked Adam off balance. My cousin hydroplaned down the ramp, waving his arms madly, until he skidded to a stop at the threshold.

"Ow!" he said.

"Nice moves," I said.

Adam smiled and bowed.

"Everybody okay?" Jesús called from near the surface. "We're completely soaked up here!"

"We're done!" I called.

"Shut the fucking doors already!" Rover yelled.

Charlie and Jesús slammed the bulkhead closed, and headed down the ramp. Usually this wasn't an issue, but Charlie slipped, banged into Jesús and they both tumbled in a heap on top of Adam.

"Holy fuck!" Adam yelled. "Get the hell off me!"

Helen, Rover and I cracked up. Eventually the other three untangled themselves. We were all a mess. Everybody was drenched. Helen was the only one who wasn't either bleeding or bruised.

"Rover, there's a foot of water at the bottom of the ramp," Jesús said, rubbing his hip and his ass.

"I know," Rover said. "The sump pump's supposed to go on automatically." He went to a panel and threw a breaker back and forth. "Shit."

Rover pried the panel off the breaker, and before any of us could say something about the danger of playing with electricity while you're standing in a puddle, we heard a loud ZAP and watched as he flew six feet backward, where he landed in Helen's lap.

"Well, hello there," he said to Helen. Then, "Ow! That really hurt."

Rover's hair was standing straight up. His fingers were steaming.

Helen took one look at Rover's face and started laughing again. We all joined in.

We were a mess of half-drowned rats, but at least we were in it together.

• • •

If the rain had stopped that first day of vacation, it would have been funny. But it didn't. It kept raining. And raining. And raining.

Rover's dad got the sump pump fixed, but then water started to come in through the seams of the concrete and cinder block bunker, and we had to get everything six feet up off the floor before evacuating our lair.

By the third day we had all been volunteered to be part of a rescue brigade stacking sand bags along the bank of the Breakneck River.

And it kept raining.

On day four, the dam in the river just south of Fectville broke and the flood rammed through Groston like an out of control steamroller over a road full of baby chicks.

Every building that wasn't brick was swept away like it was made out of toothpicks.

It was a miracle that nobody died, because the emergency evacuation sirens and warning shouts from the police over bullhorns came through only five minutes ahead of the wall of water.

Air raid sirens are deafening. I think they were left over from the Cold War, when the threat of Russian nukes frightened people like Rover's grandfather enough to build bomb shelters. It was a rising and falling wail, like a harbinger of destruction.

Everyone who was on the sand bag brigade ran like crazy for Steeple Hill.

Adam, Charlie and I were pushing Helen's chair like our lives depended on it, which I guess they did.

You might ask, what the hell was a disabled girl in a wheelchair doing out there in the first place?

Helen Beagle was not someone who ever thought of herself as disabled. She'd been born without several key bones in her legs, but she accepted that as part of her life.

"Some people have red hair. Some people have six fingers on each hand," she said. "This is my body. It's part of who I am, but not the whole thing. There's nothing I can't do if I want to – except run a mile. And since I can wheel almost as fast as you can run, I really don't care about that."

That Tuesday afternoon, Helen was in her beach chair with the big traction wheels, pushing herself through seven inches of water, delivering thermoses of coffee to the volunteers.

"Am I supposed to cower at home while everybody else is here, helping?" She'd told off Adam, when he'd expressed concern. "I don't think so." Then she'd turned away from him and went about her business.

Adam looked hurt, but got back in line tossing heavy sacks full of dirt from the Public Works garage to the river bank.

When the air raid sirens went off, everybody froze for a moment.

Charlie's Uncle James, the cop, listened to his radio and then grabbed his bullhorn, shouting, "Everybody up the hill. The Fectville Dam broke and the water's coming this way."

Everybody dropped their sand bags and took off.

I have never been in a riot, but I think I know what it would be like. We were a mob with absolutely no desire except survival and escape.

It was two blocks from the riverbank to the base of Steeple Hill.

I was halfway across Oak Street when I heard Helen shout, "Get the fuck away from me, Adam. I don't need your help."

I looked over my shoulder and saw Helen waving Adam away.

"I'm fine!" she yelled. "Save yourself!"

I hesitated. No way I was going to leave them. "Charlie!" I shouted. "Come on!"

He turned and we both ran and slid back down the hill to Helen's chair, got behind it on either side of Adam, and started to shove.

"You fuckers!" Helen was looking over her shoulder, swatting at our hands. "Leave me alone!" she said. "Save yourselves."

"Will you cut it out?" I told her. "If we're going to die, we're all going to die together."

Helen grimaced, frowned, and then faced front with her hands crossed, angrily.

Pushing a wheelchair, even one with beach tires, up the side of a slippery waterlogged grass and mud hill is no easy job. We dug in, and hustled. We pushed. We slipped. We pushed harder.

Four days into the storm, and we were almost used to the sound of pouring rain. It was a continuous wash of water, calming in a way, like white noise, or the sound of ocean waves washing into shore. At night, listening to the rush on the roof was calming, and, when you combined that with our exhaustion, we all slept like logs.

The sound of the coming flood was completely different.

Imagine a wall of water. Now imagine a wall of bricks. Now push that wall of bricks across a concrete floor. What's pushing the bricks? A fleet of monster bulldozers with no mufflers.

That's how loud and overwhelming it was.

I swear we were only four feet above what turned out to be the peak water line when the wave ripped through the town of Groston.

Still slipping and sliding and screaming like maniacs, we didn't stop pushing Helen.

I caught a flash of something orange, and I couldn't help but glance over my shoulder. Floating past was an old Volkswagen Beetle surrounded by a heap of broken boards. It looked like a joke boat in one of those make-a-raft-out-of-anything white-water competitions.

We dug in deeper, and finally got Helen to the top of Steeple Hill, where we collapsed in soggy heaps.

"Holy shit," Charlie said, panting. "Holy. Fucking. Shit."

I turned around and looked back.

Steeple Hill was an island. The river had completely washed

over Groston.

"I told you, you shouldn't have come, to the river." Adam shouted at Helen. "You could have gotten us all killed."

Helen stared back at Adam. Her lips were pursed into an angry frown. Even in the rain, I could see tears running down her face.

"My house is down there," she said, pointing toward downtown. "If I hadn't been volunteering at the river, I would have been at home. I would have drowned. Thank god my Mom and Dad have jobs in Fectville. My cat is probably dead. Thanks to the rest of you guys for saving me, but I didn't ask you to. I'm sorry if I put your lives in danger."

Then Helen turned and pushed herself away from Adam and the rest of us.

Adam stared after her. He didn't know what to say, which was probably good, because at that moment nothing he said or did would have mattered.

We watched as Helen made her way to the whitewashed Central Church, rolled through the crowd of bedraggled gawkers, and vanished inside.

"Fucking climate change," I said. "Fucking goddamn climate change."

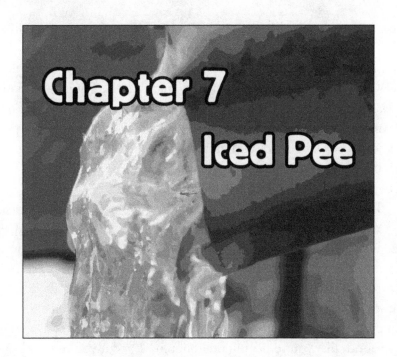

Chapter 7
Iced Pee

"Why the hell do you care about what makes me laugh? You doing a project or something? Making a survey? Trying to be all ironic?"
– Bailey "Butch" Batten

The flood wrecked Groston, but that wasn't the worst of it. You'd think that a twenty-foot wall of water blowing through downtown would be bad enough. And it was. Streets were flooded. The water and churning debris broke windows and left rubble and silt in storefronts and offices. Basements were under water. The electrical grid was fried. Wet computers became inert slabs of plastic. Sewers backed up and sewage flowed out into the streets. Cars were submerged, their engines ruined.

But then the temperature dropped and everything froze.

From Tuesday's February record high of 55 degrees Fahrenheit, 12.8 degrees Celsius, temperatures plummeted. By Wednesday afternoon, it was five Fahrenheit, or negative five Celsius. Then it dropped another ten degrees overnight, which in Fahrenheit or

Celsius is fucking cold. And everything – I mean everything – froze.

The streets froze. The basements froze. Water pipes froze. Wet computers froze. Cars that had been high enough above the flood level to escape getting waterlogged wouldn't start. Phone and power lines got coated with a thick layer of ice, and the wires drooped. Some power lines snapped. Others were so heavy that entire telephone poles fell down, blocking roads and making restoring power next to impossible. If your heat was out – which it was if you needed electricity to run your furnace – the standing water in your toilets froze.

Take a moment to process that.

You wake up in the morning to no heat, wrapped in a down sleeping bag with just your nose poking into the frigid air. Rather than unzip the bag prematurely, you hop to the bathroom, shimmy down just enough of the sleeping bag to expose your dick. Then you pee. It's still fairly dark, so nothing really registers visually, but the piss sound is off. Instead of a splashing whiz, there's a splattering sound, like you're peeing on concrete. Except you're pretty sure you're hitting the toilet. So you open your eyes and see a pool of yellow steaming on top of the ice in the bowl.

What do you do?

    A) Call a plumber.

    B) Break the ice yourself.

    C) Finish peeing and go back to sleep.

No choice as far as I was concerned. I added another layer of yellow slush on top, shook off my frozen dick, tucked it back into my boxers, zipped the bag up, and hopped back to the den, where I tried to find an empty spot in the middle of the pile of relatives in front of the wood stove.

"Everything okay?" my dad whispered to me.

"Hmm?" I looked up and saw that he was feeding the fire. "Yeah. Fine. Toilet water's frozen."

"Damn," Dad said. Then he nodded absently and put another log on. "Go back to sleep. At least you're on vacation, so you don't have to get up to go to school tomorrow."

"That's great, Dad," I muttered.

"Yaay," my cousin, Adam said, his voice muffled from his

sleeping bag.

"What time is it?" Mom said.

"Is it summer yet?" Aunt Dot said.

"No," grumbled Uncle Paul.

"It's five," Dad said. "Nobody has to be up. I've got the fire."

"Mmm," Mom said.

"Will you guys be quiet?" Ellen said. My older sister had returned home from college on break, just in time to make the rest of us suffer from her presence.

Dad didn't bother to answer. Mom hadn't really woken up. I've learned that ignoring Ellen is better than engaging most of the time, so I wedged myself in front of the fire next to Adam, and pulled the sleeping bag up over my face.

• • •

It's surprising how easy it is to sleep when it's that cold. The body shuts down, craving warmth and rest. The old Boy Scout sleeping bags were good quality, so we weren't going to freeze. The fire Dad kept burning also helped, as did the many warm bodies in the den.

We were the lucky ones. Yes, our power and phone services were out, but our house wasn't in downtown. We had a wood stove in the house, a little bit of firewood and we were up a small hill, so the water didn't hit us directly. Rover's house was okay, too. Even though the basement had flooded, his dad had the emergency generator, and had gotten the sump working before the freeze, and had the geothermal running, so they were chilled, but dry. Adam's house was all dry too, but they didn't have a working fireplace, so when their power died my folks had invited my cousin, aunt and uncle for an indefinite sleep over.

Helen wasn't so lucky. Her house was water-damaged, ice-locked and uninhabitable. As feared, her cat, Mittens, was missing. Adam told me that he'd last seen Helen getting into a yellow school bus that was taking everyone to an emergency shelter. Helen had told Adam about the lost cat, wheeled past him, been helped onto the bus and left without another word.

We still hadn't heard from Charlie, Jesús or Sean. Cell phone service was dead. Wired phone service was down. The Internet was down. It was like living in the Stone Ages. We had a hand-cranked radio that picked up broadcasts from Fectville. They were busy trying to figure out the cause of the dam breach, which was ever so helpful to those of us living downriver.

Disasters are supposed to bring communities together, but in this case it was every family for itself. Survival was key. Lots of people bugged out of town, heading to hotels or shelters or to visit relatives in warmer climes.

My dad was on call at the Emergency Room. He was all but sleeping at the hospital. Mom spent all day on the phone at a crisis hotline dealing with emotional wreckage.

Back at the house, Aunt Dot was in charge of food, and Uncle Paul got all military on us and sent me and Adam and Ellen out with our old red wagon to gather firewood.

"Make sure it's dry, if you can. Look up in the trees for dead branches. Dead and dry is best," he said.

"Like we're idiots," Ellen whispered.

"What?" Paul said. "I didn't quite hear you, Ellen."

Uncle Paul had a way of becoming very still and quiet when he was really angry; you didn't want to mess with him.

"Nothing," Ellen said. "Dead and dry."

"And don't go into other people's yards without permission," Paul said. "Times like this, people get crazy and start shooting if they think you're going to steal something they own or want. You get into trouble, give them the wood and get out. Wood's easy, bleeding's hard."

Ellen rolled her eyes, but Adam and I nodded with understanding.

If there's one thing you learn from watching multiple seasons of television about this zombie apocalypse or that communicable disease pandemic it's that people get insane and violent when they fear for their lives. Ellen might not believe it, but we did.

For the first several blocks we didn't find much wood.

My neighborhood is one of those places where everybody keeps their lawns perfectly manicured in the summer and immaculately raked in the autumn. We were high enough above the water line that there wasn't any driftwood, just some twigs and brambles, which Ellen dutifully piled into the wagon.

"What?" she said. "They're dead and dry. We're going to need kindling, right? I don't see you guys getting anything."

"We're waiting for the big wood," Adam said. Then he snickered. Ellen rolled her eyes.

"We've got to look harder," I said to her. "You pull the wagon."

"I've got to collect the wood and lug it?" she complained. "What kind of guys are you? I looked up the word 'macho' in the dictionary, and I didn't see your pictures. Maybe I should have checked under 'woosies.'"

I was this close to hitting her, but Adam got between us and said, "We're going to go ahead and look for bigger pieces like logs and big branches. We'll meet you at home."

Then we took off running.

"Really? You're ditching me?" Ellen shouted after us. "Really?!"

Adam and I laughed as we totally ditched her.

"Thanks," I said. "Everybody asks me if I miss Ellen when she's at college, but nobody likes it when I tell them the truth, that it's great being an only child."

"I wouldn't know," Adam said. "I'm always an only child. I kind of like seeing her."

"My sister is a big pain in the ass," I said.

"Yeah, but she's our big pain in the ass," Adam said. "At least she's consistent."

We wandered through the streets of suburban Groston, looking for firewood, bundled in our down coats, balaclavas, long underwear beneath our pants and snow pants, with our thick socks and galoshes. It was a weird blend of contemporary and primitive. There weren't any cars in the streets, or any other people for that matter. The whole neighborhood was deserted.

At the top of Spruce Street we looked down the hill and saw that the high school was an island in the middle of a frozen lake. The water had settled two feet up around the doors and the base of the building.

"Wow," Adam said. "That is cool."

"Cold," I said. "Icy. Frigid. Totally chill."

"Oh cut it out." He punched me in the shoulder. "Let's go down there and check it. I bet we'll be the only ones in school."

"Really?" I rolled my eyes, more like my sister than I meant to. "We're out of school on vacation and completely free, and the first thing you want is to go back into the school?"

Adam laughed. "When you put it like that, not really. Besides, all the doors open outwards. If there's an unlocked window, we could climb in, but otherwise we'd probably have to break in."

"I think we have enough problems without adding vandalism to our rap sheets."

Adam nodded and pointed to an old oak tree that had fallen across Jacobs Lane uphill from the school. "If we get a saw and the car, we'll have plenty of firewood. Let's go tell Paul."

So we did.

In the garage, Uncle Paul found a heavy ax and an old two-man saw that he'd bought at an antique shop.

"Take the wagon and get the wood yourself." Uncle Paul said. "We're not moving the car for that. We're saving its fuel for real emergencies. You guys are more than big enough to pull your weight."

Ellen laughed at us from her spot in front of the fire.

Uncle Paul continued, "Get as much wood as you can. But don't be mean-spirited and don't be brave. If somebody sees you and asks you for some wood, give it to them. If they try to take it, give them the wood, but try to keep the tools. Wood is easy. Bleeding is hard."

Uncle Paul was wrong. Bleeding is easy. Cutting wood is hard. We spent all afternoon on that oak tree, cutting and hacking and lugging logs back to the house.

By the time we got back with our first load, Ellen had vanished. Nobody knew where. Every time we returned with a wagonful, Aunt Dot handed us mugs of hot chocolate.

Rover found us a couple of hours later. He'd spent most of the day earning money with a brilliant idea. He'd found a bunch of old metal rat traps in his grandfather's shed, scoured them clean, and spot-welded long handles on to them. Then he'd gone door-to-door with a sled, selling the boxes as "ye-olde-fashioned" over-the-fire popcorn poppers.

"Amazing what people will pay when you say it's your last one," Rover told us as we loaded up our wood wagon with another haul of logs. "I made three hundred bucks!"

"I hope nobody gets rat poisoned," Adam said.

"Yeah," Rover agreed. "That would suck."

At dusk, Uncle Paul told us to stay home, because night was going to fall soon and he'd heard that Mayor Kopel had declared a state of emergency with a mandatory curfew at sunset. She probably would have declared martial law, if she'd had the authority. Politicians seem to like declaring things. It makes them feel powerful.

Rover got permission to sleep over, so when Ellen finally came in an hour after curfew, we all had a great time eating hot home-made popcorn and listening to my parents yelling at her.

"Ellen, where the hell have you been?" Mom shouted.

"Your mother has been worried sick!" Dad shouted.

She'd gone to visit some friends from high school, and said she would have called but there was no phone service...

"Do you know how irresponsible that was?" Dad barked.

"You could have been hurt or killed or dead and we'd never know!" Mom wailed.

Ellen burst into tears.

That was a satisfying end to a very long day.

• • •

I've read about disasters in books and newspapers, and thought that they were kind of cool. I've watched movies about those groups of people surviving, always wondering which character was going to be next to die. I've also seen news footage of floods and earthquakes and hurricanes happening. All those real videos look horrible, but when you're watching it you feel safe and secure and snug in your home. Those poor people, you think. I'm glad that's not happening to me.

From the other side of the camera, I can tell you with complete assurance that being on the recovery end of a natural disaster completely sucks.

By the end of that second frozen day, Adam and I were exhausted.

Our hands were chapped and bleeding. Our arms ached and our backs ached and our heads ached and our stomachs ached.

Aunt Dot served us chili that she'd been cooking all day in a massive old cast-iron pot on coals pulled from the fireplace. (In addition to losing electricity, the natural gas for the whole town had been turned off in case of leaks.) Aunt Dot had made a little cooking area by putting bricks around the slate hearth, and watching it like a hawk to make sure no sparks escaped.

"No complaints," she said, yawning. "I don't know how they used to do this all the time."

The chili was pretty good.

We ate in silence in front of the fire, crawled into our sleeping bags and fell asleep, farting. It was loud, cold and smelly.

The next day was the same. And the day after.

All we did was collect firewood, eat, sleep and fart. (And shit, too, but I'd rather not tell you how cold that is when you have to go outside because the toilet is still frozen. Don't even get me started on digging holes in the snow and then removing the stuff later for flushing when the toilets finally worked.)

Bit by bit, things started coming back. The first time we saw the streetlights go on, Adam and I nearly had heart attacks.

We were out after curfew, which by then everybody was ignoring since nobody was looting. It was dark, with bright stars and a sliver of a moon. We were in the middle of dismembering an old dead maple tree about six blocks from home.

When the lights came on, Adam dropped his end of the saw and grabbed the axe. I picked up a big long branch. Both of us spun around, looking for potential enemies. We looked like frightened dorks. We laughed and went back to cutting up the maple tree.

But streetlights meant power. Power meant that oil heaters could finally start working. It took another day, but at last the first floor of the house was warm and the downstairs toilet flowed. My parents were surprised and relieved that the pipes hadn't burst.

Until you've waved your ass outside and buried your shit under snow and fireplace ash, you don't know how good you've got it taking a dump indoors.

"Adam and Isaac, you keep getting wood," Paul said. "We're not turning off the fire until we're sure."

That evening, Mom broke out a stash of marshmallows, chocolate bars and matzah left over from last Passover, and we celebrated with stale bland kosher 'smores in front of the fire.

Everything was fine until we turned on the radio and learned that all Groston students were expected to start school tomorrow – in Fectville.

Yes, even though Ashby Bryson High would be closed for the foreseeable future, all high school students from Groston would be bussed to Fectville Regional High School.

It was on the news. Which we could watch on television. Yippee.

As Adam and I grumbled, Ellen laughed her ass off.

Adam and his family finally went home to their house and I went upstairs to my bedroom to get a good night's sleep without having to listen to everyone else snore and fart.

Then, at two in the morning, the upstairs bathroom pipes broke, and water started pouring down the stairs. Screaming expletives I didn't know that he knew, Dad ran into the basement and stood in freezing water until he found the master valve and turned everything off. Then he shivered in front of the fire, cursing his stupidity.

Yeah, disasters really bring everybody together.

Sidetrack

Dealing With It

As soon as he saw Helen wheeling toward the door of the Cool Beans Crema Coffee Company, Sean jumped up to open it, carefully standing out of the way so she could pass.

A bunch of other customers near the front glared up angrily at the long icy draft, until they saw the girl in the wheelchair, then they looked a little ashamed and went back to their laptops and lattes.

"Hey," he said brightly.

"Hi," she said, her eyes darting around the unfamiliar coffee shop.

"Can I get you something?" he asked.

"I can get my own coffee," she snapped.

"Okay," Sean nodded and smiled. "I know. I'm just offering. My treat."

"All right." Helen nodded back. "What's good here?"

"The place is a little pretentious, so they make a really picturesque cappuccino," Sean said. "My dad lives around the corner. I come here a lot."

"That'll be fine."

"I'm over there." He pointed to a table nearby.

Helen nodded and wheeled away while Sean went to the counter to order their caffeine fixes.

When he'd called, Helen had seemed surprised. He'd suggested they meet, and she'd told him that her favorite coffee shop, the Chucklehead Café had been flooded and was still closed. That was when Sean had suggested the upscale java shack in Fectville.

This whole thing felt strained.

Sean wasn't sure if Helen was still mad. Usually the two of them only hung out with each other in Rover's basement. Somehow it felt like they were sneaking around or cheating on Adam and the other guys. He hoped she didn't think he was hitting on her, which he totally never would. He was just worried. And, if he was honest, a bit lonely.

By the time he carefully walked back the two cups topped with patterned froth designs, Helen had unbundled from the cold.

"Thanks," she said, admiring the abstract brown and white design floating on top of what the menu called "artisanal crafted cappuccino, hand-pulled by a certified barista."

"So." Sean sat down, adjusted his sweater, leaned forward and asked his friend, "How are you doing?"

Helen blew on the coffee, swirling and blurring the pattern. "My house was flooded. Now it's locked in ice. All my stuff is locked in the house. My cat is gone. Thank god my parents weren't home when the dam burst, because they probably would have been killed. We're living in a hotel. Everything I own is new. I'm just glad that we're not poor, because, even though my dad works for them, the insurance company says it's going to take months to sort out the financials. Right now we're using my college savings to pay for everything. The best thing is that the hotel has a heated indoor pool. I have these plastic braces that I strap onto my legs so I can kick. There's no lifeguard, and it freaks out other people when I push my wheelchair right to the edge, lock the wheels and then dive in. Everybody thinks I'm going to drown. They made my dad sign a liability waiver. How are you?"

Sean leaned back, rocked by her breathless summary. "Better than that," he said. He sighed. "My Mom's house is fine, but the power's dead and the pipes froze, so she's moved in with my Great Aunt Mei Li in Springfield while I'm staying full time with my dad here in Fectville until everything thaws. It's not bad, but my dad doesn't know what to do with me. He's used to weekends only. I'm getting a little sick of takeout Chinese and pizza."

"Yeah," Helen agreed. "I used to think that eating out at restaurants every meal would be fun, but it's kind of agonizing. My dad is looking for another place to stay, or at least a hotel with a kitchenette, but he hasn't had any luck. Everything is full up. He jokes that maybe flooding out Groston was Fectville's economic plan for drumming up business."

Sean frowned. "I don't think so," he said, quietly. While he understood the animosity between Groston and Fectville, he'd been born in Fectville, lived in Groston, and had loyalty to both towns.

Helen noticed his discomfort. "I'm not serious," she said. "Sorry. It's amazing nobody got killed."

Sean shrugged.

"What's everybody else up to?" she asked, deliberately changing the subject.

"I don't know much," Sean said. "Cell phone service is spotty in Groston. Charlie's dad got a deal on a huge gasoline generator, so they're ok. Adam's ok too." He paused to see if it would get a reaction, but Helen didn't interrupt, so he continued. "His whole family moved into Ike's house because they have a wood stove. Jesús said that his place is the only one on their block with power and that one toilet still works, which his mother says is a miracle, although considering all his brothers and sisters there must be a huge line at the bathroom all the time."

Helen smiled. "What about Rover?"

"Rover set up webcams showing various angles in his house. The basement's just about dry. He's been going door-to-door selling old-fashioned popcorn poppers, the kind you shake over an open fire. He calls them 'Cold Poppers'. He says he's sold two hundred at $39 each."

"How the hell does Rover always manage to come out fine?" Helen laughed.

Sean grinned back. "His dad stores dangerous chemicals and hazardous waste in the lab, so they've got generators and backup generators. And Rover has a satellite uplink to the Internet."

"They have all that shit down in the basement?"

"Yep," Sean said. "Right next to where we hang out all the time. Rover claims that it's all contained and not dangerous in the least."

"Oh, sure," Helen said. "Not dangerous."

They paused and sipped their cappuccinos.

"Have you heard from your friend, Robyn?" Sean asked.

"She's mostly ok. Her house is on a hill, so they stayed dry. They have power but their cars won't start so they can't go anywhere. She says her parents are driving her crazy. We send each other lots of texts with emojis and cheer-up GIFs."

"It's crazy the way one disaster throws everybody back like a hundred years. You're the first person from school I've seen in person all week."

"Yeah," Sean said. "Speaking of which, you know what's happening with school, right?"

Helen shook her head. "No. What?"

"Ashby Bryson was completely flooded and frozen out. It's closed for the foreseeable future," Sean said. "We're all starting classes at Fectville Regional High on Monday."

"Bullshit," Helen said loudly. "No fucking way! Really?"

At this loud and violent outburst, half a dozen nearby coffee shop denizens jerked their heads up and started looking for active shooters.

"Yeah," Sean whispered, patting his hands to tamp down Helen's outrage. "I saw it on the news this morning."

"Goddamnit," Helen muttered. "I fucking hate this fucking town."

Sean tried not to take it personally. "Yeah. I can get that."

"Screw it," Helen said suddenly. "You want to play cards?"

"What?"

"I don't want to talk any more," she said. "Every time I talk I get pissed off. Every time I think about what's going on, I get pissed off. Every time I stop and think for a moment, I start to feel angry and sad. Half the time I want to cry and the other half I just want to hit something."

Sean nodded. "Yeah. I'm sorry."

"It's not your fault. Even if you were born here." Helen laughed.

Sean stood up. "I'll see if they have a deck"

"I've got one." She reached into a side pocket, dug around, and brought out a deck of Bicycle cards. "Don't leave home without it."

Sean nodded. He sat back down, reached his hand out and tapped her forearm. "It'll be ok."

"I don't know." Helen shook her head. "I fucking hope so."

They both looked out the window at the overcast sky. Outside was cold. The coffee shop was warm.

Helen began shuffling.

The riffling of cards merged with the background noise of tapping keys and the whir from the refrigerators and hiss from the espresso machines.

They played to five hundred, and Helen won by one-forty-seven.

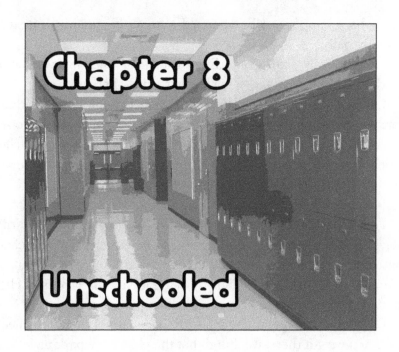

Chapter 8

Unschooled

"Ok, so I really like sitcoms from the eighties and nineties, like 'Seinfeld' and 'Friends' and 'Cheers.' I dunno. Anything that was filmed before a live studio audience."
– James Croft, Fectville High School Quarterback

Going back to school after a vacation sucks. Parents pretend that it's a great thing, probably because they're just glad to get you out of the house. They fondly remember your first days of preschool or kindergarten, when everything was exciting and new. By the time you hit high school, though, you've gone back to school after nine summers, nine Christmas breaks, nine February breaks, and nine spring breaks. In High School you start over as the new and little kids again – which is a major psychic trauma in itself – and repeat the cycle another four times.

Going back to a completely different high school as a senior after a flood-and-freeze February break where you worked your ass off just to keep warm doesn't just suck. It sucks balls. And, if that new high school happens to be your old school's biggest rival, it sucks shweddy balls.

However, my sixth grade English teacher said that we should avoid using foul language, slang and jargon, so here goes.

Going back to Fectville Regional High School after our disastrous February break was as disagreeable as slurping sweat from a pair of hairy stinking poxy eczema-spotted testicles – mismatched testicles: one of them swollen and bloated, like a lumpy beanbag, and the other shriveled and rotten like a dried raisin.

It was that bad.

First off, we were being bussed, so we had to get up even earlier than usual. Because of the short notice (not to mention the chaos caused by waterlogging and dead school department computers), we were told to report to the faculty parking lot at Ashby Bryson High an hour before school in Fectville was supposed to start.

Of course, nobody in the school department bothered to check, and when we got there, we found that the old school parking lot had flooded and was still covered with a thick layer of ice.

Groston is a small town and our high school was intelligently situated in a central location, so almost no one had to take the bus. During the school year, most kids walked a mile or less, or got dropped off.

When almost six hundred kids showed up at seven a.m., bleary eyed with coffees in hand, there was nowhere to stand, except in the middle of the road. A few kids drove themselves, but there was no place for them to park either, since the student lot was flooded too.

The three elementary school busses and the football team's two road trip busses weren't enough, and nobody really had a plan, so the busses were idling and blocking Spruce Street. It was clear they were going to have to shuttle the busses back and forth, but there wasn't a bus manager, and besides, nobody could move, so the busses couldn't turn around. It was a traffic nightmare, and because of what they called "potential liability issues," the fucking bus drivers wouldn't even let us get on until they got approval from the school department, which hadn't open yet, so we shivered outside on the hill above our partially-submerged and frozen high school.

I've read something about a proposal by educators to swap the start times of high school and elementary schools, because first thing in the morning the younger kids are always wide awake while high school students just want to either sleep or rip your lungs out.

Nobody was happy.

One by one our gang gravitated together.

"Hey," Rover muttered.

"This sucks," Charlie said.

"Word," shivered Sean.

"Word?" Jesús said. "Really? Word? Are you a poet now?"

"Hey," Sean shrugged. "You're an artist. I'm a poet. A slam poet. And a lover too!"

Rover made a retching sound.

"Listen to this one," Sean said. "Chinese food/Grandma's frozen dim sum/steamed in bamboo on a propane stove/hot and tasty/ You warm my heart and fill my stomach/family-style."

Charlie and I clapped.

Jesús sarcastically snapped his fingers, which was perfect because he was wearing gloves and they just sort of made a whisking sound.

"Sounds good," Rover said. "Makes me hungry."

"Oh, fuck I'm cold!" Adam said. He was long and skinny, and before moving to Groston, his family had spent a lot of time in Mexico and Spain, so he'd never really acclimated to New England's winters.

"Word," I agreed.

"Word." Charlie nodded.

His teeth chattering, Sean grinned at Jesús, who just scowled at the rest of us.

"Anybody seen Helen yet?" Adam asked, trying to be casual.

"I heard her family is staying at a hotel in Fectville until they can move back home," Sean said. "So her folks are driving her straight to Fectville Regional."

Adam didn't ask Sean the list of questions that occurred to me: Who did you hear it from? What hotel? How's Helen doing?

"Can't blame her for that," Jesús said. "That would be sweet. Live in a hotel with room service and a maid. Never make my bed.

Fresh towels. Have a chauffeur drive me to school."

"Word," Rover said.

"Word," Sean agreed.

"Aww, Christ, will you guys cut it out?" Jesús said.

We all grinned and spoke as a unit, "Word!"

Jesús snorted, rolled his eyes, and laughed.

• • •

By the time we got into Fectville Regional High School, the first bells had already rung and the Fecters were on their way out of their homeroom advisories.

Those of us from Groston were required to attend a mandatory assembly in their gym. It took the busses four trips to get everybody in, so it was nearly nine before we could even start.

I don't think I've told you enough about the differences between Fectville and Groston yet, so bear with me.

The short version is that Fectville is rich and Groston is poor. Or perhaps we're just resources-challenged or industry deficient.

Here's the power point version – imagine a slide show with animations, pictures and charts:

- Groston is a fading New England mill town with some suburbs.
- Fectville aims for an antiseptic urbanized suburban village motif.
- Fectville has the State University, the power plant and, until recently, the dam.
- Groston has a derelict box factory and the sewage treatment plant.
- Fectville Regional High School serves about 1,500 students, and was brand new with building costs underwritten by contributions from wealthy alum.
- Ashby Bryson High barely had 600 students, and was built after World War Two. It hadn't been more than patched in fifty years.
- Groston was on the cusp of becoming, "majority minority." And the schools had a high proportion of students who "qualified for subsidized lunches."
- Fectville was predominantly white. And wealthy.
- Fectville High's cafeteria had a salad bar, pizza bar, taco bar and

an espresso bar. No one from Fectville qualified for subsidized lunch.

- Fectville's sports teams always had new equipment, expensive uniforms and squads of coiffed cheerleaders.
- Groston's equipment was old and battered and dingy, with the cheapest possible uniforms, and nobody would have bothered with cheerleading except that Susie Wardle had managed to turn it into a near-religious cult with pom-poms. With the exception of the Fearsome Twosome's rise to the State football finals, Groston lost at everything – except the Academic Olympics, which our gang had dominated annually, until we lost interest after we started eating Adam's marijuana edibles.
- Fectville's computers were state-of-the-art, their in-school wifi was blazingly fast, and every single kid got a new laptop and a tablet every three years.
- At Ashby Bryson High, some of our computers still had floppy drives. We mostly made do with paper and pencil and our cell phones. Our teachers claimed that they were teaching us to think, not just push buttons.
- Even the guys in Fectville wore current and designer clothes.
- Except for Sean and his whole sweater thing, and our two Goth outliers (Jonah Harrison and Ilya Samson), the guys from Ashby Bryson wore jeans, tee shirts, hoodies, and ratty sneakers – not in a hip or grungy fashionable way, but because we just didn't care.

We shuffled into their gleaming gym with its video score board and cutting-edge sound system, muttering because their janitors stood at the doors ordering us to thoroughly wipe our feet on the carpets and dump our coffee cups into trash cans to preserve their pristine playing floor.

By the time our old principal, Mr. Douglas, finally squealed the microphone, our asses were hurting from sitting on the bleachers.

"Hi everybody," Mr. Douglas said. He had a deep and slow voice, sounding a bit like a punch drunk football player at half speed.

A few kids answered back with a half-hearted, "Hi Mr. Douglas." More snored loudly – or pretended to.

"Um… This situation is new to me too," he said. "So, I'm just going to turn it over Dr. Robert Smith, the principal of Fectville

Regional High School."

Ilya and Jonah, the two Goth kids, stood and clapped wildly while the rest of us groaned.

A short skinny man in a three-piece suit and a narrow tie glared at them as he walked to the microphone. He had a pinched face, a pencil moustache, and bags under his eyes. "Good morning."

Not even the Goths answered.

"Welcome to Fectville Regional High School. It's a bit of a mouthful, so we sometimes call it by the nickname F.R.H.S. My name is Dr. Robert Smith," he said. "I'm the principal here. But you can call me Dr. Bob." He smiled amiably. There was more silence. "All right then…"

Good old Dr. Bob took an entire half-hour to explain how it was going to work. Even though Fectville Regional High School was almost brand new they were already renovating part of it, so there weren't any empty classrooms and we were going to have to "squeeze in and be courteous." Our teachers from Groston and the Fectville teachers would be working together to "team teach" and "maintain the flow and integrity of both schools' curricula." Lunches would staggered, and only twenty minutes long, which was the shortest allowable by state law. First lunch would begin at nine twenty-five in the morning.

"Lunch at nine-twenty-five?" someone groaned. "I just had breakfast!" Even Mr. Douglas looked aghast.

"We're doing the best we can," Dr. Bob said cheerfully. It was clear that he wasn't used to fielding questions. "Hopefully this is going to be a brief problem. And we're all going to do our best to get through it without incident, but I'm going to need your help. Your schedules, room numbers, and maps will be online. How many of you have laptops?" A few kids raised their hands. "Tablets?" A few more. "Cell phones with Internet?" Almost everyone else.

"Okay, so if you don't have a device, there is no stigma. Please go to the main office after this assembly and we'll check you out a spare. For those of you who do, the network name is 'Regional Guest' and the password is 'FectvilleRules.' Capital F. Capital…"

A deep bellow interrupted, "You're fucking kidding me!"

That got a laugh, but my friends and I all looked around nervously, fairly certain that Butch Batten was back.

Dr. Bob looked incensed. His nostrils flared, and he actually seemed to grow an inch or two. "The password is FectvilleRules with a capital F and a capital R. No spaces. It's the same password for everyone because we want you to remember the Fectville Rules. The Fectville Rules are simple, and probably not very different from those you have at Ashby Bryson.

"No running in the halls. No smoking. No drugs. No weapons. No bullying. No cheating. No swearing."

"Fuck that shit!" someone yelled. "I need a bong hit!"

Everyone laughed.

"What about sex?" someone else shouted to a round of cheers.

Dr. Bob's eyes and nostrils widened with rage. "I had hoped to avoid starting off on a harsh note, but it's clear that we need to set boundaries for the sake of your learning and your safety. For minor offenses you'll receive a warning. Then detention. Then in-school suspension. Then full suspension. Are there any questions?"

"Yeah," someone shouted, "how do you spell Fuckedville?"

• • •

After we were dismissed from the gym, everybody scattered. Some whipped out cell phones or laptops or pads and started logging in. Others, feeling like beggars, headed to the main office for the promised Internet loaners. We stumbled and fumbled through the halls with all our stuff, because we didn't have lockers, and probably never would. By the time we figured out where to go for class, we'd already missed first lunch.

The day was complete chaos and a total loss.

It wasn't until fifth period that we discovered our entire gang, except for Rover but including Helen, were shoehorned with thirty other Fecters into a tiny room on the second floor of the "old wing" for Advanced Placement World History.

We grinned as we saw each other, and then sighed as we looked for a place to sit. The Fectville students all had black plastic ergonomic shell chairs with right-handed flip-up desk arms. We were squeezed into a row of dented folding chairs along the back wall, forced to balance our notebooks on our laps. It had been like that all day, and we should have been used to it. Probably it would have been fine since we were finally almost all together.

Except one of the Fectville students said, "Hey, look, it's Fat Charlie!"

All heads turned to stare at us, and specifically at Charlie.

"Hey, Fat Charlie!" said another.

"Hey, hey hey! It's Faaaat Charlie."

Back in the day when we'd been at Jerome Marco K-through-Eight, Fectville and Groston held a huge annual inter-school water gun battle, and lots of kids at Fectville had gotten a soaking from Charlie's amazingly accurate water cannon. His aim was legendary, and Charlie was well known in both towns as the Liquid Assassin or The Soakafier.

"I didn't know Fat Charlie had a brain," said James Croft, Fectville's quarterback. "You sure you're all in the right class?"

Like many stereotyped high school jocks, James Croft was a flaming dickhead. You wouldn't have thought he'd be taking AP World, but there he was. As much as I disliked Doug Hawthorne these days, Croft was even worse. Tall, and handsome, he had a patch of white skin over his left eyebrow, which he claimed was "a dueling scar." He had that swagger of high school jock self-entitlement – and we were in his school.

Charlie's face was grim. He bit his lip. We all looked around, uncomfortable.

"Cut it out," Sean said. "His name's Charlie, and he's smarter than you."

"We all are," Jesús muttered.

"You all can't be that smart," said a smoking hot girl in a red dress, "if you can't even remember that your big friend here's name is Fat Charlie."

"Stop it," Helen demanded. She wheeled her chair down the aisle toward the offensive girl's desk.

"Why?" the girl in red said. Her hair was raven black and her eyes were brown.

Later on, we learned that this was Diana Marley, who was the social dominatrix of FRHS. In Groston, Susie Wardle held that position as our social queen and head of the cheerleading squad. Diana Marley wasn't even on the cheerleading squad, but still managed to have the Fectville cheerleaders as minions to do her bidding. Naturally, she was going out with the quarterback, James Croft. "The boy's name is Charlie, right? He's kind of cute."

I could see that Charlie was holding his breath and closing his eyes, working to keep his shit together.

Helen nodded, waiting.

"But he's still fat, right?" the gorgeous girl in red continued. "So he's Fat Charlie. Q.E.D."

Charlie didn't move. His face was red and his knuckles were white.

"You don't get to call him that!" Helen shifted her wheelchair into full speed forward and rammed it into the back of the Diana Marley's desk-chair.

"Hey!"

Helen wheeled back and was preparing for another ram.

James Croft jumped up. "Stay away from Diana!"

What a hero. Protecting his girlfriend from a girl in a wheelchair.

Adam, Jesús, Sean, and I jumped up too to defend Helen.

Charlie stayed in his seat, which we couldn't blame him for. Even in New England, black boys learn not to get in fights with white quarterbacks. The rest of us all had our fists raised.

That was when the two history teachers finally walked into the room.

"What is going on here?" said Mrs. Hendry.

"They're crazy." Croft had his hands up and open, like he was trying to keep the peace. He pointed at Helen. "She banged her wheelchair into Diana."

"Really?" Mrs. Hendry said.

"Your kids are out of control," Diana said. "They tried to take our seats!"

Mrs. Hendry wasn't stupid. She knew something else was happening. She also knew that the odds of getting a straight answer were slim. She nodded her head, and sent all of us to the office for our first warning, except for Charlie, who'd somehow managed to keep seated and keep quiet. His face was a mask.

As we left the room, we heard Croft say, "Guess Fat Charlie's too much of a coward to fight his own battles…"

We all stopped dead in the hallway. Helen was in front. Standing behind her in a row were Jesús, and Sean. Adam was next to me, near the door. For a long moment, nobody in our group moved.

I could imagine Charlie wedged into the folding chair, listening to that shithead talk, and having to eat it.

Adam twitched and began to turn back into the classroom, but I put a hand on his shoulder and said, "Not now."

He nodded, and we all went to the office.

Fortunately, one of The Fectville Rules was no weapons, because if any one of us had been armed, somebody would have gotten killed.

And that was just our first day at Fucktville Regional.

Chapter 9

Detained

"My favorite comic actor is Bugs Bunny. He was funny. My favorite cartoon was 'The Rabbit of Seville'. I think I only saw it once or twice, but I still remember them singing and jacking the barber chairs up to the sky."
– My dad

Toward the end of that first horrific week at Fectville Regional High School, the post-school scene in Rover's basement was bleak. Adam and I were playing cribbage, and Rover was trying to crack the Fectville School Department's server.[20] Nobody else came over, because by the time the busses took us back to Groston and we got home it was already dinnertime. And then there was homework and

---

[20] Adam told us that his parents had completely ungrounded him. They said that they'd thought it over, and that our rescue of Helen during the flood was good enough for time served, plus time off for good behavior. He privately told me that he thought they let him off easy.

chores. Both Adam and I felt like we needed to keep some continuity in our lives, so we told our folks we were doing our homework at Rover's, which wasn't true at the moment. None of us felt much like doing homework.

When you come from a place where you're comfortable, and then get dumped into a shithole situation, it's hard not to feel angry and bitter and sorry for yourself. Lately it seemed as if it was one thing after the other conspiring to shove our faces into the dirt.

In Groston, our gang was not near top dog pack, but that was because we didn't want to be and we didn't really care. We thought of ourselves as the smart kids who were still fun. We were ethnically and economically diverse, not that it mattered to us. And one of our guys, Adam, had kicked the asses of two football stars and lived to tell about it.

At Fectville Regional, though, we were all Groston pond scum, squeezed into the back of classrooms. Imagine Leonardo da Vinci's Last Supper. The real Jesus and his twelve apostles, perfectly balanced facing the viewer. Now add settings for another seven uninvited guests. It kind of ruins the harmony of the masterpiece.[21]

That afternoon, a couple of players on Fectville's football team had tried to corner Adam on his way out of the building in order to provoke a fight. The Fectville team felt some kind of loyalty to the fraternity of high school jocks, and Adam was the guy who'd messed up Doug and Butch.

I'd gone out another door and only saw the periphery.

They began by taunting him and then started that chest bump thing that guys sometimes do, like billy goats butting but without the horns.

Adam didn't react to their attempt at provoking an assault. He kept his head down and rebounded back and forth off three or four Fecters until he spun out of the circle and ran to the bus.

The football jocks jeered and shouted, things like "Run away creep!" and "We're going to squash you like a bug!" But they let him

---

[21] Although to be fair, the real Jesus Christ probably would have been fine with the extra company, and just put in an order for more loaves and fishes.

go.

"You okay?" I asked.

Adam shrugged and stared out the window. That's when I'd made the plan with him to regroup later in Rover's basement. We needed to talk.

But guys suck at talking about things, whether they're important or not. Girls can talk all day about almost anything. I mean I've overheard some lunch table conversations about mascara and eyeliner that lasted twenty minutes. Yeah, some guys can babble about sports that way. Or about computers. Or barbecued pork. There are stoners in Groston who can opine for hours about complex fertilization and lighting systems for growing marijuana. Actually, young men can bullshit on almost any topic that has nothing to do with yourself, your identity, your looks, your emotions or your feelings.

We don't even know how to begin.

Rover was staring at his computer. Adam was staring at his cards. The only sounds were the motor from the sump pump and the fan of the dehumidifier.

"Uh, have you heard anything from anyone else?" I said. Really, I wanted to ask Adam how he was feeling about barely avoiding another fight, or what we should do to support Charlie against the bullying, or what was up between him and Helen?

Adam played a ten on my six and counted, "Sixteen."

Just then, Sean sidled down the stairs.

Rover glanced up. "Hey Sean. Who died?"

"We're almost done here," Adam said. "We can start a three hand game as soon as I finish winning."

"I've got some bad news." Sean dropped into a chair. "Fat Charlie's dad... I mean, Charlie's dad... Shit. Charlie's dad is in the hospital."

"He's not dead is he?" Rover said. Then he realized what he'd said and added, "I was just joking."

"No, he's not dead," Sean said. "Mr. Johnson's in the hospital. Another heart attack."

"Shit," we echoed.

"What happened?" Adam asked.

Sean shrugged. "One of his customers' brand new SUVs got stuck in the flood, and they'd towed it into the parking lot. Mr. Johnson was helping with the tow truck. He had an infarction or something. He's actually been in the hospital for a two days now."

"How did you find this out?" I asked.

"My mom was visiting my great Aunt Mei Li. She's recuperating from hip surgery. My mom ran into Charlie's mom at the hospital."

"Wait, a few days ago?" Even Rover had stopped typing. "How come Charlie didn't tell us?"

I took the opportunity to explain my theory about our inability as young men to verbalize. "Guys don't know how to talk about their feelings. I think it dates back to when we were hunters and had to keep quiet to track prey. Women, on the other hand, were the farmers. They had to learn to communicate. It's evolutionary."

My friends listened, gave me the finger, and then ignored me.

"My guess is that Charlie was probably embarrassed," Sean said. "I mean, you remember how freaked he was at his dad's first heart attack."

"Didn't want us to worry?" Adam suggested.

"Yeah," Sean agreed.

"We should visit," Adam said.

"Naah," Sean said. "If he'd wanted us to know, or if he'd wanted us to visit, he would have said."

I threw up my hands. "No. You know that, Adam and I are Jewish. When somebody dies, you bring them some food. Whether they want it or not."

"Charlie's dad's not dead," Adam said.

"And Charlie's still on a diet," Sean added.

"We could bring him healthy food," I suggested.

They ignored me.

"So, what are we going to do?" Rover said. "The Fuckwads at Fectville are treating us all like shit. They're picking on Adam. They're picking on Charlie, which given the circumstances triple sucks. I can't get into their computer system that easily. I mean, I could with a brute force password attack, but since I'm trying to be covert about it, I've got to run all my requests through a server out of Russia and I can't hit it too frequently."

"What the hell are you talking about?" Sean said.

"You know how in movies and on TV the computer guy sits down and types a few keys and cracks a system?" Rover said.

We all nodded and grinned.

"Yeah, that always looks cool," Sean said.

"Well, a quick hack like that is bullshit unless you have access to a back door," Rover explained. "Real life hacking takes time, especially if you don't want to get caught. So I can't fuck things up on the inside."

"I've got to go," Adam said. "I'm not getting any homework done here."

"Isn't that the point?" I said. "We've got to talk."

"Yeah, maybe. Or maybe I've got to keep my grades up so I can actually go to Columbia when this shit gets straightened out. Maybe I'm not going to settle for going to Fectville State."

The basement got quiet.

My cousin knew that I still hadn't heard from any other colleges or universities. Fectville State had rolling admissions and a really low bar.

Rover quickly went back to his typing.

Sean shook his head. "Dude! Harsh."

I stared at my cousin. "I've applied to other schools, Adam. Just because I didn't get in – yet – doesn't mean that I want to go to Fectville."

"I know," Adam said. "I didn't mean that, Isaac. I'm sorry. I'm just…"

Adam grabbed his coat and bolted up the stairs.

We watched him leave.

Rover shook his head. "Everything is going to shit."

"We've got to do something," Sean said.

Just then, I didn't care.

• • •

Bad shit happened continuously at our "new school". Rather than try to present you with a coherent narrative, I'm going to use a simple technique that Mrs. Maxim, my AP English teacher, told me about – a list of all the shitty shit that happened to us, and around us, at Fectville Regional High School. Some of these complaints may seem small and petty. Others, I think are quite egregious.

Here we go…

- Groston had a rotating class schedule, which was confusing, but made sense to us. Fectville had a fixed class schedule, which meant that every day all our classes were in the same boring order. For instance, I had P.E. first thing every morning, when I was barely awake. Ever try to climb a rope first thing?
- And they didn't integrate us into the Fectville lunches, but tacked on extra lunches before and after.
- High school seniors from Groston were all given the 9:25 a.m. lunch. Often food wasn't even hot by then.
- High school freshmen from Groston got the 2 p.m. lunch – which was just 30 minutes before dismissal. Often all the hot food was gone.
- Some Groston kids tried to order lunch through delivery services, but this was banned after the second time a Chinese food delivery guy was found wandering the halls.
- Groston students with cars were initially allowed to drive to school, but then were prohibited from using the student parking lot following an "incident" where a Fectville junior's car was vandalized. Somebody keyed a 2007 Porsche. That's the kind of cars the Fecters drove in high school.
- Because Fectville High was located in a suburban development, on-street parking without a permit for longer than two hours was prohibited, but there weren't any signs, so the students from Groston who drove in the next day got out of class in 20 degree weather to find that their cars had been towed – and the busses had already left.
- After that, most of us took the school bus back and forth from Groston to Fectville. These old yellow kiddie transports were irregular and frequently late – and we were marked tardy each and every time that happened.
- Some of us organized car pools, but "for our own safety," parents were prohibited from dropping us off in front of the school, so we

had an eighth of a mile walk from the street to the front doors.

- We were never assigned lockers, but were still expected to change our clothes for gym. If you didn't change, you were marked absent for that day. Under State law, Phys Ed was a required course and fifteen absences meant you failed. If you failed PE, you were required to make it up before you could graduate. Nobody was sure how that was going to work.[22]

- The wearing of boots or black-soled shoes on the basketball courts or squash courts (yes, they had squash courts) was prohibited. If you didn't have the right footwear, you were marked as absent.

- Remember that we didn't have lockers? That meant that if we wanted to change from snow boots to sneakers, we had to carry our sneakers in our backpacks – with all of our schoolbooks and any packed lunches.

- One day, shortly after it started snowing, during one gym class, somebody (presumably a Fectville fuckwad) swiped fifteen left snow boots and threw them up on the roof of the gym. Because of "safety concerns" the janitors were prohibited from going up on the slippery roof to get the boots. It took a human pyramid of ten Groston seniors (including myself, Adam and Sean) to get up on the roof and retrieve the boots. Three of them were already full of snow.

- After rescuing the boots, we were all given detention for our "recklessness."

- The next day, not one of Groston's seniors changed into gym clothes, and that afternoon the entire senior class was forced to endure an in-school assembly about the difference between "The Groston Rules" and "The Fectville Rules".

- The day after that, somebody reported that a Groston senior was carrying a weapon, so the police were called and every single backpack from Groston was opened and searched.

---

[22] The only silver lining of the early morning lunch was that I ended up spending almost all of P.E. in the locker room – first changing to get into my gym stuff, and then changing back so I could go to lunch. I really don't know why they even bothered.

- They found three multi-tools with knife blades and suspended all three students for three days, including Dave Rover.
- They also found Adam's medical marijuana, which was unopened and sealed in a bag plainly marked "medical marijuana." Even though Adam produced his medical marijuana card, he was suspended for a week.
- They also found seven peanut butter and jelly sandwiches, which were confiscated. This was the first we learned that tree nuts and peanuts were banned because somebody in the school might have a "severe and life-threatening allergy".
- When Charlie asked their principal if anyone in the school actually was allergic to peanuts, Dr. Bob said that information was "classified because of HIPPA privacy rules." When Charlie said he'd be happy to eat outside the building – even in the snow – and demanded his sandwich back because that was his lunch, Charlie was suspended for two days for "incitement."
- That's when Sean and I walked out of school in protest of our friends' mistreatment and were also suspended, but only for one day each. (Jesús said that he would have walked out too, but a suspension would have killed his needs-based scholarship to arts school. We told him we understood and not to worry, but he still looked pretty distraught.)
- The next Monday morning there was a brand new metal detector that all the Groston students had to pass through. Not the Fectville students, mind you. We said that this was a violation of our rights and staged a sit down protest in the front hall. Helen actually started the chant, "Hey hey! Ho ho! The metal detector's got to go!" This time, the whole Groston senior class was given detention. Because this was after-school, the busses had already gone by the time we were done, so we had to walk, get a ride, or call for an Internet car.
- On Tuesday morning, the Groston police were there with sniffer dogs both for intimidation and because they thought Adam was coming back to school that day, forgetting that he'd been suspended for a week.
- Meanwhile, we were expected to learn, have all of our books in

our backpacks (with our sneakers) and our school work ready to be graded at any time.

- With the exception of Mrs. Hendry, our AP World History teacher, who didn't let anybody push her around, our Groston teachers were relegated to "assistants" and our sports teams were completely sidelined.

- On the day that the official "Report on the Failure of the Fectville Regional Water Authority Dam" was released, Mrs. Hendry got into a huge argument with Fectville's AP Euro teacher, Mr. Jackson. The report was only three pages long, and said that the dam failure was due to "a confluence of unfortunate and unpreventable circumstances." Mrs. Hendry reamed Mr. Jackson out in front of our class, citing the effects of climate change, global warming, and the incompetence of the FRWA in adequately maintaining the integrity of a dam that had been built back during the Works Progress Administration. Mr. Jackson sputtered and stuttered saying that everyone in Groston enjoyed the benefits of cheap water and waterpower but didn't want to pay taxes to maintain the dam. Mrs. Hendry patiently explained that the Fectville Regional Water Authority was a quasi-government agency, and wasn't allowed to collect taxes, but did have a twelve member board of directors who were paid six figure salaries for meetings once a month – and that Mr. Jackson's wife and brother-in-law were both on the Water Authority's board. Jackson started yelling. Mrs. Hendry stood her ground and yelled right back. The police were called again and she was dragged from school in handcuffs while we all cheered.

- Dr. Bob slapped Mr. Jackson on the wrist with a warning, and threatened to suspend Mrs. Hendry. The Groston's teachers' union counter-threatened to go on strike, which would mean that the student-to-teacher ratio at FRHS would become illegal. We hoped that would happen, but instead Mrs. Hendry was permitted to return to school on the condition that she'd retire at the end of the year.

- And all that shit was just in the last few weeks of February.

Chapter 10

Smashing News!

"I've always been partial to Shakespeare's 'Taming of the Shrew'. I know it's not particularly enlightened by contemporary standards, but it is the only Shakespearean comedy that I think is actually funny."
— Felicia Capamundo, Principal, Jerome Marco K-8

It was a Saturday night in early March, and we were embedded in Rover's basement in the middle of a crucial Rocket League tournament when Sean dropped his bombshell.

If you don't know what Rocket League is, think of video game soccer, but with rocket powered cars that can fly. I know that our parents find it hysterically funny to watch half a dozen teenage boys each on different computers or laptops playing a game simultaneously, but if it wasn't shit-tons of fun, we wouldn't do it. We called ourselves Team Bomb Shelter A and Team Bomb Shelter B, and had been practicing for months. Rover, me and Charlie were the

A Team. Sean, Jesús and Adam were the B Team. Helen was still M.I.A..

This was a pretty high profile regional tournament with sponsorship and actual cash prizes for the top three winners. Of the two thousand three hundred and fifty-four that had started on Friday afternoon there were only two hundred and fourteen left.

Suddenly, Sean announced, "I'm gay."

I shrugged.

We were in a pause in the play. The B Team was already out, and the A team had just lost a match by one point. We had to win the next one if we didn't want to get completely knocked out of the tournament.

"Focus, focus," Rover said. He was always saying that. Rover wasn't much for chatter during gaming. He said that it interfered with his "neural-physical pathways". In other words, he couldn't talk and push buttons at the same time.

"Is there any more iced coffee?" Charlie asked. It was four in the morning on Saturday. No, it was Sunday, I guess, and we'd been gaming pretty continuously for over thirty hours.

"How can you drink iced coffee in the middle of winter?" Jesús said.

"You take cold coffee and you add ice," Charlie said. He stood and stretched.

"I mean, doesn't it make you cold?" Jesús asked.

"It tastes better than reheating old burned coffee," Charlie said. He looked at the pot, which had been simmering for a while and shook his head. "Never mind. I'll make a fresh pot."

"Don't waste that!" I shouted. I lifted my "Groston Rules" coffee mug. We'd printed fifty of them up, thinking that we could sell them to our former classmates as a bonding and fund raising thing. Turned out that nobody liked the look of bright blue type on bright yellow mugs. We should have listened to Jesús.

"Isaac, are you sure you need more coffee?" Adam asked me.

"I'm fine," I insisted. I held up my right hand. "Perfectly steady."

"Yeah, but your pupils are wicked dilated," Jesús said.

"I had an edible gummy bear at midnight," I said. "I'm probably crashing."

"You had a whole gummy?" Adam shook his head. "Those things have 10 milligrams each. You're supposed to bite their heads off, and then wait a while."

"GIVE ME SOME COFFEE!" I shouted.

Everyone laughed. Charlie poured two inches of sludge into my mug.

"I'm entering the lobby," Rover said. "Next game's starting."

"Let me get the coffee going," Charlie said, pouring water from a jug into the back of the machine.

"Hurry hurry!" Rover said.

"I'm ready," Adam said. Even though this was an A Team match, he and Jesús were our eyes, looking for holes and strategies.

"Set," said Jesús.

"Meeee tooo!" I sang.

Charlie hit the coffee machine's On button, jumped over a pile of pizza boxes, and opened his laptop. "All set."

"I'm gay," Sean said, a little louder.

We ignored him.

Rover said, "…and NOW!"

Team Bomb Shelter was back in action!

• • •

Or not. We got demolished by a bunch of ten year olds from Pawtucket playing under the name Team Whacko. It shouldn't happen like that, because by the time you get toward the end of the finals, just about every Rocket League team is evenly matched. That's why people actually watch live-streaming video games. They're as exciting as a real life football game, but without the commercials, time-outs, concussions and penalty challenges. We lost seven-to-one, and Rover immediately began cursing and wondering whether there was a problem with our Internet stream.

"I don't understand it," Rover muttered. He started running a diagnostic.

"They Braziled us!" I moaned. In the 2014 World Cup, Germany shellacked Brazil seven to one. In the tournament game we'd just lost, we were cut down so bad that Team Wacko, had deliberately scored our only point on themselves just to rub our faces in the mud.

"Assholes." Jesús muttered.

"I thought I had that pass," Charlie said.

"Me too," Jesús agreed.

"You did," Rover said. "It looked like there was a stutter in the video. I want to watch the replay."

"Holy shit," Adam said. "That was a long fucking series. I can't even believe we got that far."

"I'm with Rover," Jesús said. "We shoulda won."

"We got robbed," I said. "We got robbed!"

Sean slammed his laptop shut, shoved it into his backpack, and stood up real suddenly.

"Hey, where you going?" I asked him.

He shook his head at me, and grabbed his coat.

"Dude, it's only a game," Charlie said. "No need to get so pissed off."

"Yeah," Jesús said. "Your parents are going to freak out if you come home at four in the morning. Better to wait until tomorrow to go back. I mean later today. At least wait until dawn…"

"I tried to tell you guys something important," Sean said, pulling his coat on one sleeve at a time. "You just blew me off."

"We didn't blow you off," I said. "We just ignored you."

Sean glared at me. "You're the one who's always saying that we don't talk to each other enough."

"We were in the middle of a tournament!" I said.

"Losing," Jesús said.

"Badly," Charlie added.

"There! See that," Rover said. He pointed at the replay on the big screen. "That was definitely a glitch. I'm going to contest it."

"Rover, you can't contest it," Charlie said. "Nobody can challenge Internet glitches. The game plays in real time. Something breaks, you lose. That's the rules."

"But I tapped into my dad's servers!" Rover said. "We should have been solid."

"Forget it," Adam said. "That was only one point. We lost by six."

"Yeah, but we could have caught up."

"I can't believe you guys." Sean was shaking his head. He picked up his backpack. "I don't think you even heard me."

"You're gay," I said.

"You're a homo," Jesús said.

"Queer?" Rover suggested.

"Queer as a three dollar bill," Charlie said.

"Guys, this is just not right," Adam said. He always was trying to make peace, and really didn't have much of a sense of humor about anything that might offend anyone. "It's hard enough to say anything personal, without you guys doing this."

Sean nodded. "Yeah, which is more important, my sexuality or a video game?"

It was a stupid question.

"A video game." We all said it simultaneously. Even Adam.

"Yeah?" Sean said. "I'm out of here."

"Wait wait wait wait," Charlie said. He jumped back over the stack of empty pizza boxes and blocked the door.

"Get out of my way, Charlie," Sean said.

Charlie held up his hands in an "I surrender" gesture. "Look, Sean. At that particular moment the game was important to me. Right now. Your sexuality is more important to me."

"Not to me," Jesús said.

"Me either," Rover said. "Although… maybe if you asked me out on a date…"

"Guys?" Charlie said. "Give me some help here."

"Look," Jesús said. "I'm just not attracted to Sean. I like girls. So I really don't care about your sexuality."

"And I am attracted to him," Rover said, "but I care more about video games."

"Really?" Sean said.

Rover shrugged. "I've known you're gay for years. I'm bi. I've checked you out when we're at the beach. But, you know, it's not something I'm going to bring up because it would be weird."

"Rover, you're bi?" Jesús said. "How would you even know? You never date anybody."

Rover flipped Jesús off. "I started by admitting that I like video games better than social mating rituals. I don't date men and I don't date women. I'm bilaterally celibate."

"You see, Sean?" Charlie said, shaking his head at Rover. "You are important to us. We've all known you're gay forever. The announcement just didn't seem like big news."

"Wait wait wait," Sean said. "How the hell did you all know I was gay?"

"Dude," Charlie said. "You're gay. We know this. Plus, you just said."

"Yeah, but before that? Who else knew I was gay? I mean, I don't even think I really admitted it to myself until recently."

He looked around the room. Rover and Jesús had their hands up. I raised mine. Adam raised his. Charlie shrugged. "I don't make judgments."

"How the fuck did you guys know?" Sean insisted.

"You wear sweaters," Jesús finally said.

"It's cold," Sean said. "You're wearing a sweatshirt."

"Not the same thing," Jesús said. "You wear sweaters as fashion statements. Your hair is always perfect. And you wear loafers."

"Oh, come on!" Sean said. "That is such a stereotype. Half the guys at Fectville Regional wear nice sweaters and loafers."

We all looked at each other and shrugged. "Half the guys at Fectville Regional are gay."

"Q.E.D." Jesús said. He liked to use his Latin whenever possible.

"Come on," Sean said. "That's not fair. And it's stereotypical. I grew up in Fectville before the divorce and my mom moved us to Groston."

"We know," I said. "That's why we never said anything about it. Fectville is gay. You're gay. So what? We're just glad you're not a Fectville dickhead."

Sean shook his head. "I'm not sure whether that was insulting or not."

"Not," I said.

"Hey, Sean, relax. You're our friend," Charlie said. "If we can't insult you, who can? It doesn't matter to us whether you're straight or gay."

"It matters to me," Rover said. "If I was ever going to ask

someone on a date, it might be you."

Sean blushed bright red.

"Wait a second," Charlie said. "Sean, are you telling us you're gay because you're into Rover?"

Rover's eyes widened in panic.

"No no no!" Sean said quickly, but it seemed honest. "No way."

"Thanks for that," Rover muttered. "I guess."

"You must be into somebody," I said. "Otherwise you wouldn't have said anything."

Charlie posed and flexed his muscles. He was still a bit overweight, huge some people might say, but Charlie had lost some serious poundage and his biceps were bigger than grapefruit.

"Cut it out," Adam said. "Don't tease him."

"No," Sean said. "It's none of you guys."

"Oooh," Jesús leered. "But there is a somebody?"

Sean blushed again. "Yeah. There is a guy that I was thinking about asking out. I heard rumors about a rave next month. I didn't want it to come as a shock to you if I brought a guy as a date."

"You sure it isn't one of us?" I said.

"Come on, pick me! Pick me!" Rover said. "Then I don't have to ask anyone out! I figure that if I can make it through college without a massive relationship trauma, there's a chance I might find somebody to mate with and reproduce."

We all stared at Rover.

"What?" Rover said. "Ok, so if it's a guy we won't reproduce in the traditional way, but we can adopt or find a surrogate to carry a clone. I've given this a lot of thought. Hey, at least I know what my problems are."

We looked back at Sean.

"Who is it?" I grinned.

"Leave it alone," Adam said.

"Dude, somebody in this group is always saying we should be more open minded and communicative," Charlie said, looking pointedly at me. I grinned back. "This is our chance to have a real female style girl to girl conversation."

"I'm not a girl," Sean said, his voice getting really low.

"Yeah, yeah, yeah," Charlie said. "Nobody's saying that. But are you a pitcher or a catcher?"

"Don't care," I said. "Don't want to know."

"Damn, Charlie," Jesus said. You know that once I visually picture something it's almost impossible for me to forget it. And you're putting these images in my head!"

"I care!" Rover raised his hand, and winked at Sean.

"GUYS!" Adam said.

Sean's eyes were wide. His mouth was open. "You guys are such fucking assholes."

"We're Team Bomb Shelter," Charlie said. "We may have lost the tournament, but we haven't lost our sense of humor."

"I don't know," Jesús said. "But Sean, that's not what I'm interested in at all."

"What?" Sean said.

Jesús grinned. "Fucking assholes."

We looked at Sean and Jesús.

There was a brief moment of suspense.

Then Sean laughed, and we all threw pillows at Jesús.

Chapter 11

Walk On By

"I don't laugh. Ever."
– graffiti written in black marker just above the toilet paper dispenser on the wall of the bathroom inside the office of Principal Robert ("Call me Doctor Bob") Smith at Fectville Regional High School.

It was late March and the weather had finally gotten nice for a minute. Early spring in New England is a real crapshoot between rain and snow, clouds and sun. But the days were getting longer, and the air was clear.

Adam and I were walking home from yet another afternoon of what we called anal-retention detention.

A week ago, Adam had pointed out to Mrs. Hershberger, the Fectville Calc teacher, that she was being sexist by only calling on girls in the class.

Mrs. Hershberger was well built, in her early forties, and wore tight sweater dresses that made her look like she spent her nights at a cocktail lounge.

She'd argued that it was impossible for her to be sexist, since she was a woman. Male teachers had been calling primarily on boys for years. She was simply righting the balance.

I'd jumped to Adam's defense, and we'd both made the mistake of shouting her nickname, which was Mrs. Lushburger.[23] So we had ten days of punishment.

As usual, we'd missed the late bus. Jesús, who was doing detention time for doodling during calculus, offered us a ride, but we'd declined.

Jesús's car, a 1972 Dodge Dart, was older than all of us and held together with rust and Bondo. It was a shitty car, with sticky torn plastic upholstery, spongy suspension, intermittent power steering, loose brakes, a dead air conditioner, an AM only radio, and power windows that were broken. The inside was a cesspool of broken toys, used tissues, half-empty juice boxes, and something smelly that we couldn't find, but was getting worse as the days grew warmer. The car drank gas like an alcoholic frat boy at a keg party, but was useful to get you from point A to point B.

Jesús's mom had paid some Fecter who lived on a side street near the school to let him use their driveway. In exchange for the car and the parking fee, Jesús was his family's personal taxi service, ferrying brothers and sisters to and from dentist and doctor appointments, after-school activities and play dates. Jesús also liked to drive fast through the back roads, and crank up 1970s Yacht Rock with the windows down and the heater blasting.

It's nice having a ride, but it was a beautiful day and sometimes the Dartmobile was all too much.

We did take him up on his offer to drop our backpacks at our houses, so we wouldn't have to hump them the five miles home.

Adam and I thanked him and waved as Jesús patched out in a spin of gravel and a blare of Hall and Oates.

We walked in silence for a while.

The best thing about having regularly scheduled detention was that we got all our homework done before we got home. Whenever

---

[23] Rumor was that her silver coffee mug was spiked with vodka.

there was time to spare, I wrote in my journal. Jesús drew. Adam studied Japanese for fun. Charlie was reading Moby Dick, also for fun. Sean was teaching himself computer programming, and Rover used his time to try and hack the Fectville School Department on a mini computer that looked like a phone.

I found it interesting watching the kids from Fectville who had their own detentions. They usually put their heads down or stared off into space. None of them cracked a book or sharpened a pencil. I could almost understand it. Maybe they figured that school was bullshit and detention was bullshit and everything was bullshit so what the fuck? Why bother working or even trying? Maybe these kids had money or parents with connections. Maybe they didn't. Hard to tell from the back of a head and a pair of slumped shoulders. I'm not sure that our little gang really was any smarter or more diligent, but because we'd all grown up together doing all our homework every day, even the transfer to Fectville didn't seem to be a good enough excuse to slack off and quit. Besides, I think I would have died of boredom if I hadn't kept my mind busy.

"Whatcha thinkin?" Adam asked.

I shrugged. "The Fecters don't do their homework during detention."

"I've noticed," Adam nodded. "They think we're idiots, because as seniors we shouldn't have to try so hard."

"They don't know, do they?"

We walked in silence. I was thinking about the final notification emails that would start coming from colleges and wondering whether I'd get in anywhere beside Fectville State. Adam, I imagine, was thinking about Columbia and his own problems.

"Maybe none of them are taking the Advanced Placement exams," I said.

"Maybe they're all eidetic geniuses," Adam said, "with idiot-savant brains."

"Maybe they've bribed their teachers."

"Maybe they're all wannabe school shooters."

"Maybe they're aliens."

"Or vampires."

"Or just really really stupid kids," I said.

"They're not stupid," Adam said. "They just don't get it. You and I think that getting our homework done is a good way to get our parents off our backs, and to learn something. And we're trying to go to college, so it's all about education."

"Yeah?" I said. "So?"

"So," Adam said, "it is amazing how lucky we really are."

"Lucky? Really? We've got a five mile hike back to Groston because we're doing stupid detention in a stupid school, because the stupid dam in stupid Fectville broke, and they're probably never going to reopen our stupid high school. That's lucky? You're Internet famous, but it's gotten you nothing but kicked out of Columbia. And I'm going to be stuck in college with all those Fectville kids."

Adam didn't answer right away. We walked along the Route 24 breakdown lane kicking rocks and moving over whenever we heard a tractor-trailer getting close.

"We are lucky," Adam insisted. "We're white and we're male, so we've never really had to deal with racism or sexism or sexual harassment."

I raised my hand. "Personally, I would love to get sexually harassed by just about every senior on the Fectville High School cheerleading squad."

Adam looked askance. "It's not harassment if it's a fulfillment of a fantasy."

"Whatevah."

"We've got houses. We've got families," he continued. "Our parents have jobs. They don't beat or abuse us, and they're not drunks or druggies."

"We're the druggies," I said.

"No, we're not." Adam shook his head. "You've seen the real burnouts in Groston and Fectville. None of us are that bad."

"I don't know," I muttered. "Give me a few years at Fectville State and we'll see. I might not be at a good college, but I'll have my marijuana-induced psychosis to keep me company."

Adam stopped and waited until I stopped too, a few steps closer to home.

"What?" I said, turning my head.

"Look, Fectville State is a pretty good school, if you want to go," he said. "It's not prestigious, but education is education, and you can always transfer out. If you don't want to go to school right away, Rover's plan is still in effect."

"Right." I snorted. "We're all going to hang out in his basement and come up with some brilliant idea or a killer Internet app, create a dot-com startup, get venture capital, go public and retire as billionaires by the age of twenty? That's not a plan. That's a fantasy."

My cousin looked at me with a mixture of curiosity and concern. "Are you okay?"

"No." I shook my head. "I'm not okay. I'm not a genius like you and Rover and Helen and Charlie. Even Sean and Jesús get better grades than me, plus they've got the whole minority thing going for them when they apply. Sean's got a brain for business, and Jesús can draw like Degas. I don't mind the fact that every single one of my friends has a great opportunity for a successful future. What I do mind is that I don't. My future is going to be here in Fectville, grinding it out. Alone."

I found myself panting and out of breath. I hadn't said it very loudly, but I hadn't ever said it out loud before. My heart was pounding and I felt the pressure behind my eyes that meant I wanted to cry. Self-indulgent crying, like a little baby. I flashed on my father telling me that big boys don't cry, and that immediately went to that stupid song as my brain did everything to try and avoid thinking about the despair that was filling my chest.

"Hey, Isaac" my cousin said, catching my eyes. "We're not going anywhere."

"We're going home!" I said, turning away and walking faster.

"No, I mean…" Adam started walking to catch up. "Me and Rover and Charlie are sticking with you until you're unstuck."

"Yeah, you'll maybe stick around because you're fucked about Columbia," I snapped. "But Charlie's going to go to NYU. Rover's going to MIT. Sean says he's gotten into three schools, but he's not telling us which until he picks. And Jesús is waiting to see if he gets enough financial aid from Parsons. You'll be out of here too, as soon as the bad publicity dies down. Me, I'm going to be borrowing money from my dad to buy a shitty car so I can commute from my parents' house to Fectville State. Maybe I'll buy the Dartmobile from Jesús, convert it into a low rider and write, 'Born to Lose' on the side."

"Hey!" Adam shouted.

I broke into a jog.

Five minutes later he caught up to me. I was panting by the side of the road torn between rage and wanting to throw up.

"You know, you really ought to take up a sport besides video games," Adam said.

I tried to hit him, but he did his Aikido thing – moved out of the way, stepped inside, and grabbed me in a hug.

If it had been anyone else, I would have gone apeshit just then. Guys don't hug other guys. Either it's gay, which I guess would be unwanted sexual harassment in my case, or it's just plain freaking weird. But I've known my cousin most of my life. He's my best friend and a good guy, and right then I really needed that hug.

It's hard being almost eighteen. You're not a kid. You can't vote. If your parents give you permission, you can serve in the army and die, but you can't order a beer in a bar. And you have to finish high school, otherwise they won't let you into college.

Of course, you could drop out, get a shitty job, move in with your girlfriend, couch surf, or you can stay at home with your parents – who are just waiting for you to get out of the house so they can move on to the next phase of their lives, without kids.

Everybody cheerfully tells you, "You've got your whole future ahead of you!" But they don't say the truth, that if you fuck up just once you are completely screwed. Or if you're mediocre and average or just plain slow, you're completely screwed. Instead, everyone pretends "It's all good" and "We live in an age of infinite possibility." Black guys have it lots worse. They are given that talk, and know that they might die because of some stupid cop. Girls are warned about wearing the wrong makeup and sexy clothes, getting groped by strangers, date rape dangers, that female anger is interpreted as bitchiness, how having sex can make them look easy, and that all men are dangerous sex-crazed idiots – much of which is true.

But for all of us, the reality and finality of accidentally fucking up while you're a teenager is not something that's taught in schools, and the kids who post shit about it on social media are either poets, suicidal, in therapy, or all three. My dad laughs and calls any movie that deals with stuff like that, an "After School Special." My mom would probably be sympathetic, but going to her for more nurturing and hugs won't help. She'd probably suggest therapy. Like Adam said, I've grown up with good parents in a good neighborhood with a good skin color (don't take that the wrong way!) and a penis (same again). I really shouldn't need more coddling, should I?

But the hug Adam gave me felt good. Reassuring and genuine. Not sexual. Comforting, but not babying.

Then a semi blew by and blasted his air horn and we both jumped back in embarrassed fear.

Adam laughed. I grinned.

"You okay?" he said.

"Yeah. Thanks," I said. "Do that again and I'll kill you."

"No you won't. I've got a second degree black belt."

"Polonium poisoning," I said. "You'll only know it's me just before you drop dead."

"Thanks," he said. "I'm glad you gave it that much thought."

"It's a sign of respect," I said.

"Come on," Adam said. "Only three more miles."

• • •

"Adam."

"What?"

We were still about a mile from home. Sometimes you forget how long it takes for a person to get from point A to point B by foot.

"What's up with you and Helen?"

"She's fine," Adam said. "She's moved back into her house. It's dusty, but the contractors are working on it. The freeze actually might have helped, because it meant that mold didn't get a chance to set in."

"No," I said. "I mean between you and Helen?"

He shrugged. "Nothing between. Never was. Never will be."

"That's poetic," I teased. "Kind of tragic in a Shakespearean or

John Green kind of way."

"What the fuck do you want from me?" Adam snapped. "She hasn't spoken with me since that day on the hill. Every time I see her she wheels off in the other direction, or if she can't avoid me, she stares straight ahead as if I don't exist. Nothing ever got started, and even if I wanted it to, now it doesn't look like it will. I miss her. I miss her as my friend. And I miss anything that we might have had. Is that what you wanted to hear?"

"I miss her too," I said. "So how do you know that…"

"I spy on her on social media," he said. "I'm a fucking cyberstalker."

"It's not stalking if you're not creepy about it," I said. "It's normal to check out what your friends – or even ex-friends – are up to. You're not being creepy about it, are you?"

"No." Adam rolled his eyes. "Probably not." He laughed.

I said, "I know this sounds like a bullshit platitude, but it's okay to care about somebody, even if they don't care about you."

"I dunno," Adam said. "These days that feels a lot like unwanted attention, which as you know is a crucifying offense."

"You're not hitting on her. You're not even talking to her."

Adam stopped at the top of the last hill before Groston, and I stopped beside him.

"I just wanted her to be safe," he said. "We saved her life, right? I've gone over it a million times in my head, and honestly I don't think I could have done or said anything differently. I didn't mean to blame her, though."

I remembered those moments, soaking wet, after we'd heard that the dam had burst, while we were all pushing her chair and scrambling for high ground.

"She was frightened," I said. "You were frightened. Any of us could have died. She has to understand that."

"Clearly not," he said. "Otherwise she'd still be friends with you, if not with me. Right? I mean, she could have stayed in touch with all of you. But as far as I can tell, she's cut everybody off."

"She knows that you're our friend," I said. "She doesn't want us to have to choose sides. She doesn't want us to be uncomfortable."

"Screw that!" Adam said. "I just want to talk to her."

"Did you try?"

"I've sent her emails, they come back marked as spam," he said. "She's blocked my calls and texts. She's ghosted me on socials, I can only see her things on her friends' feeds. And none of her other friends let me get anywhere near them either. It completely sucks."

I nodded.

"Watch this," Adam said. He took three steps and dove off the hill.

I ran after him, thinking for a moment that my cousin had just committed suicide.

But the hill wasn't a cliff. It was a tall round hump covered with grass, and I watched with amazement as my cousin rolled like a ball or a hoop all the way to the bottom.

He stood up and shouted, "Ta daaah!"

Suddenly, a bunch of bunny rabbits of all sizes started running away from the spot where Adam stood in the high grass.

Adam jumped into his Aikido ready stance and then laughed as the rabbits scattered in all directions. "I must have landed on top of their burrow. Sorry bunnies!" he called after them.

I jogged and stumbled down the hill, taking about three times longer than Adam had. "That was amazing!" I panted.

"Years of martial arts training," he said. "You fall down a lot. You get back up. It's not big deal. Let's get the hell home."

I wanted to hug my cousin back to comfort him like he'd comforted me. But he didn't slow down until he got to his house, picked his backpack up from the front porch where Jesús had left it, waved goodbye, and went inside.

Sidetrack

Don't Sweater the Small Stuff

Sean Chang looked at his sweater closet and winced.

Maybe his friends were right. For a high school senior, he had too way many sweaters. Way way too many.

It wasn't really a sweater closet so much as a small cedar-lined room with shelf after shelf of neatly folded sweaters. They were arranged left to right by thickness and what he called "warmth-weight", and then from bottom to top by color. Starting on the left were the heavies, the bulky cable-knits and thick sheep's wools, then gradually thinning out towards the right for light silk, cashmere and a few linens that had become fashionable. The bottom shelves were bright colors, then mixed colors, and then toward the top were the darks and at the very top the whites. It was a system that he'd designed years ago to make picking his daily wear easier.

He smiled at that thought. And then he frowned.

What right did his buddies have to criticize him for his clothing choices?

They were great people, but they all dressed like it didn't matter.

151

Every single one of them wore what Adam's grandmother called schamattes, rags! Blue jeans are fine, but every day? Tee shirts are great, but every day? Sweatshirts can be comfy, but every single day?

And if it was ok to wear that crap, then what the hell was really wrong with wearing a different sweater every day?

He sighed. He knew that his habit had typecast him. He was "that kid who wore sweaters." He was "the prep." He was the "neat guy." Or worse than that, he was "that Asian guy who's always wearing the sweaters."

Which, even if it was a stereotype, was true. Sort of by definition.

As Sean stepped into his sweater closet the lights went on. He smelled the cedar and wool and smiled again. He always smiled when he came in here. This room was the heart of his home.

The sweater collection had begun innocently enough, after his parents split up and he'd moved with his mom to Groston.

He'd never seen the new house before, and Mom had told him, as they drove from the hotel they'd been staying at, that was on purpose, so he could see his room as empty and decorate it however he liked. Sean sat in the back in the stupid booster seat he thought he was too big for and fooled around on his phone. He didn't bother looking out the windows.

The new house was cold, and completely empty. Mom didn't want to bring anything that she'd "purchased with your father." Their new furniture was going to arrive tomorrow, and tonight they were supposed to sleep on the floor in sleeping bags. Like a camp out. "It'll be fun," she'd said.

Sean was a little excited about that and wanted to light a fire in the new fireplace, but Mom wouldn't let him. She said that ten years old was too little to light fires.

They went down to the cellar and tried to turn on the furnace, but it didn't work because the oil tank was empty. Mom had never dealt with stuff like that. She told him that those kinds of things had been his father's jobs. Probably she was still hoping that Dad would come back and rescue them.

So, while Mom was on her cell phone arguing with the oil delivery company, Sean had found some old logs out back, and set them up in a teepee, just like he'd seen in the movies. He found some matches in the kitchen, but the logs wouldn't light until he checked some videos on his phone and decided that he'd use the old newspaper method rather than cutting wood shavings.

Nobody online mentioned that you were supposed to open the flue in the chimney, probably because they had built their fires outside.

The house had filled with smoke, and Mom, screaming, had called the fire department. By the time the trucks arrived, though, the fire was out because the logs had been wet.

Everything was fine, but the new house was still cold and now it smelled like smoke.

After she calmed down, Mom ruffled his hair. "It's ok. You smudged our new home. It's important to purify places, so that we can move in and move on."

Sean noticed that Mom had wiped tears from her cheeks. Again.

Dad, he had gathered from snippets of whispers and snatches of phone conversations, had dumped Mom for one of his secretaries – a white one with big tits. Mom had made an effort to hide the truth.

Back then, Sean was sure that it was all a mistake. Dad would realize that Chinese women were better than white women and come back. Dad would realize that Mom was better than anybody else and come back.

Except he hadn't.

They'd sold the big house in Fectville. Dad moved into an apartment, and Mom had taken her money and bought the divorce house on "the right side of the railroad tracks" in Groston. It was smaller than the one in Fectville, and it was so empty. Their voices echoed against the bare walls.

Finally, after the firefighters had gone, Mom took Sean by the hand and said, "Let's explore our new house." He'd already seen the basement, and she led him through the empty living room, dining room and kitchen.

He'd kept silent, until she'd taken him up to the second floor. "How do you like it?"

"Is this really my room?" he'd asked, his eyes wide. It was the biggest and emptiest room of them all, three times the size of his room at home, and with its own bathroom and a walk-in closet that was almost as big as his whole room at home!

His mother had hesitated for a moment, and then said, "Of course it's your room!"

Little Sean had smiled. "I like it." Then he'd frowned. "But it's still cold."

His mother had hugged him for a moment, and then said, "Then let's go buy you a sweater."

So they'd gone to the mall and the collection had begun.

It wasn't until he was thirteen or fourteen, when Jesús came over for a visit and commented about the awesome size of his bedroom that Sean realized that his mother had given him the master bedroom.

She was such a Chinese Mom. He was her first – and only – child, something that Great Aunt Mei Li was incredibly critical about. "We don't live in China," Great Aunt Mei Li said. "Americans can have more than one child."

Mom would do anything to make Sean happy. And that meant frequent trips to the mall in Fectville for sweaters. Even after they'd filled the oil tank and figured out how to turn on the heat, and Mom had finally let him build a fire in the fireplace, she'd taken him to the mall about once a week. She'd hired a carpenter to rebuild the walk-in closet, lining the walls with cedar and putting in fluorescent lighting and the shelves all the way to the ceiling.

"Some day," Mom had said, "when you grow big and strong, you'll be able to see up into the top shelves!"

At the time, he hadn't believed it. He'd still thought that Mom and Dad would get back together. That they'd move back home. That they'd be a family again.

Sean hadn't wanted to leave Fectville. All his friends were there. He'd lived there his whole life. Fectville was cool. Groston was poor. They didn't have a mall. Groston sucked. Everybody knew that.

"You'll make new friends," Mom had said. And he had. Awesome friends. Better friends than he'd ever had or imagined in Fectville.

But his friend had always ragged him about his sweater collection.

Some people collected figurines. Some people collected Hot Wheels cars in packages. Some people collected guns. Great Aunt Mei Li collected Fiestaware, had it on display all over her tiny apartment, and wouldn't let anyone eat off it.

Sweaters were neither useless nor dangerous. And they all triggered memories.

He looked fondly at the Irish wool section and remembered the trip to Dublin with his father. For the first few years he only saw Dad every other weekend and then on vacations to Disneyworld and ski resorts. When he'd visited Dad in the new apartment, Dad had been so delighted to show off his stereo equipment and his big screen TV with both a PlayStation 3 and an Xbox. Every weekend they'd played video games and eaten take-out Chinese food. (His mother had always called that "cheating.") Dad had tried to be his pal. Which was ok. But they'd never really talked.

At least not until the summer Sean had turned seventeen, and they'd taken a trip to Ireland.

Neither of them had expected Ireland to be so wet and so cold in August. They'd only packed swim and resort gear, shorts, tee shirts and linen sportswear. Sean hadn't even packed a single sweater. Why would he? It was summer time. As soon as they got off the plane, they both started shivering. The cab driver from the airport had his window down and told them that they were lucky to arrive on such a bright and sunny day.

Their hotel in Dublin was a bed and breakfast above a traditional Irish pub.

"Nah, ther's no heat in the summer toim. This is a fi-en warm day," the innkeeper told Dad, when he'd stormed down to the front desk to complain.

Sean, who'd followed behind, had noticed the man's sweater. It was unlike anything he'd ever seen at the mall. Off-white and spotted with dirt and stains and crumbs, it had loose pulled threads, moth holes and worn spots near the elbows. It was a man's sweater, a worker's sweater, not a fashion statement. It was neither baggy nor trim, but showed off the man's muscles and broad chest.

"Where'd you get the sweater?" Sean had asked the innkeeper.

"Tha what?" the man had said. He was in his late twenties and hadn't really noticed Sean until then.

"That wool sweater," Sean had said.

"Ahh, me jumper?" The man's face broke into a broad smile. "Me ma made it for me before she passed. May she rest in peace." Then the man had nodded and winked at Sean, who felt his face flush. "What's yer name, lad?"

"It's Sean," he'd answered softly.

"Why that's me own name as well," the innkeeper had said, his face brightening and softening.

Sean's heart had started pounding.

Then the innkeeper had told them about a small factory nearby that made "the foinest Irish wool jumpers in the whole wide world."

Dad and Sean had put on their sweatpants and taken a taxi, and bought matching Aran wool turtleneck fisherman sweaters.

Finally warm, they'd retired to the Inn's pub for "pie and a pint" which meant a huge slice of Shepard's pie and tall pints of Guinness. The pub was warm with a fire going, and no one seemed to care that Sean was underage.

After the first pint, Dad began to talk, which he'd never done before. He told Sean that Heidi (the secretary) had been a mistake, but that the divorce hadn't been. "Your mother and I got married too young. I don't regret it, because I got you out of the deal, but we were never right. Everything was too much by the book. We had to buy this and go to that and keep up the right appearances. Everything was all about making sure that nobody was talking about us in the bad ways but everybody was talking about us in the good ways."

Dad had sighed and raised his pint. "I suppose that I blew that and shamed your mother when we split up. Everyone must have been talking about us in the bad ways." He sighed. "I wish it hadn't happened that way, but we'd probably both still be miserable if it hadn't blown up."

Dad went on to say that Heidi was long gone, and he still hadn't found the right one, but that didn't stop him from trying. "When you fall off a horse, you have to get right back on," Dad said.

Sean wasn't sure he wanted to listen to his father's monologue, but he was afraid that if he said anything Dad would stop talking. And they'd never really talked.

"Sean, lad," Dad said, trying to force an Irish accent, "Don't settle for second best just because you're afraid of what everyone else will think."

After the third pint, Sean had helped Dad upstairs and put him to bed. Dad was small and skinny and spent too many hours behind a computer screen. Only the fact that he didn't really like to eat kept him from gaining weight.

After Dad was tucked under the covers, Sean glanced at himself in the mirror.

He hadn't realized until that moment that he had grown taller and larger than his own father. Sean liked to stay fit and work out. He and his friend Adam often went to the YMCA and worked out on the weights. The fisherman's sweater was long and fit him well. It showed the bulge of his shoulders and the width of his chest.

He thought of Irish Sean at the front desk, and then went downstairs for another pint. At the very least he could tell his friends back home that he'd done that.

By that time there were musicians setting up in a corner. Two fiddlers were tuning up, another man had a big round flat drum, and a fourth held an odd thing that looked like a crumpled bagpipe.

"Dose're uilleann pipes," a voice lilted. Sean turned and saw Irish Sean smiling with a pint of his own. "Yer in luck. These lad's aren't half bad. A real Irish session is a gift from the gods."

They had listened to the twirling and whirling music for a while, and then sneaked out through a door behind the bar.

That first kiss in the storeroom had changed his life forever. Sean's Chinese face was still young and smooth, but Irish Sean had a five o'clock shadow that tickled and scratched. He'd tasted of stout and cigarettes.

Next morning, when Dad and Sean came down for the "real Irish breakfast" that was included in their room fee, Irish Sean had put the plates down with another wink and a grin. "Here's the sausage and eggs, beans, brown bread and black pudding for the fine Chinese Irish lad and his father."

Dad had taken one look at the mass of beans, greasy eggs and meats, turned green and run from the room. Sean and Sean had shared a laugh.

It had been a lovely week, exploring the old city and countryside during the day, and the innkeeper's hospitality in the evening – after Dad had passed out.

Dad had no idea, which was probably part of the excitement.

The next August, Dad had been in Hong Kong for work, but sent Sean a new Irish jumper as a reminder of the trip that had changed their relationship, and changed Sean's life.

Sean looked at all his sweaters, smiled and sighed. Yeah, he wore sweaters all the time, but so fucking what? He loved his friends, but they were bullshit assholes about the whole sweater thing. Fuck 'em. He shrugged and decided that their opinions didn't matter.

But they did have a point.

When he went away to college, did he really want to become known as "That Gay Chinese Kid in the sweater"?

Maybe it was time to start experimenting and looking for a new style. Maybe some leather.

Sean smiled at the thought of himself in a tight leather jacket.

But leave all the sweaters behind?

He sighed.

No. Not all. Maybe bring an Irish one. He grinned.

And maybe that crushed silk he'd found in the Salvation Army for ten bucks... And the black shawl neck cardigan from London?

Sean shook his head. It was too much to think about. Too early. Maybe later.

He turned his back on his closet and when he shut the door the light went off, just like a refrigerator.

Chapter 12

Rave On

"I liked that scene in 'When Harry Met Sally'. In Katz's deli. When she fakes the... I can't even believe I'm talking about this with my son!"
— My mom, after two glasses of wine

If it had been a Groston rave, we would have given it a pass. We knew enough about our town to know that any Groston dance party called a rave would have been lame in the extreme, with crepe paper decorations and an Internet music station playlist. My friends and I would have stayed down in Rover's basement playing video games and chewing on Moon Cakes, a new variety of medical grade marijuana brownies imported from Amsterdam.

But word had been spreading for two weeks through Fectville Regional that rich kid Diana Marley had hired "D.J. Razor" from New York City for her eighteenth birthday party in a derelict mill building.

Diana Marley was an inescapable presence in FRHS. As you

may remember she was the girl in the red dress. In fact she wore a different outrageously red outfit every day. Not only was every single piece of clothing she wore red, but the skirts were all short and the tops were skintight across the bodice. On the coldest day of February she drove up to school in a brand new red Porsche 911 with the top down. She climbed out of the $100,000 sports car wearing a full-length red fox coat, wide open to reveal her cherry red miniskirt, blood red leather hip boots, watermelon red wool tights, and a rose-colored form-fitting cashmere sweater that left little to the imagination. If I'd been directing a high school comedy, I'd have shown reaction shots of gaping guys, tripping and distractedly walking into doors. Rumor was that her father, a litigation attorney, had set her up with a multimillion-dollar trust fund.

"We have to go to this rave," Sean said. "If only to gawk and laugh."

"I dunno," Jesús said. "I understand you wanting to socialize with all your old Fuckedville friends…"

"Will you cut that out?" Sean said. "Yeah, I grew up in Fectville until fourth grade. But I'm a Groston Guy now. Through and through."

"I know why you want to go," Rover said with a grin. "I bet that guy you're into is going be there."

Sean's face turned red. "That's not…"

"Ahaha!" Rover said pointing. "Gotcha. It's true and don't deny it."

Adam shook his head. "Sometimes you guys act like a bunch of little girls."

I raised an eyebrow at my cousin, who was usually incredibly politically correct.

"What?" Adam said. "Just because gender roles are fluid doesn't mean that there aren't behavior patterns that men and women tend toward. Oh, fuck, fine. You guys are acting like a flock of diminutive cackling cisgender hens. Is that better?"

"No," Jesús and I said simultaneously.

"But I agree with Sean," I said. "Even leaving his hot monkey love life out of it, I think we've got to go so we can get Charlie out of his house. Since his dad's last heart attack he's been stuck there like he's in prison."

"It's hard worrying about your family," Jesús said. He never really talked about his family's problems, but we knew they had to be massive. Jesús was the oldest of three brothers and two sisters. His mom worked two jobs, and nobody knew anything about his dad, except that he wasn't around. Jesús didn't talk about it, and we didn't ask. Guys, right?

"Charlie won't come," Adam said.

"Sure he will," I said. "We'll just lie to him. Jesús, can you get the car?"

"It's my car," Jesús said. "And yeah, my Mamí's home Friday nights by six, and doesn't have to be out until six Saturday morning."

So, I sent Charlie a text saying that we needed him for a crucial Rocket League match on Friday night. I told him we'd pick him up to go for pizza before, and to be ready at nine.

Charlie's reply was terse. "Fuck. Fine."

• • •

Jesús drove us to The Pizza Palace. Charlie rode shotgun. Sean was wedged in between. In the back, Adam, Rover and I squirmed, trying not to touch the gross sticky seats and door handles.

I know that there are towns that claim to have the best world-class pizza. Artisanal pies baked in wood-fired ovens with only the finest ingredients. Pizza Palace wasn't that. It was a Greek place owned by a guy named Spiros, who was always there. Stained white uniform, midnight beard, looking like he never slept, Spiros was fast. He spun out cheap discs of crisp thin crust that got soggy and drooped in the middle from too much greasy cheese and sauce. We didn't care. The Pizza Palace was our place, and that night especially, the pizza was good, though I did wish we hadn't ordered extra onions on the Everything Pie.

Charlie looked like shit. He was thinner than ever and had dark bags under his eyes like he hadn't slept much. He didn't even notice that Sean was dressed extra nice, in an all-black leather outfit with polished shoes and dark black makeup on his eyes. We teased and joked and chattered as if everything was normal.

Adam blew it by asking, "How's your dad?"

Any thaw of lightness that Charlie had begun to show froze instantly. His eyes dropped, and he shrugged. "Fine."

"Anything we can do?" Jesús said, picking mushrooms off his slice.

Charlie shook his head.

"You wanna tell us what's going on?" Adam said.

I thought he was pushing too hard. "Adam, cut it out. Let him be."

Charlie sighed. "Naw, it's okay. It sucks being at home. Dad's upstairs in bed. He doesn't even get out to shit or pee. Mom dumps his bedpan in the toilet. He laughs and smiles and tells us all how much he loves us and how much he's going to miss us. Then he falls asleep. It's like every time I see him, I wonder if this is going to be the last time."

"Shit," I said. "That sucks." I looked at my friend. "I had no idea it was that bad."

"Us neither," Rover said.

"None of us did," Sean said. Jesús nodded.

Charlie shrugged. "Doctors say Dad might get better. They've got him on blood thinners and shit I don't know what. But he might not. He's got to get up and start moving. But he doesn't seem to have the energy any more. I think he's afraid that if he gets up and goes to work, he's going to drop dead. So instead, he's staying home in bed. It's like he's giving up."

"That fucking blows," Rover said.

We all nodded.

Charlie looked at us. "You guys are great. I really needed to get out of there. Mom and Desiree are always crying. Did I mention that Desiree came home from college? She withdrew for the semester. And all my aunts and uncles come over every night and hang out, like they're on a deathwatch. My mom keeps cooking. Fried chicken. Ribs. French fries. Chili. Burgers. Brisket. Fried okra. All that shitty fatty food that got all of us fat in the first place. But she doesn't know how to cook any other way. And all my aunts and uncles and cousins dig in and tell her how great the food is."

"Your mom is an amazing cook," Jesús said. "I always love eating over at your house."

We all nodded in agreement. If Mrs. Johnson ever wanted to open a restaurant, we knew that she'd get four-and-a-half stars for flavor and five stars for portion size.

"Yeah, but I'm not eating that shit anymore," Charlie said. "And my mom takes it personally. I keep asking for salads and grilled fish and tofu."

"You eat tofu?" Sean said. "My grandmother makes tofu!"

We looked at Sean. We sometimes forgot that his family were immigrants.

"What?" Sean said. "If you've only ever had that stuff that comes in plastic cartons at the supermarket, you haven't had real tofu. It's a totally different beast."

Charlie laughed. "I'd love to try it."

"I think we have to tell him," Adam said while Rover and I tried to figure out how to split the bill evenly so that Jesús would pay a little less than everyone else.

"No!" I said.

"Tell me what?" Charlie said.

"We're going to the rave!" Rover spilled it. "And Sean's excited, 'cause he's got a hot date. That's why he's wearing that fine leather jacket."

"Hey!" Sean said. "Mind your fucking business."

"What?" Rover said. "I'd date you."

Jesús just laughed.

"Damn it, Adam." I slugged my cousin in the shoulder. "You can't keep a secret worth shit."

"I didn't say anything, it was Rover."

Rover shrugged. "He would have figured it out."

"A rave?" Charlie gave us all dead eyes for a moment. "Fuck. Fine. Yeah. Okay. Let me just text my mom and let her know."

"No. You can't," Adam said. "We all told our folks we'd be at Rover's. You'll blow it for all of us."

"What's the big deal?" Charlie asked.

163

"My Mamí would never let me drive to a rave," Jesús said.

We all looked at Rover, who shrugged. "Don't look at me. My sister's at a sleepover and my parents don't care. Well, truthfully, they don't know. They're out of town visiting my dad's brother Frank in Brooklyn. They trust us."

"Fools!" Sean said. "Bwahahahaha!"

We all laughed.

"I can't tell my folks, because I'm still technically grounded, sort of," Adam said. "Except for Rover's basement."

"My loving Chinese parents don't know that I'm gay, yet," Sean said. "I keep wanting to tell them, but I don't dare tell one or the other first, and they can't stand each other, so they're never in the same place at the same time."

"And my mom and dad will tease me mercilessly if I tell them I'm going to a rave," I said. My friends looked puzzled. "They think I can't dance."

"You can't dance," Charlie said definitively.

"Unless you're choreographed and have rehearsed for hours and hours," Sean added.

A few years ago, we all did a dance number at the Jerome Marco K-8 talent show. I can't believe how much we practiced. It took me forever to get the moves down.

"That's true," Rover chipped in.

"You can't dance either," I told Rover.

"I don't try," he said. "I know my limits."

I flipped them off, and everybody laughed.

"Fine." Charlie sighed. He looked at the time on his phone. "Let's motor."

• • •

Most of Fectville is upscale. The suburban lawns are manicured. Downtown is all rehabbed or glass and steel with strategic parks and a high tech urban trolley transport system.

The rave wasn't in that part of town. It was in a back end that was known, even to the Fecters, as The Crack-Hole, where a half dozen ancient mills had been falling down since the collapse of nineteenth century manufacturing in New England.

There were no streetlights and no street signs. If we hadn't had the GPS coordinates from the rave's evite, and a driving app we'd never have found the place.

One minute we were turning down a black alley and the next there was a huge parking lot full of cars, complete with a uniformed attendant with a glowing red light baton in his left hand and his right hand up for us to stop. There was a $10 charge to park the car.

"Welcome to Area 51," Rover joked.

"You sure we want to do this?" Jesús said.

"Come on," Adam insisted. "It'll be fun."

"You paid for the gas," I said. "We got the parking."

We dug through our pockets for the fee. The attendant waited for a tip, which there was no way he was getting from us. Then he looked over Jesús's car with disdain, and sarcastically said that we'd better park it ourselves so it wouldn't get scratched.

"Asshole," Jesús muttered.

As we drove through the lot we were stunned at the number of BMWs, Mercedes, Acuras, Porsches, Priuses and even a Lamborghini.

After counting ten of them, Adam and I got into an argument about whether plural was Priuses, Pries, or Prii.

Even before we turned off the engine, we heard the solid thump of bass.

We got out of the Dartmobile.

"Leave your coats in the car," Sean said.

"Why?" I asked. "It's freezing."

"No place to put them. You don't want to leave them on the floor."

We all shrugged off our coats and dumped them in the trunk, except Sean, who kept his black leather jacket on.

"What's up with that?" I said, shivering.

"It's a fashion thing," Sean grinned.

Then we started walking. We were so far in the back that we couldn't even see the building, except for the red light over the entrance door. Our eyes had to adjust to the starlight.

"Actually, just now, I wish you guys had told me what we were doing in advance," Charlie said, "so I could have dressed a little better."

I looked at him. "You look fine to me."

Sean shook his head. "Don't worry about it. Dress up. Dress down. Whatever. Unless you're going in costume, anything and everything goes at a rave."

"Costume?" Rover said.

"Yeah," Sean said. "I know a lot of kids are going as furries."

"What the fuck is a furry?" Jesús said.

Sean grinned. "You'll see."

The bouncer at the door asked for IDs and another $10 each. Even from outside, the deep bass throbbed.

"This is pretty fucking expensive," Jesús muttered. "We aren't even inside."

"The rich don't stay rich by spending their money," I said. "They make us spend ours."

"I got ya," Sean said to Jesús. "Consider it a birthday present."

"My birthday's not until next month," Jesús said.

"An early birthday present."

"Look, Sean," Jesús said. "I know you've got piles of money, but I don't take charity."

Sean took a breath. "My dad has piles of money. My mom not so much. I live with my mom, and I don't take charity either. I've got a job."

"What kind of job?" Charlie asked.

"Day trading. Penny stocks. Turns out I'm pretty good at it. I take all the money my dad 'gives' me, and invest it. I pay myself a salary, set aside a percentage for the future, and keep the balance to 'give' back to him at some point in the future when I'm ready to tell him, 'Fuck You, I don't need your money.'"

Sean was breathing hard. We all waited.

"I'm freezin here," Rover said. "We going in or what?"

"Tell you what," Sean said to Jesús, "why don't I give… no, pay… no. Why don't I reimburse you twenty bucks for gas money for all the times you've taken me to and from school?"

"Come on already," Adam said, impatiently. "I'm freezing."

166

Jesús thought for a moment, nodded, and said, "Well all right then. You give me the twenty for gas, and I'll pay for your admission."

"But only if I can buy you a beer," Sean said.

"Deal."

The bouncer looked bored.

We handed over the money.

The door opened, and we were in.

• • •

The rave was insane.

As soon as we got inside, the music was beyond deafening. There were black lights in the hall, and strobes scattered around the huge wide-open factory floor. In between the columns and flashing lights we could see a seething writhing mass of high school and college kids bouncing up and down to the inescapable beat.

I'm a bit of a homebody. I admit it. My mouth dropped open at the sheer number of girls dressed in skimpy and scanty clothes – even guys in skimpy boxers and vests with no shirts too – and the ones dressed head to toe in furry costumes. In between retina burns I saw teddy bears and panthers, leopards, lions, tigers, and one kid who had a ten-foot stuffed giraffe's neck-and-head sticking up from a backpack on his shoulders.

It was hot and humid, and we were glad we'd left our coats in the car. There was a coat check, where you could pay another two bucks to a cute girl who was dressed like a *Lord of the Rings* elf, complete with bow and arrow and fake ears.

The beat was intense, with strobes and lasers flashing, and you couldn't help bouncing along. Every bass note shook my heart. We all were grinning and nodding. Sean was scanning the crowd for his wannabe boyfriend.

"Wait wait wait!" Adam shouted. "Before you go anywhere, I've got another present!"

He reached into his pocket and showed us a big black plastic bag labeled, "For Medical Use Only." He ripped it open and pulled out a foot-long green gummy worm. "These are called Silly Snakes. Each one's got thirty milligrams of THC with another ten CBD. Anybody want one?"

"Shit yeah!" Charlie shouted. "God, I need this."

Before we could stop him, Charlie grabbed the snake, and swallowed it whole without even chewing.

"Shit, Charlie," Adam said. "That's three times the regular dose! That was supposed to last you all night."

"You got a red one?" Jesús asked.

"They all taste the same," I said.

"No they don't," Jesús insisted.

It was an old argument.

Adam passed out the worms, and we greedily dug in.

Then we split up. Adam and I went looking for drinks. Sean was searching for his boy toy. Jesús and Charlie... I don't even know where they went.

Even before the drugs kicked in, I was having fun. It had been a long fucking freezing wet shitty winter. Everything I did was focused on getting into a better college or trying to forget that I might not be getting into a good college. Hanging out with my friends was great, and I loved playing video games, but being around so many people in a situation where they weren't trying to teach you, compete with you, or torment you was a pleasure. I didn't know shit about the kind of music the DJ was playing, but it had a pounding beat and I didn't care.

Adam and I found the keg, actually there were five kegs all in a row. Above the kegs was a sign. "Free Beer. Cups $10."

He grinned at me. "This is so awesome!"

He and I peeled out another $10 each, and gave them to another cute girl. She was wearing panda ears and a skimpy panda fur bikini. She must have handed us big red plastic cups, because a moment later we had them in our hands.

We pumped the nearest keg and filled our cups with foam.

"I can't believe that they get away with this!" I shouted to Adam. "What?"

"I mean, they checked our IDs! We're all under twenty-one."

"What? It's free beer. Are you complaining?"

"Never mind!"

We started bouncing to the beat, foam sloshing, strobes flashing.

The DJ was up on a small platform at one end of the long room. D.J. Razor was a skinny black guy with half his head shaved and the other half dreadlocked. He wore a black leather biker vest and tight black leather shorts. He was definitely not from New England. He had headphones on and was pumping his fist with the music.[24]

Standing beside the DJ, in a bright red latex dress that left nothing except her skin color to the imagination was Diana Marley, the mistress of the evening, surveying all she had wrought. Next to Diana was our old nemesis Doug Hawthorne, Groston's all-star quarterback, looking stiff and uncomfortable. He wore a blue blazer, khakis, white shirt and a tie.

I nudged Adam. "I guess Doug got his cast off."

"Is he dating Diana now?" Adam shouted at me. "I thought she was with James Croft?"

"Don't know. Don't care!" I answered back. "Hey, there's Helen!"

Adam's head spun around. I pointed to Helen's chair about two-thirds of the way across the room. She was spinning back and forth to the beat, a grim smile on her face.

Adam's face fell. He looked away. "I've got to piss."

"You want me to come with you?"

He gave me a whatthefuck look and took off.

I was just as glad. Girls go to the bathroom in pairs and packs. Guys don't. I'd only offered for the moral support.

My eyes scanned the crowd and I saw Jesús talking to some girl. Sean had found a pretty boy and was spinning with him like a ballroom dancer. Rover had pulled out his portable pocket computer and was scoping the DJ's computer system. He was probably trying to hack it. Even Charlie was out on the dance floor, making space and moving with grace.

Except for me and Adam, everyone else seemed to be moving and shaking.

Not for the first time, I wished I could dance. I am so white. My feet will bounce, but after about three or seven steps I start to trip

---

[24] According to Wikipedia his initials really were D.J., but there were disputes about whether his real name was Darius Johnson or Darby James.

and stutter. And I never know what to do with my hands. Do I move them? Wave them? Hold them by my side? Watching all the ravers, it made me appreciate punk rock mosh pits where the only objective is to thrash.

I stood off to the side, beer in one hand, waiting for the Silly Snake to kick in.

Chapter 13

Fat Charlie: Resurrection!

"Did you ever see that scene where Buster Keaton is walking down a street in the middle of a storm and the entire side of a house falls on him, but he's unharmed because he just happens to be where there was an open window? It's amazing because it was done in an age before digital special effects. They built the house, lowered the side, marked where the window was, and then pulled it back up. Even so, nobody was sure it would work, so when they did the scene, they started the camera and then the entire cast and crew left the set, except for Keaton. Everyone was sure he was going to die. That's comedy!"
— Dave Rover

The beer at the rave was free, the music was loud, and the warehouse was full of sweat and drugs and flashing lights and hundreds and hundreds of unsupervised teenagers and twenty-somethings. It was glorious!

Ordinarily, I'm a fairly laid back guy. My friends and I hang out and get loud, but we do it together in a small group. This was wildness on a level that I'd never really experienced before. You can make fun of me for being a sheltered rube from a hick New England town and I won't deny it. I'm sure that there were kids in Fectville, like Diana Marley, who'd been to Coachella or Burning Man or even an arena concert with some mega star. The biggest show I ever saw was a Music Man revival in Boston, and that was so lame that I never wanted to see another one.

The costumes were amazing, ranging from guys in gorilla suits to girls in cute squirrel outfits. Some wore next to nothing. There was a lot of leather and strategically torn cloth. Some even had masks. I spotted Helen's friend, Robyn Franklin dressed as a sexy koala, which sounds impossible but really worked. I couldn't stop staring at her. Curves and fur? Whoa!

D.J. Razor was awesome, cutting together beats that had the entire room bouncing in head-banging rhythm, fist pumping, gyrating…

I was wasted. Totally wasted. Just the memory of how wasted I was makes me feel wasted. Can you see the shit-eating grin on my face right now? I was lurching and bouncing, pretending to dance, because I can barely put two steps together, unless I rehearse something for weeks at a time. And I was having a blast. My heart was hammering. I was stoned out of my mind. I was dancing with girls I didn't know. I was dancing with guys I didn't know. I know I looked like an idiot. Who cared? Nothing mattered but moving up and down.

Which is why, when somebody banged into me, I figured it was a mosh pit starting to happen, so I just shoved back.

Then I looked and saw that a circle was forming in the middle of the room.

In the center of the circle was my buddy, Charlie. I started to wave at him and shouted, even though I knew he couldn't hear me. "Hey Charlie! Dude!"

Then I noticed that six football players from the Fectville Regional High School team had surrounded Charlie.

I grinned wider. For just a moment. Didn't realize what I was seeing.

Then I did. They were surrounding my friend. They were setting him up. It boded ill. (I actually remember thinking that at the time, "This bodes ill." Jeez, sometimes I'm a real pedant.)

By then I was about three rows back. I started to push my way forward.

The music was still pounding. The D.J. was oblivious, in his own little set list.

When the chanting started I knew that we were in trouble. It was blurry at first, a rhythmic bass shout, and then the words got clear and I sobered up fast.

"Fat. Charlie. Fat Fat Fat Charlie. Fat Charlie. Fat fat fat FAT Charlie!"

I didn't see Sean or Jesús or Rover, but I spotted Adam on the other side of the circle, also about three rows back.

The shit was about to shred through the fan.

The music stopped dead just as the entire Fectville offensive line bellowed, "FAT FAT FAT CHARLIE!"

• • •

Later on, Rover told me that he'd already hacked the D.J.'s computerized sound and lighting system and was trying to figure out what stunt to pull. Cutting the audio at that exact moment had been a fortunate accident. His home-built miniature computer had chicklet-sized keys and he'd accidentally hit the space bar, which paused everything.

When he'd heard that, "FAT FAT FATCHARLIE!" Rover just reacted, cued up his own tune, hit the space bar again to "Play," and started working on the lights.

The new music started with a rhythmic clapping.

Then the lights went out.

Then we heard it. Everybody heard it. It was loud. It was proud.

Fat Charlie you're so fine.

You're so fine you blow my mind – Fat Charlie!

Fat Charlie!

I grinned.

You know that song, *Mickey* by Toni Basil? It was an inescapable MTV dance video from 1981. It's got a stupid easy beat and a wicked hook, and the dumbest lyrics on the planet.

And when we were in our last year at Jerome Marco K-8, our entire crew rehearsed and performed it for the talent show, but remixed it with lyrics that I rewrote:

> *Fat Charlie you're so fat.*
> *You're so fat you blow my hat – Fat Charlie.*
> *Fat Charlie!!*
> *You've eaten everything and that's an awful lot*
> *You think that you are full but I know you're really not.*

Ok, I know it's not a great work of parody or poetry. We'd waited until the last minute to enter the contest. I was in eighth grade and working on a deadline. We had to have the whole routine recorded and choreographed and rehearsed in just under two weeks.

Remember that I said that I can't dance? No matter how much they deny it, multiply that by most of my friends. Fortunately, Rover's younger sister, Elspeth, was totally into the song and dance scene, and she worked our asses off. The blisters on my toes had blisters. But Elspeth was determined that if we were really going to do the dance routine in the show that we wouldn't look like losers. Her only concession was that she kicked her brother out of the number, because he was hopeless, and we needed someone to run the tech.

At the time, Charlie had joked that if he danced any harder, he'd lose weight and I'd have to rewrite the song as "Skinny Charlie."

All our work and effort paid off, and we killed it at the talent show, bringing the entire school to their feet. Even Mrs. Capamundo was chanting along at the end!

> *Fat Charlie, what a pity you don't under eat*
> *You gobble up the turkey then you gobble up the meat.*
> *Fat Charlie you're so big, you can't see your feet*
> *The food's all gone Charlie!*
> *What's there to eat Charlie, eat Charlie?*
> *Turn up the heat Charlie.*
> *Fat Charlie...*
> *Don't eat my hat Charlie!*

When the clap-track started that domp-da-domp da-da domp-da-domp da-da rhythm, I knew what I had to do. I prayed that my friends were paying attention and knew what to do too.

In the darkness I elbowed and pushed my way into the clearing. Navigating by the dim exit lights, I dodged past the football players and took my position behind Charlie and to his right.

I listened for the turnaround and prayed that Rover had the real DJ completely locked out because if anything went wrong, we were all dead.

And then… Showtime.

• • •

Lights came up.

Charlie was in the front, on point. I was behind him to the right, and Jesús was behind to my right. Adam was behind Charlie to the left, and Sean was behind him. Helen was there too, right in her position in the middle.

DOMP-DA-DOMP DA-DA DOMP-DA-DOMP DA-DA

And we were dancing in perfect sync, a routine we hadn't practiced in four years but had burned so deeply into our muscle memory that it came back in an instant.

We moved. We grooved. We clapped. We boogied.

Fat Charlie you're so fine.

You're so fine you blow my mind – Fat Charlie.

Fat Charlie!!

The looks on the Fectville football team's faces were unbelievably priceless. They were beyond dumbfounded. They were stumpified. It was like they were five-year-old kids with sticks about to beat on their birthday piñatas only to find out that the paper mache donkeys had turned into a team of Clydesdales.

Fat Charlie you're so fat.

You're so fat you blow my hat, Fat Charlie,

Fat Charlie!!

The circle around us got bigger as we stomped forward, turned on a dime. Ditched right. Ditched left. Right arm up. Left…

I caught the flamboyant grin on Sean's face, and knew we all mirrored him. Adam glanced at Helen, and saw her smiling and clapping, in between maneuvering her chair with a rolling swagger.

Even Charlie, who'd tried his best to shed his nickname, knew that by embracing it and owning it and ruling it, right now, he would be incontestably triumphant. He looked good, large and in charge!

I honestly didn't think it could possibly get better, but it did.

Rover's sister Elspeth was two years younger than us, and because she was totally into all forms of choreographed dance, any time somebody asked, she showed them the moves. She had asked her brother for a copy of the audio, and Rover gave it to her without thinking twice about it. Elspeth taught her friends, and they taught their friends. At school dances, somebody always called for the DJ to "put on that Fat Charlie Song!" Elspeth never told us about it. Why would she? She was Rover's pesky little sister. We were two years older than her, and aside from the occasional, "Hi, Pest," we never talked to her.

But Elspeth had sneaked out to the rave too. She was a sophomore now. She and her friends all had lied to their parents. They said they were having a quiet slumber party at Rover's house. Instead, they'd piled into an Internet car, got dropped at the front gate, and had been standing around on the edges, frightened by all the older kids.

When the Fat Charlie song started, they all watched and waited until the chorus came around again. They thought we'd planned it, like a flash mob. We didn't. We couldn't have.

We thought it was just the seven of us who knew the choreography. We were wrong.

Every single student from Ashby Bryson High School in Groston knew how to dance to "That Fat Charlie Song."

And they did.

It seemed like everybody from our old high school was there too, and the ones who weren't probably lied about it later.

There were about four hundred of us all in perfect lines, with Charlie at the middle, doing this cheerleading clapping boogie in perfect sync!

But there was more. Some kids from the Groston gymnastics

team and the entire Groston cheerleading squad had added in acrobatics that Elspeth hadn't dared to teach us because she'd been terrified we'd fall off the stage.

As we peeled off to the right, Susie Wardle, wearing a tight black leather Catwoman suit, signaled for her squad to form up a pyramid. She was lifted to the top, jumped up, hung from a pipe in the ceiling and then dove off, caught at the last moment before her skull could crack on the floor, by her ex boyfriend Doug Hawthorne, who had abandoned his date, the dumbfounded Diana Marley, who looked insanely pissed.

Rover remixed the song on the fly, extending it to seven earth-shattering minutes, all the while refocusing the spotlights and flaring the strobes.

If I hadn't seen the video online I never would have believed it. Somebody from Fectville had started recording when the footballers began shoving Charlie, and they kept their cell phone camera on for the entire number.

And when the song finished on a downbeat, we all stomped and stopped.

Dead perfect.

The cheers and applause from the kids from Fectville Regional and the college kids was deafening.

All the lights went dark, except for a corridor of white light, which opened up in front of us.

And with Charlie leading, the clapping crowd split open wide as we just swept out, past the coat check and bouncers, and left the building. Every single kid from Groston was done for the night.

Which was a good thing for us, because the entire Fectville police force was just pulling up outside with their lights flashing.

The parking lot was instant chaos as everybody ran for their cars.

Sidetrack

合

Harmony

Adam knelt barefoot on the dojo's white canvas-covered mat. He stared up at the Japanese scroll hanging on the front wall. His knees hurt.

At six-twenty in the morning on a Sunday, the Aikido school was empty and quiet. The first morning class wasn't until seven-thirty. It was the class he used to teach.

Adam sighed.

He'd popped awake in his bed at five-thirty, his brain still buzzing from the gummy worm. Wide awake at five-thirty on a Sunday after a rave? Fuck.

Adam always knew exactly what time it was, like he had a stupid super power. His cousin, Isaac, really enjoyed asking for the time at odd moments. Adam was only wrong twice a year, when the shifts happened to and from Daylight Savings Time, and then only by an hour either way.

He'd been dreaming of watermelon. Again. Sometimes he was driving an out of control truck full of them. This time, he was riding a giant watermelon falling out of the sky. Ground coming closer and then a jolt awake that sent his heart racing.

Both the weird dreams and inability to fall back asleep seemed to be side effects of the medical marijuana. Maybe he should switch from sativa to indica, which by all accounts had a more soporific effect, but the few times he'd tried it, he'd realized he didn't like becoming one with the couch.

Instead of lying in bed ruminating, Adam had decided to go to the dojo and try his hand at meditation. Even though he'd been banned from practicing, he still worked at the dojo and had a key.

"If you don't know your own mind," Sensei often said, "how can you change anyone else's?"

So he'd written a note for his parents, turned off the home security alarm, and jogged downtown.

Suburban Groston was quiet at sunrise. The dew glistened on tightly cut lawns. A few robins and cardinals pecked at fresh seeds in front yard feeders. A guy drove by in a car even older than the Dartmobile, hurling thick plastic-wrapped copies of the *Groston Gazette* toward front porches.

Downtown Groston was mostly empty. Shopkeepers were having a hard time after the flood and freeze. Most of them were waiting for disaster relief funds and the lawsuit against the Fectville Dam Authority to rebuild, so most businesses were closed. The smell of fresh-baked bagels from the new Brooklyn Bakery was a welcome exception.

Adam was warmed up by the time he got to the dojo. He unlocked the door, swept the mats, and then changed into his white uniform. He looked at the blue hakima Paul had bought for him after he'd passed his second-degree test, and after a moment's hesitation tied it on.

Hakimas were just one of the cool things about Aikido. Originally they were a form of riding chaps for Samurai, but for some reason Aikido's founder liked them, so everybody who earned a black belt got the privilege of learning how to tie and fold the bizarre baggy pants.

"They ground your energy," Sensei said. "They make you pay

attention. Plus they hide your footwork."

Adam took a moment to bow in, knelt down, sat up straight, and then tried to meditate.

"The purpose of meditation is to settle your mind," Sensei said. "Follow your thoughts and let them go."

It wasn't working.

Twenty minutes in, it seemed like Adam was doing nothing but ruminating, rethinking, reminiscing, reliving and replaying. He was, it seemed, nothing but his thoughts.

For instance, he realized that when he first started doing Aikido his knees had never hurt. Of course that was when he was little. Back then, Dad was alive and they were stationed in Japan. He remembered going in early, before school, to the wrestling room at the army base to sweep the mats. Dad would unroll the scroll and hang it up with the picture of Morihei Ueshiba, the founder of Aikido. Then they would kneel and wait for other students to show up. Sometimes there were five, sometimes ten. If one of the senior Japanese instructors was coming to class there might be as many as twenty. Sometimes nobody showed up, and Dad would just practice with Adam.

At the time it had seemed normal, but in retrospect, it was strange being a six-year-old white American kid studying martial arts with his dad on an Army base in Japan. All these huge American guys (and a few huge women) swapped their mottled camouflage fatigues for the clean white of a traditional gi. Dad was the only black belt in a hakima. They would all line up and bow to the kamiza at the front of the room, clapping their hands to begin practice. Then the giants would throw each other around the room, always taking turns throwing Adam too.

Adam took a breath, tried to let the thoughts go away. Stay in the present. But the past wouldn't leave.

The first lessons Dad had taught his son had been all about falling down and getting back up again. Adam learned how to roll like a ball – forward and backwards. He learned how to hit the mat from any angle and distribute his weight, slapping out.

He would run like a tiny grinning maniac at his father, who would step aside, grab him by the wrist and then launch him through the air. It was like flying for a very short period of time.

"It's called, 'ukemi,'" Dad said, laughing between throws. "It's all about receiving an attack. Don't fight back. Don't resist. Accept it. Go with it. Survive it. Then come up ready."

Dad had always said it the same way every time. Adam remembered his words exactly: Don't fight back. Don't resist. Accept it. Go with it. Survive it. Then come up ready.

Then a jeep had rolled over on Dad, crushing him to death.

Adam had been six. One morning he and Dad had gone to the dojo before school. The next morning Mom was packing to go "home" to the States. They didn't have a funeral on the base, but they did have a little ceremony. Some of the guys from the dojo came over and gave Adam squeezes on the shoulder. One of them, a huge soldier nicknamed Gentle John gave Adam the Aikido scroll.

"Aren't you guys going to need it?" Adam had asked.

"Nah. There are scrolls everywhere here. We'll get another," Gentle John had said. "This one was your Dad's. He'd want you to have it."

The rest of their departure was a blur. One day his family was in the army in Japan. The next day Dad was dead. Two days after that he was living with his Mom in her old bedroom in Groston. The day after that, they buried Dad in the family plot on Steeple Hill in a military service complete with a twenty-one gun salute. And a week later they moved again; Mom had gotten a job at an elementary school on the navy base in Wilmington, Delaware. Two years after that, she'd married Paul and they'd been sent abroad (again) until Paul finally retired and the whole "family" had returned to Groston.

Everywhere Adam had gone, he'd hung his Dad's scroll in his bedroom next to a photograph of his father, smiling in his army-issue glasses.

Years passed and the only things Adam really remembered about his father were the photo, the scroll, and the words: "Don't fight back. Don't resist. Accept it. Go with it. Survive it. Then come up ready."

What ever happened to Dad's hakima? Probably it got left

behind in the locker room at the base.

Adam blinked. He stared at the scroll on the wall of the dojo in Groston.

He'd been amazed to discover that this small town in New England had a real Japanese-style martial arts school.

Paul had brought him in after the first day at Jerome Marco K-8 and introduced Adam to the instructor, Joseph Leguzamo, who bowed and said, "On the Mat, I'm Sensei. Off the mat, you can call me Joey Legs"

Adam hadn't been impressed. Joey Legs was small and skinny and had long hair pulled back in a ponytail. Even though the guy wore a gi and a hakima he didn't look big or scary or particularly martial. He looked like a hippy burnout.

"I hear you did Aikido with your Dad," Sensei Joey Legs said. "You want to show me what you remember?"

Adam had glanced at Paul, nervous that his stepfather would be offended at the mention of Adam's real dad. Paul had just smiled and nodded.

Adam stepped onto the mat, felt its spring, and then launched himself into a long diving roll. He came up and did seven more, making a circle around the room before standing up at the end, feeling dizzy, and then toppling into an unexpected back fall.

Joey Legs was laughing. "That was awesome! First we work on your breathing."

And then Paul did something Adam hadn't expected. He didn't stay to watch. He left.

Adam took a breath.

They had given him a small gi and a clean stiff white belt.

Sensei had shown Adam where to line up with the other students. Then they'd bowed, clapped, and bowed again.

Even though he hadn't practiced Aikido in years, it came back to him quickly. The Groston dojo was a lot more formal than the wrestling-room classes he'd attended with Dad in Japan. The walls were white and severe. Instead of the sticky wrestling mat, the practice area was covered in canvas. But on the wall at the front of the room was a picture of Aikido's founder, and of course the calligraphy scroll. Ai, Ki, and Do – harmony, energy, and the way. The path.

Still kneeling, still staring up at the scroll, Adam's knees hurt even more.

He hated meditating. Aikido was about self-defense, about throwing. About joint locks and tapping out. And falling.

Sensei often said that meditation was part of the path. "Pay attention to your thoughts and then let them go. New thoughts arise. Let them go. Watch your breathing. Let that go." It never made sense.

What was the purpose of it?

"No purpose," Sensei said, laughing. "If you think there's a purpose, then you're not meditating."

Fuck that shit. Let that go, Adam thought. Fuck that shit. Let that go.

He took a breath.

But he missed practicing Aikido. He hated being banned from the dojo. Even though he had helped with the rebuilding after the flood – ripping out and replacing the moldy sheetrock and tying down the canvas to cover the new mats – the Groston dojo didn't feel like his home anymore.

He missed warming up. He missed practicing with weapons. He missed his private lessons with Sensei, teaching his Sunday morning class, and especially teaching the little kids. Sensei didn't even want him watching classes from the back.

"You still aren't ready," Sensei had said just two weeks ago. "I can feel your anger. So can everyone else. Aikido is a martial art with compassion. If you practice from anger, it will pollute your technique and you'll pass that on to others. Yes, anger can be a tool or a fuel. But if it's in your core, if it's where you come from, it's like poison and you're no longer practicing Aikido."

Adam considered that.

Was he angry? Of course he was angry. He was pissed that he wasn't allowed to practice Aikido.

He took a breath.

What else did he have to be angry about? He had a good life. Harder than some. Easier than many. Dad had been dead for two-thirds of Adam's life. Paul had been around for half of it. Mom had been there always. He was surrounded with good people: his cousin, Isaac, and all his great friends. Helen.

It came to him in a flash.

He was angry at Dad for dying.

He took a breath and stared at the scroll. He was angry. The kanji was the same as the Aikido scroll that had belonged to his father. Furious. The one that had hung in his room so long that it was almost invisible on the wall. Outraged.

Don't fight back. Don't resist. Accept it. Go with it. Survive it. Then come up ready.

Dad hadn't. He'd been crushed. They wouldn't even show Adam the body.

Had he really been mad at Dad all these years? For leaving? For dying? Dad didn't want to die. Intellectually, Adam knew that. But at age six?

Adam took a breath and then let it out.

In that instant, he felt a weight lifting from his chest.

Let it go.

Dad, I miss you.

Let it go? Hell yeah.

Dad, I'm not angry any more. I just wish I knew you...

He smiled. Cool! Who knew this whole meditation thing could be so therapeutic?

And then an annoying thought rose up.

Butch Batten. Adam was still mad at Butch.

That day in the hall, Butch had been taunting Helen, and Adam had decided to destroy Butch. He had been furious then, and he was furious now.

Kneeling on the mat, Adam remembered it vividly.

They'd been friends once. Way back at Jerome Marco K-8. Big Butch and Little Adam. Not buddies like with Charlie, Isaac or Rover but they'd all hung out together. Gone camping. Played football.

Then in high school, Butch had become a star football player and a big man. He'd turned back into a bully. Inconsiderate. Abusive. Mostly Adam had ignored it.

But that morning, seeing Helen's pain, Adam had decided to teach Butch a fucking lesson.

Adam took a breath. Tried to hang on to the release of the anger at his Dad.

Tried to let go of the other thoughts. Stop replaying the memories.

He'd hurt two people badly.

He'd almost been kicked out of school.

Clear your head. Don't think of anything.

Sensei had fucking banned him from practicing Aikido because Adam had lost control with Butch. Fuck that shit.

Meditate. Focus on the now. Let the thoughts go like ripples across the water.

But he'd seen the taunting smile on Butch's face, and Adam's sole and immediate intention had been to wipe it off.

So he'd rammed Butch's head into the wall.

He remembered that. He remembered how it sounded – like a watermelon hitting concrete.

Jeez. Watermelons.

In a moment of rage, Adam had done what he'd intended and completely destroyed Butch. His friend, once.

Adam remembered the watermelon thud, and Butch collapsed on the floor, still.

I did it on purpose, he thought. I'm sorry

Adam felt tears welling and blinked them back. Who the hell am I crying for?

Butch? Or myself?

He took a breath. And then another.

Let it go? He couldn't.

It wasn't a mistake. I should have been punished. Instead, because we had a good lawyer, I got off.

Butch went to the hospital and Adam went back to school a hero. Fuck.

Adam looked up at the scroll.

Sensei was right. I don't know how to control myself.

In the dojo, everyone knew how to fall. You knew how to get thrown or take a hit. Students cooperated to learn without getting hurt. It was fun. You could enjoy throwing someone across the room, knowing that they would fly, roll, and then get back up.

Sure, Butch was a football player, who should know how to take a hit, but he hadn't known Adam was a black belt. And Butch didn't know the secrets Adam had learned from his father. Adam hadn't really learned them either. Not then.

Now his knees really were killing him. It was almost seven. Sensei would be arriving soon to open up.

Don't fight back. Don't resist. Accept it. Go with it. Survive it. Then come up ready.

Adam looked up at the scroll and realized that somehow he wasn't angry anymore, except maybe at himself. And that was more sadness than rage.

And then he let that go too.

I'm done with the anger.

Really? Am I really?

Yes. The anger really was gone, and that brought a smile to his face. He felt good.

Was it really that easy?

No.

Because another annoying thought popped into his head, and try as he might, he couldn't let it go: Butch knocked unconscious. The sound of the watermelon.

I'm so sorry, he said to himself.

Then he whispered it aloud, like a prayer, even though no one else was in the room. "Butch, I'm sorry. I'll try to make it up to you."

He didn't know how, but it felt right.

Adam nodded, took a breath, and then clapped his hands twice, sealing the practice.

He bowed deeply from the waist, and stood, wobbling for a moment. He hobbled off the mat, stretching his aching knees as he walked. Then he knelt back down, quickly folded his hakima, changed back into his clothes and put his uniform back on the shelf.

By the time he got outside and locked up most of the stiffness was gone.

Perhaps it was finally time to come back to the dojo for classes.

He'd have to ask Sensei. But not today.

First he'd have to talk with Butch. Apologize in person. That would be hard. And Butch might not take it well. Still it needed to be done.

Meanwhile, he'd surprise Mom and Paul by picking up bagels on the way home.

He squinted in the early morning light.

It looked like a nice day.

Chapter 14

Black Monday

"Why do you think they call it dying?"
— attributed to Charlie Chaplin, when asked
how it feels when no one laughs at a joke

Sunday morning after the rave, Charlie's father died.

He passed away just after breakfast, surrounded by his family. Charlie was there, his sister Desiree too. All of Mr. Johnson's brothers and sisters and even some of his cousins. Mrs. Johnson had spent all morning in the kitchen baking and frying and stirring.

"If I stop cooking, he's going to die" Charlie heard her whisper this to his Uncle James, as she added okra to a huge pot of gumbo.

That morning she'd already made bacon, eggs, pancakes, waffles, sausages, biscuits, homefries, and grits.

The kitchen had always been always the center of the Johnson house, and the whole family was watching her.

"Etta, he wants to say goodbye to you," Uncle James had told her.

Mrs. Johnson's head dropped. Then she lifted it, nodded, tasted the gumbo, and dropped in two more dried red peppers. Then she set the spoon down, untied her apron and hung it on a hook by the refrigerator. She took a moment to check her hair in the dark reflection in the microwave's door.

She nodded again, set her shoulders, and walked out of the kitchen, slowly up the stairs.

Charlie was behind her. Desiree too. They all stopped outside the bedroom for a moment.

"I didn't see Mom's face," Charlie told me later, "but I know what she did. She set her shoulders back and put on a big old smile. That's what she called it. 'Charlie, no matter how bad things are, if you put on a big old smile, everybody feels better.' So she put a smile on, and she went into their bedroom. Desiree and I went in after."

Charlie didn't tell me what those last moments were like, and I didn't ask.

I know that our generation is supposed to be famous for publicly oversharing everything, but I don't know about that. There are, it seems to me, some things that ought to be private and respected.

All I know is that when George Johnson died, they all got to say goodbye, and then he was gone.

In this world, everybody dies. So far in my life, I've been pretty fortunate and death has been far from my day-to-day. I've read about it in the news, seen my share of TV reports too. I've watched thousands killed in video games and movies, but that's not real. Adam's real dad, my Uncle Robert, died a long time ago, and I don't remember it. Now it seemed as if death was circling closer. First, Helen's cat Mittens was lost and presumed drowned in the flood. Now, Mr. Johnson was dead of a heart attack. He'd been on the waiting list for a heart transplant, but because he was so overweight he was pretty low down, and a matched donor didn't die in time to save him.

I was at home, doing homework early Sunday night when I got the group text from Charlie.

Dad's gone.

I stared at my phone.

= That sucks. Rover texted right back.

• I'm so sorry. Adam texted.

:-(was all Jesús could manage.

> What do you need? Helen asked.

I stared at my phone. I needed to say something, but words failed me. Words never failed me. Not written ones anyway. I liked writing and fancied myself good at it. What could I tell my friend whose father was dead?

– I'm with you. I typed at last. Not knowing what it mean, but knowing it was true. Then just before I hit send I changed "I'm" to "We're."

– We're with you.

I sent it.

I waited a moment, stared at my screen. The text app glowed green, and then faded to save battery life.

Texting isn't like phone calls or conversations. You send texts off, knowing that they might land immediately, or only be seen after a delay.

Then I went back to studying for AP World History. What else could I do just then?

• • •

We all skipped school on Monday and went to Charlie's dad's funeral. We didn't really talk about it. We didn't have to. It just happened.

I slept in, woke up at about ten, and put on black jeans, a black tee shirt, a black button-down shirt, a blue blazer, and a pair of high-top Converse sneakers, which were the only black shoes I owned.

I was waiting outside, thinking about nothing, until Jesús picked me up, last because my house was closest to the Central Church up on Steeple Hill.

Adam was in front, riding shotgun. Rover was in the front middle. In back were Helen and Sean. Helen slid herself over, and I squeezed in beside.

We didn't say anything as we drove. The radio was off.

Silence in our group is a weird and rare thing. I often think that we try to avoid it. Probably not consciously, but the radio is always on. Or a video or the news. Or we're talking on our phone, or to each other. Or listening to someone else's conversation or playlist.

Jesús's car's engine was loud. The Dartmobile needed another new muffler soon, but not quite yet.

The road to the church was full of cars parked on both sides, so we found a spot in the lot at the bottom of the hill and walked up.

By the time we got there, the service was already underway. We sneaked into the church and found some space along the back wall, while we looked for empty seats.

The Johnsons were a big family and had already fixed things up in preparation. They didn't believe in waiting long to bury their dead, and hadn't really planned on such a large funeral, but Mr. Johnson was well liked, and everybody in Groston who was anybody was there. Mayor Kopel was there in a black mourning dress. I saw the school superintendent, Pedro Gonzales in a charcoal suit and Police Chief Brennan in his formal blues, looking tired. Mrs. Capamundo sat on an aisle, her head barely visible. She happened to turn and catch my eye. She had a sad smile and her face dropped in a nod, then she raised her finger and bobbed her head to the left. Beside her was Mr. Douglas. I moved back a little, out of his line of sight. The guy from the fish counter at the supermarket sat next to the town's head librarian. Adam's lawyer, Bob Billings wore a dark suit. My parents were together near the front, and beside them were Adam's mom and my Uncle Paul, all dressed in black.

Groton's Central Church is an interesting anomaly. Architecturally, it's a typical large New England church with white shingles, a slate roof and a high steeple. Inside there are rows of dark wooden pews and white walls. There's an altar and a podium, but no crucifix. That was taken down, before I was born, when the Unitarian Universalists merged with the Congregationalists who owned the building. There wasn't a Jewish synagogue in Groston, but on the high holidays, the town's Jews (my family and Adam's included) attended services in the Central Church with a rented rabbi and a rented ark of the covenant. All in all, it's about as diverse and non-religion-specific as any house of worship could possibly be.

I tried to listen, but I can't say that I heard much. I kept staring at the huge casket at the front. It wasn't as big as a piano, but it wasn't that much smaller. Charlie's father, George Johnson was inside that box and unmoving.

My grandparents were dead, but I don't remember their funerals. I know that people die every day all around the world.

Is it strange to live in a part of the planet where death is so far removed? People talk about every life being precious, but I don't think I had ever given it much thought. I guess I was lucky that way.

When the service was over, we got out of the church before the slow rush and joined the motorcade to the cemetery.

Nobody new was buried on Steeple Hill. That old cemetery is full. Instead, there's a site on the outskirts of town, up on a hill out by a bend in the Breakneck River that's kind of scenic and popular for walking – if walking in a cemetery can truly be something popular.

We watched from a distance, and when our turn came to drop a handful of dirt on the grave, the pile was already so big that we each only took a small handful.

I let the clumps of white rock and brown dirt fall from my hand and slide down the edge of the small hill atop what used to be my friend Charlie's father.

I wanted to cry, but I wasn't really sure why. I knew Charlie's dad only slightly. We called him "Mr. Johnson." He was a good man. A big man. About the only times I saw him were at school events or when I was at Charlie's for dinner or a barbecue. He always asked me, "Are you okay? Do you need any more food?" That's really the only thing we'd ever talked about.

Back at Jesús's car, while we stood around, I looked at my watch. It was just before noon.

"By the time we get to school in Fuckedville, we'll have missed three quarters of the day," Rover said.

"We're not going," I said. "We're going to Charlie's."

"I don't know," Helen said. "We weren't invited."

I guess, after the rave, Helen was back with us. Adam kept quiet. It wasn't something to talk about.

"We're his friends," Sean said.

"We've got to go," I insisted. "Trust me."

193

Jesús nodded. "That's fine with me. I just have to be done in time to pick up my sisters and take them to their ballet class."

I snorted.

"What's funny about that?" Jesús asked. "They're cute."

I shrugged. "It just seems weird that somebody would be dancing the same day that Charlie's dad is buried. But I guess it's not really weird. Somebody's dying all the time, and somebody else is going to dance."

"Goddamnit, man," Rover said. "You either have to be a writer or see a shrink."

"Or both," Sean said.

"Or maybe be a philosopher," Helen suggested. She wheeled herself to the car's door, turned her chair sideways and slid in. It was always amazing to watch how easily she moved. Her strength was all upper body above a skinny waist and thin legs.

Once she was settled, Adam collapsed the chair and threw it into the trunk. It was like the whole schism between the two of them had been healed, or at least patched up and temporarily forgotten. None of us, especially Adam, were going to say "boo" in case we'd jinx it. We took our seats, Jesús revved the engine, and we were off.

It was probably the quietest morning that our group had ever spent together.

That vanished the moment we pulled up in front of Charlie's house. Instead of draped in crepe and awkward silence, it sounded like there was a big party going on, with loud New Orleans jazz blaring out the front door.

Inside was warm and humid, dense with people and the stewing smell of thick gumbo wafting from the kitchen.

Mrs. Johnson, Charlie, and Desiree were already there, eating and laughing. Charlie's uncles were serving food and barking orders.

"Better than school lunch," Rover said.

"Much," Jesús agreed.

My friends and I grinned at each other.

"Before you boys get settled," Charlie's Uncle Jeff, the DA said, "clean some dishes, because we're running out."

Helen got herself settled into a corner of the living room,

keeping company near Charlie's older sister Desiree, who she was friendly with.

"I'll be fine," Helen said. "Get to work."

Sean and Jesús started collecting dirty dishes and plates. The rest of us went to the sink and set up a scrape, rinse, wash, rinse and dry brigade. The old clichéd saying, "Many hands make work light" is totally true when it comes to dirty dishes. It didn't take long and then we helped ourselves to huge bowls of Mrs. Johnson's amazing gumbo and jambalaya.

There is something gracious and life affirming about thick stew and rice. Especially the way Mrs. Johnson made it, which was hearty and flavorful, rich with a spicy kick and a zing that I've never really tasted anywhere else.

We scarfed and devoured and then went back for refills. The gumbo and jambalaya pots were huge and only half empty, even though the house and yard were full of laughing mourners.

I was still bewildered. Most of my experience of funerals is from TV and movies. In those, it's always raining, and there are thin women wearing expensive black mini dresses and high heels walking across muddy grass without sinking. And there's usually a bunch of guys in dark glasses despite the weather who are taking down license plates or scanning the crowd for suspects. Wakes in movies are Irish with fiddle music and people getting drunk, or Italian with wailing old women. I've been to a few shivas, and they tend to be dimly lit and quiet, with the mirrors all covered, people talking in hushed tones, and with bagels and cold cuts piled on the dining room table. None of those are multicultural madhouses with laughter and tears and music and hot food.

We ate and cleaned, and ate some more, and cleaned some more. The day went by in a blur and a blink.

At last the only folk left were me and Adam, Charlie, his sister, and his mom. Everyone else had left. The music was off. The chairs and tables were all reset back in their places.

It was dark already. Desiree didn't say anything to us. I told her that my sister Ellen had texted and asked me to send her condolences and love. Desiree nodded. Her face was red and puffy as she went upstairs.

"You boys have been so helpful," Mrs. Johnson said. "Thank you."

"No need," Adam said.

She was sitting in the kitchen, watching as we polished the last few dishes and put them away.

"Good friends," Charlie said. I could see that he was holding back tears.

"We've got to get home soon," Adam said. "Is there anything else we can do?"

"No, no," Mrs. Johnson said. "The hard part's over. Now it's time to begin again."

I didn't quite know what to make about that. I imagined that the hard part would begin the moment we left the house, which was now empty and missing Charlie's father.

"Mrs. Johnson," I said to her, "I didn't know your husband well. But I do know that my friend Charlie is one of the kindest and smartest and nicest kids I know. And I know a lot of good kids."

Adam snorted, and I saw him roll his eyes.

But I kept going. "I know this seems like a long time ago, but back in seventh grade I was having a really hard time. I kept it to myself. And there was this baseball game, like a pickup game, and I kept striking out. And I couldn't throw the ball worth shit." I blushed. "Sorry."

Mrs. Johnson smiled. "Go on."

"Charlie, um. Well he told me afterwards that I probably could use some practice. I got really mad and started to yell at him, 'cause I thought he was making fun of me. But what he was doing was just saying the truth. That I needed some practice. And he said that he would practice with me. So, every day after school we'd go to the field and throw and catch and practice hitting. I'm no great athlete." I heard Adam snort another laugh. "But I got better.

"What I'm getting at is that Charlie's a great guy, and he wouldn't be like that if it wasn't for you and Mr. Johnson."

Mrs. Johnson smiled at me. "Bless you."

I shrugged. I looked up at Charlie and saw that he was crying now. Tears were running down his cheeks. I didn't say anything more to him, but I put a hand on his shoulder and squeezed it.

"See you soon," Adam said.

My cousin and I left the house, and walked home in the dark.

"You never told me that," Adam said. "About the baseball."

"Why would I?"

My cousin smiled. "I would have practiced with you."

"I know."

The air was cold, and we shivered a little. Up above, the sky was black and full of stars.

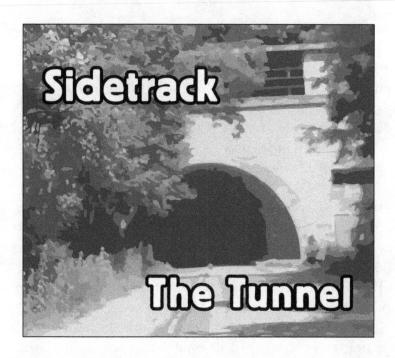

Jesús slowed the Dartmobile to a crawl, took his foot off the gas and allowed it to coast to a stop just inside the mouth of the tunnel.

He smiled, and then shook his head. Even calling the short bend in the road a tunnel was a bit of an exaggeration. Really it was a long underpass, cut through the side of a hill to avoid having to build a bridge over the railroad spur that cut between Groston and Fectville and ran to the old derelict box factory.

Jesús stared up at the smooth concrete ceiling and dreamed of graffiti.

Back in the day in New York City and London, Los Angeles and even Pittsburgh, graffiti had transformed from disfiguring scrawls into legitimate works of art. Rebel art. By artists who weren't afraid to draw big and bold, and in danger, and in public. Rip the art out of the galleries and museums and off the walls of the rich and stick it in real places where people could see it. They didn't beg for funding. They didn't apply for grants. They didn't suck up to donors and patrons. They just did shit. They just tagged or slapped up their posters, admired the work and ran.

They were rebels and artists and guys who were just saying, "Fuck you" to the whole system. They probably didn't have a single mom and bunch of brothers and sisters who depended on them. They probably didn't have a scholarship to art school that might get rescinded if they got arrested. They probably didn't have anything to lose. Just something to prove.

Jesús leaned back in the driver's seat, but when he did he lost sight of the roof.

He sighed, turned on the headlights, put on the flashers, and got out of the car. Since they built the highway, traffic was rare on Two Town Road, but still he didn't want to get hit by some dumbass checking a text.

He stood on the shadow line that divided the light of the sun from the dark of the tunnel.

It was rare for him to have moments alone like this. After school, his job was to ferry the little kids around from activity to activity, and usually his friends too. Most of the time he didn't mind. Having the only car in the crew was a privilege and a bit of a burden. And he knew he was helping Mamí keep her job and her sanity by making sure all the rug rats were safe and taken care of. But always being the driver cut into time like this. Time to stare and think and imagine.

It was amazing to think that building a box factory had once been so important it could get a railroad line built and a tunnel like this dug. There weren't any lights on the tunnel's ceiling, though there had been talk for years. Half the tunnel was in Groston and the other half was in Fectville and cooperation between the two towns was slow and inefficient, and since nobody had ever been killed in the tunnel the priority was low.

Jesús walked to one edge of the tunnel's arc, bending his knees so that his left foot could just touch the wall. He put his hand on the wall for balance. It was smooth and cool to the touch.

Then he paced across. His sneakered foot was eleven inches long. Twenty-eight shoe-lengths and a bit more. He multiplied in his head and came up with twenty-six feet. Only two feet wider than the standard Interstate two-lane road.

Then he went back to the Dart, took off his shoes, and as lightly as he could, climbed on the trunk. He moved gingerly, staying near the edge, so his weight wouldn't buckle or dent the trunk lid. Then, with a long light step, he clambered over the back windshield onto the Dodge's roof, balanced a moment, and stood up.

How high was the ceiling? The Dartmobile was 54 inches high. Jesús was five ten, so that was another 70 inches. He reached up and just touched the tunnel's ceiling with his left hand. Another 18 inches. Simple math: 54+70+19 divided by 12. Just under twelve feet. But he wasn't at the very center of the arc, and the tunnel probably went up another foot or two in the very middle.

That was actually pretty low. Of course when the tunnel had been dug, back in 1915, they probably hadn't had semi-trucks.

Still he wondered why there wasn't a height warning sign outside.

The thought of a tractor-trailer barreling down through the center of the tunnel at forty miles an hour jolted him briefly from his reverie. If a truck hit him, he'd be flung off and flattened. He bent his knees, lowered his fingers to the roof of his car, and hopped down onto the cool asphalt. He found and put on his shoes.

Then he paced the tunnel's length on both sides.

A hundred and fifty feet on the outside curve. One-twenty-seven on the inside. He tried to do the math in his head, but with the curves and the arch, his brain wasn't that good. Even with the calculator on his phone, he realized that he couldn't just multiply length times width, because of all the arcs.

How ever much surface area the roof of the tunnel had, it was going to take a shitload of paint to cover it. And that was if the whole thing was smooth. If he needed to patch bits of concrete…

Stupid to just speculate. He turned on the phone's flashlight and aimed it up.

There were some moisture stains, and a few cracks, but again the tunnel was in remarkable shape. The roof was smooth. They really knew how to make concrete back then.

It really was a perfect canvas.

But for what?

He imagined a Stygian river scene. Cover the walls black, like

Rembrandt, and then paint on the whites and colors. Fires of hell in the distances. An illusory branch of the river rolling off downstream just around the bend. Demons with pitchforks. Devils with shotguns. Tormented souls on chain gangs, or just suffering. A row of hanged men and women like Billie Holiday's strange fruit. A field of Mexicans picking fruit while being guarded by Hell's Coyotes. A white man, clearly in charge, watching from a guard tower. His eyes bright. Is he even aware that one of the demons has a hand up his ass and is manipulating him like a puppet? Over there, maybe a tour boat on the river. A gondola with an angel of heaven pushing the oar, showing off the dark side to a group of gawking Japanese Buddhist priests with cameras.

The broad strokes were easy. Should he literally draw the line between Groston and Fectville? Probably not. This vision was human but not political. He did like the idea of showing the boulders and rocks that were native to the region. Paint in the tree roots as if they were descending from above. Maybe embed a broken and bent train rail running along the top with just a hint of the disaster the next train would encounter.

Jesús pictured more details. The warts on the demons. The foam and drool on the coyotes' snouts. The missing fingers on the hands of the peasants making it impossible for them to harvest the bright red apples – were these the fruits of the tree from Eden, or just a hellish variant? Were there worms inside, or was the fruit untasteable simply because the farm workers didn't have teeth? Hell was seeing what was worthwhile and beautiful and delicious but being unable to experience it.

He closed his eyes and in his mind, he saw the entire tunnel transformed. He imagined the morning after the work was done, when the first commuter from Groston drove through, sipping on donut shop coffee, not really paying attention and then wondering what she saw. As the day went on, though, others would notice. Some would stop. Someone would call the police. Someone would call the news. Crowds would come, and they would walk into the mouth of the tunnel, into the mouth of hell. Would they see it as a metaphor for their lives? As a warning to do better? Would they understand that the life they were living was so close to hell that all it took was a brief turn underground?

Maybe he should paint the roadway, too. But covering the double-yellow line would be dangerous for drivers, and most people wouldn't be looking down in the tunnel. So no.

Jesús was almost in the middle, at the darkest part of the curve when he heard the low rumble of a car approaching.

He cocked his ears, and glanced in both directions, but couldn't be sure which way it was headed. He'd parked on the Groston-bound side, and realized that if the car was coming from there it would hit the Dartmobile before him, which would be bad, but also the safest side.

He moved to the edge and was relieved when the car – a Lexus SUV heading back to Fectville – whooshed past, well over the speed limit.

Jesús's heart was pounding as he jogged back to his car, opened the door, turned off the flasher and started her up.

"It's ok, baby," he whispered. "I'm not going to let you get trashed."

He put the Dartmobile into gear and stepped on the gas.

Some day. Some day soon. Something. He would do something.

Chapter 15

"People use comedy as an escape from the misery of their ordinary lives. It's a bit like heroin, but not quite as addictive nor self-destructive. Unless you decide you want to be a professional comedian."
— From *"What Makes Us Laugh?"* A.P. English thesis by Isaac Cohen

There was a hush in Groston as The Week of College Admissions finally arrived. Throughout the town, throughout the country, and around the world, high school seniors were learning their fate, and I'd had nothing in the way of good news.

My friends all knew — as I told you at the beginning of this book — that I'd applied to Harvard early acceptance

That week, at last, the great and mighty Haavahd had finally and officially declined to make me part of their alum-to-be. I was never going to wear crimson, or be on staff at the Lampoon.

I kept it all quiet. I knew my friends would try to cheer me up, but I didn't want their sympathy.

So I didn't tell them, nor did I tell my parents, as the rejection letters continued to trickle in. I should have told Adam at least.

Yale? No. Princeton? No. Hopkins? No.

University of Michigan? No.

Tulane, which had rolling admission and usually accepted or rejected you within about fifteen minutes after you applied, apparently had lost my file for months. They found it. And they too were a no.

In the old days, university rejection letters arrived via snail mail. It had been the only way that a large institution could effectively communicate with a body of potential students. My dad told me that you either got the skinny small envelope, or the big fat envelope, so you knew as soon as the mail arrived. Before you opened it, you saw your fate.

I'd set up a special college application email account, and didn't give my parents the password. I hated logging into it. That week, I checked my email almost every fifteen minutes, and every time I wanted to throw up or cry.

Berkley? No. University of Chicago? Nope.

Way back in May of my Junior year, Lauretta Mount, the guidance counselor at Ashby Bryson had warned me that my "only above average" grades, "frankly anemic" activities, and "not too shabby" test scores were so weak that I should probably settle for Fectville State. I don't think that Mrs. Mount was trying to be cruel or mean. She was a kind-looking lady, who wore grey suits and would have blued her hair if styles had permitted it. She'd been a guidance counselor for nearly thirty years, and had lots of experience.

"Fectville State is your safety school," she'd said. "And then maybe you should shoot for something in the middle. Like Connecticut College."

I'm sure there's nothing wrong with Connecticut College. I mean no insult. If you attended or work at Connecticut College, I'm sure it's a great place. But New London is a lot like Groston, only bigger.[25] If I was going to go to a school in a small town, I wanted

---

[25] And wealthier.

prestige. If I was going to go to a mid-level school, then it better be in an interesting place.

Yes, of course, I'd applied to and gotten into Fectville State. Rolling admissions. But they took anybody in-state who had a pulse and a wallet.

Then I'd applied to 12 other schools, just to say "Fuck You" to Mrs. Mount.

Whenever I got another email telling me to check my status, my heart started pounding. I'd spend a long minute kidding myself that I'd wait until later, and then quickly log into that school's website to find another politely-worded door to a bright shiny future slamming shut. Then, I'd check my face to make sure that nothing showed. Neutral. Nothing to see here. Move along. Then, I had to make sure I got home before Mom or Dad, in case the school had decided to physically send the snail mail rejection too. I was terrified that all my fears of being a loser were coming true. It was beginning to look like Mrs. Mount was right.

Stanford, University of Detroit, and McGill all said no on the same day.

The only school left was Columbia, which I'd applied to because I knew that Adam had applied there early, and my dad had gone to their medical school, so maybe I was a legacy and that might give me a boost.

Columbia's answer finally came.

They didn't reject me. They didn't accept me either.

They put me on their wait list. Swell.

If enough other idiots decided to blow off the only Ivy League college in New York City, then the Lions would deign to allow me to enroll.

It was like being picked last for an afterschool pickup baseball game and then assigned to warm the bench.

I stared at the web browser, trying to decide whether to celebrate, or cry, or slit my wrists.

When the hard copy letter came to the house, I stuck it under my bed, between the mattress and box spring.

I didn't tell anyone.

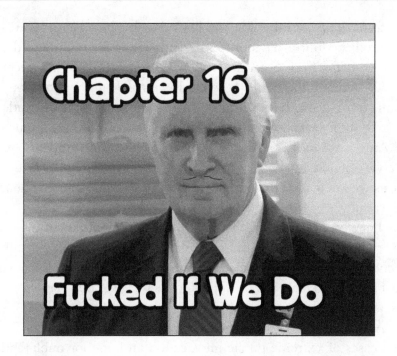

Chapter 16

Fucked If We Do

"I particularly love being in an audience full of people who are laughing. One person starts, and then it keeps going and builds. Everyone shares the laughter. It's wonderful!"
– Eleanora Beagle, Helen's mom

After our impromptu Bollywood-style flash mob at the rave, we'd thought that the kids from Fectville Regional High would have some respect for us. At the very least, they'd leave us alone. I mean, we'd done this amazing thing. Right?

We were wrong.

Remember that me and my friends, and all our old Groston classmates from Ashby Bryson High, had exited the rave in a triumph of applause, just as the Fectville police department arrived?

Yeah.

Everybody from Groston got away.

And everybody from Fectville got busted.

The cops had surrounded the old mill, then rushed in through the front doors and the side and back doors. They had arrested six hundred and fourteen people. Five hundred and forty-seven of them were students from Fectville Regional High School. They included 377 seniors, the entire Fectville Regional High School football team, track team, baseball team, the cheerleading squad, student website staff, yearbook staff, and most of the Future Entrepreneurs of America Society. (The rest of the arrested were students from Fectville State and about twenty miscellaneous random old farts. As far as we knew, D.J. Razor somehow managed to escape, although he was never heard from again.)

They brought in a PCPC – a portable criminal processing center – which was basically a tricked out trailer for use after riots, that Fectville had purchased with Homeland Security money. Even with the high-priced tech, it took hours for the police to take names, photos, and fingerprints.

Almost everybody got off with warning tickets, except for fourteen cases of extreme public intoxication and one for public indecency and public urination.

Diana Marley was cited for engaging in a criminal enterprise by holding an illegal dance assembly without an entertainment permit and operating an illegal drinking establishment and serving alcohol to minors. Her fine was five thousand dollars, which I'm told she immediately paid in cash, probably from the pile she'd collected at the door. My guess is that even after her Daddy paid her lawyer she'd made a profit.

All through that long night, the Fectville cops took mug shots and fingerprints, and called parents.

By four-thirty Saturday morning, someone, probably one of the Fectville cops, tipped off a reporter for the *Groston Gazette*. The reporter called the superintendent of the Fectville school department, a guy named Ron Glover who we'd never met, and asked for a comment about the record number of Fectville high schoolers under arrest.

By four forty-two Saturday morning, Fectville's Superintendent Glover had called Robert, (call me "Dr. Bob") Smith, the esteemed principal of Fectville Regional High School, and ripped him a new asshole.

When his phone rang, I'm sure Dr. Bob woke up fast. Almost nothing will provoke a tight-assed bureaucrat more than being called out and humiliated by the boss. Even worse, he didn't know what to do about it. I'm sure that Dr. Bob spent his whole weekend pissed off and mortified.

By Monday morning, Dr. Bob was just plain furious, but he had a plan.

The cops, he learned, had been fairly lenient. Nevertheless, his precious, precocious, and prosperous students had embarrassed him, and broken his famous Fectville Rules.

Dr. Bob was determined to lay down the law, set an example, and exact retribution.

On Monday morning, while my friends and I were sleeping in or getting ready to go to Charlie's dad's funeral, all of the 614 Fectville Regional High School students who'd been arrested at the rave had been summoned down to the gym.

After a late night of partying, and an entire weekend of parental punishment, the Fectville Rule Breakers were grumpy and exhausted.

As soon as the busted Fecters were all settled on the bleachers, Dr. Bob subjected them to a forty-five minute harangue about school spirit, delinquency, betraying the sanctity of The Fectville Rules, and the dangers of underage and under supervised drinking. Dr. Bob pretty much lost his shit, and if you watch the video somebody posted online, you can see him red-faced and practically foaming at the mouth.

When Dr. Bob finally ran out of breath, a school bell rang, and everybody in the gym got up to leave.

Dr. Bob told them to sit back down. They sat.

That's when Dr. Bob introduced my father, who hit them with a forty-five minute talk on the dangers of illegal drugs.

Yes, my dad.

On his way to Charlie's dad's funeral, my father had stopped off at Fectville Regional High School, where Dr. Bob put him behind the microphone.

My dad works in an emergency room, and over the years has

taken great pleasure in tormenting me and my sister Ellen all in the name of "scaring you kids with the truth."

Dad told the Fecters horror stories about teen parties ending with vomiting and asphyxiation. He told them about burn victims maimed from fireworks explosions. He described decapitations from drunken drivers. He talked about kids suffering dehydration because of ecstasy to heart-stopping heroin and fentanyl overdoses, brain damage from too many hits of LSD, insane behavior resulting from methamphetamine addiction, and all about steroid rage. He made a brief detour through date rape drugs, unwanted pregnancies, AIDS and other STDs resulting from drunken and unprotected sex. He closed by saying that he was wearing a black suit because he was "on the way to another funeral." (He didn't mention that the funeral was for Charlie's dad, an obese middle-aged man who over ate and never exercised.)

Yes, my father told my fellow students every single "scared straight" horror story he'd beaten into my skull over the years.

It's one thing to grow up with a father who tells you that playing with firecrackers can result in a missing finger or that riding a motor-cycle – with or without a helmet – is an invitation to brain damage. It's another thing to be the son of the guy who lays all that medi-cally graphic horror shit on you in one go first thing on a Monday morning.

Fun, right?

Dad shook Dr. Bob's hand, left Fectville Regional High School, and sped to the funeral, where I'd seen him up near the front of the church with my mom.[26]

Back in the gym, the busted kids were in shock.

According to a report in the Fectville student blog, "The gym-nasium was dead silent, except for the sobbing of several girls. Four

---

[26] I don't know where my mom was during this interlude. She hates dad's lectures as much as we do, but because she's a grown-up, she usually excus-es herself from the room. Maybe she went out to get a cup of coffee. I can just imagine my dad finishing his talk, leaving the school gym, expecting his ride, and seeing the empty space. "Where are you?" Dad would say into the phone. "I'm pulling up now," she'd answer back. "Get in."

freshmen had passed out, but recovered before the school nurse arrived."

Then another bell rang.

Everybody stood, again.

Dr. Bob told everybody to sit back down because they weren't leaving the gym for a fortnight.

"Welcome," he said, a nasty smile on his face, "to the first morning of your two-week in-school suspension."

• • •

We didn't know about any of that. Not yet. Nobody from Fectville ever talked to my friends. Worst of all, my dad didn't bother to tell me that he'd given the Fecters this cheerful talk. Maybe he thought I was up there in the bleachers. Or more likely, Dad had completely forgotten that my friends and I weren't going to Ashby Bryson High in Groston because of the flood and freeze.

When we got back to FRHS on Tuesday morning, after we'd skipped school Monday for the funeral and wake, I learned about Dad's talk the hard way.

It was a semi-organized low-key assault.

Adam and I walked in the front doors and the next fifty kids that passed by "accidentally bumped" into us on their way from homeroom to the gym for day two of their detention sentence. They even banged into Adam, despite his mystical magical walking-in-the-empty-spaces shtick.

I was clueless, angry and a bit frightened. I had to hold my cousin back from retaliating with extreme martial arts.

Then things got even worse.

The day before, on Monday, after Dad and Dr. Bob had stopped talking and their mass in-school torture had begun, every student imprisoned in the Fectville gym had pulled out a cell phone or laptop and started posting on social media. Instead of getting reprimanded by their parents (who were mostly at work), the students collected kudos by the thousands.

#FreeFectvilleHigh became a thing and went viral.

In a world of mass school shootings and rising drug overdoses, it galled Dr. Bob that a bunch of over-privileged teenagers in his charge were getting any sympathy or support. It also pissed him off that they were watching movies and videos, chatting online, and pretty much enjoying their time out of class.

So by seven a.m. Tuesday morning, Dr. Bob had installed narrowband cell phone and wifi dampeners in the gym to make sure that nobody in detention could access the Internet.

Imagine if you will an entire gymnasium full of hormonal, outraged, and frustrated Internet junkies.

Those of us from Groston who were in the nearby nearly empty classrooms could hear the outrage echo through the building. They were shouting and screaming and banging their feet on the bleachers. It sounded like the howls of ten thousand rampaging monkeys.

Three police cars pulled up in front of the high school. The cops stormed into the gym, and the noise quieted.

If life was fair, Fectville's teachers would have reveled in the smaller classroom sizes and taken the opportunity to teach and get to know us kids from Groston better.

Instead, the teachers looked angry and frightened, knowing that their turn at in-school suspension duty was only a matter of time.

By then me and my crew had been clued into the whole scene, and none of us were surprised when the intercom summoned us to the main office.

We collected our books and backpacks, grinned at the other Ashby Brysonians, and shuffled through the halls.

To be clear, over the weekend, but before the funeral, we'd had a group chat about what to do if anybody asked, and we had our plan down.

We hadn't been arrested. Nothing could be proved. We'd learned from Adam's attorney Bob Billings to keep our mouths shut and say nothing. We were going to be fine.

Dr. Bob's secretary, Gladys Farmington, who looked liked she'd gotten plastic surgery about the time the high school was last renovated, told us to take a seat in the conference room.

Adam and I sat next to each other. Rover was at the far end of the table, with his back to a wall. Jesús and Sean sat next to each other across from me. Helen wheeled herself in near the door, next to Adam, who'd shifted one of the conference room chairs so she could fit comfortably.

Dr. Bob finally appeared in the doorway, silent for a moment. He wore a dark grey suit, a thin black tie, and black penny loafers with white socks. Yes, white socks. He stared briefly.

"I'm going to talk with each of you separately," he said, softly. "While you're waiting, don't talk. Don't say anything to each other. You may think you're smart, but you're not. This room is monitored by video and audio surveillance." He pointed to the three shiny graphite-colored bubbles in the ceiling.

Suddenly, Dr. Bob realized someone was missing. "Where is the other one? Charles Johnson?"

We were quiet for a moment, then Adam told him. "Charlie's father died on Sunday."

Dr. Bob shook his head with angry disbelief, as if Charlie had killed his dad on purpose just to avoid this confrontation.

"Ms. Beagle." He pointed to Helen, "You first." He nodded his head, and left the room. Helen wheeled out, following.

Rover reached into his backpack and pulled out his laptop.

"No," I said. "Don't." I knew that Rover was itching to hack the monitoring system. "It's not worth it."

"Aww, man," Rover said. He shrugged. "Fine."

Ten minutes later, Dr. Bob came back and pointed to Sean. "Mr. Chang. You next."

"Where's Helen?" Adam asked.

Dr. Bob didn't answer. He left and Sean followed.

Then he took Adam. Then Rover. Then Jesús.

I was going to be last.

Later on, I found out what Dr. Bob had been doing. Instead of showing the slightest amount of compassion or understanding for a group of students from another school whose best friend had just lost his father, every single one of my friends was accused, humiliated and threatened. Maybe Dr. Bob thought he was doing the right thing, like my dad, trying to scare us straight.

Instead, he came off as mean-spirited and spiteful.

He'd told Helen he was surprised that a girl who had overcome such physical challenges would risk everything for a party. He'd told Sean that as someone who had grown up in Fectville, he was betraying his origins. He'd accused Adam of being a violent drug-addled sociopath. He'd warned Rover that he was collecting evidence implicating Rover in cyber terrorism. He'd told Jesús that poor kids who want to go to art school should know that college scholarships were dependent on a clean police record. He'd actually looked Jesús in the eye and said, "You know what they call art school graduates who pay full tuition? There are two answers." Dr. Bob didn't wait. "Answer number 1 – trust fund babies. Answer number 2 – unemployed hacks with a crushing debt load who will take any job they can get, starting with waiting tables."

And then Dr. Bob came for me.

• • •

By that time, I'd been sitting in the conference room for about an hour and a half. It was hard and more than a little bit frightening watching my friends vanish one by one. I pulled out a book and tried to read, but I can't even tell you what the name of the book was. The last ten minutes were the hardest.

Dr. Bob appeared, pointed a bony finger at me. "Mr. Cohen." He beckoned, turned, and I followed.

By now you probably think that my friends and I were always getting caught, but that's not really true. When we were younger, at Jerome Marco K-8, we did spend a fair amount of time with Mrs. Capamundo, but by the time we'd gotten to Ashby Bryson we'd figured out that it was better to be smart and not get busted, than spontaneous and in detention.

Dr. Bob had a nice office. I'd never been in a high school principal's office before, so I don't know if his was typical. It was big, with a huge black desk, empty except for a laptop and phone.

He sat down in a large black executive chair that had been pumped up to raise him higher than the small straight-backed middle-school chair he told me to sit in.

The wall behind him was covered with diplomas and awards and signed photos of famous Fectville Regional alumni. TV newscasters, a soap opera star, a state rep, two pro football players, and a ballerina. The wall to my left was a picture window with closed wooden blinds and a closed door into the main hall. The wall behind me had nothing but file cabinets and the door into the main office.

The wall on my right was filled by a giant video monitor, and another door that led into Dr. Bob's private bathroom.

"So," Dr. Bob said. "This."

He held up a remote, pushed a button, and on the screen appeared a single frame from a high definition cell phone video of the rave that had been uploaded to the net, showing our whole gang frozen in mid-dance formation.

Dr. Bob is a mean-looking man with a pencil-thin moustache. He looks a lot like a cartoon villain. When he's angry, his face turns red and his moustache vibrates like a wriggly motion line in a low-budget animation. I was the last one in for interrogation, and Dr. Bob's face was as pink as a well-slapped baby's bottom. His moustache was humming.

He stared at me.

Then he spoke, quietly. "Why weren't you in school yesterday? I know you were at the rave on Friday night. How did you escape arrest? Who is this with you in this video?"

What a fucking prick, I thought. We'd already told him that we'd skipped school yesterday to go to Charlie's dad's funeral. He also knew I was at the rave and exactly who else was in the video. You couldn't help but recognize all of us. It was a great still. Contemporary digital cell phone cameras are amazing. You could see the tiny patch of twelve hairs on my chin that I'd missed shaving. We were all staring out at the crowd with grins on our faces, all had our hands up in a perfectly synchronized cheerleading "Yaay!"

For a moment, I actually thought about telling him the truth. That's what my parents taught me to do. Maybe it's the right thing, too. But fuck him. I wasn't going to give him the satisfaction.

Of course, we'd been at the rave. Had we broken the law by being there? Maybe. Had we been drinking illegally? Damn straight.

Doing illegal drugs? Well, yeah.

But we hadn't been arrested.

No, we hadn't been arrested.

Could you actually prove we'd done anything at that rave beyond busting out in an amazing dance, and then getting clean away?

Nope. I didn't think so. And I thought about saying all that.

But, I kept my mouth shut. I smiled.

Dr. Bob leaned in. The pores on his face were large and the stubble of his beard seemed to grow as I watched. He smelled of antiseptic aftershave and failing deodorant.

"Mr. Cohen," he hissed, "your father was here yesterday morning. He spoke to your peers. He is a respectable physician. Your mother is a well-known psychiatrist. Your sister is attending an Ivy League college. I'm sure that they had high expectations of you.

"You, Isaac Cohen, are a failure. A complete and utter failure. Your friends are worthless troublemakers. Your family must be ashamed of you."

I said nothing. Smile rigid. It's actually hard to keep a smile when someone is insulting and threatening you at length. Not only emotionally, but the muscles get tired. My heart was pounding. I wondered if I could have a heart attack and die in his office. It would serve him right.

"Isaac, you would like to think that you're safe, and that you are surrounded by your good friends, but they are all going to leave you alone. All of your friends, every single one of them is going to go away to a decent college, except for you. Not you. Even your cousin is eventually going to weasel his way out of his troubles and leave you alone.

"Now, I understand that you are on the wait list at a very good school. Ivy League? Given your grades, that's astonishing, but I gather you're a bit of a legacy. Couldn't do it on your own, huh? But that final acceptance – that happy letter that tells you that you've gotten a golden ticket – that acceptance depends on good grades in your final semester. And good recommendations from your teachers and school staff about the last half of your senior year.

"Do you really think that you are going to get those good grades? Good recommendations? From me?

"You sit there quiet and smug, thinking that I'm a fool.

"I've been dealing with little shits like you for more than twenty years. You think you know everything, but you don't know how easy it is for someone like me to destroy you.

"You won't be able to prove anything. I can wreck your life.

"Then, your friends are all going to move away and leave you behind. And you are going to be stuck here. Forever.

"Now, I'm going to give you one last chance.

"Tell me, you little shit, what happened at the rave. The drinking. The drugs. I know you are guilty. Tell me!"

I was nearly in tears with rage and the painful truth of his cutting words. My teeth were clenched. It felt like my eyeballs were going to burst. I felt the hard cold plastic of the chair. My hands were folded in my lap, and I dug my fingernails into my palms.

For a moment I completely whited out.

There was an instant when everything was gone. I couldn't see Dr. Bob or his desk. I couldn't see my blue jeans. It was like I was suspended in ether or floating in limbo.

Then I looked up at the video screen and saw the frozen image of my friends and I, standing together and grinning in our spontaneous and complete unity.

I turned my head to good old Dr. Bob, and said, "My name is Isaac Cohen. My student id number is AB-235. I refuse to answer anything without my parents and my attorney, Bob Billings."

Then I smiled, just a little bit more than was natural, and let my eyes twinkle.

If he had really been an animated cartoon, Dr. Bob's head would have exploded like a pumpkin stuffed with dynamite. His eyes went wild. Spittle dripped between his thin lips. He wiped it with his sleeve.

Dr. Bob sputtered, slammed his hand on the desk, and told me that I was suspended for school for the rest of the day for an unexcused absence, and then he sent me home.

I picked up my backpack and left, wishing that I'd been suspended for the rest of the year.

My friends were all waiting outside in the parking lot.

"You okay?" Adam asked. "You were in there for a while."

I nodded.

"What did he say?" Sean asked.

"Nothing. Bullshit." I shrugged. "Just tried to scare me."

"Us too," Sean said.

"All of us," Jesús nodded, then shook his head sadly.

"I wish I'd thought of recording it," Rover said. "Did you?"

I shook my head. "Next time. Although hopefully there won't be a next time."

"You know that I usually respect authority," Helen said. "But Dr. Bob is a flaming fuckface asshole."

We chuckled, except for Jesús who practically fell over laughing.

"I didn't think it was that funny," Helen said.

"I'm going to design a tee shirt with a full color image of Dr Bob's flaming fuckface asshole," Jesús said, practically choking with laughter. "Lots of flames."

That got us all going again.

"I'd buy it," Sean said. "But I don't think I'd wear it."

As we walked to Jesús's car, we compared notes. Dr. Bob had asked us all the same questions. And we'd all taken the fifth, each of us threatening him with Bob Billings.

"I hope Mr. Billings doesn't find out," Adam said. "He might send us a bill."

We laughed, squeezed into the Dartmobile, picked up Charlie at his house, and headed off to the park for a quiet day of freedom in the sun.

Charlie Johnson lay on his back on the hard wooden bleacher overlooking the Ashby Bryson football field. He stared up at the early afternoon sky, but didn't see much of anything. The clouds were... just clouds. White puffs, silhouetted against the blue.

He remembered so many times lying on a blanket in Breakneck River Park while Dad and Uncle James manned the grill. Mom always made too much potato salad and said that everybody "better eat up or it'll go to waste." Then she'd pat her belly and say, "my waist" with a laugh. Uncle James would look at Dad and say, "Game on!" And the two of them would have a race to see how much potato salad and cole slaw they could pack on top of the burgers and dogs. Desiree would shake her head sadly at the spectacle, but she would do her part. Everybody would eat up until they were almost comatose, and not a speck or crumb would be packed up or thrown out. The clouds back then were filled with adventures and monsters and animals and pirates.

"Mister Johnson?"

As soon as he heard the woman's voice, Charlie blinked back the tears and rubbed his cheeks dry. "Huh? Wha?" He sat up, catching the balled up jacket he'd been using as a pillow just before it could fall down behind the bleachers.

"Hello?"

He looked down and saw an old woman bundled in a long puffy down coat, standing on the decrepit rubber track that surrounded the football field. It took him a minute to place her. Mrs. Hendry, one of his favorite high school teachers. Somehow she managed to make A.P. European History interesting.

Charlie raised his left hand in a half-hearted wave. "Hey."

"May I join you?" she asked.

Charlie shrugged and made a 'make yourself at home' gesture to a spot on the bench.

Mrs. Hendry slowly climbed up the bleachers, like they were a set of dysfunctional stairs. One up. Half down. One up. Half down. Her legs weren't that short, but it was clear that she wasn't a hundred percent surefooted. As she got closer, Charlie stood, and reached out a hand, which she took to steady herself.

"Thank you," she said.

"You're welcome." He used his jacket to dust off the bench, and she sat.

He waited for her to say something else, but she didn't. Instead, she stared out at the football field. So he looked too.

To call the thing behind Ashby Bryson High a football field was a massive overstatement. Far from a noble gridiron, it had always been a mud pit pocked with humps of scraggly grass. Every few years the town promised improvements. One year they'd laid sod. It didn't stick. Another spring they'd planted four hundred pounds of Kentucky bluegrass seed that was devoured by a flock of nasty black ravens. In December, after Doug and Butch had led the Pioneers to the finals, the council had taken a vote and promised AstroTurf. The flood and freeze had wrecked those plans. Now the football field was just a mucky swamp heaped with piles of dirt, rubble and demolition debris from the school's nascent renovation.

In one of his infrequent newspaper articles, Ike had theorized that the decrepit state of the field had contributed to the team's success. "Our Pioneers trained and played under the worst possible conditions. No wonder that when the turf was perfect they could outrun and outmaneuver their fiercest opposition."

Finally, Charlie couldn't take the silence any more. "Aren't you supposed to be in school in Fectville?" he asked.

Mrs. Hendry smiled. "Aren't you?"

"I'm skipping," Charlie said.

"Me too," the old woman answered.

Charlie glanced at her. Mrs. Hendry wasn't all that old, maybe half way between his Mom and his grandmother. Her hair was short and gray. Her glasses were large and thick with brown plastic rims shaped like twin old-fashioned television screens.

"I didn't know teachers skipped school."

"Oh, Mr. Johnson." She tisked. "Teachers do so many things that are wrong." She reached into her coat and pulled out a thin silver flask, unscrewed the top and took a swig. "Coffee," she said to his quizzical look.

"Really?" he asked.

She offered him the flask. He took a sip and nearly spat it out as the liquor burned his throat. No way was that coffee.

Mrs. Hendry chuckled, took the flask back, took another snort, screwed the lid back on, and slipped it back into her coat pocket. "So, why are you here?"

"My Dad died," Charlie said, bitterly. "School seems kind of pointless. What about you?"

"My husband died," Mrs. Hendry said. Her voice was flat. "School seems kind of pointless to me too."

"I'm sorry," Charlie said.

Mrs. Hendry shrugged. "Your loss is more recent. Henry died seven years ago. We were planning on moving back down south to North Carolina after we both retired at the end of this year. He was a schoolteacher too. In Fectville, I'm afraid. A little home in Chapel Hill was the finish line for the marathon. Our goal. Our plan. Our reward."

"That sucks."

"Yes, it does," Mrs. Hendry said. "Today is our anniversary. And I always skip school and come here. This is where we met. Pretty much where you and I are sitting. It was a beautiful day in late October. Fectville was demolishing Groston in the regional finals, and when we lost, Henry was so excited that I slapped him."

"You what?" Charlie sputtered.

"I didn't know who he was. It was my second year up here in Groston, and I thought he was just another rude Fecter who was having fun insulting the kids that I taught."

"What did he do?"

"He kissed me. Then I smacked him again. Then he kissed me again. I kissed back. Times were certainly different then," she mused. "We went out and got coffee. That turned into dinner, and then breakfast, and then a mad rush in the morning to get to our respective schools. And then, twenty-six years later, he died."

"That sucks," Charlie repeated.

"Vocabulary has never been your strong suit, has it Mr. Johnson?"

Charlie tried to load up a sarcastic retort, but decided she was right and gave up. "You win."

"Aren't you cold?" she asked.

Charlie shrugged. "I'm too fat to be cold."

"No," she said. "You are not fat any more. I've been very impressed by the changes you've implemented over the past few months. You were always a handsome man, but now you're looking much healthier."

Charlie, thinking about all the fat blobs in his family, and his father dead of a massive heart attack, didn't answer.

"Was that insensitive?" Mrs. Hendry asked. "I can never tell these days. You young people have so many triggers. When I was a girl we were taught to hide our feelings and suppress our emotions. That meant our psyches were traumatized and therapists got rich, but it also afforded a certain amount of protection and freedom of speech. If I was a young teacher just starting out, I'd be terrified of losing my job over some stupid off the cuff remark."

"No offense taken," Charlie said. "My dad was overweight. So am I."

"No," Mrs. Hendry insisted. "You're not fat anymore. You're not thin. I doubt you'll ever be. You are a large man. But you are not going to repeat the mistakes of your father."

Charlie snorted. "That's what he always told me. 'Charlie don't do what I did. Don't make the same mistakes as me. Don't play football and get your head bashed so many times you can't think straight. Don't get your girlfriend pregnant so you have to marry her and can't go to college. Make something of yourself, boy. Make something of yourself.'"

Charlie fell silent.

Mrs. Hendry nodded. "I always wondered why you didn't play football."

"Now you know."

"That also explains quite a lot about your older sister. I had her in class. Desiree was a good student, but always trying to prove herself worthy."

Charlie grinned. "Now that you mention it, yes it does explain a lot."

They sat for a while and watched as a flock of ravens descended on the field and began pecking at the dirt.

Mrs. Hendry sighed, took out her flask, unscrewed the lid, and offered it to him. He shook his head. "Do you know what the worst thing about getting old is?" she asked.

"Going blind, deaf and incontinent?" Charlie said.

She laughed, snorted and coughed. "Ow!"

He laughed. "Sorry."

"No, no," she said. She removed a tissue from a plastic pouch, blew and wiped her nose. "I retract my comment about your wits.

"The worst thing about getting old is that all the people you rely on die or move away. Yes, you don't have to clean up their dishes or put up with their socks on the floor. But you lose your mirror, your conscience, and your guide."

"My Dad always told me what to do," Charlie said. "I didn't always listen to him. Most of the time he was right, though. And even when he was wrong, he meant well."

"My father was a prick," Mrs. Hendry said, "who beat my

mother and thought I was a cow, fit for nothing but providing him with grandchildren."

Charlie glanced at his teacher, wondering how much she'd had to drink. "I guess I was lucky."

"Yes, Mr. Johnson, you are lucky. As was I. When I found Henry, I made damn sure that he wasn't my father. We had some fights, and sometimes it got physical, but I always hit back and held my own. And I wouldn't have stuck around if I hadn't. Don't be a victim. That was the lesson I learned from my father."

"Don't be a fat fuck is what I learned from mine," Charlie muttered.

Mrs. Hendry turned and smacked Charlie on the cheek.

He recoiled from the stinging blow.

"Your father was never a fat fuck," Mrs. Hendry said, her face an angry scowl. "And neither are you. From your father you learned to be kind and strong, and that education and knowledge are power. You learned to take what you have and make the best of it, and then go beyond. As Charles Bukowski said, 'We are here to laugh at the odds and live our lives so well that Death will tremble to take us.'"

"Who's Charles Bukowski?" Charlie said, astonished that his history teacher had used such blunt profanity.

"A drunk and a great poet. Did I hurt you?"

"No."

"Should I hit you again?"

"No!" Was the old lady crazy?

"Good. When you speak of your father that way, you hurt his memory."

"Yes, Ma'am." Charlie nodded. "But he's gone. And I miss him. I'm all alone. And I got no one to talk to."

He felt the tears coming, and blinked them back.

"You are so not alone," Mrs. Hendry chided. "Even if you didn't have your family, you have that remarkable group of friends. Almost everyone else in this school relies on parents or money or good looks or even brains to get by. You and your friends are different. You hold up mirrors to each other and you're brutally honest, which is rare. You all make some spectacularly dumb choices, but you all stick together."

"You mean the dork squad? Team Bomb Shelter?" Charlie said. "Come on. We are just a bunch of misfits that no one else will take in."

"That's what all good friends are," Mrs. Hendry said, shaking her head. "In my many years of teaching, I rarely have seen anything like it. You all are fortunate. Trust your friends. Keep talking with them. Only one more piece of advice, and then I have to go."

She stood up slowly.

"What's that?" Charlie asked. He rose and offered his arm to hold on to.

"Keep making new friends," she said. "For your entire life. Don't stop. Don't get stuck. Don't settle for the few that you know and are comfortable with. Keep adding to your friends. Even when you get old like me. Make new friends, but keep the old. To hell with silver and gold. Friends are better than money in the bank."

She fell silent as Charlie helped her down the bleachers, until they both stood on the chewed up running track.

"Come here," Mrs. Hendry said, beckoning his face down to her level.

For a moment he was frightened that the old lady was going to kiss him. Or hit him again. Instead, she reached up, brushed his cheek with her knuckles, patted him twice, and tottered off.

"Are you ok to drive?" Charlie called after her.

Without turning around, Mrs. Hendry lifted her hand and gave him the finger.

Charlie gaped as his history teacher vanished around the corner and down the path back to the old gym.

He sighed, smiled and shook his head.

The sky was bright blue. It was clear and almost empty now, but just on the horizon moving west into the sunset was a swirling cloud like a puff of smoke from the fiery snort of a dragon.

He laughed, turned, and headed for home.

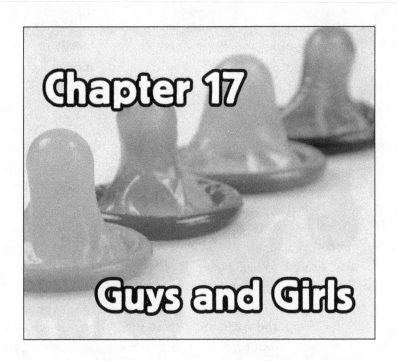

Chapter 17
Guys and Girls

"Honestly? I love snappy, witty, intelligent dialog with an undercurrent of heat. Spencer Tracey and Katherine Hepburn's movies were brilliant. That TV show 'Moonlighting' was good, but doesn't hold up as well."
– Susie Wardle, Captain, Ashby Bryson Cheerleading Squad

By now you may have noticed that I haven't really talked about girls much. (Helen doesn't count. She's sort of an honorary guy. Helen, if you're ever reading this, I meant that in the best possible way.) It's not that my friends and I weren't into girls. Except for Sean, we totally were. Although who the hell really knew when it came to Rover. We just didn't talk about girls much. It didn't seem weird to us.

We spent our hours on the couch and chairs in Rover's basement shooting the shit about video games and sports, memes and stupid songs. We used all our several-years-old technology to play those much-discussed video games, did a little hacking and even a little crypto-currency mining, too. Sometimes, almost by accident, we did our homework. As always, Rover's basement was our bomb shelter clubhouse, warm, dry and a bit ratty. A few years earlier, Rover's mom had decided to redecorate upstairs, so she'd tossed a dozen old throw pillows down the stairs just to add color. After a few years, though, they'd all turned a uniform shade of grubby brown.

If you were to sum us up just then, you might say we were a bunch of lazy pampered bored moderately over-privileged American teen-age guys.

Plus Helen, of course. She was part of the gang, too, and we mostly treated her like one of the guys, except that Helen was a girl and she was proper. When Helen was around, other girls and sex were rarely mentioned. I don't know if she noticed it. If she did, she didn't say.

Between video game tournaments and pillow fights, (also usually when Helen wasn't around,) we talked a little bit about other girls.

Sort of.

Here's an example:

"Hey, Charlie," Jesús would say in the middle of a heated gun battle.

"Yuh?"

"Did you see Barbara Moody today?"

"Nah."

Barbara Moody was in Jesús's AP Biology class at Fectville Regional. She was a white girl with dark brown hair, green eyes, and wore form-fitting sweater dresses. Even though she was from Fectville, Jesús liked her. We all knew that.

Jesús: "She looked sweet."

Charlie: "Huh?"

Rover (snapping): "Focus!"

And the conversation would stop.

Like that.

The only really detailed sex conversation that I can remember the entire gang having happened a few years ago, when Helen's parents had taken her to Berlin for a week.

There'd been a flurry of braggadocio about losing our virginities. Charlie, for example, claimed that he'd lost his at Camp Waredaca when he was a Counselor in Training. He said that he and Donna Naismith, one of the girl's CITs, had "done it" on the beach behind the canoes after supper. Of course he didn't tell us this until months later, so there was no way to know if it was true. Jesús said that his first was a distant relative, but he refused to give us any more details. Sean never said anything for obvious reasons now, but then we thought he was just being discrete. As far as I knew, me, Adam, and Rover were all still virgins, and embarrassed about it. We didn't go so far as lie, but we pretended to have more first-hand knowledge than we did.

Can you blame us?

In one of our more uncomfortable father-son talks, my physician dad told me about the Playboy magazine collection he'd kept under his bed when he was my age and the complaints his mother – my grandmother – made about his using too many boxes of Kleenex.

"So, Isaac," Dad said, "if you have any questions or need to talk, I'm here."

Then he gave me a condom. The wrapper said, "Safe sex is great sex."

Right, Dad. Thanks.

My generation has had instant Internet porn available at every moment for our entire lives. We can watch tits and ass and dicks on our laptops, our tablets and our phones. And we do. Nothing is left to the imagination. Intellectually, we know that a huge chunk of the sexweb is staged acting. We also know that almost none of the girls in our school look like porn stars. Although there are three who seem like they might have had breast augmentation, I'm not going to name names.

From home experimentation, I know that there's no way that I'm going to be making a forty-minute sex video, ever. And even if I shaved my balls I'm not that big.

Then there's all that weird kinky stuff. I've watched it, and while I find that almost anything will turn me on, half (or more than half) makes me feel a little nauseated during or after. I don't believe that girls really like some of the stuff that they do on the videos either. And this makes me feel a little bit sicker on a morality level. I'm wondering if they're getting paid, or being exploited. Or both. You read about sex slavery. It's out there, and it's real. I mean, even if it is consensual is it all acting? There aren't any special effects, right? Pornography seems very realistic to a curious teenage boy with a raging hard on.

And then after five minutes of streaming porn, we're done with that bit of business, and back to checking social media or playing a video game. So as far as informational or even inspirational value, pornography is completely fake.

More recently there's that whole #MeToo thing that's made almost every conversation about sex completely uncomfortable.

Lord, I should probably delete or censor this entire section of the book.

But I want you to understand, I didn't want girls to feel threatened by me, so I tended to avoid them.

Imagine me at a party (not that I go to that many, but simply for the sake of the illustration) with a red cup of beer in my hand. I'm dressed normally, in jeans and a tee shirt and a sweatshirt. And there's a girl I want to talk to. We're part of a big group of people who are laughing. She's right next to me. She seems to be enjoying my company. One by one the others drift off. The music shifts and…

Scenario 1:

I lean over to kiss her and she tells me, "I'm gay."

Scenario 2:

I lean over to give her a kiss and she belts me in the face.

Scenario 3:

"Hi," I say. "Wanna dance?"

"Get the fuck away from me!"

Scenario 4:

She says, "Wanna dance?"

I agree, and after watching me dance for two minutes, she flees in horror.

Scenario 5:

She puts her hand on my crotch and asks, "So, I guess you're into tranny guys?"

Turns out in this fantasy that sh/e is a cisfemale thinking about becoming a gay transsexual, and while I find the direct physical contact sexually stimulating, I have to admit that no, I think I really prefer women who are born women who like men who are born men…. It's all very confusing.

Scenario 6:

I decide to take it really slow and introduce myself. "Hi, my name is…"

"I know you. You're Icky! Get the fuck away from me before I call the cops!"

Scenario 7:

After a session of hot and sweaty making out, we're getting naked in a hot tub and she says, "No, stop, you're pressuring me. I'm calling the cops!"

My imagination goes on and on and on like that.

The easiest way for me and my friends to survive with our egos intact and our criminal records clean is to completely avoid dealing with the reality of sex and relationships.

• • •

So it was more than a little surprising to me when Charlie proposed that we all pool our resources to rent a limo for our Senior Prom.

"What Senior Prom?" Rover said, sensibly enough. "I know you're not talking about going to the Fectville Prom, because that was two weeks ago, and as far as I can tell, we don't even have a high school. Last I heard they were thinking of knocking down the old gym rather than rehab it."

There weren't any big ballrooms in Groston, so the Ashby Bryson High senior prom had always been held in the gym. As you know, the gym was old school, literally – cinder block walls, a warped parquet floor laid over concrete, hard metal bleachers, static-blaring loudspeakers, buzzing fluorescents, and an incandescent bulb score-board that never worked. Every year the prom committee tried to make it look pretty with a disco ball, streamers and banners. They always managed to make it look pitiful. The streamers looked like fly paper, and the disco ball and banners were dwarfed by the size of the room. They tried to make it sound good by renting a PA or hiring a DJ with his own sound system, but the acoustics sucked. Every year people complained afterwards that their hearing was wrecked and their feet were killing them.

"Word," Sean said.

"Fuck you with this 'word' shit!" Jesús hissed. "Word is a word. It's just a word. It doesn't mean anything!"

"Word." Sean grinned. He really enjoyed teasing Jesús. "Meanwhile, planning for the prom is well underway. The ABHS student council has been meeting in exile."

"Like a Vichy government," Charlie snickered.

"You're on the student council?" I asked Sean.

"Yeah." He shrugged. "I was elected back in September."

"Really?" I looked puzzled. "I don't remember that."

The rest of the gang chanted, "Vote for Sean. He's the One!" (Making it rhyme.) Hearing Sean's campaign slogan clicked something in my memory banks.

"Oh. Right," I said, and I began to wonder if I was doing too much medical marijuana

Sean smiled like a politician, gave everybody two thumbs up, and continued, "Since we still have all the funds collected during the first half of the year, and haven't spent anything this semester, there's a big pile of cash. So the prom committee rented the ballroom at the Fectville Biltmore. You guys didn't know?"

Adam, Rover and I were clueless. As usual.

"So, the Groston prom is supposed to happen in Fectville?" Adam said.

"We really need to work on publicity," Sean muttered.

"Yep," Jesús said. "Even though she's my baby, there's no way I'm taking a date to the prom in the Dartmobile. It's a good car, mind you, but it's never going to get me laid."

"You could be driving a Lamborghini and it wouldn't get you laid," Rover dissed.

Jesús shook his head. "If I had one of those I most certainly would get laid."

"Not sure I'd want a girl whose head was turned by a car," I said.

"Did you really say that?" Sean asked. "You?"

I blushed.

"Leave him alone," Adam said. "He's old fashioned."

"There's a difference between being old fashioned and stupid," Sean said. He looked at me. "No offense."

"None taken," I answered.

"But let's face it, you're not going to marry your prom date," Sean continued. "The whole purpose of prom is to say that you went, and to try and get laid. It's an American rite of passage."

"Yeah," Rover said. "Pointless expenditure with horrible costumes and terrible music all based on the precarious hope of a happy ending."

"Exactly," Sean said. "Like a real reality show."

"Are you taking your guyfriend?" Charlie asked Sean.

We all glanced sideways. Not that there was anything wrong with it, but we never really talked about Sean's preferences.

"Ayep. Me and Clyde are wearing matching tuxedoes."

"Clyde?" Rover said. "You're dating Clyde Jessdale? The lacrosse guy? Long, lean. Blonde hair?"

"Mmm hmm," Sean said.

Rover nodded. "He's yummy."

"He's mine, Rover," Sean said, a warning tone in his voice.

Rover raised his hands in a shrug. "A guy's got to dream. Let me know if you ever want to do a threesome."

Adam and I shuddered at the image.

Sean threw a pillow at Rover, who batted it away. "Hey, watch out for the equipment."

"Who are you asking, Charlie?" Jesús said.

"I already did," Charlie said. "Diana Marley."

"What?!" We all said. "No way!"

"Way," Charlie said.

The girl in the red dress, Diana Marley was rich and popular. Her family had owned the box factory in Groston, reaping the profits and then moving the operation overseas where labor was cheaper. Diana was into power. She'd dated James Croft, Fectville's star football quarterback. Then she'd dumped him and gone for Groston's even better quarterback, Doug Hawthorn.

"Are you kidding?" I said. "I thought she was still going out with Doug."

"Not any more," Charlie said. "She's been pissed at him ever since the rave. Dumbass Dougie dumped Susie Wardle for Diana Marley, and then he didn't even ask her to go with him to the prom. Fuck that shit. I did."

"You asked her, and she said yes?" Adam asked.

It didn't make sense. Diana Marley was at the top of the Fectville Regional High School female food chain. She had looks, money and fashion sense. Or to put it in teenage guy terms, she was hot, rich, and dressed like a hot rich girl with style. And she was in a few of our AP classes, so she wasn't a complete idiot.

"Yep," Charlie said. "Diana said she likes how I look. All those workouts paid off. And she knows I can dance. Early bird? Worm."

"Word!" Sean said.

Jesús threw a pillow at him.

I have to admit that after hearing about his date, I looked at Charlie with newfound respect. Charlie had lost a lot of weight, and he did look good. Yes, he could dance, but he was also wicked smart and was always one of the nicest guys on the planet. That should have been enough, but hearing that he'd asked and been accepted by Diana made him seem even more impressive. Stupid, right? But there's this male hormonal, hierarchical pack thing that happens when one of your pals claims a desired mate. Let's put it this way, it's one thing to know that your friends are great. It's another when a smoking hot rich chick validates it. This probably shouldn't be the case, but it was. And yes, I know that's a gross exaggeration of what was going on, but it still made an impression.

"Booof," I said. Sometimes the gap between what I think or write and what I actually articulate out loud is Grand Canyon wide.

"Yep," Charlie agreed. He looked pretty damned pleased with himself. "Hey, Isaac, who are you going to ask?"

Everybody looked at me.

"What about Adam?" I said.

"You gonna ask Adam to be your prom date?" Sean said. "You guys are cousins! That is so wrong."

Everyone laughed. I threw a pillow at Sean.

I deflected the conversation by asking my cousin, "Are you going to finally ask Helen?"

Now, everybody leered at Adam, who blushed red. We all knew that he wanted to ask her. Adam had been pining after Helen since way back at Jerome Marco K-8. Nobody needed to say anything. We just smiled and waited.

"I will," he said at last. "I will. I promise."

"Don't wait too long," Jesús said. "You don't want to miss your shot."

Adam nodded.

"What about you, Jesús?" I said. "Who are you bringing?"

Jesús smiled. "That's a surprise."

"I bet you haven't asked anyone," I said.

"Who says I had to ask?" Jesús's eyes twinkled.

"Someone asked you?" Rover said. "No way."

Jesús shrugged. "When you're as good looking as me, you have to fight them off. I had my pick."

Rover grabbed a pillow and threw it back at Jesús, who laughed.

"Are you going?" I asked Rover.

"I'll go with you," Rover said to me.

"No way!" I said, probably too quickly. We all knew that Rover was a professed albeit untested multisexual. "No no no no. Not into it. Let's just be friends."

"Oooh!" Rover said. He made a seppuku self-stabbing motion. "Wounded to the core. Gaak!" Then he shrugged. "Don't worry about me. I'll figure out something. Count me in."

"So, you're going too?" I asked. "Even though you don't have a date?

"Oh yeah," Rover said. "Stag in the bag."

I didn't know what that meant, so I ignored it.

"So, everybody's going?" I said, bewildered.

They all nodded and shrugged.

"You in?" Charlie asked me. "You can always ask Helen's friend Robyn."

I flashed on the image of Robyn Franklin in a furry prom gown, and smiled. Then I blushed and shook it off. My friends were all staring.

Talk about peer pressure. Ten minutes earlier, my only worries had been finishing an AP World History essay and getting into a good college. Now I was worried about being outed as a social failure in front of my buddies.

"Yeah," I said, reluctantly. "Sure. I'm in. I'll go. Of course."

"Awesome!" Charlie said. "And, tßo answer Jesús's concern, I already lined up a deal on the limo through my dad's old car dealership."

"Who are you going to ask?" Adam mouthed silently toward me.

I mouthed back, "I have no fucking idea."

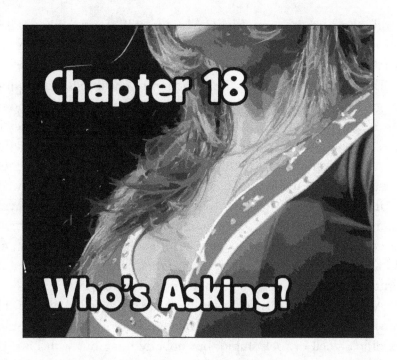

Chapter 18

Who's Asking?

"Nothing really makes me laugh anymore. Not out loud. There's too much bad shit happening in the world. I'd like to have a sense of humor, but it seems to be broken. You really want to know what I think is funny? Really? I picture a cartoon of a seed. It's buried under ground. The camera pulls back and you see the seed in a cutaway with bulldozers laying asphalt. They're building a highway over top. Somehow, though, enough water gets to the seed and it starts to grow as cars and trucks zoom by overhead. The seed hits the bottom of the road, but it finds a slender crack and slips up and up closer to the surface, where it finally breaks through. A beautiful flower blooms! Then WHAM! It's run over by a station wagon."
– Bailey, "Butch" Batten (way earlier in the year)

Wah wah wah. I didn't have a date to the prom.

Talk about a bullshit problem. There are so many people in the world who have it worse, right? My dad still gets two newspapers delivered every day, so even if I didn't get shit through my feeds and social medias, I see the headlines on the breakfast table.

Famines and refugees. The addiction to cheap oil that requires our government propping up dictatorships, creates terrorists and requires military actions. All that shit with Russia. Internet privacy issues. Sexual harassment. Racism in every form, from discrimination through cop shootings to ethnic cleansing. Homes flooded. School shootings. Political corruption. Homophobia. Anti-Semitism.

It's fucking overwhelming how many horror shows are playing out around the world at this very moment, and my biggest worries are getting into college... no, getting into a "good" college, because I'm already in at Fectville State... and that perennial teen angst favorite, who am I going to take to the stupid senior prom?

A few years ago this kid at Jerome Marco K-8 killed himself. His name was Jeremy Francis. He was my age. Nobody really liked him. He didn't smell or look stupid, but nobody hung out with him. He was just another kid in gym class. And when he hanged himself in his bedroom we all joked about autoerotic asphyxiation that went too far. But it leaked out that he'd left a note that said, "I just don't matter." They brought a grief counselor in to school to comfort us, but aside from a few hyper hysterical drama-queen girls, nobody really had a problem with his death. Months later, when Mrs. Cap read his name at the school promotion ceremony a bunch of us looked at each other and said, "Jeremy who?" We felt kind of shitty about that.

I'm not saying I was anywhere near suicidal, but I often wondered if I mattered to anyone beside my friends and my parents.

All this is a long way of saying that when I got to my last period AP Spanish class on that Thursday afternoon before prom, I dumped my books on the floor and put my head down on my hands.

Yo no hablo Español bueno. After four years of high school Spanish, I can't understand a Telemundo program without closed captioning translation. The only reason I was getting a B in the class was that I did all the homework, all the extra credit, and crammed vocabulary with Jesús before every quiz.

Back at Ashby Bryson, our old Spanish teacher, Señora Gutierrez, had always talked about the beauty of the Spanish language. Señora was a short Rubenesque woman in her late thirties or early forties who seemed comfortable with her big and shapely form. She wore barely "appropriate" clothes that fit her swooping curves. Lots of tight fitting sweater-dresses. (I guess sweater dresses were a thing that year.[27]) It wasn't a bad look on her. Some of the cruder guys called her a Milfita. She would recite Cervantes and even though I never understood more than a word or two, it sounded pretty sexy. When we all got dumped into Fectville, Señora Gutierrez gave up, put in for early retirement. I later heard she'd moved to Barcelona, where she became active in the Catalan separatist movement. I missed her.

Now our Spanish teacher was Señor Desmond McKenzie, an immigrant from Jamaica, who spoke Spanish with a deep baritone West Indian accent. Evidently he had seniority in the teacher's union and couldn't be fired. He seemed nice enough, but I couldn't understand him in English, let alone en Español.

"Awrite, Arright," Señor Mac rumbled. "Klaro k hablen cun un compañero sobre el baile llamado prom."

"Wha he say?" someone from Fectville muttered. Those of us from Groston knew better than to say anything.

"He wants us to partner up and have a conversation about prom."

Shit.

"Easy peasy," someone else on the other side of the room said.

"En Español!" Señor Mac reverberated cheerfully.

"Simple-a-fucking-mente," someone cracked.

Double fucking shit. I kept my head firmly down. Maybe if everybody thought I was asleep, I'd vanish like a chameleon.

Somebody nudged my shoulder. "Hey."

"Fuck prom," I muttered into my desk. "Feck-o prom-o."

"Si," said a girl's voice. "Odio el baile, tambien."

---

[27] When I was going over the fourteenth draft of this manuscript I realized that just about every woman I've mentioned wore something tight that showed her shape. I think it was freshman year that we all had the talks about gender bias and the false media image of women. We did listen and learn. But all I remember are the tight dresses. Chalk it up to hormones.

She had a pleasant voice, and it took me a second to translate that she hated the dance too.

Fine. I'll play along. "¿Por que?"

"Porque mi novio me abandon."

"That sucks," I muttered. My eyes stayed closed. So what if you got dumped, I thought. At least at one time you had a boyfriend. I didn't have anyone. Never had. Never would.

"En Exxxpañol, Señor Cohen," Señor Mac's voice growled nearby.

"Muy malo," I said, over emphasizing the syllables. "Mucho sucko."

She giggled, which made me kind of laugh and lift my head up.

The girl I was talking with in Spanish was Susie Wardle, the head of Groston's mostly disbanded cheerleading squad.

• • •

I'd known Susie since first grade. Or more accurately, I'd been aware of her since then. She was the bouncy girl with the blue eyes and bright blonde hair who sat next to me in the reading circle. Once, when Mrs. Martin wasn't looking, I'd leaned over and kissed her on the lips. Today that prepubescent peccadillo would probably get me thrown out of school for sexual harassment or unwanted promiscuity, but Susie didn't tell and I didn't tell and Mrs. Martin didn't see. In my memory, she'd even kissed me back, smiled, and then promptly forgot that I ever existed.

To say that we grew up and grew apart would imply that we were ever together for more than that momentary lip brushing at age six. She didn't ignore me, but she never really breathed the same air as me. Susie had a completely different set of activities, interests, classes and of course friends. She was pretty and popular, and I was boring and invisible and inconsequential. Different circles. Different cliques.

By our senior year, Susie Wardle had become the most beautiful girl in Groston. She was Doug Hawthorne's Homecoming Queen, and the two of them had been so striking that the *Groston Gazette* had put their picture on the front page with the headline, "Groston's Hometown Heroes."

If I'm being honest, and I've tried to be, I had indulged in many many many private fantasies about Susie that ended with a Kleenex wipe.

Boy. Hormones. Imagination. Q.E.D.[28]

But as far as I could recollect we hadn't had anything like a conversation since first grade. The only reason we were in the same AP Spanish class was because of the whole school shift. And now I had to talk with her about the prom. In Spanish.

"Tu novio es un idiota," I said. "Estúpido. Que cabrón."

"What?" she said. "Como?"

"He's a dumbass," I said. About the only Spanish I really knew well were the slang and profanities that Jesús had taught me.

She smiled at me.

Susie Wardle actually smiled at me! My heart skipped.

Be cool. I told myself. I did everything I could to keep my face straight and avoid blushing.

"¿Por que no?" she said.

"Verdad?" I asked. Really?

"Si."

She didn't know why I thought Doug was an idiot? Was she fishing for a compliment? Fine. I shrugged. I'll tell the truth. "Porque eres la chica más hermosa en toda la escuela."

"De toda?" she corrected me.

"En dos ciudades," I told her. She really was the finest looking girl in Groston and Fectville, like a wholesome but still sexy hand soap model. I thought for a moment, and continued. "Tus ojos son del color del cielo en un día perfecto. Tu pelo es tan brillante como el sol."

I watched her parse the words, and as they dawned in her mind I added, "Y tu sonrisa es una luz en la oscuridad."[29]

---

[28] Susie, if you're reading this, I apologize for objectifying you, but please keep in mind that boy hormones are both voracious and shameless. I'm pretty sure I was never creepy. Was I?

[29] "Your eyes are the color of the sky on a perfect day. Your hair is as bright as the sun.... And your smile is a light in the darkness." A bit hokey, but it really was how I saw her.

She smiled more than a grin. Her red lips opened, and her teeth shined like a bright white beacon lighting up my heart.

You're a fucking idiot, I told myself. You're supposed to play it cool. Shit.

"Gracias," she said. "¿A quien invitáste?"

Who did I invite? I snorted. "Ninguno." Nobody.

"¿Ninguno? ¿Por que? Eres un buen chico."

"Sí," I laughed. "Pero buenos chicos terminan el último." Nothing like quoting Vince Lombardi en Español to explain why you're a loser.

Susie laughed and then said, "¿Quieres ir El Prom conmigo?"

I wasn't sure I'd heard her correctly. Did she really just ask me to go the prom?

I said, "¿Que?"

Which was when Susie Wardle looked into my eyes and asked, "¿Quieres ir al baile conmigo?"

She did. Holy fuck! Time stopped. I held my breath. My heart was pounding.

That was when I noticed that we were the only two people in the classroom who were still talking. Everyone else, including Señor Mac, was looking at us.

Shit. So much for playing it cool. Still, I took my time.

"¿De verdad?" I asked. Really? "¿O es solo para la clase de Español?"

"Sí. De verdad." Yes, she said. She said YES!

I didn't hesitate. "Joder sí." I shrugged.

Señor Mac snorted. Nobody else got it.

Susie looked puzzled. "Joder?"

"No importa," I said, quickly. "Sí! Solo sí. El gusto es mio."

Susie Wardle looked at me, right at me, and said, "Gracias."

"De nada," I said. "Totalamente!"

Señor Mac cracked up, and boomed, "Perfecto. Y así es como hablas en Español."

Someone on the other side of the room said, "What the hell?"

Which was exactly how I felt.

But as the bell rang, Susie gave me a pink business card with her name, social media tags, email address and phone number.

"What color suit do you have?" she said.

"Suit?" My voice cracked a little. "Blue?"

"Good," she said. She nodded. Then she picked up her designer backpack, and left.

I stared at the pink card with two thoughts colliding in my head.

Are Susie Wardle and me really going to prom?

And why does she have business cards?

Then, I decided that the last question didn't really matter.

I floated out of school and have absolutely no memory of how I got home that afternoon.

Chapter 19

Let's Dance!

"Last week a friend emailed me a video of a cute little puppy with its tail caught in one of those robot vacuums. The puppy wasn't in any danger, but it couldn't get its tail free. Watching that little doggy yapping and pulling at the vacuum, and then get yanked off its feet and dragged across the kitchen floor was hysterical! I know it's cruel, and I have to say that when I describe it, I feel ashamed that I ever thought it was funny. Can I change my answer again?"
— My mom

On Friday nights my family and Adam's usually have a family dinner together at one of our houses. Because we're Jewish (except for Paul, Adam's step-dad), we light candles and say blessings over the wine and bread, but it's not really a religious event. There are often other guests. Sometimes my friends and their parents, and sometimes other random grown-ups. Mostly, the adults chatter, laugh a lot and drink too much wine. If my sister Ellen is home from college, she often brings one of her friends and she drinks wine too.

For some reason, that Friday was quiet, just us without any extra guests, which meant that when Adam quietly asked me, "So, Isaac, what's going on with you and the prom?" my parents and Ellen were paying attention.

It was like one of those old TV commercials where everybody stops and stares.

"What?" I said. "Is my private life everybody's concern now?"

Ellen grinned at me. "Yeah, dog breath. Who even knew you had a private life?"

"Now, Ellen…" Mom warned in that singsong voice she'd used since we were children.

"I'm curious, too," Aunt Dot said. "Adam hasn't mentioned anything about prom to me either."

"I bet Adam is going with Helen," Ellen said.

At least now everybody was on Adam's case too. Their heads swiveled and their eyes focused on my cousin.

Adam blushed.

"What's the deal, guys?" Paul said, trying to sound like one of the cool kids, which truthfully he pulled off from time to time.

"We're just going to the prom tomorrow," Adam said. "It's not a big deal."

"Not a big deal?" My dad laughed. "I remember Ellen's senior prom. It was a nightmare for months. 'Who am I going to go with? Nobody likes me. What am I going to wear? What if my date stands me up? What if I get a pimple!'"

Dad's echoing of my sister's whining was so dead on that we all laughed, except Ellen. He'd had a bunch of wine, so he kept going. "'What about my hair? I can't believe I picked out this dress! Does it still fit? Did I gain too much weight? Where am I going to get shoes that match his tie?'"

Ellen scowled and threw a dinner roll at Dad, who looked surprised when it bounced off his forehead.

"Hey!" he said. "Don't throw food at the table."

"Don't be such a jerk," my sister told my dad.

I waited for him to yell at her. My dad can be really loud and frightening when he gets angry, but that didn't happen. I could see his face starting to get red, and then he was interrupted.

"Ellen's right," Mom said to him. "You should apologize."

Did all the house rules change when you went away to college? I'd probably never find out.

"Why?" Dad blustered. "It was just like that."

"I remember," Paul said, coming to Dad's rescue. "She even made Dot take off work early to finish restitching the dress."

"See?" said Dad, but you could see his heart wasn't really in it.

"Senior prom is very important to young people," Aunt Dot said. "It's a life passage event. It's one of those turning points in our culture that mark the change from childhood to adulthood."

Allright... Aunt Dot was off and running on one of her sociological indigenous people's diatribes, comparing prom to Quinceañera and the Bantu coming of age rituals.

Maybe even without the extra guests, all the grown-ups had too much wine.

While they were all busy, I glanced at Adam and bobbed my head toward the kitchen. Together, we quietly got up and started to clear our plates...

"Wait a second," Dad said, cutting off Aunt Dot in the middle of a horrifically graphic description of an Indonesian ritual mutilation ceremony. "Do you need the car or something?"

"No," I said. "We're not going out right now."

Dad shook his head. "Not tonight. For the prom."

Again, everything stopped. I sighed.

"We rented a limo," Adam said. "No problem."

"A limo?" Paul said. "You guys aren't old enough to..."

"Charlie's dad used to work at a car dealership. Remember?" I explained. "Charlie got us a deal."

Everybody got quiet for a moment as they thought about Mr. Johnson. Still dead. The adults nodded their heads.

"Okay," Dad said.

Then Aunt Dot asked Adam, "What are you going to wear?"

"I have a tux," Adam told his mom.

"You do?" I said. It was news to me.

"Yeah." Adam shrugged. "Of course I do. I rented it."

"Do you have a corsage?" Paul asked him. "Girls love corsages."

"Yes," Adam said, slowly, and deliberately, like he was a little bit tired of explaining something simple to children. "Of course I have a corsage. And a boutonniere too."

"What the hell is a boutonniere?" I asked.

"It's a flower that goes in your tuxedo's button hole," Paul told me. "It's supposed to match the girl's corsage. Back in the day, girls would make them for their guys, but I doubt they do that now."

"No, they don't," Adam said. "You order them as a set from the florist."

I gaped at my cousin. Nobody had told me anything about this shit!

Ellen nodded her chin at me. "What about you, butthead? Corsage? Boutonniere? Tuxedo? Black socks?"

I set my chin. "I'm fine." I grabbed my silverware and turned to go.

"Wait a second," Dad said, slurring just a little. "You don't have a tux, do you?"

"I…" I shrugged. "I'm going to wear my suit."

"Your Bar Mitzvah suit?" Mom said. "There is no way you're going to fit into that."

"I'm not fat," I said.

"No, you've grown," Mom said. "Taller. And in all directions. It's been four years!"

She was right. I hadn't really thought about it. "I'll squeeze," I said. "I'll hold my breath. This year's fashion is really tight clothes."

Dad and Uncle Paul snorted genuine laughs.

"Loser." Ellen shook her head.

"You can't take a date to prom in a suit that doesn't fit," Mom said.

"He doesn't even have a date," Ellen said, dismissively.

"I do too," I said, opening my stupid mouth without thinking.

"Yeah? Who?"

I set my jaw. Don't answer. Don't answer.

Everybody waited. Everybody looking.

"Come on," Adam said, tugging my elbow toward the kitchen.

"He couldn't get a date if he paid one," Ellen said.

"Ellen," Mom warned.

"It's true," my sister said. She held up her index finger and thumb to her forehead making an L for Loser sign.

"Ignore them," Adam said to me.

I looked at my cousin. "You don't think I got a date either."

He winced. "Let's go wash some dishes."

Really? Nobody in my family believed that I could possibly get a date for the prom. Sheeeyit.

"Susie Wardle is my date," I said.

"What?" Ellen gaped.

"You heard me," I said. "I'm taking Susie Wardle to the prom."

"No way." Ellen stared. "You? Ech, she would never even talk to you."

Adam stared.

"Who's Susie Wardle?" Aunt Dot asked Adam, who for once kept his mouth shut.

"Susie is the captain of the Groston cheerleading squad," Ellen explained. "She is beautiful, blonde and blue-eyed. She is the most popular girl in Groston. She was dating Doug Hawthorne, the star quarterback? Pimplebutt here has had a crush on her since elementary school. That Susie Wardle?"

"Isn't that the quarterback whose arm you broke?" Paul asked Adam. He was quick on the uptake.

Adam nodded.

"No way," my dad said. "You? Dating a cheerleader? Really?"

Are you fucking kidding me? My whole family thought I was completely worthless. Yes, I was the dumb guy in our gang, but my friends didn't rub it in. It was general knowledge that I hadn't gotten into any good colleges, and most people in Groston and Fectville thought I was a loser. I had kind of grown to expect that sort of thing from kids in school, but not from my family.

Fuck it.

I shook my head, gritted my teeth, slammed my plate and silverware back on the table, said, "Do your own damned dishes," stormed off to my bedroom, and slammed the door.

• • •

My bedroom is right upstairs from our dining room. I could hear them talking and laughing through the floor. I picked up my phone and stared at it. Not sure what to do. Take a selfie? Post #ParentsSuck #embarrassment #teenangst #ihateprom #humiliation?

A few minutes later there was a soft knock at the door. I ignored it. I kept opening and closing phone apps, like some kid with OCD.

The knock got louder.

"Hey, Isaac," my dad's voice was muffled. "May I come in?"

"It's unlocked," I muttered.

My dad came in.

I didn't bother looking up. They design phone apps to visually zoom open and zoom closed. It's kind of soothing. He shut the door behind him and hung something on my closet door.

"Sorry, kiddo," he said.

"Wow," I said, "apologizing to both your children in one night, this must be a new record. Maybe I won't need therapy later in life." I stared at my useless phone.

To his credit, Dad kept his mouth shut and his anger in check. He stood awkwardly, looking for a place to sit.

My room is a mess. It's always a mess. When a friend comes over, they just clear a space to sit and throw whatever on the floor. Dad needed instructions, which I didn't feel like giving him.

"What?" I said.

"You're really going to the prom with that girl?" he asked, gently.

"Yeah," I said. "Her name is Susie Wardle. She actually asked me."

"Really?" Dad said, his skepticism showing again. He quickly added, "That's great. But you do need a tux."

"Well, I guess I'm not going then," I said. It really had been too good to be true. "Can't get into college. Can't get a date for prom. Or more specifically, can't keep a date for prom. I guess everybody's right, and I'm just a fucking loser."

"Nobody said that," Dad said.

"Ellen did, and the rest of you thought it," I snapped. "You thought it." I pointed at my dad.

He decided not to argue. "I got you something."

"A trust fund? A job at the dump?" I asked. "A gun?"

"Don't joke about suicide," Dad said, instantly putting on his physician's authority voice. "I see a lot of kids who… Really. Just don't joke about it."

I shrugged. What I really needed was a mindless video game. I started flipping through the online app store. I'd avoided Fortnite, because I knew I'd lose months of my life, but maybe tonight would be a good time to start.

"I brought you this," Dad said. He whisked the thing he'd brought into the room off the door, and laid it flat on the bed beside me.

I looked up from my phone. It was a suit bag.

Dad unzipped it.

Inside was the brightest baby blue tuxedo the world hasn't seen since the nineteen seventies. It was as blue as the sky on a clear spring morning. It had wide pointed lapels with dark blue piping and diagonal-cut blue pockets. There was even a light blue ruffled shirt and a pre-tied deep navy almost black velvet bow tie folded over the front of the shirt.

I was almost speechless. "Wow."

"Yeah," Dad laughed. "This thing was pretty hip back in the day. I don't know if it's stylish now, but beggars and choosers and all that. You're just about the size I was then. I think it will fit you. You want to try it on?"

I poked my cheek with my tongue. "No. But I don't have much choice, do I?"

"You might as well," Dad said. "You want me to leave the room?"

I rolled my eyes. I hadn't gotten undressed in front of my father since I was eleven and he took me shopping for a pair of new jeans, which I refused to wear because they were too stiff. "No, just turn around."

A few minutes later, I was adorned, and said, "Ok. You can look."

Dad turned. "The shoulders are a little broad, but Dot can take them in. And you're a little taller than me, which is weird, but she can let out the legs." He grinned. "Not bad."

I looked at myself in the mirror, and I had to smile too.

I know some people think that clothes matter, and they probably do. But I've always felt that the attitude of the person wearing the clothes was more important.

I actually looked dapper and well appointed. Yes, I was almost certainly completely out of sync with the latest styles, but at least the tuxedo, shirt and bow tie all worked together in a unified look.

"You want to wear my shoes?" Dad said. "I've got a pair of patent-leather black shoes with pointy toes."

"No fucking way," I said. "Black Chuck Taylor high tops. They're still in the box."

"Classic." Dad nodded. "All right. Let me call Dot and get her up here to measure you. Your mom's dusting off the old sewing machine."

"Hey, Dad," I said.

"Yeah?"

"Thanks."

"Come here," he said.

And we had one of those moments of awkward family bonding shit.

Dad wrapped me in a big hug. "I love you."

"I love you too, Dad."

It was so corny I almost wanted to cry. But it was true.

And it was getting late, so he left, and a few minutes later, Aunt Dot came in with her measuring tape, pins, and soap marker and started clucking. Adam came in and started laughing. And Ellen stood at the doorway, scowling and shaking her head.

Not the worst Friday night ever.

• • •

Saturday morning zipped by in a blur.

Our group chat was all about logistics. Sean started it off with a ping at nine a.m., "What time are we getting picked up?" Rover immediately went all paranoid and needed to know every detail of the itinerary. Jesús texted that he wasn't even going to be done ferrying his siblings until six that evening. Adam mentioned that the doors opened at the Biltmore at six-thirty for the breathalyzer line and pictures, and that dinner was being served at seven, so there wasn't a lot of time. Jesús offered to be picked up last. Rover said that he could be ready any time after noon if that would be easier. Charlie's phone was off, and he didn't even get into the mix until just before noon, when he said he needed a list of all our dates' addresses. Rover immediately pinged back that as soon as he got them, he'd run a geographic travel algorithm to determine the most efficient route. Jesús suggested that using a GPS driving app would probably work just as well. Rover fired off three messages that read, "Really?" "Who are you?" "And why are you my friend?"

Of course, I realized that I didn't even know where Susie lived. I needed to call her.

I stared at my phone and watched the digital seconds tick by. I had her pink business card with all her social contacts and phone number.

Finally I sighed, punched in the numbers and hit the green call button.

"Hi, Isaac." She answered on the second ring. "You're not ditching me, too. Are you?"

"What?" I said. I recognized her voice, but not the anger.

"I've been waiting for your call," she said. "Are you calling to cancel?"

"No," I replied. "I'm not. Are you cancelling on me?"

"Gah," she muttered. "No. Shit. Do you even have a tux?"

"Yes," I said, my eyes drifting toward the blue beauty hanging in my closet. "It's blue, like I said."

"What color blue?" she asked.

"Powder," I said. "Light blue sky."

There was a long pause and then a sigh of relief. "All right. That will work."

"I'm glad that my sartorial choice meets your expectations."

"I wouldn't go that far," she said. "I haven't seen it in person yet."

"I live to please you," I told her.

"Really?" she said. "Then why the fuck did you wait until the last minute to call me?"

I stared at my phone. "Because I didn't have anything in particular to say. You really don't know me. I really don't know you. We're going to prom together because neither of us have dates, right?"

There was a long silence on her end.

I literally hit myself in the forehead with the palm of my hand. Had I actually said that aloud?

"Yeah," she said at last. "So, why are you calling me now?"

"I need your address," I told her, "so I can tell the limo where to pick you up."

"You got a limo?"

"Don't sound so surprised," I said. "I told you, you're special to me."

She laughed. "Right."

"My friends and I all chipped in together."

"The whole dork squad?" she said.

I shook my head, glad I hadn't done a video call, so she couldn't see that I was flipping her off. "If that's how you think of me, then why the hell did you ask me to the prom?"

"I was desperate," she said.

Now I paused. Right. Of course.

"Look," she said, "would you rather I lie to you?"

"No," I grumbled. "Are you even going to dance with me?"

"Can you dance?" she asked.

"Not very well," I admitted. "It took me forever to learn the whole Fat Charlie dance routine. But still, you're my prom date, and I'd like to manage my expectations a little."

"Yes," she said. "I'll dance with you. At least one dance."

"My pick," I told her.

"Not if it's a slow dance."

"My pick," I insisted.

"Fine," she said at last. "Look, I'm sorry. I don't mean to be a jerk with you."

"Me either," I told her. "It's a marriage of convenience."

She laughed. "I wouldn't go that far."

"I would…" I started, but quickly continued, "…not either. Right. So I need your address and I'll let you know what time we'll pick you up as soon as Rover maps the logistics."

"Dave Rover?" she said. "Did he get a date?"

"Nope," I said. "He claims he's playing the field."

"Right," Susie chuckled. "My friend Marcie still needs a date. I think she's going solo."

"Marcie Kahn? I dunno. Rover's not as desperate as I am."

She snorted. "You really know how to charm a girl."

"Just being honest." I fed her words back. "Would you rather I lie to you?"

Susie gave me her address and told me that her parents wanted me to come inside to take pictures. I said that was fine, so as long as they emailed copies to my parents, who wanted them too. Then she made me promise never to repost them on social media without her permission.

I asked her if she was that embarrassed by me.

There was another long pause. "No," she said, lying. "But I don't want you to think there's more here than there is. And I know how people are. Everybody in Groston and Fectville thinks I'm some kind of human Barbie doll. It's not fair to either of us."

I scratched my head. "Yeah, all right. I'll see you tonight."

She ended the call.

I stared at the phone and looked at the picture of her on my contacts that I'd snagged from some social site. Susie Wardle looked perfect. Blue eyes, blonde hair, fair skin with a bit of a tan. Big white teeth smile. A light blue dress with just a little bit of cleavage. I don't know if she was every straight guy's fantasy, but she certainly was mine.

And she was right. I really had no idea who the hell she was. No wonder she wanted to keep her distance.

It was going to be a strange night.

Chapter 20

Naught Prom

"Comedy is a rough sell for me. There are so many challenges in this world. I feel that entertainment is a waste of my time. Years ago I read a book called, 'Amusing Ourselves to Death.' I don't mean to sound judgmental about the choices that other people make. When I was a kid? Oh, I used to love The Three Stooges."
— Marvin Beagle, Helen's dad

Hummers are weird cars, grotesque, oversized, and frightening. Rover's dad calls them Urban Insult Vehicles because they're so horrific for the environment. Stretch Hummers are even weirder. They look like a cross between a bus and a tank.

Still, I had to grin when the bright white stretch Hummer pulled up in front of my house at five-thirty on the dot. Yeah. This was it.

I was ready to go: tuxed and flowered, with a yellow rose boutonniere pinned to my lapel, and a yellow rose wrist corsage in a clear plastic box for Susie Wardle.

I also had fifty bucks in my wallet, and a condom, just in case.

I grabbed my stuff, checked my zipper, and headed out the door.

"Have fun, loser!" my sister Ellen shouted from her room.

I smiled, and gave her the finger, which she couldn't see but still felt satisfying.

Fortunately, Mom and Dad weren't home, otherwise they would have wanted pictures – solo pictures of me before the prom without a date.

Rover's head popped up out of the sunroof. "Hello there!"

Charlie's Uncle James, the cop, came out the driver's door wearing a chauffeur's cap and uniform. He held open the door

"Your ride, sir," he said with a grin.

"Seriously?" I asked him. I'd known Charlie's Uncle James for years and never figured him for a limo driver. "Why are you dressed in the monkey suit?"

"Undercover," Uncle James said. "Prom's in Fectville, so I can't go in my real uniform. Besides, none of you guys are old enough to legally rent a car. Somebody has to drive, right? This will prevent any possible DUIs."

I nodded, not really sure what that meant. Was Uncle James going to enable us or cramp our style? Not that our gang had much in the way of partying style. Yes, we like the occasional beer or shot, but we weren't addicted to massive alcohol consumption like so many of the kids in Fectville. Adam's medical marijuana and the occasional hallucinogen that Rover manufactured when he could crack open his dad's lab were about it, and we'd been steering pretty clear of those for a while because of all the shit troubles we'd been having.

Uncle James made a "this way" gesture, and I got in the back.

It was like being inside somebody's high-end living room with a really really low ceiling. The seats were plush. There were side tables, a flat screen TV, a full bar, and white shag carpeting.

"Word!" Sean said, raising a glass of what looked like rum and Coke.

Jesús rolled his eyes.

"Hi," Helen said. She was snuggled in next to Adam, who smiled and waved at me.

"Welcome to the prommobile," Charlie said. "Just so you know, the carpet's removable, but they'll charge us an extra two-hundred-and-fifty bucks to clean it if anybody pukes on it."

My guy friends were all wearing black tuxedos with black bow ties. Helen was wearing a beautiful white dress. I stuck out like a baby blue sore thumb.

"You want a mojito?" Adam asked me.

"Uncle James is cool with it, as long as we don't get caught," Charlie said.

"What about the breathalyzers?" I said. "Don't we have to breathe into a tube and pass a test to get into the prom?"

Rover pulled his head in from the sunroof. "I've got a neutralizing chewing gum that I designed to fool the breathalyzer. It tastes a lot like raw squid, but it works."

"Besides, we've got another plan," Sean said.

"What other plan?" I asked.

Rover and Charlie grinned at each other.

"It's a surprise," Jesús said, smiling.

"You guys suck," Helen said. She turned to me. "They won't tell me either."

"Ike, don't be pissed. I know you usually like to organize these things," Charlie said. "It's mostly Rover's plan."

Rover's eyes twinkled "Are you in or not?"

I looked at my cousin.

"I'm totally in." Adam stirred his drink. "Prom, shmom, let's get this party on."

"But I've got a date," I said. "She's expecting to go to the prom."

"Yeah, right," Jesús said.

"Really?" Rover said. "Then how come you didn't text me her address?"

"Seriously? I forgot," I said, simultaneously flipping Jesús and Rover middle fingers. "I don't know if she'd be up for it. Whatever it is."

"All right, all right," Rover said. "Fair enough." He looked at Charlie. "We said we'd give our dates votes, too. This is a consensus-based decision. Anybody's a no, and we go to the shitty boring prom in Fectville. Right?"

"I know that Clyde'll be fine," Sean said.

"He is fine," Rover said. Sean blushed. Then they fist-bumped.

"I'm not a part of the gang? I'm just a date?" Helen said.

Adam's face turned crimson, and he began to sputter.

"Relax. I'm good with that," she said to Adam. She patted his cheek, which somehow got even redder.

"I'm pretty sure Barbara will say that she's in," Jesús said.

Charlie looked at me. "Who's your date? Maybe you want to call her first?"

I looked at my cousin. He really hadn't told anyone? Adam smiled and shook his head. One good thing about my family and friends: gossip was kept to a minimum. Suddenly, though, I didn't want to tell them. I don't know if I was frightened about the ragging my friends would give me, or if I was worried that Susie might blow me off at the last minute.

The intercom snapped on. "Any more destinations before we get going?" Charlie's Uncle James asked.

"Yeah. We've got one more to pick up." I told him Susie's address.

"Susie Wardle?" Rover's eyes widened. "Susie Wardle? You're bringing her to the prom?"

I looked at my cousin. "I thought you didn't tell anyone."

"I didn't," Adam said.

I looked at Rover. "How do you...?"

"Hey, in third grade, I memorized the entire Jerome Marco K-8 School Directory." Rover shrugged. "I can't help it if my brain retains everything."

"Susie freaking Wardle?" Jesús said. "Is your date?"

"Hubba, hubba!" Rover said. "She's hot."

I looked at my friends. Jesús was shaking his head with disbelief. Sean's mouth was open in a jaw-dropping look of amazement. Charlie and Helen were both nodding and grinning.

"Way to go, dude," Helen said. "I didn't think you had it in you."

I licked my lips, and tried to decide whether to take offense. Screw that, these were my friends.

"Yeah," I grinned. "Jackpot."

"So, you want that mojito?" Adam asked. He had been crushing mint with a mortar and pestle. It smelled awesome.

"I think I'll wait a bit and see what my date wants to do," I said. It felt good saying that, my date. Pride.

Charlie tapped on the glass and said, "Drive on, James." He looked at us and whispered, "I always wanted to have a chauffeur and say that!"

● ● ●

When we finally got to Susie's house, the limo was full of laughing and well-lubricated teenagers. We'd stopped along the way and collected all the other dates. Sean's guy, Clyde Jessdale wore a black tux and a bow tie with pink polka dots that matched Sean's. Jesús's date, Barbara Moody wore a long dark green dress that matched her eyes. Charlie's date, Diana Marley wore a designer ball gown in her trademark color – blood red, of course. All my friends and their dates were drinking and smiling and looked relaxed and fabulous.

I felt awkward and nervous.

"Hey," Diana whispered to me. "Don't tell Susie I'm here. I want to surprise her."

I got the feeling that this was an evil girl kind of surprise, not something well intentioned, but I nodded anyway.

Uncle James opened my door, and I got out.

Susie lived in a small mansion on a few acres of rolling grass. The front door was under a portico with six Doric columns. To be honest, I hadn't realized that Susie's family had that much money, because her parents hadn't given her a car for her sixteenth birthday. Sure she always dressed nicely, but I'd assumed it was thrift store chic.

Windows on the Hummer limo rolled down to watch as I walked up the steps to knock.

Rover stood up and stuck his head back out the sunroof, of course.

My heart was pounding. They had one of those video camera doorbells. I waved. Then I pushed it, and heard a carillon toll. I expected something by Bach, but instead it sounded like a church bell version of the introduction to that old David Bowie song, "Heroes".

Susie's mom opened the door. "You're Isaac Cohen?"

Susie's mom looked just like her daughter, but older. Her eyes were blue and her hair was blond but thinner. She wore more make-up than Susie, and was about fifteen pounds heavier. Most of it in her bust, which stared at me like a pair of halogen headlights.

I nodded and tried to look away from the immense cleavage, but wasn't fast enough.

Susie's mom followed my eyes to her boobs, smiled, and whisked me inside, waving at my friends before closing the door behind with a soft thud and a click.

We walked down a short marble corridor to a spiral staircase. My sneakers squeaked.

"Susan," her mom said in that singsong voice that mom's everywhere have perfected. "Your date is here."

Susan? I'd never thought of her as a Susan. It was always Susie or more frequently SusieWardle like her name was all one word.

I waited, clutching the clear plastic flower box. Suddenly, I had to pee. Was there time?

I heard a door upstairs open and close, so I looked up.

Susie Wardle came down the staircase like an angel or a movie star.

Susie Wardle was perfection. Her blue dress was nearly the same color as my tux, but infinitely snazzier. It was short in the front, exposing her shapely tanned calves, and most of her thighs, and had a long train trailing behind. The dress fit her like a glove, showing amazing curves and a swelling bosom with a deep swath of cleavage. Her hair was pinned up like French royalty, and her shoulders were bare and exposed. I have no idea what shoes she wore. Maybe glass slippers, but they were probably blue high heels.

It was a perfect entrance, and I was entranced.

Susie smiled at me.

I definitely needed to pee.

Instead I stared and grinned like an idiot.

Just then, her father hurried into the room carrying a heavy SLR digital camera, like a gun, but with a flash mount.

"Hey, baby," he said, "give me a smile."

Susie turned her head and the flash popped half a dozen times.

"Keep coming down the stairs," he said. "Take it slow. Good.

Ok, turn a little."

Kinda weird.

"A little more," Susie's dad said. "Good. Chin out. Turn. Tilt. Another step."

"Don't trip," her mother said.

I could see Susie's face stiffen. A frown flickered across, but then was replaced by a plastered-on grin.

"Ok, you, whatever your name is, go to the bottom of the stairs," her dad said, nudging me. "Look up at her. You see her. You want her."

"Dennis, stop that," Susie's mother said. "His name is Isaac. You'll embarrass them."

Too late, I thought.

"Hey, you wanted these pictures," Susie's dad said. "I'm just doing my job."

It was the longest forty-five seconds of my life. Susie floated down the stairs like a goddess, while the flash popped over and over, and I stood at the bottom stiff as an awkward troll, glad at least that Aunt Dot knows how to trim a suit.

Her dad made me reach a hand up for her, and when Susie didn't reach out for me, he had her go back up the stairs twice until he got what he wanted. We had to open the flower box slowly, and slip the corsage on her wrist even slower.

When I finally touched her hands and her arms, my heart started beating faster.

It's one thing to know that you're just a date of convenience. It's another to convince your body that there's not a beautiful young woman in easy reach. Civilization is a thin veneer of manners and unnatural behaviors that hold our instincts in check. Barely in my case. I wanted nothing more than to pick Susie Wardle up, throw her over my shoulder, and run for the nearest haystack. Fortunately, I'm neither strong nor stupid. Also, we didn't live on a farm.

I followed her dad's directions. "Reach your hand out," he told me. "Susie, take his hand. Good! Now, go slowly. Slowwwly."

We posed the whole way down the hall, pausing every so often to look over our shoulders, as I escorted Susie to the front door.

On her father's cue, we both stopped again, looked over our shoulders toward each other this time, and smiled at his camera. Flash. Flash. Flash.

When we turned back to each other, for a brief moment I saw her face close to mine. God I wanted to kiss her. Her bow lips were perfectly red. Her eyebrows were dark perfect lines. Her skin was perfect. Her breath was sweet.

Those thoughts fled when I saw what she was thinking.

Her face was a mask. Her grin was forced. Her eyes were pleading.

"That's enough pictures," I said. "Our friends are waiting. We're going to be late."

It didn't stop her dad and mom from following us outside and snapping away while Uncle James opened the door for us.

Her mother gave her a dark black frock to wear, "in case the air conditioning is too much."

Rover watched the whole thing from his perch through the limo's roof, and he took pictures with his phone of them taking pictures of us.

"Be sure to ring the bell and wake us up when you get home," Susie's mother told her. Probably so they could tune in, rewind and rewatch the doorbell's video feed.

I was about to get into the Hummer, but her dad was right behind me. He put a hand on my shoulder and quietly said, "If you hurt my daughter, I will kill you."

I glanced at Charlie's Uncle James, the cop disguised as a chauffeur, who shook his head, no.

I smiled. "I'm sure that won't be a problem, sir. I'll take good care of her."

His hand pinched my shoulder hard. "You'd better."

Uncle James "accidentally" bumped him, which broke the grip. I got in the car, and the door shut with a satisfying thunk.

• • •

By the time I got settled, Susie had squeezed into a slot between Diana Marley and Barbara Moody, safely as far away from me as possible. Looked like her dad had nothing to worry about. I sighed and waved at her parents as we drove off.

Susie sat still, her shoulders thrown back like an ancient Roman marble statue.

The back of the limo was suddenly quiet. Nobody really knew what to say.

In general, the kids at Groston's Ashby Bryson High School were pretty cool about dealing with each other. There were some of those rich/poor, majority/minority, jock/burnout straight/gay tensions, but not much. Still, everybody knew that even though we'd grown up together, Susie Wardle was in a different class from the rest of us. Even Diana Marley, who was completely loaded and hot, didn't have the same zest. But Diana had stolen Susie's boy friend, Doug. And then Susie had embarrassed Diana by stealing him back at the rave. After that, Diana had dumped Doug. It was a wonder they weren't clawing each other's eyes.

Susie took in the scene in the enormous rolling room. "Hi."

"Girl, you've got to relax," Diana told her. "You're making the rest of us nervous."

Susie tried to smile.

"Hey, Susie," Rover said. "I've got a great idea. You want to completely blow off the prom with the rest of us and do something really fun?"

"Like?" Susie looked at Rover like he was a gigantic bug, which considering the way his eyes were bulging at her wasn't much of a stretch.

"We have something absolutely cool and totally awesome planned as an alternative to the ultra-boring Fectville-centric prom," Rover said, bobbling his head.

Susie coughed, clearing her throat. "I bought a prom dress. I have a ticket to the prom. I have a prom corsage on my wrist. I even have a prom date." She nodded at me, in case anyone was confused. "Why wouldn't I want to go to prom?"

"Cause it's going to suck," Rover said, his words coming out quickly. "It's supposed to be our senior prom, but it's not even in Groston. Half the kids there are going to be Fecters from Fectville."

"Hey!" Clyde and Diana said, simultaneously.

"Present company excepted," Rover continued, "most of you kids from Fectville just don't get us. You all think that we're losers because your town's dam burst and wrecked our school, so we can't even have our own prom at our own gym, like that's our fault."

"True," Diana said.

"All my friends are going to be at the prom," Susie said. "I'm expected…"

"Yeah, we're all expected," Charlie said. "We're expected to be-have like proper young adults and do what we're supposed to. Have fun, but within certain limits. We've got another idea. A different plan."

"What is it?" Susie asked. She looked at me. "Isaac?"

"I actually don't know either," I said. Then I looked around the limo. "Remind me why you're my friends?"

Diana shrugged. "They said they wouldn't tell me until after I agreed to go. And then Charles said I'd have to wait and see." She whacked Charlie on the shoulder. He smiled.

"Charles?" Sean mouthed the word and the rest of us smirked.

"I don't know anything about this either," I said. "My so-called friends won't tell me. They thought I was bullshitting about having a date, and that I needed cheering up."

"It's some biiig secret," Clyde said, squinting at Sean. "But I'm okay with that."

"I'm fine. I don't care," Diana said. "Anything has got to be more interesting than prom. At our prom, they put the punch into big water dispensers, so nobody could dump anything into it. I heard that Dr. Bob told the chaperones at your prom to make sure nobody dances too close."

"Not a problem for me," I muttered.

"I'm a little unsure about this," Barbara told Susie. "But I'm game too. The driver's a cop, so I'm not worried about them slipping me a roofie."

Puzzled, Rover looked up at the sunroof.

"A roofie is rufinol," Sean told him. "The date rape drug?"

"Oh," Rover said. "Wait! That's outrageous. I would never need a drug to…"

"I didn't mean to offend you," Barbara said, looking apologetic. "But these days you have to be careful."

"Okay," Rover grinned. "No problemo."

"Look, Susie," I said. "We don't have to go. I trust my friends. But our group operates on consensus. That means that if anybody says no, we'll all go to prom, and it's not a big deal. Nobody will hold it against you. Right? I told everybody that I'd support you, whatever you want. I do know that I'm probably embarrassing to you as a date…. Look, don't say anything. You really didn't want to go with me. And if we show up at the prom, you're going have to fake smile again, there are going to be kids taking pictures of us together that'll get posted forever on the Internet. If you want to hang out with your friends, fine. Probably you do. My friends, though… We may be the dork squad, but we're cool. We have our moments."

"Yeah," Jesús said. "And tonight we've got a no social media rule. No pictures, no texts, no posts, no videos, no recordings, just us. Switched off." He looked at Barbara. "No roofies either."

"Thanks for the memories," sang Helen.

"Does that mean I can't upload the pictures of her parents chasing after you?" Rover asked. "They looked so cute!"

Susie winced.

"Shut the fuck up, Rover," I said.

"What happens at naught-prom stays at naught-prom," Jesús said.

"Word!" Sean said. Jesús winced.

"Rover organized this really cool set up," Charlie told Susie. "We're calling it naught prom."

"Not N O T." Rover spelled it out. "Or K N O T. But N A U G H T. It's nothing like prom."

"No adults," Charlie continued. "Just us. We think that it'll be a shit ton more fun than prom. If you want, you can come, and check it. If you want, you can invite some of your friends. One last set of messages out to the world, before we go in. Or, if you change your mind, I'll tell Uncle James to take all of us to the real prom."

Susie looked at my friends. Then she looked at me.

God she was pretty. I really wished she liked me. "I'll do whatever is going to work best for you," I said. "If you want to go to prom, we'll go. If you want to ditch me, I'll stay behind. Whatever you want is what I want."

I was lying. I really didn't want to do that. I wanted to hang out with my friends and dance with Susie Wardle without everyone in the world staring. I imagined the two of us slow dancing on a beach, with a full moon and a reggae band and warm water lapping over our bare feet.

For a moment, Susie actually looked like she was going to cry. Her eyes softened. It was just a moment. Then she nodded and smiled and said, "I so fucking didn't want to go to the prom anyway. Yes, of course I'll check it."

I wasn't sure I liked that, but Sean, Jesús, Clyde, Adam, Charlie and Helen all cheered "YES!" at the same time, like they'd rehearsed it.

Barbara smiled and patted Susie's knee. "Good call."

Diana Marley leaned over and kissed Susie Wardle on the cheek. I added another lurid variation to my sexual fantasy library.

"I promise that you will not regret this," Rover said. And, even though there wasn't any need for it now, he started telling her about his anti-breathalyzer squid gum.

Just then, the Hummer stopped.

"That was fast," I said.

"Are we there already?" Diana asked.

"Where are we?" Susie asked.

Uncle James opened the door.

• • •

We got out of the limo, and stood in the empty back parking lot for the gym behind Ashby Bryson High.

I heard Susie let out a little deflated sigh.

I agreed. "Really?" I said. "We're going to break into the school?"

I looked at Charlie's Uncle James.

"No." The cop-turned chauffeur shook his head. "It's not breaking in when an authorized officer of the law opens the doors to check for any signs of vandalism. Which I did not find, do not expect to find, and if I do find, there will be a problem."

He gave us all the policeman's deadeye stare.

"Got it!" Rover said. "Can we go in yet?"

Man, Rover was excited.

"Not yet," Charlie's Uncle James said. "A few more things. First off, you have to understand that my job is on the line if you, any of you, or any of your friends fuck this up."

He was staring right at Charlie, who nodded.

Uncle James continued in his deep cop voice, "I want to be very clear. I am completely unaware of anything that goes on tonight. The alarm was never disabled. There are no high school students on the premises. There is no food. There are no alcoholic beverages, nor illegal substances. No signs or traces of any of these will be found. If I am asked, I dropped you off at the Fectville Biltmore ten minutes ago. And I believe that the GPS tracking in the limo will reflect this?"

"One hundred percent!" Rover said. "Already taken care of."

"Seriously guys," Uncle James said. "Don't fuck this up. You have a long history of fuck ups. I probably shouldn't trust you, but I do. Don't create a disturbance. Don't get caught. I do not want to have to lie. I will not lie under oath. And I do not want to lose my job. That's it. You got it?"

"We'll be good," Sean said. He was holding Clyde's hand. Clyde looked nervous. They were cute. "Can we go in yet?"

"Everybody, cell phones off!" Jesús said.

"I thought we were going to be able to leave whenever we wanted," Susie said, quietly.

Barbara nodded in agreement.

"You still can," I reassured them. "We're not going to leave the phones in the car, just turn them off. Right guys?"

"Absolutely," Jesús said. He nibbled Barbara's ear, and she giggled.

One by one, everybody got out their devices and powered them down.

"I'm going to hang around for a few minutes," Uncle James said.

"Then I'll be back around midnight. I'll give you my cell phone number if there are any problems. Which there won't be. Right?"

"There won't be, Uncle James," Charlie said. "I really appreciate this."

Diana was already pulling Charlie toward the gym.

Uncle James nodded. "You guys deserve more than the shit you've gotten this year. Have a good time."

Susie, Barbara and Clyde still looked wary.

Adam had pulled Helen's wheelchair from the trunk, and got her settled in.

"Shall we?" I said, bending and offering Susie my arm.

Susie hooked her hand in the crook of my elbow.

She touched me! I thought. Oh my god! Don't be a jerk. Be cool.

I smiled, and led the way.

Just before we got to the doors, Rover shouted, "Wait wait!"

We all stopped and looked at him.

"Hang on." Rover took out his little pocket computer that's about the size of a big phone. He had it open. He tapped a few keys.

"Now!"

I pulled open the gym doors just as the loud Techno music kicked it.

• • •

The Ashby Bryson High School gymnasium was an antique wreck even before The Rains, The Flood, and The Freeze. Constructed of cinderblock and steel girders with a metal roof, it was always too cold or too hot. The wooden basketball court's floor was warped, which should have given our team a major home court advantage, but didn't because the warping kept changing throughout the season. The scoreboard was old. The sound system sucked. The bleachers were long metal aluminum monstrosities that killed your ass if you sat on them for more than a minute.

Even when they'd had proms and homecoming dances there, the place had reeked of disrepair, neglect and budget woes. The best the Ashby B dance committees had ever managed was to string banners and streamers and shine strobes off a broken disco ball. Which always made the place look a bit like the aftermath of a small bomb explosion.

During the flood and freeze, water had leaked in, staining the walls, and warping the floor even more.

But that evening it had been completely transformed.

Instead of looking up at a rusted ceiling, we saw the stars, planets and then the green flickering of the Northern lights.

"Holy shit," Clyde said.

And the music seemed to come from everywhere all at once with a loud, but not overwhelming, bass thump.

"Holy shit!" Clyde repeated.

I was right there with him.

There were four long tables set up in the middle of the room. Two had chairs, tablecloths, and candles. One had a punch bowl, an ice bowl, a metal beer cooler, bottles of wine, red plastic cups and bottles of soda. The other had paper plates, plastic silverware, chopsticks, and boxes of Chinese food.

"Holy shit!" Clyde said. Not much in the way of imaginative verbal variation. I looked at Sean and wondered at the attraction. Must be physical.

"Happy naught-prom," Adam said to me.

"You did know about this, didn't you?" I demanded.

"Yeah," he said. "But I figured that the surprise would do you good."

I looked at Susie, who was staring up at the planetarium-like ceiling. "How is that even possible?"

"First I rewired the power." Rover grinned. "Those are high intensity projections of digital images from NASA. I have five high-def projectors scattered around the gym. Each of them is tuned to the original ceiling topology. So, they're compensating for all the interference from other obstacles like the girders and lighting fixtures. It's sort of like the camouflage that salamanders use, but not anything like that."

Susie nodded, like she actually understood what Rover was talking about, which I rarely did. "What about the sound? I don't see any speakers."

If it was possible, Rover's grin got even wider. "I figured out the resonant frequencies of the bleachers. Sound is all about vibration.

Pretty much anything can vibrate. Turns out that if you hook them up just right, and feed in enough power, bleachers make an awesome sound system. Just don't sit on them. You hear that guys? DON'T sit on the bleachers. They're wired with a lot of electricity. I don't know what will happen if you do."

"You did this?" Susie said.

"We helped," Charlie said.

Jesús was already twirling Barbara around the dance floor. Sean and Clyde were dancing too. They looked good together.

"Do you want to see?" Rover asked Susie, who nodded, eagerly.

He took her by the hand, and carefully led her under the bleachers.

And that is how Dave Rover stole my date.

To be honest, I was only pissed for about five seconds. I knew Susie wasn't into me at all. I was just her revenge or paper tiger or beard or something to keep her so-called friends from giving her a hard time at the real prom.

Adam gave me a mojito and slipped me a 10 mg medical grade THC chocolate bar the size of a poker chip.

I stared at the drink and the candy. Did I need drugs to have a good time? No. But they were there and I took them. I chewed the illicit candy and downed the mojito and asked for another. The music and the food and the lighting and the dancing and my friends probably would have been enough.

But the drugs certainly didn't hurt.[30]

I remember laughing and spinning in the middle of the gym, staring up at the ceiling, but seeing through to the night sky. Rover had downloaded and remixed a planetarium show from the Smithsonian and mashed it up with a natural history documentary, so we flew among the stars. Saturn's rings spun in webs, and exploded into a

---

[30] Except for the massive booze hangover I had the next day. I really don't get why anyone would ingest that much alcohol more than once (or twice), since it kills so badly. That shit hurt. There are kids in Fectville who brag about binge drinking every weekend until they throw up, and then they can't even get out of bed until after noon. At least marijuana never gives me that trouble…

million bands of color before scattering into millions upon millions of monarch butterflies that flew into the sun sending halos of light and solar flares twirling. All to a thumping bass line.

It was fucking awesome.

Just after midnight we all started to run out of gas. Diana asked if we had any cocaine, but we didn't, which was probably a good thing.

Charlie said he'd gotten a text from his uncle, so we had to get moving soon. It only took us about twenty minutes to clean up the mess, which was mostly shoving paper plates, plastic cups, broken chopsticks and empty boxes of lo mein and General Tso's chicken into big black plastic garbage bags and wiping up a few spilled drinks. Rover said that he'd come back tomorrow to get his equipment. We all agreed to help.

In the limo, Susie sat next to Rover and across from me. But when we got to Susie's house, she leaned over the middle and kissed me on the cheek. "Thanks. It was fun."

"You're welcome," I began. I wanted to say more. Make one last pitch...

Then Uncle James opened the door, and Rover got out and escorted Susie to her front door.

Rover gave Susie a long and slow and deep kiss, right in front of the video camera, just before ringing the bell.

Damn. I still couldn't believe that Rover had stolen my date. Simultaneously, I couldn't blame him.

To compensate, I stood up, poked my head out of the stretch Hummer's sunroof and used my phone to take more pictures of her parents as they came out.

They looked at Susie. They looked at Rover. They looked at me. I waved and took more pictures. They looked really confused.

Susie waved goodbye and was gone.

Chapter 21

Wake Up Call

"People think it must be fun to be a super genius, but they don't realize how hard it is to put up with all the idiots in the world."
– *Calvin in "Calvin and Hobbes" by Bill Watterson*

Even though I slept through most of it, Sunday morning hurt. I sort of thought that going to bed early – I was home and in bed before one – would have taken care of the pain, but it didn't.

When my phone bleeped at 11:30, it sounded like a gong in my brain. Then it gonged again. And again. And again!

I reached over, grabbed, peered.

Group chat. Cleanup at the gym to help Rover disassemble and remove his shit. Everybody was checking in. Gong!

"Fine." I replied. Then I put my phone into airplane mode.

I rolled over and a minute later, Mom was yelling into an echo chamber that Adam was downstairs, waiting for me.

Like I cared.

She yelled again. Came upstairs and banged on my door with a jackhammer.

"Fine," I muttered.

Now she fired bazookas at my door.

"FINE!" I yelled. And that hurt!

It was clear that the bombardment wouldn't stop, so I pried myself out of bed, peed, stuck my head under the shower, took four ibuprofen, and stumbled downstairs. I needed more drugs to counteract the previously consumed drugs. No wonder some people did that whole wake and bake, bloody Mary, mimosa, first line of the day thing.

"Good morning sunshine," my cousin said, brightly.

I flipped him off and headed for the coffee.

Which was gone. My mother makes a big pot of coffee every morning, and then cleans it up before she goes to work or leaves the house. She doesn't understand that I don't care if coffee is stale. I just needed the caffeine.

I stared at the empty carafe.

I stared at my cousin.

"Looking for this?" He waved a styrofoam cup of donut shop coffee at me.

I nodded.

"It's for you." He asked, "Do you need some food?"

I shrugged. Probably. Couldn't actually open my mouth to speak. I needed the coffee before I could have my coffee.

Adam handed me the cup. I peeled off the lid and chugged. Fortunately it had already cooled or else I would have been screaming and in more pain.

While I drank, Adam made me a peanut butter and jelly sandwich, wrapped it in a paper towel, nodded his head at the door and said, "Come on."

The light of day was death ray bright. I squinted and stumbled on the front steps.

"Man, you're hurting," Adam said. "Didn't you drink any water before bed? Dehydration's a bitch."

I didn't bother to answer. Coffee in right hand. Left foot. Right foot. Eyes narrow slits barely open to avoid banging into trees and cars.

I finished the coffee and threw the empty cup into one of the neighbors' trashcans.

Adam handed me the sandwich. I chewed as we walked. It tasted like peanut butter-flavored caulk. I wanted more coffee. I barely had enough saliva to swallow.

I briefly imagined myself dying in the street from a bolus of PB&J wedged in my esophagus, too deep for a Heimlich rescue or even one of those tracheotomies where they cut a hole in your throat and stick in a stripped-out ball point pen.

I blinked. My brain seemed to be coming back online.

• • •

By the time we got to Spruce Street I was nearly functional. I looked down at the scenic empty Ashby Bryson High parking lot and I sighed.

It was a beautiful spring day. A Sunday morning. And we were going to break into our old high school. Again. Whee!

"Fun time last night," Adam said.

I nodded. Shrugged. Still not a hundred percent. Maybe at thirty.

"Are you going to be okay with Rover?"

I gave my cousin a quizzical look.

"He stole your date," Adam said. "Remember?"

I shrugged and mumbled, "Susie wasn't really my date."

"Yeah, she was," Adam said.

"She asked me," I said.

"Yeah. That makes you her date. She was your date. And she dumped you for Rover."

I shrugged. And shrugged again. "So?"

Adam looked at me. "Doesn't that make you feel… something?"

"Sure. It was nice to be asked," I said. "For a little while I felt like I might be something special. I'm not."

"Yeah," Adam nodded. "You're acting like that a lot recently."

"What?" I stared at my cousin.

"Like you're not worth anything," he said.

I didn't feel like saying anything, so I started walking down the hill.

"Wait," Adam said.

I flipped him off.

He put a hand on my shoulder and stopped me. "Isaac."

I spun around, made a fist and punched my cousin right in the face. My knuckles hit his nose with a crunch, and he went down like a sandbag dropped from a rafter.

"Holy shit!" I said. My eyes widened. "Adam, are you okay?"

He sat on the sidewalk with his nose in his hand, blood gushing.

"Doh, I'm dot okay," he said. "You bwoke my dose. Ow! Add fudckin hurds."

Shit, I thought.

"Shit," I said. I handed Adam the paper towel from my sandwich. "What the hell do we do?"

"I fuckin bweed for a while," Adam said. He lay back on the sidewalk, pressing the paper towel up into his nose.

I stood for a while. I stared down at him. I pulled out my phone, stared at it. Thought about calling for help, but who would I call and what would I say? His parents? My parents? An ambulance? Adam wasn't screaming with pain. He was just bleeding. Then I sat down next to him.

"I'm sorry," I said.

"Dodt apowogize," he mumbled. "Fukin jerk."

"I thought you were supposed to be a black belt. Get out the way and all that shit."

"I tot you were by frend," he said.

"I am."

"So, wha da fuk?"

I shook my head. He was right. What the fuck? Because Adam was asking me about Susie, I hit him?

I started to feel sorry for myself, but then realized that was pretty fucking selfish considering that I'd just socked my cousin in the face.

"I guess I am a little pissed off," I said.

"You tink?" he said.

"But I can't blame Rover," I said. "I mean, as far as I know, Rover's never had a date in his life. And to catch the fancy of Susie

Wardle on merit? I mean, that's pretty fucking cool for him."

"I wasn't dalking bout Rover," Adam said. "I was dalking do you."

"I know. I know. I knew last night that Susie didn't care about me, but I figured that if she liked Rover…" I trailed off. Thought about my friends. My fantasies. My dreams. What the fuck were they?

"Real doe-ble," Adam said. He still sounded like he was talking through a tube.

"What?"

"Doble. Like a king."

"Everybody's got something," I told him. "You've got Helen, and you've got your Aikido."

"Dot so it's youfful," Adam mumbled.

"And you've got straight As. Charlie's the nicest guy on the planet, and he's black and he's got great grades. Jesús is Hispanic and poor, and he's got great grades. And he can draw like Leonardo Da Vinci or Picasso. Man he can draw. Sean's got money, he's Asian, good looking, and he's got great grades."

"Dis is still all about cowedge?" Adam said. "You're a great guy and you've got good grades too." His nose was clearing a bit. Maybe I didn't break it. "Cowedge doesn' madder."

"It matters," I said. "And I've got nothing extra. I'm just an average or above average white male nobody. Doctor Bob was right. Everybody else is going somewhere. I'm just going to Fectville."

"So, you're just a loser?" Adam said. He sat up and blew his nose like a cowboy, and red snot spewed on the green grass. "No need to fight with Rover about Susie. Right? You're a loser, so he deserves her more than you do."

I shrugged. "Something like that."

"Then why the fuk did you hit be?"

"Because," I shouted, "fucking nobody fucking likes fucking being fucking reminded that they're a fucking loser!"

My shout echoed around the neighborhood. Fortunately it was still early enough in the spring that nobody was outside having a lawn party.

I lay back on the sidewalk next to my cousin and stared up at the clouds going by. They were white and fluffy against a background of pure blue.

After a while, Adam stood up, wiped his glasses on his tee shirt, spat some more blood onto the grass and said, "Leds go. Rover could pwababby still use some heb."

I laughed.

"Wad?" Adam said.

"You look like a raccoon clown," I said. "You've got two black eyes and a big red nose."

"Fug you," my cousin said. "Next time I'm going to throw you across the room."

"Black belt my ass," I said. "I am sorry."

He shrugged. "I'm a fugin' bwak bewt. I wud suppod do duck or dodge or do someding. Leds go."

I laughed, and followed.

• • •

The gym's doors were open, and the musical bleachers were playing some kind of New Orleans big band number. Fortunately, my hangover had faded with the coffee, peanut butter, ibu, and violence.

All my friends were there, laughing and dancing, like the party hadn't stopped, just taken a twelve-hour break.

The ceiling still looked like a dimmed Northern Lights, and while everyone asked Adam what had happened (he told them I'd punched him, but it wasn't a big deal), I went to the center circle, and lay back on the floor, and stared up at the swirling green and gray sky.

Rover's projections were harder to see in the daylight, but they were still cool. I really couldn't blame him for busting a move on Susie. She'd practically asked him for it. When they were smooching on her doorstep, I saw her actually lean into his kiss. She couldn't get away from me fast enough. No, that wasn't really true. Susie had been nice to me. Except we'd had no chemistry. But it seemed like she was drawn toward Rover, as weird as that sounded. Odds were it was a one-time thing, forgotten in her never-ending quest to be top girl in the school. And Rover's tech was magnificent.

I'd have helped with the cleanup, but I didn't feel like talking to anybody.

One by one, my friends came and joined me, lying down at center court, while the sound system played a sax version of "Iko Iko".

Adam even lifted Helen out of her chair and lay her between us.

"Are you ok?" Helen asked him. She shot me a look. "Isaac?"

"Yeah," Adam said. "Like I said, I accidentally walked into his fist. We're fine."

"Hey guy," Rover said, nudging my leg. "I didn't mean to steal your date."

I laughed. Rover flinched. "I'm not going to punch you."

"Thanks," he said. "I like her."

"Hey," I said. "If she likes you, and you like her, then go make some really smart and pretty babies."

"What?" Rover looked panicked.

We all laughed. He laughed too, but still looked nervous.

"It's too bad they're knocking this place down," Jesús said.

"Bullshit," Sean said. "This gym sucks. It's always sucked. When they knock it down, anything they put up will be better."

"Yeah," Charlie agreed, "but it looks pretty awesome right now."

"Sounds good too," Helen said. "Better than the old PA ever did."

"Rover, you're a freaking genius," I said.

"Yeah," Rover said, not really accepting the compliment. "But I'm not sure how the sound system would work if there were people sitting on the bleachers. Either they'd muffle it, or it would electrocute them."

"That's a problem," Adam said. (Except it sounded like, "Dads a probrum.")

"Can you really project anything up there on the ceiling?" I asked.

"Yeah, pretty much," Rover said. "As long as it's a high def image."

It was quiet in the gym. No hum of HVAC. All of us lying on the hardwood floor. No buzzing from the fluorescent lights.

All ideas start somewhere. They had to. Sometimes it's an apple falling on the head. Or the hand of god reaching out for Adam. Or a homemade computer in a garage. Or Helen dressed as Eve, giving Adam a piece of apple pie...

I closed my eyes, started to doze and dreamed of greatness.

Chapter 22

Warped

"As a cop, it would really help if I developed a sense of humor. Now shut the fuck up!"
– Officer James Johnson

Even though the gym's floor was bumpy and hard, we were all lying down and half asleep. Rover had programmed the bleachers to play some kind of mellow ambient music. Imagine fields of grass and birds, except with electronic chirps and trills. It had been a long night and a long winter and a long spring. We'd been battered and beaten and abused by the system. We were sick of high school, so lying down in mid-court on a lazy Sunday was a perfectly ironic respite from the cares of our first world woes.

If you're thinking that it was too good be true, you're absolutely right.

I was dreaming of world-shaking ideas, just on the cusp of something absolutely brilliant, when a loud voice barked, "NOBODY FUCKING MOVE!"

Do they really expect that to work?

Black men, young and old know the terror of that shout.

Try it on yourself for a moment. Imagine that you're in the middle of folding laundry or something equally mundane and someone shouts, "NOBODY FUCKING MOVE!" You'll lose your socks.

Helen screamed. Jesús screamed.

Charlie, Sean and I sat up like somebody lit matches between our toes.

Adam did a backwards Aikido roll and came up onto his feet in a martial arts ready stance.

Rover flinched, didn't get up, and pressed a button on his hand computer. A loud techno-dance track began blaring from the bleachers while his projection lights suddenly became disco laser strobes.

The two Groston cops who had sauntered into the gym while we were all asleep went into panic mode.

Charlie's Uncle James spun around, wondering what was going on, drew his weapon just in case.

His partner, a rookie named Delbert LeRoi Wang, freaked out, drew his gun and began firing rounds into the bleachers.

BLAM! BLAM BLAMBLAM! It was loud.

Without thinking, Adam stepped up behind Officer Wang, grabbed the gun, twisted, disarmed the cop, and threw the weapon across the room.

"Ow-ow-ow!" Adam yelped. His hand had been burned by the gun's hot barrel.

Officer Wang grabbed Adam and tried to bring him under control.

Adam spun out of the cop's grip, reversed the hold, feinted a punch to the cop's face, and then brought the rookie to the ground in a wrist and elbow lock.

"UNCLE JAMES, UNCLE JAMES," Charlie was yelling. "IT'S US. DON'T SHOOT! WE'RE UNARMED."

The strobe caught the action in mid-flow. Charlie's uncle locked and loaded. Wang on the ground. Adam standing above him, pinning the young cop with one hand. Sean and Jesús backing away. Helen crawling towards Adam. Charlie's hands to his head. I was getting ready to run straight at Charlie's uncle to distract him from firing.

"TURN THAT FUCKING MUSIC OFF!" Uncle James said.

Rover hit a button and the room fell silent. The lights still twitched. Then he killed the strobes and brought up the room's fluorescents.

Gun still trained at Adam, Uncle James shouted, "Adam! Let him go! NOW!"

Adam stared at Charlie's uncle. Nodded. He pushed Officer Wang away as he let go and backed off quickly out of arm's reach.

"HANDS UP!" Charlie's uncle kept the gun trained on Adam.

Adam raised his hands.

"Wang? You okay?" Uncle James said. "Wang!"

Now, to be clear, until this point we didn't know that the other cop's name was Delbert LeRoi Wang.[31]

"Wang?" Charlie's Uncle shouted. "Get your head in the game Wang!"

Rover snickered.

"I lost my gun," Wang said.

Sean snickered. So did Jesús and I.

"Wang, where is your weapon?" Charlie's Uncle said. His voice was 100% cop. Not a glimmer of the nice guy we knew. The kindly chauffeur who had driven us to naught-prom the night before? Gone.

"Where is my piece?" Officer Wang said. He started moving toward Adam and I. "Where the fuck did you throw my piece?"

With one hand, Adam and I pointed in the direction it had gone. With the other hand, we covered our mouths. We were both suppressing grins and trying not to laugh.

Officer Wang backed away, moved in the direction we'd indicated, while keeping his eyes on us.

Which is when he tripped over Helen's wheelchair, fell on his ass and yelled, "Jimmy, they got me!"

---

[31] Yes, that really was the cop's name. I know that it's completely politically incorrect to make fun of someone because of their name, but... Come on! At least he wasn't a white cop shooting at black kids. Right? Ok forget it. It was the morning after an excellent party and we were all still a little high.

Charlie's Uncle sighed, shook his head, holstered his gun and said, "Holy shit, Wang, you fucked this one up."

That was it. We all broke up laughing.

• • •

Here's a piece of obvious advice: avoid pissing off a police officer before he restrains you. After he found his gun in a far corner of the gym, Officer Wang lined us all up sitting down in the middle of the court with our hands on our heads. One by one he went down the row. The whip ties he used bit into our wrists like thin bear traps. He even cuffed Helen.

Charlie's Uncle James watched, letting his humiliated partner vent, but making sure he didn't lose his shit and go too far.

By then, things were a bit less stressful but a lot less funny.

There was a series of moments when Wang finally realized that Helen was disabled, and couldn't get into her chair without assistance. He reached out to help her, but she hissed, "You touch me and I'm going to say you copped a feel."

Wang froze. He cut the whip tie around her hands, let Helen crawl into her chair, and recuffed her. Then he realized that she needed to use her hands to push her chair. So he cut the new tie, and then whip tied her legs to the chair's footrests. Satisfied, he stepped back. Helen flipped him the bird, and he looked like he wanted to hit her.

I could see Adam's blood pressure rising and he started to tense.

"Let it go," I whispered to my cousin. "It's okay."

Adam nodded, but kept his eyes on the rookie.

"So, what the fuck are you doing here?" Uncle James finally said. "We nearly killed you, you little fuckers!"

"We didn't break anything," Helen said.

"We're cleaning up!" Rover said.

"What are you doing here?" Charlie asked.

"The department got a tip about a break in," said Uncle James. "Someone had to respond. I'm just glad I caught the call."

"You're trespassing on town property," Wang said. "There are signs of illegal entry. Vandalism. Defacing public property with graffiti. Resisting arrest. Assaulting an officer."

"What graffiti?" Sean said.

"We're cleaning up!" Rover repeated.

"You started shooting at us!" I said. "We're kids!"

Charlie's Uncle James raised his hand.

Everyone got quiet.

"Yeah," Uncle James said. "The gunfire is a real problem. If rounds hadn't been fired, we could have gotten away with just giving you idiots a warning. But the situation has escalated into something more serious. We're going to have to file a weapon discharge report."

Officer Wang's face paled. "I thought I saw…"

"Shut the fuck up, Del," Charlie's uncle said. "If we write this up the way it really happened, you're screwed."

"Yeah," Sean said. "First you started shooting at a bunch of unarmed high school kids and then one of them took away your rod, Wang."

We snorted.

Wang kicked Sean who yelled, "OW!"

Uncle James flinched and looked like he wanted to reprimand his partner, but he didn't.

"Don't fucking say another word," Wang hissed. "Just because you're Chinese doesn't give you the right to make fun of me. Got it?"

Sean nodded.

"We're not going to say anything," Helen said. "To anyone. About anything."

"Or maybe we'll say whatever you need us to say," Jesús offered.

"They're tearing down this building this summer," I said. "Nobody's going to be looking for bullet holes in the walls."

"Uncle James," Charlie said. "We'll keep our mouths shut."

"The truth could look really really bad," Rover said.

"We could go to the firing range," Wang said. "Shoot a bunch of rounds. Lose track of how many we fired."

Uncle James was nodding. "That could work…"

We were in the middle of concocting a pretty plausible series of explanations. It all could have been fine.

Yes, we'd been busted for trespassing, but that was a misdemeanor and our ace attorney Bob Billings could probably get the charges dropped since the doors to the gym were clearly broken before we…

Then a loud evil voice said, "No. No fucking way are they getting away with it this time."

We looked up and saw Butch Batten walking across the gym with his phone up, obviously recording the whole conspiracy scene. Maybe he was even broadcasting it live.

We hadn't seen Butch in months. After he'd been released from the hospital, he'd been in rehab. Even though there were rumors that he'd been seen lurking at FRHS, he hadn't officially gone back to school yet.

Butch didn't look the same. Old Butch had been a small grizzly bear with an attitude. New Butch looked like an overweight gorilla with a speech disorder. He was unshaven. He lurched like he had a hard time keeping his balance. And he slurred a little. Brain damage? Shit.

"Yeah," Butch said. "I'm live streaming this whole thing. It's already out there on the Internet. You fucking losers. I saw you breaking in here. I called the cops. You're supposed to be the good kids. You're supposed to be the smart kids. You're the multicultural wondergang with a disabled girl thrown in for even more fucking diversity! You're a bunch of sneaks and cheats. You think you can get away with anything. Bullshit. You fucked up my life. Now I'm fucking up yours. Nothin' you can do but go to fucking jail."

Charlie's uncle tried to reason. "Son, can you turn off the camera, please."

"No fucking way you loser cop," Butch said. "I know Fat Charlie's your nephew. Nepotism. Collusion. Conspiracy."

"Didn't know you knew so many big words, Butch," I said.

"Listen, Butch, I want to apologize to you," Adam said. "I've been thinking about it a lot. I know I hurt you. I said I didn't do it on purpose, but I did. And I'm sorry. I'm sorry."

Everybody was very quiet.

For a moment, Butch reached back, like he was going to throw the phone at Adam's head. Then he stopped, grinned. "Not this time, Adam. Fuck you. You don't get out of this. Fuck you all. You're busted."

"Fuck you, too, Butch," Helen said. "Fuck you too."

Butch just grinned at her, and backed out of the gym.

And the rest of us? We all went to jail.

• • •

The Groston town jail is small. Just three cells. There was a drunk in one. Helen got her own private room, and the rest of us were in the other.

The walls were concrete covered in thick layers of grey paint. The stainless steel toilet squatted like a shiny throne in the middle of the room. There were bars on the door, just like in the movies, and there were two cameras on the wall outside the cell with red lights. A suicide watch, they told us. There were two stainless steel shelves for beds.

We sat down on the metal bunks and said nothing. Admitted nothing.

Except for Adam, who held an ice pack to his face. He squatted at the wall next to Helen's cell, and whispered to her all afternoon.

I don't know what anybody else was thinking, but I thought that Butch had done a pretty good job stitching us up.

He had a point, too. No, we weren't rich like the kids in Fectville, but we acted like we were entitled to anything and everything. Why? Because we were smart? Because we paid attention in class and did most of our homework? Because we had decent parents and good friends? Because when we did drugs or drank we didn't get caught? Did that give us the right to break into the old school and do whatever we wanted? Clearly not.

On the other hand, fuck that. The school building was empty. The gym was going to be torn down. What use was it doing anyone? What harm did we do to it?

Yeah, society has rules. Are all of them good rules? Why protect an old building slated for demolition? And what did the building have to fear from a bunch of high school students? We didn't have explosives. (Well, Rover probably could have made us some, but that wasn't our thing.)

291

We weren't even doing graffiti. It was just pretty lights on the ceiling.

And if we had really done graffiti, damn it would be epic.

I had a lot of time, sitting there on that hard ass stainless steel shelf, trying not to think about the fact that I needed to take a dump.

No way were any of us going to sit on that disgusting toilet, bare assed in the middle of the cell with a video camera recording our every movement through the bars.

Even though it was Sunday, Bob Billings had us out before dinner, which at my house at least was completely silent.

I went to bed, and wondered how many of the Fectville Rules were going to crash down on us on Monday morning.

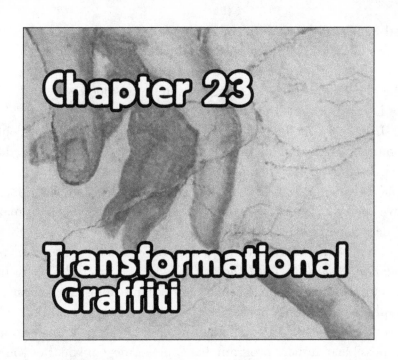

Chapter 23

Transformational Graffiti

"When I was a kid, I laughed my ass off at random videos online. Now that I'm in college, I try to find my humor in literature. It's not easy. I've learned that the things one generation finds amusing often sour within decades. Freud wrote a book about 'Jokes and their Relationship to the Unconscious.' In the book, he tries to tell a few jokes. They're not funny. Not at all. Sigmund Freud really can't tell a joke."
– My sister Ellen

My parents took away everything. They grounded me forever. No car privileges. No phone calls. They confiscated my laptop. When I had homework, they gave it back, but made me work downstairs in the kitchen. They even took my phone.

And they made me go into therapy.

I know I mentioned this before, but I was only seventeen. My birthday is in September. All my friends were eighteen already. Jesús and Sean's birthdays were in December, and are only a few days apart. Charlie's birthday was in January. Rover's eighteenth was some time last summer. Adam's was last month.[32] I don't remember when Helen's birthday was, but I'm sure Adam does.

Legally, almost all my friends were adults.

Legally, I was still a child. If they wanted to, my parents could commit me to a mental institution. Which they sort of threatened to do if I didn't go into therapy.

Can you and I agree that I clearly was not mentally ill? I might have been a little fucked up, but I wasn't psycho or schizoid or manic, depressive or even ADHD.

I realize that there's an entire thick book called the *Diagnostic and Statistical Manual of Mental Disorders*, also known as *The DSM*. It's the shrink's handbook, a huge catalog of human mental illness from agoraphobia to xenophobia and every gradient in between. Probably, if you comb *The DSM*, you'll identify a mental illness and appropriate possible treatment program that could fit me – or you. But you're not crazy, right?

Okay, so maybe you are nuts. Maybe not. I don't know you. This isn't about you.

Now that I'm thinking about this, writing to you as if I'm in a conversation with you right now might be a little bit doo-wacky.

This might not be the world's finest literary conceit, but is it institutionalization-worthy insanity? Nah.

My parents however were adamant.

The three of us were having a "family meeting" in the kitchen.

"Isaac, we're worried about you," Mom, the shrink said. "You've had a rough year. Everything was going so well, but now it seems as if every week there's something new and troubling…"

"Son," Dad interrupted her, "if you don't see Doctor Dave, we're going to check you in to Routledge."

I stared at my dad in disbelief.

Routledge is the local loony bin. It's a 100-year-old institution located on a beautiful campus on a hill in Fectville, overlooking

---

[32] He'd been grounded, so we didn't really celebrate.

a scenic bend in the Breakneck River. It's the place that kids get "checked into" when they overdose, become bulimic, or start cutting themselves.

I looked at my mom. My eyes were a cross of disbelief and sad puppy.

"You didn't have to go that far," she said to Dad.

"We agreed," he reminded her. "This isn't just me." He waved his finger back and forth between himself and my mom. "We're united on this."

Then he turned to me. "Either you get help the easy way, or the hard way. Mental illness isn't a joke."

"I revivah fa fafaser," I spoke the gibberish with a completely straight face. "Flumbagee fa. Bliga ferstaf."

They stared at me like I'd lost it. I smiled. I shrugged. "Flingo."

"Mental illness is not a joke." Dad repeated it in that firm I'm-not-fucking-with-you-but-you're-going-to-die-if-you-don't-stop-smoking-drinking-eating-cheeseburgers-and-snorting-crystal-meth physician's voice. "I've seen the consequences too often."

I was smart enough not to roll my eyes, but I did look out the window above the kitchen sink. It was a beautiful late spring afternoon. Ordinarily by then I'd be downstairs in Rover's basement shooting up zombies with my friends or herding gigantic soccer balls with my souped up video game car and trying to rank up. My lips were a tight frown.

Part of me thought, you know, maybe checking into Routledge would be interesting. They'd probably give me some primo drugs, and I'd have a legitimate excuse to blow off finals. I could take it easy, go along, and make some really strange new friends.

Part of me thought about the whole social stigma of checking into Routledge. My friends wouldn't care, of course. Once I told them the whole story they'd be fine. But everybody else in school? They'd label me a nutjob. Which wouldn't matter if I was going away to a college where nobody knew me, but since it looked like Fectville State was likely to be my alma mater, I'd have to deal with these cretins for another four years.

Part of me was in despair that my parents really thought I was so fucked up that they needed to pull this shit.

I briefly wished that my sister Ellen was around so I could talk with her. Usually, Ellen and I don't get along, hoever since she's gone off to college she's become more human and every so often I can get an almost honest answer from her. If Ellen agreed with our folks and thought I'd gone over the deep end, then I'd have to seriously consider it. But she'd already gone back to school.

Physical wounds are easy to self-diagnose. When you get stung by a bee, break an arm or lose an eye, it's pretty obvious that something's wrong.

When you lose your mind, how can you tell? Maybe all the weed had driven me insane. Or maybe I was just naturally crazy. Whacko?

I stared at the kitchen table. Such a familiar and ordinary piece of furniture. The table was round, made of some kind of brown hardwood. I'd grown up eating breakfast, lunch and dinner on it. Cereal. Eggs. Pancakes dad made. Canned soup. Mac and cheese. Cheeseburgers. Homemade ice cream sundaes. Pretty much every meal except formal dinners and times that we'd gone out. I'd finger painted and done homework there. I'd barfed on that table.

Soon, I'd be graduating and leaving the round table forever. Not soon enough though. Fectville State didn't have dorms, so I'd probably still live at home. For another four years. If I'd gotten into a better school, I'd be out of Groston in a second. Yeah, I'd be gone, Juan. Sure, I'd probably be back for Thanksgiving and summer vacations, but it wouldn't be the same.

"Fine," I said, softly. "I'll go to the shrink."

My parents were still arguing. They didn't hear me at first. It took a few seconds for it to register and them to stop dealing with their own issues and refocus on mine.

"What?" Mom said.

"What did you say?" Dad underscored.

"I said, fine. I'll go."

Mom smiled. "I am so relieved." She had been pushing me to go into therapy since third grade, when I'd complained that I felt like an outsider, because they made me sit down during the "teach the kids how to dance" enrichment assembly. Win for Mom.

"When does it start?" I asked, resigned.

"Tomorrow morning," Dad said. "You already have an appointment."

"You already made…?" I started to get really angry.

Dad looked triumphant, too.

I stuffed my reaction down. I wasn't going to give them the satisfaction. "If I'm not going to school, I'm going to need a signed permission note, and you'll have to fax it over, because I'm supposed to have a history quiz tomorrow morning."

Dad nodded. "I'm proud of you."

"Really? You're proud that I'm going to see a shrink? You really have a skewed sense of my accomplishments."

"Look," Dad said, "I didn't…"

I got up and left the table. Mic drop.

• • •

Doctor Dave's office looked like the ultra neat den of a middle-class family with too many children and a live-in maid – lots of stuff, but nothing out of place. There was a playpen, a box of blocks, a unit of three cubbies labeled with "Toys for girls" and "Toys for Boys" and "Toys for You." There were three bookcases. One had board games on the bottom two shelves, then board books, picture books, chapter books and a selection of young adult fiction. Another was full of various highbrow literature. Toni Morrison, Paulo Coelho, Harlan Ellison, Faulkner, Ayn Rand, Sylvia Plath, and the James Taylor songbook. The third held medical books. There was a brown faux leather Freud couch (of course), two overstuffed chairs upholstered with stain-resistant tree bark brown colored fabric. There was a small blue plastic kiddie table and two matching blue plastic kiddie chairs, a sad looking grey cloth love seat, and a skinny prefab desk with a laptop on it and a low-budget office chair tucked under. A sign on the desk read, "There is no try. Only do!"[33] There were two windows with slatted shades that were down, and a sound machine making ambient noise. There was a mini basketball hoop over the trashcan, and another Nerf hoop on the back of the door.

---

[33] I had a childish impulse to add another "do!" to the sign.

Doctor Dave sat in one of the overstuffed chairs. I sat in the other. It was comfy.

We knew about Doctor Dave because Ellen had seen him one summer when she'd briefly developed an eating disorder. She'd taken to bringing a large purse to the kitchen or dinner table and hiding food in it. When Mom smelled the rotting fish in Ellen's room three days after we'd had baked salmon for dinner, they'd gotten the referral.

Dr. David Schwartz was an adolescent social psychologist specializing in "infant through adolescent mental discomfort." (I'd read his brochure while we were waiting.) He'd gotten his Ph.D. at Rutgers and had worked in New York's famous Bellevue youth psycho ward. "For the past twenty years, Doctor Dave has taken pleasure in easing the suffering and pain of more than 4,000 young people and families."

I didn't know if 200 patients a year was a good or bad statistic.

Mom and Dad had both taken the morning off and we all drove together like a real family to his office, which was on the second floor of a once-flooded building in downtown Groston. In the small waiting room, my parents filled out the paperwork, insurance stuff and waivers.

Then we'd waited about fifteen minutes until another door opened and a small girl and her father came out. The little girl was crying. Her dad looked angry. They left and shut the door behind them.

Five minutes later, in came Doctor Dave.

I'd never met him before. His sessions with Ellen had been private.

Doctor Dave was in his late fifties with thin hair and a wannabe moustache. He wore blue slacks, brown loafers with no socks, and a blue tee shirt. Neutral colors with no sense of style or flair. He looked like he needed a cardigan or one of those jackets with patches on the elbows.

He shook my parents' hands, told them it was good to see them again, and suggested that they come back in fifty-five minutes.

Dad nodded and immediately headed for the exit. Mom looked

at me and said, "Are you going to be all right?"

"He'll be fine," Doctor Dave said. He had a soft voice.

"Yeah," I agreed. "I'll be fine." I tried to echo his voice.

Mom gave me a hug. Dad took her hand and they left.

"All right, listen," Doctor Dave said. "I've gotta go to the can. Why don't you go in and take a seat?"

He opened another door to a small bathroom, and closed it behind him.

For a moment I considered ditching. Why not, right? Why should I stay? Because my parents had paid for it? Because I was already there? Because maybe I was nuts? Nah. I wouldn't ditch because maybe it was expected that I'd ditch. Of course I could reverse psyche him out by doing the unexpected but for a different reason...

The problem with seeing a shrink is that no matter how sane you are, once you open the oyster shell of your brain and peek inside you wonder if you've got a pearl in there or just a bunch of gooey salty muck.

That's when I went in and sat in one of the overstuffed chairs, trying not to think about all the snot and tears that had been shed there.

A few minutes later Doctor Dave came in. His hands looked damp, like they hadn't been fully dried after he'd washed.

He sat in the other overstuffed chair.

Then we stared at each other. For a while.

Was this that psychiatrist game of, "Who's going to talk first?"

"Look, I'm not crazy," I said. "My parents made me come. Can we get this over with?"

He nodded. "We're here for an hour."

Tick.

"Actually, fifty minutes," I said, looking at a clock on one of the bookcases.

He shrugged. "I'm here for you, not for your parents."

"But they're paying you."

He shrugged. "Mostly the insurance company is paying me."

I looked around the room. Chutes and Ladders. Candy Land. The Game of Life. "Right."

Tock.

"What's troubling you?" he said.

"That my parents think I'm crazy," I said without hesitation.

"Is that all?"

I scanned up the bookshelves. The Carrot Seed. Green Eggs and Ham. The Phantom Toll Booth. Harry Potter.

"Pretty much," I nodded. "I really don't want to be here."

"I'm getting paid," he said. "Think of me as an expert. Whatever we discuss is private between us."

"Unless it's incriminating," I said.

"Unless you're planning self-harm or a crime of violence, I really don't care," he said. "Even if you admit to a crime, I'm bound not to testify. But if you're planning to hurt someone or yourself, that's where I draw my own line."

"I'm not."

"Good."

We sat some more.

I nodded my chin at his diploma on the wall. "Did you like college?"

He shrugged. "Mostly. I was in a fraternity. It wasn't like Animal House, but it had its moments. What college are you going to?"

Now it begins, I thought.

• • •

My parents were waiting when I opened the door into the waiting room. Appropriate. I kind of wished that there had been another exit from Doctor Dave's Den so I could have sneaked around and surprised them.

Dad and Mom jumped to their feet.

"Shut the door, would you?" came Doctor Dave's voice.

I closed his door.

"He's not going to talk to us?" Dad asked.

"Nope," I said, cheerfully. "It's private."

"How'd it go?" Mom said.

Despite their threat of institutionalized commitment, my parents really aren't that bad. We've been together my whole life, which may seem obvious, but lots of kids don't have that. They claim that I can talk to them about anything, and I do talk to my parents about most things. But not sex or drugs or shit like that.

"It's private," I repeated.

Dad squinted at me, probably wondering if I was being what he sometimes called, "a sneaky little shit."

As we walked down to the car, I said, "Doctor Dave said that you can stop punishing me."

Dad stopped in his tracks. "I'm going back to talk with him."

"He won't tell you anything," Mom said. "Remember we had the same issue when Ellen saw him."

"It's confidential," I said. "Patient Doctor Privilege."

"Did he really say that?" Dad asked.

"Do you trust me?" I asked Dad.

"No," he said. "That's why we're taking you to see Doctor Dave."

"Hmmm." I nodded, like Dad had said something psychologically profound.

Then I smiled.

Yes, I was being a little shit.

"It's all right," Mom said. She put her hand on Dad's arm to calm him down.

"We'll think about it," she told me. "We'll let you know tonight."

"Come straight home after school," Dad hissed.

It was just after eleven. They drove me to Fectville Regional High School in silence.

• • •

For once I didn't have detention.[34] I got most of my homework done on the bus home. Adam sat next to me, asked, "How did the shrink thing go?" After I told him that I didn't want to talk about it, he'd cracked his books and worked too. It seemed wrong to be seniors doing so much homework so late in the year, but both of us

---

[34] I'm sure that Dr. Bob would have assigned us detention for the rest of our lives, but somehow the word of our arrest never reached the administration at FRHS. Thanks Uncle James!

were in the same boat. Our futures weren't decided. Not yet.[35]

Per our earlier agreement, when I got home, I turned on my inactive cell phone and texted Mom that I was home. There were about ten million unread messages and texts, but I ignored them. Which really isn't easy. But it's easier than getting caught. I know that Dad checks the phone every night to see if I've done anything with it.

I got Oreos and milk from the fridge, and finished the rest of my homework at the round kitchen table.

Then I went upstairs to my room, closed the door, lay on the bed, and stared at the dripped stucco ceiling.

Our house was built in the late sixties and has a real old TV sitcom feel to it. My ceiling in particular is a very random entity with craters and valleys and sharp peaks like a lunar landscape viewed from orbit.

I've looked at it forever, trying to find meaning where there is none.

Which was when I got an idea. A fucking great idea.

The Idea.

I remembered Rover's projections on the ceiling of the Ashby Bryson gym. I remembered Officer Wang accusing us of defacing public property. I remembered reading a blog about graffiti artists and the transitory value of disposable art.

And I was suddenly inspired. I had a vision of something pretty amazing.

Now, if only my parents would let me free from my home prison, I thought I knew how to make it real.

---

[35] No, I'm not going to tell you what Doctor Dave and I discussed. It really is private. Suffice it to say that he honestly agreed that I'm not crazy. He did say that Ritalin, Adderall and Prozac could be helpful. I told him that I didn't want more drugs.

Chapter 24

Breakout

"I'm embarrassed to admit that I really enjoy silly kid comedies like 'Home Alone,' where Macaulay Culkin gets violently inventive on the robbers. The blend of slapstick and Rube Goldberg leaves me laughing and cheering at the same time."
– Paul Davis, my uncle

Helen was the one who finally broke us out of solitary home confinement. She did it by playing the cripple card.

It was the fifth or sixth night of our post-arrest imprisonment. I was studying for Mrs. Hendry's AP World History final. All the kids in the Fectville half of the AP class were done. Their teacher, Mr. Jackson said that the Advance Placement test we'd all taken was good enough for him to count as the final exam. He even excused the Fecters from attending his class, as long as they signed into the library for "study hall." Mr. Jackson had already started his summer vacation.

Mrs. Hendry, however, insisted that the AP exam didn't cover the depth and complexity of everything she'd taught us. This was true. She was an awesome teacher. We all learned a lot. Knowledge was her mission, not grades. She had a point, but as usual, it meant that us kids from Groston were getting screwed.

I was deeply immersed in reviewing the run-up to World War II, going through my notes and the textbook, when Mom knocked on my bedroom door.

"Hon, you have a phone call."

"Really?" I said. "I thought my phone was confiscated, turned off, and stored in a Faraday cage."

Mom ignored that. She opened my door a crack and peeked her head into my room. "It's Helen Beagle. She's calling on the old landline. I almost didn't answer it because the only people who call on that line are telemarketers and pollsters. Helen sounded a little distressed. Is everything okay with her?"

My parents love Helen. Everybody's parents love Helen. She's small and pretty and cute and smart and polite. She's an A Student in a wheelchair. They've never seen her tripping on hallucinogenic mushrooms or clearing a roomful of zombies.

"I wouldn't know if she's okay, Mom. All I know is that her house was destroyed in the flood and she's been living in an extended stay hotel in Fectville," I said, laying it on thick. "I'm not allowed to have communications with any of my friends outside of school. We're allowed to sit together on the bus. And in school, they make us sit at different tables during lunch. Other than that, we're all too busy cramming and taking finals."

Mom waited a beat, ignored the jibes, and said, "Helen's on the phone. You can take it in the kitchen."

"So, I have your permission?" I asked.

"Yes," she snapped, turned, and went downstairs.

I sighed melodramatically, closed my notebook inside my textbook, and slowly stomped down the stairs to the kitchen, where the heavy antique telephone receiver lay sideways on the counter.

"Hello?" I said, as cheerfully as I could muster.

"Hey Izzy," Helen said. "Are you alone?"

I raised an eyebrow. "Not really." Mom was lurking in front of the stove, sautéing onions with an olivewood spoon she'd bought in Italy. She had an open can of tomatoes and half a bottle of red wine ready to make into sauce. It smelled good.

"All right," Helen said, "then we're going to keep talking in code until everybody's clear."

"What?" I was confused.

"Hold on. I'm conference calling everybody else in."

There was a click on the line and then Helen said. "Everybody there? Sound off."

"Here," said Sean.

"Me too," chimed Jesús.

"Yep," said Charlie.

"The Turks massacred the Armenians, starting in April of 1915," Rover said. "But they still won't admit it."

"I'm here for you, Helen," Adam said earnestly.

I rolled my eyes. Then there was a pause. I realized it was my turn.

"Oh, yeah." I grinned. "I'm here, Helen. What's up?"

"My parents are upstairs," she said. "I can't believe they go to bed this early. Anyway, they gave me permission to call someone for help with my AP World History exam. They didn't say I couldn't call everybody, so...Anyway, they're probably asleep by now, but if I suddenly start talking about the Battle of the Bulge, that means somebody came into the room."

"Helen, you don't need to lose any weight," Adam told her.

Charlie laughed. "True."

Even though it was a lame joke, we cracked up. It was really good to hear everybody's voice. It had been too long.

"I don't know about you guys," Helen said, "but I'm sick of this whole being grounded thing."

"Yes, that is correct," Rover said. "The South African government's imprisonment of Nelson Mandela just made him and his cause stronger."

We all processed Rover's remark for a second. Rover wasn't actually taking the AP World History Class, but a while ago he'd told us that he'd read the entire textbook just for fun. Who knew that he

305

was so quick with history, too? Damn that kid was smart.

"Thing is," Helen said, "we didn't deserve this. Right?"

"Right," Sean and Charlie said simultaneously.

"A lot of shit has gone down on us this year," she continued, "and us getting caught napping in the gym was probably the least offensive thing we did."

I was searching for some kind of a world history analogy to answer her, but by the time I came up with the British Intelligence service's use of a corpse to distract the Nazis from the real D-Day plans the conversation had already moved on.

"We need to stand up for ourselves," Helen said. "It's crazy to allow our parents to keep punishing us for something so insignificant. Next year we're all going to be gone. They won't have any say over what we do then. We're all legally adults. Why not exert our independence now?"

There was a chorus of cheers on the line. Except from me, since I still wasn't a legal adult.

"I'm in," said Sean. He always was first to agree.

"Me too," said Charlie.

"Reagan was ready to push the button," said Jesús.

"Declaration of war between the US and Grenada," Rover said, trying to top Jesús.

"Whatever you need, Helen," Adam said.

I kept quiet. Seventeen. Sometimes it seemed like I'd never reach eighteen.

"Not me. I'm almost up to that part of the book," I said, "but I'm not there yet."

"You're close enough," Charlie said. "The answer is all of the above."

"The Irish chafed under British rule for centuries," Rover told us. "Ultimately, however, enough time passed and their rebellion created the independent Republic of Ireland."

"Yeah, but Northern Ireland is still dominated by the Brits," I said, frustrated. I put my hand over the phone's mouthpiece. "Mom, listen, would you mind? It's hard enough to think without you monitoring my every word."

Mom smiled, nodded, put the lid over the pot, and turned the temperature down to low. "Give this a stir every so often with the wooden spoon. The pot is non-stick, and you'll scratch it if you use metal. And if you smell something burning, turn it down a little more and call for me."

I gave her the thumbs up as she picked up her wine glass and left the kitchen.

"All right," I told the gang. "She's gone. Listen, I've been doing a shit ton of thinking, and I have an idea for a big end of the year prank that's totally awesome. It will require all of us to work together. It's dangerous, but not in a lethal or maiming sense. More like another huge problem if we get caught again."

"Which we won't this time," said Charlie. "No matter what."

"Why are you bringing up civil disobedience when we're studying for World History?" Rover asked.

"Rover, are your parents even listening?" Helen asked.

Rover ignored her, and I went on.

"Because if I'm going to get busted for something, I want it to be something real and profound and magnificent, not something just plain stupid, like getting ratted out by Butch."

"The American Monument Men did save a lot of important art from destruction during the end of World Two," Jesús said, getting into the spirit. It was like he was reading my mind.

"'Who will make sure that the Statue of David is still standing or the Mona Lisa is still smiling?'" Sean quoted, sounding just like George Clooney. "'Who will protect her?'"

"Exactly!" I said. "It's just like that. A grand adventure against impossible odds. Even with an artistic twist."

"Can you explain the logistics supply chain for the Boer War?" Rover asked.

"Oh my god, Rover," Helen said. "Stop it. You're making my brain hurt!"

"I just want to know what the hell Izzz is talking about," Rover said.

"Me too," said Charlie and Adam together.

"Okay," I said, walking over to the kitchen door to make sure my mom wasn't eavesdropping. "Here's the plan…"

• • •

Listen, I know that I'm going to cheat right now, but if I tell you all the details of my plan, it will spoil the big ending.

In a movie or TV show, this would be that music-video-like montage scene, where the team of heroes builds some intricate contraption, or does massive amounts of research on the Internet in a matter of seconds, or masters a complex and lethal martial art move, or lays booby traps by rolling out spools of wire and digging trenches full of sharp punji sticks.

Suffice it to say that I explained the whole plan to my friends.

Rover thought for a moment and said that my audacious plan was possible. "If a bunch of PhDs in Chicago and New York can create an atomic weapon that will stop the war in Japan, this is the least we can do."

I'm not sure I was comfortable with his analogy, but we all agreed that we would all wrap up our homework and studying, and walk out (or in Helen's case roll out) of our houses at 10 p.m., and meet at the old gym to work out the real details and logistics.

Our priorities were clear.

1. Finish high school without failing.
2. Graduate and exit Groston with a bang.
3. Don't get arrested. Preferably never again.

"Are you sure about this?" Helen asked me. "We all know that you haven't been accepted to any other colleges besides Fectville State…"

"Not yet," Adam said, hopeful as always.

"Fuck it," I said. "It's my idea. I'm totally in. What about you guys?"

"I already said the answer to that one," Sean said. "By making the Western world dependent on our products and addicted to our synthetic opiods, the Chinese will rule the world!"

"The Spanish Armada," Jesús began. "Ummm… They lost, but this time maybe not."

"Kim Phiby totally was a Russian spy!" Rover added,

triumphantly.

"Helen, whatever you need," Adam said. "I'm with you."

"Get a room!" Jesús muttered.

"I agree," I said. "Jeez, Adam, take a stand for yourself."

"Yes, the US will come to the aid of its allies. Mom, leave me alone. I'm working!" Then Adam hissed, "I'm in."

"Oh," I said. I hadn't realized my Aunt Dot was eavesdropping on him. "Sorry."

"I'll need transportation," Helen said. "Jesús?"

"All right here goes," Jesús said. He covered the phone and shouted, "Mamí, necesito mi coche para llevar a Helen. Okay? Sí?" His voice got clearer. "I got ya, Helen"

"Then I'm in," she said.

"The allies met at Malta to crush Russia's hopes," Charlie said. "FDR put severe limits on Stalin's power."

"Aww, Man." Rover sounded disappointed he hadn't thought of that one.

"All right then," I said. "At the old gym, as soon as you can get there. See you guys soon. Bye."

We all said goodbye.

Mom walked into the kitchen and and lifted the lid on the pot. The smell of caramelized onions with tomatoes and wine, dried basil and oregano filled the kitchen. "Tonight what?"

"Tonight I'm breaking out," I told her. "I'm not a kid any more. If you want to take away my allowance, that's fine. I'll get a job. I'm going to finish my homework and studying now, but then I'm going to meet up with my friends. This is our last chance to spend time together before we all start to scatter. I'm not going to spend any more of my life locked in my room. If you don't like it, I'm sorry. If you want to kick me out, I'll find a place to crash. You and Dad raised me, and I think you did a pretty good job. But this is my life, and I have other things to do than stay inside and feel sorry for myself. My friends and I have plans. Oh, and I'm taking my cell phone, because I need to be able to be in touch with you, or so you can call me so you won't worry too much."

To my surprise, my mom listened to the whole speech. Then she nodded, but didn't say anything, except, "So, is Helen okay?"

"She's fine," I said. "It was a deception. She knew you wouldn't give me the phone if anyone else called."

Mom nodded again, and then added some already-cooked spicy Italian sausages to the sauce. "Dinner's going to be ready in about half an hour. Go finish your homework."

"Yeah," I said. "I'm going to do that. Because I want to, not because you're telling me to."

She laughed. I went upstairs.

At dinner, Mom told me to tell Dad what I'd told her.

It's one thing to take a heroic stand in the moment. It's another to try and repeat yourself. It came out abbreviated and fumbled.

"I'm breaking out," I said.

"You've got acne?" Dad said. "Let me see. Any really good pimples?"

"No!" I quickly said. When I went through puberty, my dad the doctor took great pleasure in popping some of my most monstrous zits. It was the creepiest and most disgusting thing a father could do, aside from actual physical or sexual abuse. "I'm going out tonight to hang out with my friends."

"Really?" Dad said. "You're not taking the car."

"I'm walking."

"If you get arrested, I'm not bailing you out."

"I have my Bar Mitzvah money."

"That's supposed to pay for college."

"Fectville State is cheap."

He nodded. Twirled some pasta on his fork.

"So?" I said.

Dad shrugged. "I'm not handcuffing you to the bed. You're almost an adult. Time to start acting like one."

I was confused. It's one thing to fight with your parents. It's another when they seem to back down and give in.

"I'm taking my cell phone back, too," I said.

"I don't know where it is," Dad said.

"I do," I said. Teenagers always know where their cell phones are.[36]

"It's in the drawer," Mom said, in case I didn't.

"Fine," I said.

I'd been expecting a fight, but the whole conversation was both disconcerting and somewhat anticlimactic.

At 10:10, Adam and I met and started walking through the dark suburban streets of Groston.

"Hey," he said. "All good?"

"Surprisingly so. You?"

He nodded. "Yeah. Me too. Mom and Paul told me not to make too much noise when I came in. They didn't even set a curfew. It was weird."

It was a warm night. The crickets were chirping.

And for a moment we were free.

---

[36] Unless we lose them. Which I've only done twice.

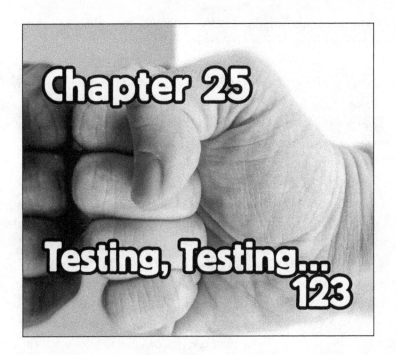

Chapter 25

Testing, Testing... 123

"Comedy specials on TV are such bullshit. You know why? Because they kill all the spontaneity. I mean you've got a cameraman and a sound guy and some director who's calling the shots. Real comedy is a guy with a microphone. Or a girl with a mic. And an audience and it's either make us laugh, or we're going to kill you. It's life or death. That's comedy."
— Robert "Bob" Billings, Attorney at Law

Final exams for high school seniors are usually forgone conclusions. The auto shop kids don't care. The art kids don't care. The kids that have gotten into the Ivy League colleges just have to pass, they didn't have to care.

And then there was us. We didn't want to care, but we had to.

I had to.

So far, I'd been rejected everywhere, except by Columbia, which put me on it's wait list. So far, the only college or university in the world that had officially "accepted" me was Fectville State. And they accepted everyone.

Nobody, except Doctor Dave, knew that I'd racked up a pile of rejections, though. I kept pretending that good news was just around the corner.

Every day, my mom asked if I'd heard. Every day I told her no. Then she gave me a cookie. Pavlovian.

But, in the back of my head I was percolating another idea, one that I hadn't told anyone about.

I wasn't going to Fectville State, ever.

After months of complacent depression, I was covertly planning a gap year.

The plan was to ace all my finals, retake the SATs and nail them, then travel and have some wild but academically correct adventures with Doctors without Borders or AmeriCorps or intern at a homeless shelter, whatever, and reapply to a bunch of schools that had rejected me because of my average junior year grades and less than top-notch test scores. Or apply to other schools that I hadn't the first time.

So what if I was a freshman a year older than everybody else. I wouldn't be "behind" I'd be "more experienced." All the freshman girls would be into me because I'd have a tan, a five o'clock shadow and stories of treating malaria in Borneo.

I was determined not to be that lame transfer student guy.[37]

Doctor Dave thought a gap year was a great idea. I wondered what my parents would think if they knew he was encouraging me.

Still, unlike all the Fecters who were blowing off finals, I both needed and wanted to kick butt and get the good grades that most of my friends usually achieved without even breaking a sweat.

Except I wasn't any smarter this year than I had been the year

---

[37] The guy who shows up three or four semesters in, doesn't know anybody, and never makes any friends. He eventually graduates in the middle of the class, becomes an office worker, steals staplers, and tries to go postal, but his gun jams, the cops wound him, and he's sent to Federal prison where his nickname is Mary Jane... I have no idea where that image came from, but I couldn't shake it.

before. I really wanted to be smarter. I worked hard, maybe as hard as I could. I'd read and reviewed all the chapters in my textbooks. I did all the assigned homework and extra credit. I'd stopped taking any medical marijuana a month ago, and even tried cutting back on the coffee, so I could sleep a bit better. That only lasted two days. For me, coffee is a necessity. Hi. My name is Isaac, and I'm a caffeine addict.

Mostly, I went above and beyond.

For English, I wrote draft after draft after draft of my research thesis on "What Makes Us Laugh?"

When I finished, I printed it out on high quality stationary stock and bound it in a leather cover. As I turned my paper in, Mrs. Maxim, one of my favorite teachers from Groston who had survived team teaching in Fectville, welled up in tears and thanked me.

"No no no," I told her. "You're not supposed to cry. The thesis is about comedy. You're supposed to laugh."

"I don't know what's in this," Mrs. Maxim said, hugging the thesis and laughing a little through the tears, "but it is the best looking paper I've seen in years."

I made my English Teacher cry.

And she hadn't read it yet. Hopefully it was good. Hopefully it was A++ material. I needed it.

Finally, all we had left was Mrs. Hendry's AP World History exam.

I had read the entire textbook. I had crammed the AP World History Test Book. And I'd watched a History Channel marathon called "The Sweep of Civilization."

I even made the world's most detailed crib sheet, shrinking down forty pages of time line notes to an almost microscopically detailed three by five card that I folded three times and stuck in my blue jeans watch pocket. I had created the tiniest guidebook to world history ever.

Yes, I knew that if I got caught with the cheat sheet, I'd fail and be expelled. Would that be any worse than going to Fectville State?

Honestly, that probably would be worse, but I wasn't thinking too clearly that morning. I'd been up all night, drinking a blend of iced coffee and my dad's diet cola and figuring out which forty pages of my two hundred pages of notes were the most important.[38]

Just having the cheat sheet in my pocket, even without using it, was enough to get me suspended.

And yet, simply having the thing in my secret pocket gave me such a feeling of comfort and relief. I had a lifeline, an extra life, the cheat codes for history!

I never got to sleep that night. Before going to school, I practiced at my desk in front of a mirror, surreptitiously wriggling the note card from my mini-pocket, opening to the proper decade, repalming it, and then raising my left hand to my forehead where I could peer up and read the tiny type. Then the "ah ha!" nod of realization (in case anyone was watching). Finally, while the answer was written on the test by the right hand, the left hand refolded the crib and surreptitiously reached around and slipped it back into the watch pocket. Calm, cool. Putting it away looked a little like I was scratching my balls, but I didn't really care.

You don't have to use it, I told myself as I walked toward the staircase. But if you get stuck, it's there...

Dishonest?

Yeah, it rubbed me the wrong way too.

Did I really want to have to cheat to get into a good college? What would that mean? Was it good gamesmanship, or was I never going to be good enough and base my whole life on lies?

Well, if all else failed, I could go into politics.

Adam met me at the staircase for the long and final walk to the final final.

Which was when Butch Batten decided to make his final play.

• • •

The "history department" in Fectville Regional High School consists of four classrooms on the second floor of the "old wing." It's the last unairconditioned section of the old part of the building and

---

[38] Yes, writing this now, I realize that I had probably had overdosed on caffeine, and actually could have used an anti-stimulant of some kind. Fortunately, I didn't have a stash of gummies.

as far away from the main office as possible. Supposedly, they were going to tear it down or rehab it over the summer. That doesn't really help those of us who were suffering through to the end of school. For the past three weeks, temperatures in the room had fluctuated from really hot to hot as hell. It was going to be hard to pay attention and be at our best for a history final on a day like today when the temperature hit eighty outside and the temperature inside would get close to ninety.

Adam and I were ambling along, trudging up the stairs, trying to get in the doors just before the bell rang, but not a moment sooner. Mrs. Hendry had a thing about tardiness. We had a thing about not being too early.

Butch Batten was lurking on the landing as we climbed to the top of the stairwell. "Hey, assholes," he said, cheerfully blocking the doorway to the hall.

"Fuck," I whispered.

Adam and I stopped still.

"Goin' somewhere?" Butch growled.

"History final," I said. "Excuse us, please."

"Oh, yeah." Butch grinned. "No problem. You want me to carry your books too?"

He didn't move.

The bell rang.

We were late.

We were alone.

"You don't want to do this," I told Butch.

"Really?" Butch said. "Yeah, I think I do want to do this. You guys fucked up my life." He pointed a thick finger at Adam. "You fucked up my life."

"He didn't fuck up your life," I said. As soon as I said it, I couldn't believe I'd even opened my mouth. Butch looked at me like I was insane. I kept going. "You did that yourself."

"What the fuck do you know about it?" Butch said. "You and your perfect little gang of perfect little assholes. Team Bum Fuckers, with your own private set of rules. You got everything lined up. For me, it's all wrecked. I'm the washed up high school football star stuck here forever. For you? A whole future planned out. Get away with anything. Get away with everything. Everything's gonna be swell."

Butch really didn't know me at all.

Adam stood still. And silent. I shifted nervously from foot to foot.

"It doesn't have to go this way, Butch," Adam said softly. "I really don't want to hurt you."

"That makes one of us," Butch said. Then he looked at me. "I hear that you guys really need to ace this test. Hendry takes ten points off just for being late, doesn't she? And then it's another one point per minute. Am I right?"

Adam didn't move. I nodded. Mrs. Hendry always said that being on time meant being early and being prepared.

Butch smiled at me. It was a surprisingly gentle smile, considering the fact that he was a gigantic muscle-bound idiot who was already getting a bit chubby because his football career was over and he'd stopped training.

"Well, you can both go then," he said. "In about fifteen more minutes." He looked at an imaginary watch on his wrist.

Then he pointed at me. "Or you can just leave him alone now. So far, you're only down about twelve points."

Butch was going to let me go? I wasn't sure I believed him. I looked at my cousin. Adam stood still.

"You're seriously thinkin' about taking off, aren't ya?" Butch said. "Some friend, huh? Some cousin. I guess it's all relative. Haha! Get it? He's just going to leave you here. This is how your family treats each other, huh?"

I felt the edge of caffeine wearing off and exhaustion hitting the soles of my feet. I felt the weight of the cheat sheet in my pocket and the sweat dripping down my back.

"You can go ahead if you need to," Adam said quietly. His eyes didn't leave Butch. "I'll be fine."

"Yeah," Butch said. "This little tree fucker will be fine."

Adam winced.

Butch smiled again. I couldn't help but notice that Butch actually had nice brown eyes. When he smiled, they twinkled a little.

Yeah, I know it's weird that I observed shit like that in the middle of a crisis. But I'd never really spent that much time close up in Butch's face. Who would want to?

I realized that my thoughts were drifting. Too much caffeine. The history final seemed very far away.

"I don't trust you," I told Butch. "Even if I wanted to go, I don't think you'd let me."

"Really? My beef is with this jerk. You? Not so much. You can go now." Butch stepped to one side of the doorway. He lifted his hand in a, you-can-pass-right-this-way kind of gesture. "Now you're down fifteen, no sixteen points. Better hurry."

I looked at Adam, then nodded. "Sorry, Adam. This test is really important to me."

"I know," he said. "I'll be along soon."

For a moment I hoped Butch might really let it all go.

"Me and Adam? We're just going to talk." Butch's eyes narrowed, hardened, and the smile vanished. It was like watching a heavenly angel falling for Lucifer's call to battle.

• • •

One of the things that happens when you grow up with a close friend is that you can practically read each other's minds.

In Butch's head, I was a coward, betraying my cousin.

Adam and I both knew better.

As soon as I stepped past him, Butch opened his arms and charged straight at my cousin.

You'd think that he'd have learned his lesson from the last time, but maybe his plan was an upgraded variation: grab Adam, then throw him over the railing and down the staircase.

Butch was fast. There was a reason he and Doug had been star football players. He went from zero to a thousand like a cross between a jaguar and a snarling grizzly.

I barely had time to turn my head and watch.

Adam stood still and waited until the very last moment. It looked like he was going to take the hit...

Which was when I shouted, "WATCH OUT FOR THE BUNNY RABBITS!"

Even as he kept rushing, Butch turned his head just a little and gave me a curious look. He couldn't help it.

Adam stepped out of Butch's way and ducked all the way down, his hands touching the floor.

Butch completely missed the grab.

He sped past Adam and down the stair case, where he tripped, stumbled, fell and tumbled end over end like a two-hundred-pound sack of potatoes, thudding and thumping and cracking before hitting the wall at the bottom of the landing with a muffled crunch.

"Oh shit," Adam said. "Oh shitohshit oh shit."

"Holy fuck," I said. My heart was pounding.

"Bunny rabbits?" Adam snapped at me. "Where the fuck did that come from?

"I have no idea." I shrugged. "Do you think we killed him?"

We stared down the stairs at the still and crumpled heap.

"I don't know," Adam said. "We should check."

"Don't go down there. He might be faking."

"No," Adam said. "But he's still breathing. I can see it from here. I'm going to take responsibility for this."

"No, you're not!" I said, grabbing Adam's tee shirt. "No DNA. You didn't touch him. Butch provoked it. You just moved out of the way. You know how this will look. It's just like last time. The truth doesn't matter."

"Then what?" Adam asked.

"Now we go to class," I said. "You're not staying here by yourself."

"I wasn't angry," Adam told me. He looked sad. "I really wanted to apologize to him."

"Adam, either we're both going, or we're both staying."

Adam looked at me for a moment, then nodded.

"When we get to class," I said, "I'll tell Mrs. Hendry what happened."

"If the cops come, I'm taking responsibility," Adam said. "I don't care if they arrest me, but you need to stay and finish your test. Okay?"

I didn't like it, but I nodded in agreement.

When we opened the classroom door, Mrs. Hendry looked furious. She inclined her head toward the two empty desks with their blue books, waiting.

"Mr. Cohen, Mr. Siegal. You're late. No excuses," she said, handing me the test questions.

I nodded, and then whispered in her ear. "I think one of the students, a member of the football team, fell down the stairs."

Her eyes registered surprise, and then understanding. Mrs. Hendry might have been old, but she was quick and sharp. "Did either of you two…?"

"No," Adam said, shaking his head as he took his test papers from her. "We didn't."

Mrs. Hendry looked from Adam to me. Some schoolteachers you can lie to; they'll believe anything. Mrs. Hendry wasn't one of them. She had an amazing bullshit detector. She nodded. Then she pointed to our chairs with the exact same you-can-pass-right-this-way gesture Butch had just used.

"Class, I have an errand to run. You have the rest of the period to finish your exam. I trust you to adhere to the Ashby Bryson Honor Code. No talking, no cheating. When you're done, please put your papers on my desk."

As Mrs. Hendry left the room, we sat down.

Helen, Jesús, Charlie and Sean looked up from their tests.

"You okay?" Helen mouthed.

I nodded. Adam nodded.

I got out my pencil and read the first question.

"Describe from the Japanese perspective, the events that brought the United States into the Second World War…"

A kamikaze question? I had to laugh. Piece of cake.

I started writing, and got into the zone.

I don't remember the rest of the test. I don't remember hearing the EMT ambulance or any kind of commotion in the hall.

By the end of the day, everybody at FRHS had heard that Butch Batten had nearly killed himself falling down the staircase. Speculation was that it was a botched suicide attempt. Or just a dumb accident.

Butch was out for the rest of the school year. Over the summer, his parents moved with him to Florida, and we never heard from

321

him again. Years later at a high school reunion, we'd probably learn that he'd become a used car salesman or something like that. But for all practical purposes he was gone from our lives forever.

Maybe it seems like I'm being callous, but we didn't even have a school assembly to talk about it. What was there to say? Thank fucking god!

Did I feel guilty? Yes, but only a little. If you can think of a better way for us to have resolved the situation, please let me know. In my mind, Butch did it to himself. We just made sure that he didn't take us down with him.[39]

Adam and I kept waiting for the police or Dr. Bob, or at least a call over the loudspeaker for us to come down to the main office.

But Mrs. Hendry didn't give us away. She didn't report us as tardy. She told everyone that she didn't know what happened, except that she'd heard somebody fall. She didn't even take any points off my test.

Adam passed with a seventy-five, because he blew the question on the Opium Wars in China.

And I got the first perfect grade anyone in her class ever got on a final exam.

It wasn't until a week later that I remembered the cheat sheet in my pocket, and even then it was only after Mom did the laundry, when I found it crumpled up in my jeans.

I smiled at the damp ball of blurred paper, that I hadn't used.

Was there some lesson there? Maybe rewriting my notes had focused my thinking. Maybe just having the safety net had been enough. It didn't matter. I hadn't needed it.

For a moment, I thought about drying the crib note out and framing it. Or maybe selling it to a publishing company as the world's most perfect AP World History cheat sheet. Then I tore it into little bits and threw it into the trash. All that confetti looked suspicious. I could imagine my mom asking questions, so I got most of the bits out of the trash, and flushed them down the toilet.

---

[39] Months later, Rover told me that Susie still kept track of Butch on social media, and that he enrolled in the University of Miami and had a girl-friend nicknamed Fifi.

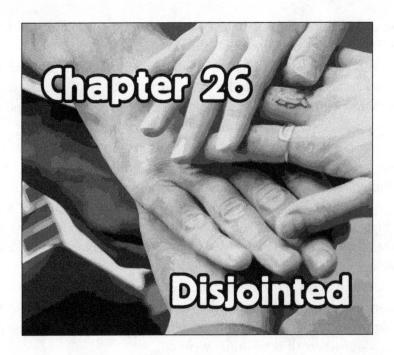

Chapter 26

Disjointed

"I think it's the duty of the comedian to find out where the line is drawn and cross it deliberately."
— George Carlin

It was the Monday after Hendry's AP World History exam. We were into the last few days of high school. All the other seniors had been done for weeks. They weren't even bothering to show up any more. It was supposed to be over for us, too. You got that part, right? Finished. Complete. Done. Finals were done. Papers were in.

But Doctor Bob wasn't going to let Adam and me slide, so we still had to attend FRHS every day. At least until Thursday.

Graduation was on Thursday.

And then, as usual, something threw a monkey wrench.

For months, rumors had been floating around that they might have to relocate our graduation. Our graduations were always held in the gym at Ashby Bryson (mostly because the gym was big enough and didn't cost extra), but Mr. Douglas, Superintendent Gonzales and the Groston School Board were seriously considering shifting the venue because of the whole flood-n-freeze.

Fectville Regional High always had their graduation at the swanky red velvet Savoy Theater in Fectville, but that date had been booked a year ago with a touring show that was either an Abba cover band or the original Abba band in some kind of virtual reality concert.

The heartbreaking news came after school on the Monday afternoon before we were supposed to graduate, while we were in Rover's basement playing a massive multiplayer first-person zombie shooter.

Adam and I had already wasted yet another day of our lives in Fuckedville doing bullshit make-work and eating lunch. Now we were wasting the afternoon, blowing off steam by slaughtering video zombies in a coordinated attack on a barn.

Charlie, Jesús, Helen and Sean were circling around the barn. Rover was acting as commander, monitoring the situation and issuing orders. Adam and I were on point moving toward the barn's front door when all our phones went off.

Every single one of our cell phones pinged, rang, donged, chirruped and vibrated at the same time.

"What the fuck?" Charlie said.

It's rare enough that one signal gets through the cement into Rover's basement bomb shelter. Let alone all seven.

If there's one thing we've learned in the past few months it's not to ignore our phones, especially when there's a group text.

Everybody (except Rover) snatched a look at the message.

It was from the Groston School Department: "Ashby Bryson graduation ceremony to be rescheduled. Date, time and location, TBA."

"What?" I said.

"Bullshit!" Sean shouted.

"Fuck me!" Jesús agreed.

"No no. No, that is not true," Helen said. "My mom said that they couldn't possibly move the graduation date because all the out-of-town relatives have already bought plane tickets and have hotel reservations."

"They fucking did it," Charlie said.

"Let's focus on…" Rover began, but then his avatar's head got bitten off by a zombie. He threw down his controller. "All right, fine. What's going on?"

"My phone is saying the same as yours." Jesús showed Helen.

"This text is from the Groston school department," I said. "It's official."

"It doesn't really mean anything. It's not settled," Helen said, trying to reassure herself. "TBA means To Be Announced. It means that they haven't committed to anything yet."

"Except that they are clearly committed to rescheduling," said Sean. He threw his phone across the room (into a pile of cushions we kept in the corner for just that purpose). "They are committed to rescheduling."

"This is not fair," Adam said. "I mean, really not fair."

"Fair?" Charlie said. "What about this whole fucking year has been fair?"

"Wait a sec, wait a sec," Rover said. And then, "Holy shit!"

"What?" we all asked.

"I just logged into the Groston school department's network," Rover said. "I'm looking at the superintendent's emails now. Yeah. Here it is. They are planning to move our graduation to the Fectville High School gym."

"Bullshit!" Sean said.

"After all we've been through?" I said the words slowly. "They want us to graduate in Fectville?"

It felt like the universe was rubbing our noses in dog shit.

"You really just hacked into Dr. Gonzales's email?" Helen said.

"No," Rover said. "I did that three years ago. I looked over his secretary's shoulder. She's never changed her password. Anyway, they had some construction guys go out to the Ashby Bryson gym today. They're worried about it being too hot, so they're recommending the change."

"Damn," Charlie said. "Well, Isaac, I guess it's a good thing we actually didn't get around to doing any work on your big project."

"No," I said quietly. "It's the reverse. This decides it. We're not finished. Not yet. We're going in."

Everyone looked at me.

• • •

I may have given you the false impression that Team Bombshelter and I were already working hard on my big project. We really weren't. We'd barely begun. Cut us a break. All the plans and ideas were in place, but the motivation to actually make it happen had been pretty low.

Can you blame us? It's one thing to start on a big undertaking in the winter, when you're trying to avoid doing homework. It's another to get it rolling in at the end of the year, when you're completely burned out.

As you might have guessed, my plan involved a lot of covert work in the gym at Ashby Bryson, and Charlie was totally right, if we had already started, and been there when the inspectors came by, we'd be in deep shit right now.

I realized that I'd opened my mouth and spoken before I thought, and while everyone waited, I chewed it over.

We could accept defeat. That would be easy.

Part of me was already disappointed.

But another part of me started to vibrate – not in a pornographic way, but sort of a juiced-up caffeine buzzy way.

I think I've made it clear that I'm not the smartest kid in my bunch. I'm not the tallest, biggest, shortest or even the nicest. But I do have a knack for ideas. And that's when the buzz in my head started to rev up.

"No... Wait a second, wait a second." I held up my hand. "Rover, that email said that their big problem is with air conditioning, right?"

"Yep." He looked at his screen, and did that cool flick thing they do in the movies so that the Superintendent's email box was spun onto the front of the big screen monitor.

In the background, the video game zombies finished slaughtering the rest of us. Oh well.

In the foreground was a letter from Crowther Construction to the school board. Dave Crowther thanked Dr. Gonzales for accepting his bid to install temporary air conditioning in the ABHS Gymnasium. Crowther then apologized because, "Even though it's a quick job, my crews are on other projects and we can't start sooner than Friday."

Graduation was Thursday.

"Are there any other reasons not to hold graduation in the gym?" I asked Rover. "Is there anything in the emails about the building's current safety code? Its occupancy permit? Is it still valid?"

Rover tapped away. Another email popped up. This was a summary from the building inspector. The gym was still structurally sound, but needed rewiring, the AC, and probably a new sound and light system if it was going to serve for graduation. According to the building inspector, the cost for rehab wouldn't be worth spending the disaster insurance money.

"I don't see anything about it officially being condemned," Rover said.

"Perfect." I nodded. "And we all know that the rest of that report isn't all true."

"What do you mean?" Helen said. "Climate change is making everything warmer. You know the gym gets sweltering…"

"Yeah," I said, "But that's just the air conditioning problem. The gym's power works well enough, and Rover managed to blast sound and lights at the naught-prom, right?"

"Yeah?" Adam said. "So?"

I quickly ran through the numbers in my head. We had tonight. We had all day Tuesday, and Tuesday night. We had Wednesday, Wednesday night, and Thursday morning. That was more than 60 hours of total time.

Could we pull it off?

It wasn't like we didn't have a choice. We could have punted.

Even then we could have let things go the way they were supposed to. Allow the school department to move our graduation. Get our diplomas in the sterile gym at Fectville Regional High School.

Or we could dare to greatness. Or at least something approaching a big "Fuck you and Farewell" but with style.

So I kept talking to my friends.

"First, we create a dummy construction company that offers to install the air conditioning at a lower bid than Crowther's. Then we kick into high gear, and actually put together our project. We have until this Thursday to pull it off." I grinned. "Then we hold our graduation in our own gym as we planned and blow everybody's minds! Bwahahahaha!"

My friends looked at me like I'd lost my mind.

"Izzy, you're crazy," Sean said.

"I am seeing a shrink," I admitted.

"Create a construction company?" Adam said.

"Not real. On paper. Emails.

Charlie looked skeptical. "You're thinking that we can do all that, and have it done so we can graduate in the gym at Ashby B. By Thursday?"

"Honestly, I don't know if my bleacher sound system will work without electrocuting people," Rover said.

"So, we'll test it," I answered.

"I'm not going to test it," Sean said, unhelpfully. "Last thing I need is to be zapped."

"We can get Rover's sister to do it," Jesús said. "We just won't tell her it's a test. Zzzzt!" He shook like he was in the electric chair.

Rover looked thoughtful. Charlie laughed and slapped Jesús five.

"I like Elspeth," Sean said. "And like Helen said, there's no AC in the old gym. It gets wicked hot! If we're shining Rover's lights and blasting his sound, that's adding even more heat."

He had a point. Old New England schools didn't have air conditioning because they were usually finished for the year before it got too hot. Now that global warming was real, and people were wimps, air conditioning was becoming more of a necessity.

"Who cares?" I said. "Even if it's hot, I'd rather be miserable for a few hours in our own gym than graduate in fucking Fectville."

"But they're already planning to move graduation," Helen said.

"Yeah." Charlie shook his head. "The school department isn't going to say, hey, those crazy kids, they just might make it work. And even if they did, my great-grandmother is old and overweight. I don't want Nanna to die of heat stroke just so I can graduate near home."

Adam nodded at me. "He's right."

I took this in. "Rover, you got any ideas?"

Rover's eyes were looking up at the bomb shelter's low ceiling. "The gym has those big ceiling fans, which make it impossible to hear anything when they're running. They move a ton of air around. If we used them to move hot air up and cool air down with some kind of refrigeration and ventilation system we could probably cool the place off, but the noise would be brutal."

"What if we cool the gym down in advance," Sean said, "and then use your bleacher sound system to compensate?" He was a bit of a science geek too. "Can it neutralize the resonance of the fans?"

"Maybe," Rover said. "But all that stuff will draw a ton of power. And I have to run major juice through the bleachers, which means that if I do electrocute someone they'll probably become barbecue."

"What if there was a shit ton of ice on the roof?" Jesús said, getting into the spirit of things.

"It would be all kinds of hipster and ironic," Charlie said, "to chill the gym with ice after it was wrecked by ice."

"Crazy!" I cheered, trying to keep them going.

"It might work," Rover said. "It doesn't have to be for long. A couple of hours…"

"We could skip the whole ritual of accepting diplomas one at a time," Adam suggested. "That would speed things up."

"No way," Sean said. "Getting the diploma is really important. It's sort of the whole point of graduation. Chinese families, even though we're American now, are still totally into formal recognition ceremonies."

"I agree. I know my Mamí wouldn't like it," Jesús said. "She's really proud that I'm getting honors."

"Wait a second." Helen frowned. "You guys are seriously talking about the possibility of killing people just to graduate on our own turf?"

That put it rather starkly in focus.

"No," I said. "But yeah."

I looked around the room at my friends.

"Look, we've had the worst possible luck this year. Everything that could go wrong has. We were supposed to be coasting for the past five months. Instead, we are suffering. I say that we take back control, and we go out with a bang."

I could see they were still skeptical.

"Right," Helen said. "The loud banging sound of all our parents being zapped."

"I can see the newspaper headline," Adam said, "Groston Graduation Gets Griddle and Gore."

"That's pretty good," Sean said. Adam shrugged.

"Here's the deal," I conceded, "if Rover can't figure out how to prevent zapping people on the bleachers, it's off. If Sean can't figure out how to cool the gym, it's off. Nobody dies. Nobody gets killed. Nobody gets hurt.

"But," I said, "in the meantime, we're installing air conditioning and going ahead with our own renovations. And then of course we're going to have to keep everybody away from the gym at Ashby B until the very last moment, while still making sure that they all show up for graduation on Thursday afternoon."

"Dude, today is Monday," Adam said. "And it's nearly dinner time. What you're proposing is a shit ton of work."

"We'll need lots of help," I explained. "We're going to have to open this up to other seniors. Other kids from Groston."

"Like who?" Sean said.

"Anybody and everybody who might pitch in. I'll take any warm bodies."

"Why would they do this?" Jesús asked. "Except for you and Adam, the rest of us are already out of school forever."

"And how are we going to get everybody to show up at the right place and the right time?" Helen said. "When the school department sends my parents an email..."

"Oops!" Rover said.

"What now?" Sean asked.

"Would you look at that," Rover said. "The school department's server just crashed. They just lost all access to their email and records. I modified the NSA's ransomware virus."

Charlie shook his head. "I don't know if this is nefarious or genius."

I gave Rover a tip of the hat salute. "That's a real shame. Rover, can you show one of us how to keep track of what's going on with the school department? And show somebody else how to manage your video projection stuff? We're going to need you to focus on the sound and cooling systems."

"Yeah, all right," Rover said. "I think so."

"Dibs on communications," Helen said.

"I want to handle the ceiling redesign," Jesús said. "I've been thinking a lot about your concept. I like it. But Rover's projectors were dim during the daylight. Remember? And they generate too much heat. For maximum impact, what we're doing has to be visible and probably permanent. So the projector's aren't going to work. I've been watching videos online, and I know how to make it happen."

"Isaac, what do you need the rest of us to do?" Sean asked.

Everyone was looking at me.

I didn't mean to become the leader, but I guess I'd opened my mouth and stuck my foot down my throat.

"Put together crews," I said. "We'll need a bunch of other people to help."

"I'll get my brothers and sisters up to speed," Jesús said. He shrugged. "They're small but they'll do whatever I say as long as I feed them ice cream."

"Cool," I said. "But we need more. There's not much time, so we'll need a big crew who can keep secret, otherwise…"

"On it," Charlie said. "I'll talk with the football team."

"The football team?" I was surprised.

"I've been reaching out." Charlie shrugged. "Make friends, man. That's my motto."

Rover said, "I'll see if Susie will get some of her cheerleader friends…"

"Wait a second," Charlie said. "You're still talking with Susie Wardle?"

"More than talking." Rover grinned. "We're dating. She's my girlfriend!"

Sean and Jesús exchanged looks. Helen shrugged.

"Can she keep a secret?" Adam said.

Rover rolled his eyes. "Did you or anybody else in school know that Susie and me are dating? No. Why? Because she doesn't want to advertise it. Do I care about that? Yes. A little. But if it's a choice between making out with her in secret and not having her at all... No choice. Right? So yeah, Susie can keep a secret."

This was a lot more information than any of us were prepared to deal with just then, so we were quiet for a moment.

"Are we really going to do this?" Adam asked.

"Consensus vote," I said. "It's all or nothing."

I raised my hand.

One by one my friends all raised theirs.

I grinned. We all grinned.

Game on.

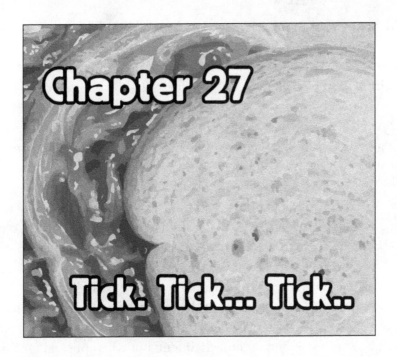

Chapter 27

Tick. Tick... Tick..

"The slow burn is the most challenging and rewarding move in comedy. Guy One insults Guy Two. Then Guy Two builds a reaction with glacial speed. The setup is important, but the crucial element is absolute commitment to the explosion. Once in motion, it's like watching molten lava oozing toward a cache of fireworks. The pleasure is in the process, and the final blow-up is the button."

– Attributed to Oliver Hardy, on comictrainingwithoutthe.net

After our breakthrough, we turned off the video games and kicked into high gear.

We told our parents that we'd all be hanging out in Rover's basement, and used the bulkhead to sneak in and out so his folks wouldn't catch on. Rover took great pleasure in hijacking his Dad's security camera feeds, just like in the movies!

Helen and Charlie started working the phones. While Rover

and Sean were brainstorming, Jesús, Adam and I began loading Rover's video and sound projection shit back into the trunk of the Dartmobile. Then we broke into the gym at Ashby Bryson High (again) and started filling it with equipment and volunteers.

We stayed up all night at the gym, prepping and testing.

And then suddenly it was Tuesday morning. Adam and I were trudging from the parking lot to FRHS, when my cousin threw me a curve.

"Do you ever think about sex?" Adam said.

"What?" I mumbled. I'd taken a lot of donut shop caffeine and some Ritalin to stay awake. My brain was toast – avocado toast... day-old brown avocado toast on soggy bread with flies circling around.

"Sex," Adam said. "I think about it all the time."

My head was still spinning from the ride to Fectville.

Jesús had taken a break from the gym project and driven like a madman to get us to school before the late bell rang. On ordinary runs, Jesús is a safe and careful chauffeur, but when pressed for time he rolls stop signs and blows through red lights. He'd teleported us from Ashby Bryson High to Fectville High at record speed, skidded to a stop on the edge of the bus lane, and as soon as we'd closed the doors, shouted, "Later" and patched out to get back to Groston.

" Uh-huh," I said. "I think about sex, too."

All the freshmen, sophomores and juniors heading into school were moving slowly. Nobody wanted to be there.

We, of course, were the only two seniors left in the building.

We would have skipped, but we knew that he'd be there. Our nemesis.

And there he was.

Waiting by the front doors was good old Doctor Bob Smith, Fectville's anal-retentive vindictive douchebag of a principal ready to check us in or kick us out. Even though it was a hot June day, Dr. Bob wore a black suit with a skinny tie and his collar buttoned tightly. He was frowning. At me. Of course.

"I think about sex all the time," Adam said. "In my dreams. And when I wake up. And in the shower. And at breakfast. And in the car."

"Adam," I said. "Stop."

"What?"

"You're a guy. You're supposed to think about sex all the time," I said. "I saw a statistic that guys between the ages of thirteen and twenty think about sex on average every seventeen seconds."[40]

"This is almost constant," he said. "I think about it every three seconds."

I shrugged. "Same difference."

The sun rises on the front doors of Fectville Regional High School, and I could see the sweat beading on Dr. Bob's tiny moustache. I looked at my phone. We had seventy seconds to get into the building before Dr. Bob locked us out and we'd have to sign in tardy at the office, and get a slip for after-school detention – which we all knew he'd enforce.

Still by then, Adam and I had our swagger down cold. We ambled and dawdled, making him wait.

"Helen and I haven't ever had..." Adam's voice trailed off.

I almost stopped walking, which would have been bad, because we had a shit-ton of work to do after school. Fortunately, my survival instinct kept my body moving even while my brain glitched.

"Haven't had sex? You two haven't?"

"No." Adam shook his head. "I don't know if Helen can. With her legs. You know?"

"How would I know? She's not my girlfriend. Have you even talked about it with her? Ever?"

"No," he said. "And she's never brought it up. And I'm not gonna. I don't want to pressure her."

"You could say..."

I thought for a momecnt, kept walking, and timed it just right.

I was right next to Dr. Bob when I said, "Hey, I am really hot, hard and horny and I want to fuck you." Then, as if surprised that he was even there, I looked up at the principal. "Oh, hi, Dr. Bob."

Dr. Bob's face was red and getting redder. The tips of his ears were scarlet.

"Good morning, sir," Adam said, fighting back a laugh.

---

[40] Research results vary based on climate and culture.

Who says that boys ever progress past fourth grade humor?

We brushed past the principal and were inside just as the first bell rang.

• • •

Adam and I slept through school that Tuesday. We walked from class to class like mental patients on Thorazine, slipping into our seats, folding our hands, and dropping our heads on our desks for a series of 52-minute naps interrupted by a shitty school lunch.

Actually, this was the first hot school lunch that I'd ever eaten in all my twelve years of public school.

When I was a little kid at Jerome Marco K-8, Mom used to make me peanut butter and jelly sandwiches every day. She'd spread creamy peanut butter on one slice of white bread, store brand grape jelly on another slice, gently press them together, slice off the crusts with a sharp knife, and then cut the sandwich it into four triangles. She'd wrap it in waxed paper, and put it in a brown paper bag with a big handful of potato chips, an apple or a clementine and a napkin. Then she'd give me money for milk and I was set.

One morning, Mom rebelled, yelling that she was sick and tired of doing everything for everybody who didn't care or appreciate anything.

"I'm done," she shouted. "DONE!"

Bam, the kitchen door slammed, and she walked out of the house.

Ellen and I had stared in slack-jawed disbelief as Mom got into the car and drove off.

Dad, who had set her off by asking, "Is there any coffee?" had the same deer in the headlights look.

Ellen started sniffling. I looked at the loaf of bread, my partially peanut-buttered slice, and the grape jelly slowly oozing onto the counter from the overturned jar.

"Is Mom leaving us?" I asked. "Are you guys getting a divorce?"

"No, no," Dad said, putting on his I'm-a-doctor-and-I-know-everything voice. "She's just going through something called peri-menopause. It's a hormonal change that happens to women as they

336

age."

"Mom's not that old," Ellen said.

"She's not going to die, is she?" I asked.

Ellen burst into tears.

"No no no!" Dad said, trying to be reassuring. "It's normal. She's fine. She'll go to a yoga class or something. She'll be fine. She'll be home later, after work."

"Today?" Ellen said.

"Yeah," Dad said. "Probably." He opened the freezer, took out a can of coffee, and began scooping grinds into the machine.

"What about my lunch?" I asked.

Dad smiled at me. "I'll make you lunch today."

He proceeded to massacre that sandwich, tearing it to absolute shreds.

I ate it though, sort of balled up sticky pieces of doughy bread and a mess of purple-brown stuff.

Mom was back for dinner, with takeout fried chicken. Next morning she showed me how to make my own damned lunches.

Which I had done every single day since then. Most of the time, I made my lunch the night before. I'd upgraded the bread to a hearty sourdough, and the peanut butter was this awesome natural crunchy kind. I'd stuck with the grape jelly through tenth grade, but one day we'd been out and I tried a jar of farmer's market strawberry preserves, and my life changed for the better. And every day I took a big handful of potato chips, and threw them into the paper bag. In AP Environmental Science, when we talked about recycling and the Great Pacific Plastic Garbage Patch, I felt very proud that I'd been a pioneer in minimizing waste.

But last night had been an all-nighter, and I hadn't gone home from the Groston gym before going to school. So I had no option but the school lunch.

I stared at the tray in front of me.

Limp hot dog, soggy bun, and greasy flaccid tater tots on a Styrofoam plate.

It was the end of the school year and they were out of ketchup. They were out of mustard. They were out of everything. Usually there's a salad bar, but all they had were shredded carrots and parsley. Usually there's a frozen reheated pizza option. That was gone too. No taco bar. There used to be ice cream bars and ice cream sandwiches, but the food police had outlawed them. They'd switched to frozen yogurt and frozen juice bars, but the Fectville freezers had overheated and created a fly-attracting puddle.

The only other choice was the vegetarian option: raw tofu with a vegan brown sauce that looked like chunks of albino-colored gelatin doused with motor oil.

I can't believe that kids ever eat the shit they serve. If I still give a fuck when I grow up and have kids, I'm going to make the school board eat hot lunches for a month before they approve any catering contract.

"So, what do you think I should do?" Adam said, sitting down across from me as I tried to choose between going hungry and eating the slightly grey hot dog.

"Huh?" I was still tired. We definitely needed to bring a coffee machine to the gym for tonight's shift.

"About me and Helen?"

"Adam," I said. "I don't give a rat's ass. You have a girlfriend you love and care about. You'll figure it out. You'll either get laid or you won't. Probably you will. Then you'll be happy. I'm not happy. I don't have a girlfriend. I don't even have lunch."

"Yeah." Adam reached into his backpack and pulled out a submarine sandwich from Jake's Sandwich Hut.

"Where the hell did you get that?" I said.

"I ordered it online. They deliver. Turns out their driver, Dave, is a brown belt at my dojo. He handed it to me through the window during Latin. I gave him a three dollar tip."

"Fuck!"

Adam grinned. He pulled out another sandwich and handed it to me. "I've got your back. Or at least your stomach."

Chapter 28

A Thin Slice
of Montage

"*Since I started working on this thesis, finding things to really
laugh at has become challenging. I took on the project thinking that
it would be a great excuse to watch a lot of comedy, and get school
credit. I imagined my mom saying, 'Turn off that video and do your
homework.' And my reply, 'This is my homework!' The problem is
that the more I analyze comedy, the less funny it is in the moment.
I'm hoping that my appreciation, sense of humor and real laughter
will return when I turn this paper in. I'm terrified that it won't.*"
— *Intro to "What Makes Us Laugh?"*

For me, the next few days were a blur of frantic focused random
and coordinated nonstop activity in the Ashby Bryson High School
gym, interspersed with blank spots of brain-dead enforced inactivity
at FRHS.

Somehow, I had become the undertaking's unofficial leader.
Everybody came to me with questions about logistics, priorities,

personnel, and persnickety details.[41]

That said, we had some massive challenges.

Yes, both the Groston cheerleaders and the Ashby Bryson football team, as well as a whole bunch of other underclassmen and women, got involved.

But bringing more people in also caused friction.

As we were gearing up for the final push, at two a.m. on Wednesday morning, Jesús and Susie Wardle got into a heated shouting match about colors. They were screaming so loudly that it cut through the boom-thump of a DJ Razor bootleg track that Rover was blaring through our fully functional bleacher-speaker system.

Rover had solved the general concern about bleacher electrocution early on, by powering it up while Jesús's younger brothers and sisters were playing tag on them. Jesús didn't seem to mind, but Adam started freaking that we could have killed a bunch of little kids. Charlie calmed him down by pointing out the obvious: it had worked, and everybody was fine.

I personally had visited Charlie's Uncle James the cop, and filled him in on our nefarious scheme. He'd begun by shaking his head, saying, "Absolutely not. No way. Are you kids fucking crazy?"

However, after he looked at Jesús's inital design through Rover's Virtual Reality headset, he agreed to do whatever he could to run interference – as long as we didn't set off any alarms, light anything on fire, blow anything up, or draw "any kind of undue attention" to ourselves.[42]

We'd blown through $5,000 pilfered from our college savings and arranged for the delivery of a refrigerated container full of

---

[41] I realize that by not getting into the specifics about what we were doing, I'm being more than a little cryptic. I'm trying to maintain the suspense, so I can't really go too much into the nitty gritty without giving away the big finish. If you're a blogger or reviewer, please no spoilers!

[42] Remarkably, no one in town noticed, or cared enough to report the various pickup trucks, delivery vans, and cars filled with young people driving in and out of the Ashby Bryson High School parking lot at all hours of the day and night. Maybe they thought we were doing construction. Which we were.

five-pound bags of ice. Charlie had spent Tuesday morning convincing an old friend of his dad's who worked construction to bring a crane to the parking lot and hoist the container up on the roof. Fortunately, the roof didn't collapse and Sean's modification of Rover's ice-conditioning plan worked. By dawn the building was cool inside.

All of a sudden, it was late Wednesday afternoon. We had less than 24 hours to go. I'd finished another hideous day at FRHS, been picked up by Jesús and was back at the gym.

Things were surprisingly way on schedule. All the prep work had been done. The designs were complete. The scaffolding was up. (The football team had "borrowed" the boards, end frames, braces and outriggers from the renovation/construction site at Fectville Regional High School.)

Our pirated satellite wifi network was buzzing and the printers were chunking. All the supplies were laid out in rows.

We had a whole crew standing by, waiting for the go.

We even had three buffet tables set up for the crew, like a movie set, with pizza, doughnuts, fresh fruit and veggies (for the health-conscious), a big platter of Mrs. Johnson's fried chicken and ribs, and a huge bowl of salad with a spicy Cajun balsamic dressing she'd made for Charlie's sake, plus takeout Chinese and four coffee makers on full rotation. To her eternal credit and my undying gratitude, Susie had brought in a burr grinder and ten pounds of locally roasted gourmet coffee. We'd already chugged through two pounds, because every time somebody made a fresh pot it smelled soooo good.

So, when Susie started shrieking, "BORING BORING BORING BORING!" in her cut-through-the crowd cheerleader voice, everybody's heads whipped around terrified that she'd fallen from a scaffold and broken her neck. (Yes, she was yelling and couldn't possibly have broken her neck, but fear isn't logical.)

I relaxed when I saw that she was just facing off with Jesús (again), and I would have let it go. But Rover came up to me and asked me to intervene.

"You've got to do something," Rover begged. His eyes were nervous and wide. "I think they're really going to kill each other."

By then I'd become somewhat complacent about my role as honorary foreman. I even grumbled a little, because I'd been on my way to snag an artisanal doughnut and a fresh cup of java for my IV drip.

"Fine," I told him, "but cut the music so we can hear ourselves think."

Rover whipped out his remote and instantly the music snapped off.

The silence would have been deafening, except just then Jesús yelled, "This is my design, and I don't want some bimbo telling me how to lay it out!"

His words echoed through the gym.

Awkward.

Susie had her fists clenched and a look like she was going to claw out his eyes.

I sighed and said in as big a voice as I could muster, "All right guys, coffee break!"

Jesús, Rover and Susie spun their heads toward me and simultaneously said, "What?"

I shrugged. "I'm out of coffee. And I think we need a break."

"What we need is to get moving on the last stage," Jesús said. "Tick tock!"

"What we really need," Susie said, "is for this greaser to get his head out of his ass."

"Did you just call me a greaser?"

"Did you just call me a bimbo?"

I pushed the button on the burr grinder, which made a hideous buzz saw whine that was impossible to ignore. It frazzed for a good minute and a half, while Susie and Jesús and Rover's heads spun from each other to me and back to each other, and then back to me.

Adam sauntered over. "Do you know what you're doing?"

"Not a clue," I whispered back, smiling. "Help me out here?"

"Not a chance." He laughed. "I think you're on your own. Keep your eye on the goal. But don't lose any friends in the process."

Some fucking peacemaker.

I looked around the room. Jesús's brothers and sisters were clearly on their sibling's side. The cheerleaders and football players were on Susie's.

Helen gave me two thumbs up.

I have no idea where Charlie and Sean were. Probably out on another food run.

Fine.

I walked to the nearest coffee maker, lifted the empty carafe, and nodded my head for Jesús and Susie to join me.

• • •

Susie and Jesús backed away from each other, and with slow measured steps made their way from center court to the edge of the gym where we had the catering services set up.

They both snatched mugs, keeping their distance from each other.

By then, I'd put in a new filter, dumped in the fresh-ground dark-roast, refilled the machine with water from a jug, and pressed the start button.

We waited. Everyone waited. Rover bounced from foot to foot.

Fortunately, it was a pretty fast drip machine. As soon as there was a decent amount in the pot, I slid a mug under.

Then, because it's polite, even in the era of sexual equali-ty, I poured coffee for Susie first. Then Jesús. Then I swapped the drip-catching mug with the pot, and found that I'd timed it right and had my own perfectly full cup of fresh black heaven.

"Milk? Sugar?" I asked.

Jesús shook his head. "Black. Like it's meant to be."

Susie smiled viciously. "I like cream and stevia," she said. "It's important to drink what you want, and not get stuck in absolutism."

Rover was instantly at Susie's side, pouring her cream and squirt-ing two shots of natural calorie-free sweetener into her mug, stirring it with a spoon, and then licking the spoon.

"Thank you, honey," Susie said, giving him a quick peck on the cheek.

I both wanted to barf and was completely jealous.

Rover shrugged, and started to walk away, but Susie grabbed him by the elbow, spun him around and lip-locked my friend in a deeply passionate French kiss.

Rover's sister Elspeth shouted, "Woot! Go bro!"

Rover, out of breath, blushed.

Jesús looked furious at Rover's betrayal.

I took a sip of my coffee. It was delicious.

"You know," I said, "I used to like my coffee with milk. Never much of a fan of sweeteners. But this coffee is so good that I'm trying it black, and finding out that I kind of like it."

"There are plenty of opportunities for everyone to have coffee the way they like it," Susie said through gritted teeth. "Everybody doesn't have to drink it the same way. Do they?"

"No," I agreed. "But what we're doing isn't really like individual cups of coffee, is it?"

"Exactly!" Jesús said. "If you add sugar or stevia to a pot of coffee the whole thing is ruined!"

"Only if you don't like your coffee sweetened," Susie said.

"Which I don't!" Jesús insisted.

"All right," I said, stepping in between the two. "All right. Let's talk about the real problem. Which is what?"

Jesús started. "She still wants to use different colors than what's in the specs. My design is meant to create a unified whole."

"But we've already modified the original design," Susie said. "It's been modified from day one! I'm just saying that if we add a few more modern colors we can maybe even improve on..."

"IMPROVE ON IT?" Jesús shouted. "IT'S A MASTERPIECE!"

"BUT THIS IS OUR VERSION!" Susie yelled back. "WE CAN DO WHATEVER WE WANT!"

For a moment I thought about dropping the coffee pot on the floor with a loud shattering crash. It would have interrupted their argument, but also would have made a huge mess and been a tragic waste of dark roast.

"OH MY GOD, LOOK!" I screamed at the top of my lungs. "IT'S BUGS BUNNY!" I pointed at the ceiling.

Everybody looked up.

While Adam and I had been dogging it at Fectville Regional High School, our crews had spent most of the day cleaning and prepping the ceiling. It was bright and shiny and new. Probably better than new.[43]

There was no Bugs Bunny up there on the ceiling.

Everyone looked at me.

"What the fuck, Izzy?" Jesús said.

Susie was silent, but her face said the same thing.

"We could do that, right?" I asked Rover. "Put a video of Bugs Bunny up on the ceiling? Right in the middle, like saying that this whole year has just been one big ass Loony Tunes cartoon?"

"Yeah," Rover said, reluctantly. "But everything else is ready to go. And Jesús spent a lot of time working on the designs."

"No way are we putting Bugs Bunny up there!" Susie and Jesús said it at the same time.

"Jinx," Susie said. "You owe me a coke."

Jesús pointed to the catering tables. "Get it yourself."

"All right," I said. "Forget about Bugs. But Susie came in late and didn't have a chance to be in on the initial design part."

"No, I didn't," Susie agreed.

"At Fectville, we form a decoration committee," said Diana Marley, "we always ask for everybody's input. Even if you're late, you're still given a say."

I took a breath. Diana, as Charlie's girlfriend, was one of the few kids from Fectville who had been allowed to help with the project. She wasn't being very helpful just now.

"And our gang's always been about consensus," Rover agreed.

"Look," Jesús said, "most of these guys, including you Diana, just found out about this the other day. We need to have one person who says yes or no. Otherwise it'll be a mess!"

"What if we gave Susie her own section," I said. "A unified section that all was the same color scheme? You pick it, Jesús. Or work it out between the two of you. But Susie, it can't slow us down and it has to fit within Jesús's overall vision. Can you two please make that

---

[43] Think Tom Sawyer white washing the fence, but on the ceiling, with fifty kids, and without the apple cores or dead cat. Also, we'd had to put down big blue tarps to keep the drips off the basketball court. I don't know why we bothered with that.

work together?"

Both of them stared up at the blank ceiling.

"Yeah," Susie and Jesús nodded and spoke at the same time.

"I can make it work," Jesús said.

"Me too," Susie said. "I can see it."

They fist bumped each other.

Everyone started to breathe easier.

"Wait, a second," I said. I pointed to Susie. "You've got something else to say. Right?"

"What? Oh." Her eyes widened, and she blushed. "I'm so sorry about that greaser remark."

"Yeah. I called you a bimbo. Sorry," Jesús said. "I think we're even. Let me get you that coke."

"Oh thank Christ," Rover muttered. Force a guy to choose between sex and male friendship and he's between a rock and a hard-on.

"All right everybody," I shouted. "Let's get back to it. We've got a shit ton to do and a hard deadline of noon tomorrow."

Everyone started to move.

Charlie and Sean banged through the doors carrying boxes filled with refried beans, rice, and burritos from an all night Mexican joint in Fectville.

"What'd we miss?" Charlie asked, taking in the end of the scene.

"All good," I said.

"What is it with you and the rabbits?" Adam asked me.

"I have no fucking idea," I said.

Just then both our phones vibrated.

"Who's texting us at this hour?" I wondered. Our parents were asleep and all our friends were in the gym.

We both looked at our phone and saw the message was from Martin Douglas, the principal of Ashby Bryson High.

"Boys, I hope this text isn't waking you. I'm sorry to report that Principal Smith is insisting that you attend your morning classes today at FRHS for an early dismissal prior to graduation. Dr. Smith has convinced the superintendent to rule that if you skip or are tardy your diplomas will be withheld and you will have to attend summer school."

We were speechless.

Then another text blipped in, also from Principal Douglas. "But congratulations! You're almost there."

"What's up?" Sean asked.

"Fucking Dr. Fucking Bob!" I cursed.

Adam showed Sean his phone. I showed Charlie mine. "Even though it's Groston graduation day tomorrow, we've got to go to school in Fectville tomorrow morning. This morning. Today!"

They were speechless too. I mean, all of us were thinking variations on, "They can't..." or "What fucking assholes..." or "No fucking way!"

But they could. And they were. And that was what was happening.

Finally, I sighed. I shoved my phone into my pocket.

"Somebody give me a bucket and a brush," I said. "I need to blow off some steam. I've got a lot of work to do before finally finishing fucking high school tomorrow."

Chapter 29

Fuck Off Fectville

"Puns are funny. Or maybe I should say, 'Puns are punny.' I appreciate truly clever wordplay. For some reason, other people don't seem to enjoy punishment as much as I do."
– Dr. Robert J. Smith, principal of Fectville Regional High School

The final tick-tock in the Ashby B gym began Thursday morning at 7:45. Rover's bleacher sound system blared a solo bugle reveille, which kicked into a full New Orleans horn section boogie. None of us were asleep. A bunch of Elspeth's friends started dancing. Helen rolled up, handed me and Adam iced coffee in travel cups, gave him a kiss on the cheek and said, "See you guys soon."

Jesús had already pulled up in his Dart. "You sure you don't want to go home and shower first?"

I looked at my cousin and we shook our heads, no.

We were hot and smelly and our shorts, tee shirts, grubby sneakers, hair, legs and arms were all covered with dried wheat paste and scraps of paper.

"Let them think that we're total losers," I told Jesús.

Charlie stuck his head out the gym's door and hollered, "They already think that."

I flipped him off. I'd been up for thirty-nine hours straight.

Charlie grinned, waved and vanished back inside.

"Are we going to have enough time to change after school?" Adam said. "My mom will kill me if I show up to graduation looking like this."

"Relax, man," Jesús said. "We've got it all scheduled out."

Jesús patched out the Dartmobile and we did the Groston to Fectville run in under twelve parsecs.

Dr. Bob, in his button-down suit, was waiting at his post, pacing in front of the school, cell phone in his hand, his face red as he shouted into the phone, "What do you mean you can't find the Groston graduation diplomas. There are four boxes of them! They were supposed to be delivered by today."

We waved as we walked past, "Hi, Dr. Bob."

He glanced at his watch, glared, and thumbed us inside just as the bell rang.

"No," he was screaming into the phone, "the Groston diplomas were not delivered to my office. Yes, I am sure!"

Adam and I snickered, and I nearly gave Dr. Bob the finger, but I held myself back.

As the only two seniors left in the entire school, we'd recently been reassigned to Mrs. Hendry for homeroom and every other class. They knew we respected her.

"I am sorry that they are making you boys do this," she said. "Where are your caps and gowns?"

I shrugged as we slid into our desks. "We won't be here long."

Mrs. Hendry stared at us. "Is there something happening that you boys want to tell me about?"

Mrs. Hendry was smart. Adam and I exchanged grins, but shook our heads. I said, "No. Not yet."

Adam said, "You'll find out soon enough."

Mrs. Hendry sighed, logged into her laptop, signed into the school's network, and recorded that we were "present and on time".

Adam pulled out a deck of cards, and we continued our game of gin. When anybody asked, we said we were playing to 100,000 – but the truth was that after a month of nearly continuous play, Adam was winning 15,432 to 14,429, and were both getting pretty sick of runs, triplets and sets. After a while, the cards all look the same, which makes sense because there are only 52 of them.

Time crawled. I would have napped with my head down, but I was afraid that I wouldn't wake up. I think I'd had a total of four hours sleep since Sunday night. Mrs. Hendry suggested that if we wanted to learn something, we could we take out our textbooks and read about the Sherman Anti Trust Act and its effect on world trade. We opened our books and set them in front of us while we played cards. Mrs. Hendry didn't mind. Or if she did, she didn't say.

I looked at the clock on the wall. 11:12. Less than an hour to go.

Rover and Helen were late.

Then, Mrs. Hendry frowned at her computer's display. "That's odd," she said.

I compared the wall clock with my phone, which said 11:11. Nope. Right on time!

"What's going on?" Adam asked her innocently, as he picked up the seven of hearts.

"I just got an email from the Groston school department," she said, "announcing last minute changes to the emergency backup plan for today's graduation ceremony!"

"Really?" Adam said. "What's strange about that?" He discarded the king of clubs.

"Because there is no emergency backup plan. Or at least this is the first that I've heard of it. And here's another email. A news release congratulating the Dorothy Gale Commercial Construction Corporation for its quick work installing a temporary air conditioning systems in the old gym. This one says that because cooling has been effected, in case of a gas leak at FRHS, graduation could be relocated back to the Ashby Bryson High School gym."

Her laptop pinged as a new email arrived.

"And now here's an email from the Fectville Fire Department confirming the gas leak…"

Mrs. Hendry's voice trailed off and she stared at us. "What did you boys do?"

"Us?" I said, innocent as the Unabomber. "We're sitting here with you. We're just playing cards."

I snatched up Rover's king and said, "Gin" just as the fire alarm went off. Flashing emergency lights. Ringing bells. Cheers from the classrooms full of juniors, sophomores and freshmen.

"About time," I muttered.

"Cutting it close," Adam answered.

We could barely hear each other.

Mrs. Hendry raised an eyebrow as she raised her voice. "I know for a fact that we've done all our fire drills for the year," she shouted over the blaring klaxons.

"Maybe it's a real fire!" I said. "But I wouldn't rush."

We could hear the freshmen, sophomores and juniors pouring out into the halls.

"Thanks for teaching us, Mrs. Hendry," Adam yelled, as he put the cards away. "You are the best!"

"Hey, hey hey," I said. "Don't forget to score me."

"You got fifty-two, plus the twenty for gin," he said.

"All right," I said, "Fourteen thousand, six-hundred and seventy-four. I'm catching up."

"In your dreams," Adam shouted.

"We'll see you at graduation," I told Mrs. Hendry. "Be sure you get in early, if you can. Sit on the right side of the old gym."

"Why?" she asked.

"You'll see," I said, cryptically. I waved as we left.

Adam handed me a banana. He had one too. We chewed slowly as we walked down the stairs, past blaring alarms and flashing strobes, and through the emptying school.

Rather than going to our designated assembly area, we walked right out the front doors.

Dr. Bob was back on his cell phone. Even outside, the fire alarms were deafening, nearly drowning out his voice.

He was screaming, "No. There is no gas leak in the gym! There can't be. Yes, I am certain. Because there is no gas line into the gym!"

Adam and I dropped our banana peels at his feet.

Dr. Bob saw us sauntering past. Still shouting into his phone, he pointed an accusing finger at us.

What? Adam and I raised our hands in dual shrugs as we kept walking.

Jesús screeched up in the Dartmobile. Squeezed inside were Charlie, Rover, Sean, and Helen.

Dr. Bob beckoned at us with his finger. Come back here, he was mouthing. He pointed at us, then at the banana peels on the ground. I could read his lips saying, "Come back here now and pick this up!"

The Dartmobile's door swung open.

Both Adam and I waved at him.

We shoehorned our way into the car, and Jesús patched out again. Slower this time, because there were way too many people in the vehicle.

We didn't mind.

I barked an order, "Pre-sent fingers!"

And, as we zoomed out of the parking lot, every single one of us flipped off Dr. Bob with both hands.

Giggling, Jesús had to grab the wheel to avoid hitting a slow-moving freshman.

Dr. Bob's face was maraschino cherry red as he chased after us, stepped on one of the banana peels and started to slide.

We watched him slip, waving his hands in a frantic panic. His cell phone flew through the air, flashing like a digital bridal bouquet at a punk rock wedding before smashing to bits on the sidewalk in front of Fectville Regional High School.

No, Dr. Bob didn't fall and split his trousers open. That would have been too perfect.

But if it was a cartoon, he would have landed on his ass, and his head would have exploded.

We laughed like a carload of monkeys on nitrous oxide.

• • •

We were all grinning and laughing, slapping high fives and cheering. Then I realized that everyone was still wearing their work clothes.

"I thought you guys were going to be dressed and ready by now."

"We added a few last minute changes to Jesús's design," Charlie said.

"Susie's idea," Rover said, proudly.

"What?"

"I'm cool with it," Jesús said.

"Relax, man," Sean said. "It's done. All taken care of.

"We've got time," Helen said. "We're going to zip everybody home, get dressed and go."

All of our cell phones went off simultaneously as an emergency text announcement came in:

"Due to a gas leak at FRHS, Groston's Graduation Ceremony will be re-relocated to the Ashby Bryson High School gym. New start time will be at 12:15 p.m.."

"See," Helen said. "I even gave us an extra fifteen minutes." She smiled. Helen had orchestrated the entire fraudulent exchange of emails, leaving a post-dated paper trail back and forth between the school department, building inspectors, the fictional Dorothy Gale Commercial Construction Corporation, and the natural gas division of the power company.[44] Rover had also hard-wired the FRHS fire alarms so they couldn't be disabled without cutting the power to the entire building.

"I can't change at home," Adam began. "My parents…"

"No, Adam," Helen said. "Your folks are already at the Fectville gym. All of our parents are. I asked my folks to get everyone a section near the door so they could get good seats, but we could get out quickly when it was over. We factored everything in. By now they've gotten the alerts, so they'll start to leave here and drive straight to Groston, but they'll get stuck in a traffic jam, and we'll have plenty of time to shower and change."

Adam and I looked out the rear window. Helen was right. The FRHS parking lot was over-full of cars and minivans. Confused

---

[44] Helen had fun building a fake website, complete with a rainbow logo and the slogan, "Making the Dreams that you dare to dream come true since 1939."

parents and grandparents were filing out of the gym, half were plugging their ears and the other half were still looking at their phones, as the fire trucks pulled up, blocking the road, and began rolling out hoses.

"I'm glad I told my Nanna to wait at our house until the last minute," Charlie said to Jesús.

"What?" Sean said. "We promised to keep this secret."

"Hey, she's in her nineties," Charlie said. "I promised her that my uncle would take her to graduation in the squad car. So we're going to have to be careful not to run into them."

Jesús sighed. "That is so not fair. I had to pull all my kid brothers and sisters off the project this morning, so my Mamí wouldn't get suspicious. She's already dragged them here to Fectville to get good seats. They were pissed at me. I had to give them each five bucks to keep their mouths shut."

"Hey, it's not my fault you didn't think of a good excuse," Charlie said.

"I'm dropping you off last," Jesús told him. "You'd better change fast."

"Guys, guys, don't worry," Helen said. "I roped off a section at the old gym for all our families."

I won't bore you with the logistics of our final costume change. We all moved like the Flash or Superman in his phone booth. But it was easier for us, since we didn't have to squeeze into spandex.

I didn't have time for a shower. That had been a pipe dream. I ran my head under the faucet in the kitchen sink to get out the goop, but adding water to the wheat paste made it worse, so I toweled off and ended up with a Sid Vicious spiked hair look.

I looked at the new suit Mom and Dad had insisted buying me for graduation, and remembered how hot it might get in the gym with all the extra bodies, despite Sean's hacked ice-conditioning system, and said fuck it. So I just put on a clean tee shirt, fresh underwear, filthy shorts and slid the nylon royal blue graduation gown over my head. Flip flops instead of my tight black leather dress shoes. This was my graduation. My parents would still get their pictures, but I was not going to be uncomfortable. I almost forgot my cap, ran back, grabbed it, ran outside, and was back in the car.

"Three minutes, twelve seconds," Rover said. "Not bad."

The only notable delay was when Adam carried Helen into her house at a run.

We all had to wait for nine excruciating minutes.

"You ever wonder how Helen gets herself dressed?" Rover said.

"What do you mean?" Sean asked.

"She can't move her legs, right?" Rover said. "Can she put on her panties by herself. Are all her dresser drawers at the same level? Does she need help getting in and out of the shower? Even if she does, how fast can she change?"

Jesús made a frowning face and told Rover, "You know, I have never thought of that stuff and really didn't need to put any of those images in to my head."

Finally, the door to Helen's house opened, and Adam quickly hefted her back out, fully dressed in her cap and gown with her hair wet.

"See what I mean?" Rover said. "Hey, you think those guys were getting it on?"

My cousin did have a big fat grin on his face.

Sean, Jesús, Charlie and I cracked up.

"What?" Helen asked as she and Adam scootched into the car.

"Hey, you lovebirds," Rover began, "I was just wondering…"

I leaned over and punched Rover in the shoulder.

"Ow!"

"What?" Helen said.

"Nothing," Rover and I said simultaneously.

"Go GOGOGO!" Charlie bellowed.

• • •

As soon as Jesús hit the breaks in front of Charlie's house, Charlie had the passenger's door open and was out at a run. He had his keys in his hand, unlocked the front door and left the keys dangling, turned off the alarm and raced upstairs.

The clear plastic bag holding his cap and gown and tassel were on his desk, and he briefly thought about just grabbing them and going. But Helen had said that there wasn't enough time, and there wouldn't be enough elbow room to put it on in the car. So he tore the crinkly wrapping open and shook out the royal blue nylon graduation gown.

Then he slipped it over his head, stuck his arms through the sleeves and turned to look in the mirror.

Which was when he saw the family photo on the wall. Mom and Dad. Dad still alive. Himself and Desiree. All at the beach last summer. Looking like a pod of whales. But happy. All of them. Even Desiree had taken a week off from being a pain in the ass.

He remembered that particular day. They'd rented the house nearby for a week and had gone to the beach every day.

There had been a guy who offered to take a picture of them with their backs to the ocean. Their heels were downhill on the sand, so they were almost falling backward. Dad's arm was around Mom. Their kids, Charlie and Desiree, were in front, elbowing each other playfully.

The guy had captured the moment just as the seagull had pooped on Desiree's head. It was a long, wet, green and white splash.

Desiree's laughter and smiling had ended instantly, as she started screaming her head off. Dad and Charlie had laughed and laughed while Mom put an arm around Desiree as she yelled at them to stop and shrieked about the ruin of her hairstyle. All the while the guy who took the picture kept saying, "No, it's good luck! It's good luck!"

Dad had been relaxed and happy that week. Mom hadn't cooked, even breakfast. They'd played Bananagrams for hours at a time, and had put together that 1,000 piece puzzle of the Statue of Liberty.

Charlie looked in the mirror, and almost didn't recognize himself. The gown looked huge, and he looked small.

"I miss you, Dad." He said it out loud.

He felt himself starting to well up with tears, but Jesús honked the horn and that got him back in gear.

He grabbed the cap and tassel, ran back downstairs, turned on the alarm, locked the door, pulled the keys and tried shove them back into his pocket but couldn't, because his pockets were buried under the blue gown.

So, he just ran back to the car, threw his keys on the dashboard, slammed the door and shouted, "Go!"

• • •

Graduation day at last! Twelve minutes after noon on Thursday, and we were racing through the meandering back roads of one of Groston's nineteen-seventies suburban housing developments.

The seven of us were crammed into Jesús's 1972 Dodge Dart in our usual slots. Charlie was shotgun, Rover was wedged between Charlie and Jesús. I was in the back passenger side behind Charlie. Sean was behind Jesús. Adam and Helen were in the back middle. Helen was sitting on Adam's lap. Adam had a big smile on his face. Still.

"Go faster!" Charlie yelled.

"Don't go faster!" Helen yelled back. "The speed limit is 25!"

Jesús was doing sixty. The Dartmobile's muffler was roaring.

"Turn Right. Right," Rover shouted, his head ducked down as he squinted at his phone's screen. "No nono. Left. Left!"

"Does anybody have any gummies?" I asked.

Adam shot me a look. "You really want to be stoned for graduation? Really?"

"I'm nauseous," I said defensively. "It's for anxiety."

Then I looked at my friends. In our bright blue nylon gowns, we all looked like a bunch of blueberries about to be turned into jam. If we hit a tree it would be a strawberry-blueberry blend. I didn't need to disconnect from our last triumphant moments in high school.

Adam was right. I shook my head. "Nah. I guess not."

"Are you sure?" he whispered with an evil grin. "Because I've got some...."

I was just about to slug Adam in the shoulder when Jesús spun the wheel left and we all leaned right, hoping that we wouldn't flip over.

"Oh my god. Who just ripped ass?!?" Sean demanded.

"I can't smell anything," I said. But I did feel my stomach lurch from too much coffee and not enough food as we topped a hill and went airborne for a moment before bottoming out with an excruciating thud of antique Detroit iron scraping on asphalt. We heard Helen's wheelchair crash around inside the trunk.

"Stop bouncing the car!" Helen shrieked.

Adam, who had his arms wrapped tightly around Helen like a seat belt, didn't say a word, but he kept that big wide smile on his face.

"Graduation's in seven minutes," Charlie said. "We're late."

"I'm working on it," Rover was punching his portable computer.

"I'm working on it, too," Jesús said. He stomped down on the gas, and a moment later the Dartmobile started to pick up more speed.

That's when I smelled it. A thin trace whiff of sulfur grew into a round and deeply nauseating stench of rotten egg and rancid dog shit.

"Jesús, these windows still don't open," Helen wheezed.

"Rover, what the hell did you eat?" Jesús coughed.

"Hard boiled egg and bean burrito," Rover said. "Like I do every day."

"It stinks!" Sean moaned.

"He who smelt it dealt it," Rover snorted.

"Real grown up," Sean said. "I haven't heard that since fifth grade."

"Rover, I need to know the next turn." Jesús coughed. I could see from the back seat that his fingers were white on the steering wheel. "They fucking closed down roads due to Helen's so-called gas leak. And there's backed up traffic on Main Street from all the parents still driving in from Fectville."

"Working on it!" Rover said, squinting as he tried to tap something on his phone.

"Rover," Charlie asked, "why the fuck don't you make your phone's screen brighter?"

"See, I told you there was a gas leak!" Helen giggled.

"Happy to oblige," Rover said to Helen. "I'm working on it," he said to Jesús. "Because my battery's about to die," he told Charlie.

"We're all gonna die!"Sean, Charlie and I said it simultaneously, and then we laughed hysterically. "Jinx, you owe me a coke! No you.

359

No, YOU!"

Looking back, it was probably way too much to expect that those last moments of bondage in the public school system would be uneventful. Considering the monumental prank we had set up, and our recent history of back-to-back shitstorms, it was entirely possible that we really would die before crossing the gym floor and collecting our diplomas.

My heart was pounding. I could have sworn I heard a police siren.

"Rover," Jesús said. "The road is dead-ending in about five hundred feet."

"Go right!" Rover shouted.

"NO, LEFT!" everyone else screamed.

Jesús turned left.

That's when he saw the three police cars, their lights flashing, heading straight toward us. Jesús kept the wheel turning, and did a power slide 180.

"HOLY FUCK!" Charlie screamed as the front passenger door unlatched itself and flew wide open. "My keys...!"

Rover threw up.

Fortunately, Rover aimed it over Charlie and out the open door. His barf spun out and away and splashed across the front window of the lead squad car. It spun and wobbled, and the two cop cars behind it slowed.

Charlie, tightly buckled into the old fashioned lap-only seatbelt, gave up on his keys, groaned, reached out, pulled the door shut as Jesús straightened the Dart and put the pedal to the metal.

"Hold on," Jesús said.

"To what?" Sean screamed.

Jesús reached under the dash and flicked a switch.

I think that if any of us had known that Jesús had installed nitrous oxide after-burners in the Dartmobile, we would never have agreed to the whole making a grand entrance scenario.

But Jesús hadn't told us.

It was like popping over the top of a high roller-coaster hill and, instead of a slope, hitting a free fall.

Adam clutched Helen. Sean and I slammed the back door locks

down.

We didn't have time to do anything except hold on, and hope that we weren't going to lose our breakfasts like Rover.

I looked back and saw the squad cars vanish in the distance.

We saw the school ahead, but there were cars parked everywhere along the road. The parking lot at Ashby Bryson wasn't big enough to fit the entire senior class and all their families.

"Almost there!" Sean shouted.

"This car doesn't have airbags, does it?" Rover yelled as he rolled himself into a ball in the front seat.

"Short cut!" Jesús yelled. He jerked the wheel right, banged over the curb and began bouncing us across the football field toward the small parking lot behind the gym's back door fire exit.

Despite the seat belt, Charlie's head kept hitting the ceiling. "HoOhOLy FuhuhUHCK!"

The gym's cinder blocks got closer and closer.

Sounding like a train conductor, Jesús said, "Last stop, Ashby Bryson High School graduation and points beyond!"

We popped over the curb onto the asphalt at near light speed.

Jesús spun the wheel, stomped the brakes with his right foot, and simultaneously mashed his left foot down on the old-school emergency foot brake.

The Dartmobile whipped around and came to a stop, parallel to the building and inches from the back door.

"Perfect," Jesús said. He turned off the engine. His face was white. "Nice job, baby"

"Jesús, you're blocking the gym's back door!" Sean yelled.

"Move it!" Charlie and I both screamed.

We had to wait another thirty seconds while Jesús restarted the Dartmobile and inched it away from the building so he wouldn't scratch the paint.

Then we spilled out of the car like our legs were made of mud.

Helen crawled out and fell on Adam.

"I gotcha," he said.

She kissed him. Sweet.

"So," Jesús said, "we didn't die, did we?"

"I don't think so," Sean said.

Rover looked like he was going to hurl again. Kept his mouth closed. Shook his head.

Helen reached under her robe and handed Rover a stick of gum.

"Eww!" Rover muttered. "Is this my squid gum?"

Helen shrugged.

Jesús opened the trunk, yanked out Helen's wheelchair and opened it.

Adam picked her up and helped her get settled. She gave him a kiss.

We all straightened our caps and gowns.

"Anybody know which side the tassel goes on?" Sean asked.

"The right," Helen said. "You switch it to left after you get your diploma."

"Are you sure?" Jesús asked.

Helen gave him a look, and Jesús flipped the tassel to the right.

"Ready?" I said.

Adam, Helen, Sean and Jesús gave me thumbs up. Rover nodded. Charlie grinned.

"Lets go," I said, smiling.

Charlie pulled himself up to full size, grabbed the back door, and tugged.

"It's fucking locked," he said.

"What?" I said. "No. No. No."

"Yeah," he nodded.

"Gimme a second," Rover said. He pushed a button on his portable computer. "No. Wait."

"What's your sister's phone number?" I asked him.

"I don't usually give guys my sister's number without her permission.

"Just tell me!"

He did. I called Elspeth. A minute later, she opened the back door. And we strode into the gym.

Chapter 30

Sky High

"Also, I've always liked splat humor. A cartoon character hits a wall, or gets a safe dropped on its head, and gets flattened with a loud clang! and splush! For a few moments, they're slightly disoriented or impossibly thin. Then, poof! Everything's fine! The splat is always funny. It's that reset that makes it okay to laugh. Otherwise, it's horrific or ultra violence."
— Dave Rover

Half of me expected everybody to be already seated and staring at us as we sneaked in the back door of the gym.

The other half expected chaos. With hundreds of parents and relatives and graduating students converging at the last minute in the Ashby Bryson gym, there would probably be kids running around, parents shushing, our fellow seniors texting or slapping high fives or squealing with excitement.

Part of me wanted a standing ovation.

Instead, nobody noticed us.

The room was as quiet as a church, except for the occasional squeak of a sneaker on the wavy old parquet floor.

Although some people were sitting on the bleachers on both sides of the basketball court, a majority were standing around the middle of the room, staring up and pointing at the ceiling.

They were soooo quiet. Almost everyone was whispering in awe.

What we'd done – what Jesús had designed and Susie augmented, what Rover and Sean had engineered, and the rest of us had chipped in with the grunt work was, in a word, spectacular.

You know the Sistine Chapel, Michelangelo's masterpiece fresco in the Vatican?

Imagine that. Full size, in all its glory.

Got it?

Now move it to Groston. To the gym at Ashby Bryson High School. Change up the images here and there. Add a bit of Day-Glo color.

And WHAM!

That's what we'd done.

It was stupendous.

You've probably seen pictures of the real Sistine Chapel. Maybe you've even visited. Go to Rome. Go to the Vatican, go to the top floor of the Apostolic Palace, the Pope's official residence.

There, you'll find an enormous room with high ceilings triumphantly covered by an epic tour de force painted in wet plaster by Michelangelo in only four years.

We did ours in under four days.

On the ceiling in Italy, there are nine scenes from the biblical *Book of Genesis*, including *The Creation of the Universe*, *The Creation of Man and Woman*, *The Fall of Man and Woman*, and *The Story of Noah and the Flood*. Surrounding and supporting the ceiling's central panels are more murals with prophets and sibyls, more biblical stories, and trompe l'oeil depictions of marble supports and busts.

Finally, at the far end of the room in the Vatican is an enormous wall depicting *The Last Judgment*. Added on at the end of his life, Michelangelo used this ultimate fresco to settle scores, give shout-outs to patrons, and blow the minds of other Roman artists. He was sixty-six years old by the time he finished, and was so fed up with the project that he painted himself, hanging on the wall as a dried-out husk, skinned and empty.

The Sistine Chapel is indisputably one of the most glorious works of art the world has ever seen.

And we had recreated it. To scale.

Splashed across the ceiling of the gym at Ashby Bryson High was a one-to-one full-sized reproduction of Michelangelo's masterpiece, except instead of fresco paint on plaster, we'd used ten thousand two hundred and sixty-six 300 dpi color laser prints and twenty-four buckets of wheat paste, like street graffiti artists.

And instead of the faces of ancient Romans, or Michelangelo's fantasies of his lovers, we'd substituted the scanned and photo-shopped yearbook portraits of all one hundred and thirty-seven Groston graduating seniors.

It really really worked!

The ceiling of the Sistine Chapel is only a hundred-and-thirty-three feet long by forty-six feet wide. A standard high school basketball court is eighty-four feet long and fifty feet wide. But with the bleachers and sidelines in Groston, Rover and Sean hadn't had to do much to adjust and scale Michelangelo's paintings.

And although covering the ceiling and wall was a shit ton of stretching on tiptoes and getting drops of glue splashed in our eyes, it wasn't really that hard to do.[45] After Rover projected the images up onto the ceiling it was sort of a street art graffiti paste-by-the-numbers project.

Yes, it had taken us a lot of practice slapping up the pages one at a time to get them smooth, straight and overlapping. And it had taken a while to figure out how to move around the scaffolding that we'd swiped from Fectville. (One of the last things the football team had done that morning was dump the scaffolding out back behind the gym. Somebody was supposed to move it back to Fectville later,

---

[45] Helen insisted that we clip ourselves to safety lines, so there were no accidents.

but I'm pretty sure that never happened..)

And with the help of the entire Groston football team, cheerleading squad, various friends, and assorted brothers, sisters and relatives, we'd gotten it all done.

The biggest challenge was making *The Last Judgment* fit on the far wall, which we'd done with a little bit of cropping, and by painting the doorway to Hell over the rear exit of the gym. Which was kind of appropriate.

No wonder everybody was gaping.

When I was thirteen, my grandparents took me on a Bar Mitzvah trip to Italy. To be honest it was pretty boring, except for the catacombs for the dead and the daily gelato tastings.[46] Seen through the eyes of a thirteen year old, the Sistine Chapel was only moderately impressive. Mostly what I remember were all the guards hissing loudly in Italian for everybody to shut up and stop taking pictures.

Today, though, I found myself grinning with delight and amazement at what we'd accomplished and how fucking good it looked!

Even though I'd done my fair share of climbing the scaffolding and slapping up sheets of paper with a makeshift paste-brush broomstick, I hadn't really taken the time to step back and look at the whole thing.

You couldn't take in the whole thing. It was that big.

From Zechariah to Jonah, it was all there. A combination of intensely detailed and graphic Renaissance mastery with substitutions from Groston's contemporary history and our sense of humor.

Later on, TV people interviewed me about what they called The Ashby Bryson Sistine Gymnasium Project.

"How did you, a bunch of high school students, manage to do all that?"

"It was easy," I said, thinking they wanted a technical explanation. "Rover downloaded the Vatican's 3D interactive virtual reality website and turned it into a VR app. Then he and Sean mapped out how to shrink, compress and divide the mural into grids for eight-and-a-half by eleven sheets of copy paper. There was a brief panic

---

[46] My favorite is still pistachio. Mmmm.

early on when we realized that our laser printers weren't printing all the way to the borders, but Charlie went to an office supply store and bought three guillotine paper cutters. Then Sean and Rover reconfigured the grid to take the crop marks into account.

"Meanwhile, the design team had their own challenges. After long discussions,[47] Jesús and Susie compromised by maintaining Michelangelo's color palate with only a few bright highlights here and there, and mostly focused on inventive ways to honor and memorialize our soon-to-be former classmates."

The TV people didn't really care that much. They used the sound bite of me saying, "It was easy," and a clip of Susie in her cheerleading togs, then long shots of the ceiling.

Now that I had a moment, I took a little time to enjoy what we'd done.

Helen was depicted in robes as the Biblical hero *Judith, Carrying the Decapitated Head of Holofernes.* She sat on a Romanesque version of her wheelchair and balanced a gruesome platter on her head. Naturally, we'd given the dead Syrian general's face a passing resemblance to Butch Batten. Near the front wheel of the wooden chair, playfully rubbing its head against Helen's foot was her lost cat, Mittens.

Sean was painted as the *Drunken Noah,* with his boyfriend Clyde pointing at Sean's semi-erect dick. I squinted and noticed that in Jesús's illustration, Sean's Noah wasn't completely unconscious, but was peeking at Clyde to gauge his reaction.

Charlie was *The Prophet Jeremiah* glowering down with doom in his eyes. Standing behind him in the picture was Charlie's dad. The late Mr. Johnson had a comforting hand on his son's shoulder. It was a darker aspect of Charlie than he usually presented, but he looked strong and powerful.

I was sketched as *Jonah, Being Eaten by the Whale.* Given the miserable and waterlogged year I'd had, it seemed appropriate. I really felt like I'd been swallowed alive by a huge mindless fish, only to be vomited up on shore where nobody really believed what I'd been through.

Rover and Susie were drawn as *Adam and Eve,* naked, being

---

[47] And loud fights.

chased from the Garden of Eden. Rover's sister Elspeth was the red-draped angel prodding Rover's neck with a sharp sword. Gotta say that in Jesús's interpretation, Susie was a heck of a lot more sexy and Rover was a lot less buff than Michelangelo's versions of Eve and Adam. I still can't believe that Susie agreed to the nudity. I glanced over, and saw the two of them holding hands and blushing.

We had decided to take a somewhat Hindu approach to the portrayals of God, giving each image of the Deity a different face.

Our artistic director, Jesús had featured himself as *The God of Creation*, dividing the heavens and forming the sun and the moon. In this self-portrait, Jesús's face was a lot more gleeful than Michelangelo's stern original, and God's beard was clearly a cheesy costume clip-on.[48]

Our former principal, Mr. Douglas, was a blushing *God Creating the First Woman*. Both Helen and Susie had insisted on keeping Michelangelo's original Adam and Eve for that portrait. Susie said that we shouldn't be arrogant, splashing ourselves everywhere. Helen was more political. "No way are we making a statement that modern girls are second fiddle."

And in the middle of the ceiling, in the center of the gym, in *The Creation of Man*, Adam was pictured as my cousin Adam.[49] But he was being created by a female God, who looked a lot like a gigantic version of Mrs. Capamundo, sans beard and surrounded by angelic versions of the old front office support staff from Jerome Marco K-8.[50]

One of the reasons it had taken us until the last minute to get the project together was the level of care and detail that Susie and Jesús put into selecting who would go where.

David and Goliath were remapped as Doug Hawthorne and Butch Batten (although because Butch's face was turned, you couldn't really

---

[48] While Jesús had been picking us up from Fectville, Susie had slapped a big red handprint on the naked butt cheek of an assisting angel, as if God had just spanked the angel for making a mistake, and in retaliation the angel was mooning him. Fortunately, instead of being livid, Jesús laughed.
[49] Of course.
[50] There had been a lively debate about whether to have Adam and God giving each other the finger. Ultimately we decide against.

tell). Butch showed up again, more respectfully, as *The Prophet Ezekiel*.[51] Robyn Franklin and Marcie Kahn were two of *The Sibyls*, and so on...

I could continue but, like watching somebody else's kids walk across the stage to collect their diplomas, it would probably bore you.

That said, nobody was bored, and there weren't any guards shushing or yelling, "No photographia!"

Every parent, grandparent, aunt, uncle and second cousin was scanning our mural, and looking for their students, clapping in delight as they found the faces.

Susie's dad was grinning; her mom looked more than a little concerned. Rover's dad looked at his son and winked broadly. Charlie's mom was in tears. His Nanna had a big smile on her face. Jesús's mother looked gobsmacked. I wasn't sure if she was impressed or thought her son had committed blasphemy. She kept crossing herself and smiling and then looking uncomfortable. Helen's parents were smiling too.

Sean's Mom and Dad both looked confused. He still hadn't told them that he was gay, so they didn't know what to make of his scene.

Adam's mom, my Aunt Dot was staring at the ceiling with her mouth open. Uncle Paul was grinning and taking hundreds of pictures with his SLR.

My parents waved at me. Ellen just shook her head, but then gave me a reluctant thumbs up.

Suffice it to say that I had to give Rover an elbow in the ribs to remind him that it was time to turn on the sound system and get the ceremony started.

The folks sitting on the bleachers jumped as the metal vibrated loudly with the brassy synthesizer intro to Emerson Lake and Palmer's old prog rock version of *Fanfare for the Common Man*.

Everyone in the middle of the room quickly headed for their seats on the bleachers.[52]

---

[51] Even though Butch was an asshole, we couldn't in good conscience erase him from history or only paint his misdeeds. After all, he had helped take the football team all the way to the state finals, and once upon a time, he'd been our friend.

[52] Nobody except us ever knew that there had been a chance of electrocution.

Rover assumed his position at the mixing board. Simultaneously, Helen wheeled out to center court with a microphone and mic stand on her lap, while I rolled a podium across the warped floor. Sean and Jesús carried one long table with boxes of diplomas. Charlie and Adam brought in another table with more diplomas.

Mr. Douglas, clearly shaken, took the cue and stepped up to the microphone. Helen handed him a bottle of water. He drank from it and thanked her. He tapped the microphone. "I guess it's time to…"

At that moment, Dr. Robert Smith, principal of Fectville Regional High School, breathlessly burst into the gym, his suit disheveled and his face red with sweat and anger.

Dr. Bob banged in through the gym's front doors and strode to the center of the room, straight toward the seven of us.

His eyes were wide. His small teeth were clenched.

You know that moment on a playground after a really little kid falls down and gets hurt, when you can tell how much pain the child is in and how loud the yell is going to be by the length of the inhale before the scream?

Dr. Bob had started that long squinched-up inhale.

Simultaneously, all seven of us smiled at him and pointed at the far wall of the gym where we'd pasted up our version of *The Last Judgment.*

There had been a lot of discussion during the final phase about whether or not we had any right to pass judgment on our classmates.

Ultimately, Jesús and Susie had decided that since graduation was supposed to be joyous, no one from Groston would be pictured as one of the damned.[53]

That said, Charlie and I both had insisted that Dr. Bob completely deserved to be Charon, the ferryman bringing the damned across the River Styx into Hell. But Adam had argued persuasively for a completely different interpretation. In the end, Adam won, and we all agreed where Fectville's principal, Dr. Robert Smith should go.

In the center of *The Last Judgment,* the seated figure of Christ

---

[53] Not even Butch.

was transformed into Dr. Bob – solemn and holy and moustached, surrounded by the lights of heaven, draped in robes, but with a thin black tie, because Dr. Bob was unimaginable without one.

In retrospect, the entire scene could have backfired. We might have accidentally created something impious or offensive. Back when I'd first pitched the idea, we'd had a long discussion about religion, multiculturalism, the purpose of art and the separation of church and state.

Ultimately, though, what won the day was that larger-than-life-sized portrait of Dr. Robert Smith as *Jesus Christ The King* sitting on his throne at *The Last Judgment*.

Just as he was about to let loose with his scream, Dr. Bob followed our outstretched fingers and beheld the muraled wall.

He didn't recognize himself at first. Dr. Bob's eyes registered confusion, and disbelief, but he couldn't look away.

As Dr. Bob stared at himself portrayed as the holy messiah, the rage and tension left his face and his tightly balled fists unclenched. His shoulders dropped. His mouth fell open.

Softly at first, small tears leaked from the corners of his eyes, but then, like the flood wiping the earth clean, Dr. Bob wept. Tears rolled down his cheeks in dripping streams. His body jerked with sobs, while a strangely beatific glow that was almost a smile spread across his face.

Adam had argued that the reason Dr. Bob was such a total dickhead was because he thought of himself as our savior.

I caught my cousin's eye, nodded, and gave Adam the thumbs up. He shrugged and nodded back.

We both smiled.

We had made our enemy, the high school principal who had taken such pleasure in tormenting us, cry.

Sure, Dr. Bob was crying tears of joy. He felt revealed and righteous.

But half the kids in the school were taking pictures of him on their phones. I knew that the videos showing up on social media wouldn't have our context.

High school principals aren't supposed to break down in public, and my guess was that within a year, Dr. Bob would quit and become a priest or a social worker, some job with less rigid anxiety and more compassion. Maybe that was just wishful thinking on my part.

Susie stepped up and escorted Dr. Bob to a chair next to Mrs. Capamundo, who handed him a tissue to wipe his eyes.

The music faded to silence.

We all joined our class on the bleachers.

Mr. Douglas cleared his throat.

"Ladies and Gentlemen, parents and families, students and former students and soon to be former students, welcome at last to Groston's Ashby Bryson High School Graduation Ceremony!"

The crowd went wild.

Chapter 31

Diplomatic Impunity

"Humor is relative. The best comedians surf a room, provoking ripples of laughter here and there. They float back and forth, testing the waters. Then, they're in a groove, and the laughter builds a wave that crescendos, crests, and breaks with a sidesplitting sense of relief."
— from "What Makes Us Laugh?"

Considering the run-up and our exhaustion, the graduation ceremony itself was a blur of cheering and clapping, handshaking, fist bumping, fist pumping, little boogie dances, cell phone selfies and the longest sustained feeling of utter relief I've ever experienced.

Fortunately Sean's improvised air conditioning system worked, so we weren't sweating like dogs.

If life had been fair, Adam would have been the valedictorian. Instead, Charlie had the honors, which wasn't so bad. Mr. Douglas called him to the microphone, and we all stood. The football team stood, the cheerleading squad stood, and of course Charlie's entire family stood up and whooped. His 95 year-old great-grandmother couldn't stand, but boy could she wolf-whistle and bang the arms of her wheelchair!

"It's been a long year," Charlie said. "So, I'm going to keep it short." More cheers.

"Students of Groston, you have endured flooding and ice, persecution and disgrace."

Boos and jeers. "Damn fucking straight!" someone yelled.

"We've had losses," Charlie said softly.

"Sorry about your dad, man!" someone shouted.

Charlie's eyes dropped for a moment, and then he looked at his mother. She smiled at him, patted her left hand on her heart, pointed to heaven, pointed to the ceiling, and pointed at Charlie.

After a while, Charlie cleared his throat. "And we, the ones who are here today, we are the lucky ones."

"What the fuck you talking about Fat Charlie?" someone else shouted.

Charlie stared into the bleachers, looking for the heckler. "We've been called names."

"Fat Charlie!" half a dozen hollered cheerfully.

"You're so fine!" someone shouted, to laughter and applause.

Charlie held up his hand to prevent everyone from busting out into the song.

"We've been bussed and we've been dissed. We lost the keys to our houses. And we are the lucky ones.

"We have our families. We have our friends. We have our town and our country. We have our education. And soon – real soon – we will have our diplomas!"

Pandemonium for a full minute.

Charlie waited. Then continued. "Today in this holy place of learning, washed clean by flood and freeze, and restored by our commitment and hard work, we are together for the last time."

The room grew quiet.

"There are only a hundred and thirty-seven of us left," Charlie said. "Yet we have the power to shape and change and improve the world.

"And I know that we will. Because thanks to our parents, our friends and our teachers, we already have!"

The cheers began again, but Charlie talked over them.

"They say that high school is just a beginning, just a pit stop, a rest stop on the highway of our lives.

"I, for one, am glad to flush that toilet and get the hell out of here!"

Charlie raised his fist to a deafening wall of cheers and applause.

Mr. Douglas looked stunned, but quickly retook control, and began passing out the diplomas.

We'd had a brutal rehearsal a week earlier in the gym at Fectville Regional, but nobody had really paid attention, so when it was my turn, I was surprised to hear everyone cheering and calling my name.

I floated off the bleachers, walked across the floor, got my diploma and handshake from Mr. Douglas, and paused for a moment.

It wasn't very long, but long enough to look up at the Ashby Bryson High School version of the Sistine Chapel that we'd made. Long enough to see all my friends standing (except Helen, who was sitting in her chair in the aisle of the front row) and clapping with their hands over their heads. Long enough to see my mom crying, and my sister Ellen staring at her cell phone, and my dad wipe a tear from his cheek.

Then I got the hell off the stage and made way for the next grad.

• • •

As soon as all the diplomas were distributed, "Pomp and Circumstances" began – a hip hop brass and drum corps rendition that rocked the gym through Rover's sound bleachers.

On cue, Jesús's brothers and sisters flung the back doors of the gym wide open.

An aisle of sunlight streamed in across the floor.

Our class stood, and to a standing ovation from our families and teachers, filed out through *The Last Judgment*'s portal to Hell and into a party.

The back field at Ashby Bryson High School was covered with a huge white tent that had been hastily erected during the ceremony.

There were round tables, and chairs for seating, long tables spread high with premade sandwiches, bottled water and soda, bowls of salad, boxes of chips, trays of hors d'oeuvres, and platters of freshly baked chocolate chip cookies. Charlie's Uncle Eugene had driven his barbecue rig up from New Orleans, and had an entire pig roasting that smelled delicious.

A large banner read, "Congratulations to all the Groston Grads! Buffet sponsored by the Law Offices of Bob Billings. It's never too late or too early to call your attorney."

Helen had arranged the whole thing through a series of emails and requests.

She'd found two wedding photographers to take professional family and graduation pictures on commission, and even managed to get three photo-booth guys hooked up with special software that jacked their green screens to project scenes from Jesús and Susie's rendering of the Ashby Bryson Chapel as a backdrop. It was totally cool to see everybody taking pictures of themselves with their biblical counterparts, sort of like a neo-renaissance mash-up selfie. The lines got to be huge, but aside from the few people who'd made late lunch reservations in Groston or Fectville, no one was in a rush.

Everyone was saying stuff to everyone. It was one big gleeful gushfest.

Across the parking lot, Mrs. Hendry caught my eye, and started waving her hands, applauding us in American Sign Language. Mrs. Capamundo made me bend down and gave me a kiss on the cheek.

As soon as our elementary school principal was out of sight, Helen's friend Robyn Franklin came over and shook my hand.

"Nice job," she said.

I shrugged. "I didn't do much."

"Yes, you did," she said. "It was good working with you." Then she stepped in close, gave me a kiss on the lips and whispered, "Call me," in my ear.

I was dumbfounded and tongue tied. That kiss sent a shiver from my lips to my dick. I could barely breathe. By the time I snapped out of it, she'd vanished in the crowd.

I had no idea that Robyn even liked me, wasn't sure what it

meant, but damn I was looking forward to finding out.

My sister Ellen saw me smiling, rolled her eyes, and said, "You're still a loser. But a cool loser."

Dr. Bob came up to me, shook his head, and then shook my hand. He opened and closed his mouth twice, searching for words. Then he shook his head, nodded, and walked away. I never saw him again.

One by one our gang came together and drifted back into the gym.

"So, what are we going to do now?" Charlie said to me.

"Party in my basement?" Rover said. He looked over at Susie. "As long as that's okay with you."

Sean rolled his eyes, but he was holding hands with Clyde, so he really couldn't talk.

Adam pushed Helen's chair into the circle. He put his left hand on her shoulder. She reached across with her right, and held his.

"I don't know if I can come," Jesús said. "My Mamí wants me to go home."

"She'll understand," Helen said. "Tell her we need you to drive."

"Really?" I said. "That's it? We've been through all this, we've come this far, we've worked this hard, and we're just going to go back down into Rover's basement and pretend like nothing's changed? Seriously?"

We all got quiet for a moment.

Then my face broadened into a grin, "Psyche!"

I turned and threw my arm over my cousin's shoulder. "Let's go!

"*While I understand the purpose of black comedy and satire as political tools, for instance during the Cold War in Russia, I don't find them amusing or funny. For me, a real comedy has to have a happy ending.*"
– *Mrs. Hendry, A.P. World History, Ashby Bryson High School*

Word got out about what we'd done in the gym. It went viral and made international news.

We formed a company, "The Groston Rules – Multimedia Murals and More." Bob Billings helped us create an S Corporation.

Even though Rover had invented most of the intellectual property, he said that he wouldn't have done it without us, so all the patents and copyrights were jointly held by the seven of us. (Except for the bleacher sound-system patent, which ultimately made him independently wealthy.)

Suddenly, instead of high school graduates stuck on the college and higher education track, we were an artistic dot-com production team that traveled around the world.

Yes, I finally did get into Columbia College off the waiting list.

I never got an email notifying me about my status change.[54] The thick envelope arrived exactly two weeks after *The New York Times Magazine* did a spread on our work. We'd transformed the entire Park Avenue Armory in Manhattan into *Hieronymus Bosch's (USA! USA!) Garden of Last Judgment.* It was a lurid reinterpretation of the crazy psychedelic Dutchman's work that featured the President of the United States, his Cabinet and advisors, as well as a good chunk of both houses of Congress in a frenzy of naked greed, larceny, lust and bondage. *The New Yorker's* art critic raved, "The fact that this powerful piece of contemporary political art was created by a team of seven recent high school graduates makes it all the more disturbing."

I looked at that fat acceptance envelope with Columbia's blue crown on it, feeling its thickness in my hands, and yes, I grinned my ass off.

I did a little dance. It was no Fat Charlie Dance, but it was mine.

Then, without asking my parents for permission, I said, fuck you to Columbia, and I deferred. I sent an email telling them that I'd already made plans, but would be glad to reconsider their offer in a few months.

Thanks Ivy League, but I wasn't in a rush to go or do or be anything else.

Down in Rover's basement, I told my friends first. They didn't bother to cheer.

"Cool," Jesús said.

"Word," Sean said.

"Will you stop that fucking 'word' shit?" Jesús threw a pillow at Sean.

"Never!" Sean laughed.

"Not bad," Charlie said.

"Awesome," Rover said. "Now, come on, guys. Focus, focus. We're supposed to be sketching a proposal for the Venice Biennial and the deadline is next week!"

"I'm proud of you ," Helen said. She gave me a kiss on the cheek.

---

[54] Or maybe I did, but by then I'd stopped checking.

Adam grinned and gave me the thumbs up. "Told ya."

That was it. It was done. My friends and I had made promises to each other, and we would stick together a little while longer.

At breakfast the next morning, when I told my mom and dad that I was taking a gap year they both choked on their coffee, like they were drinking motor oil.

I sipped my coffee. It tasted just fine.

THE END

9 781940 060422